The Forests of Norbio

Also by Giuseppe Dessì

The Deserter

GIUSEPPE DESSÌ

Translated by Frances Frenaye

A Helen and Kurt Wolff Book

Harcourt Brace Jovanovich

The Forests of Norbio

New York and London

Library of Congress Cataloging in Publication Data

Dessì, Giuseppe, 1909–
  The forests of Norbio.

  Translation of Paese d'ombre.
  "A Helen and Kurt Wolff book."
  I. Title.
PZ4.D4647Fo [PQ4811.E67]   843'.9'12   74-30087
ISBN 0-15-132505-7

First edition
B C D E

HISTORICAL PREFACE

Sardinia, the largest island in the Mediterranean except for Sicily, is a land of mountains with no clear ranges and of lowland and coastal regions that until modern times were malarial. The island was named Sardo by the Phoenicians who founded settlements there for the purposes of mining and trade. Many of these communities became important towns, among them the Phoenician Caralis, now Cagliari, the capital. The mines in the Iglesiente mountains mentioned in this novel were known from ancient times. The Carthaginians and the Romans colonized the island; the Vandals and the Arabs invaded it.

In the fourteenth century, Sardinia passed to the House of Aragon and remained under Spanish rule for four hundred years. In 1720, the peace which concluded the War of the Spanish Succession awarded Sardinia to Victor Albert II of Savoy. As a result, he and his successors were known as kings of Sardinia, and the history of the island was linked with that of the House of Savoy whose seat of power was far to the north, on the Italian mainland in Turin, the capital of Piedmont.

In 1802, during the Napoleonic wars, Victor Emmanuel I lost Piedmont to France and found his realm limited to Sardinia. He resided in Cagliari from 1806 until 1814. In 1815, the Congress of Vienna reinstated to the kingdom its former possessions and added Liguria and Genoa.

The House of Savoy made sporadic attempts to reform Sardinian agriculture, taxation, and the administration of justice, but the Piedmontese frequently met with local resistance and were unable to overcome the differences between their language and culture and that of the Sardinians. King Charles Albert (1831–49) made the most vigorous effort on Sardinia's behalf. In 1836 he abolished signorial rights and the consequent division of land formed the basis of the agrarian economy of the nineteenth and twentieth centuries.

In Europe, the first half of the nineteenth century saw an increasing national spirit, a demand on the part of the people for greater freedom and representation, and the formation of secret revolutionary societies. This tide of liberalism culminated in the revolutions of 1848. It brought two important changes to Sardinia the island, and Sardinia the kingdom. In 1847 the island was united with the continental domains of the House of Savoy, its administration integrated with that of the mainland. In 1848 the king granted his subjects a liberal constitution which was to rule the new nation of Italy, founded in 1861, and to endure until the dictatorship of Mussolini. However, while Sardinia in 1847 and 1848 gained in one sense, by being given equal standing with the other provinces in the kingdom and being able to send its representatives to sit in the Piedmontese parliament, it lost its administrative autonomy. As part of the reorganized kingdom, Sardinia found itself subject to remote and, in the view of many Sardinians, "foreign" Piedmontese officials unfamiliar with the traditions, language, and problems of the Sardinian people.

During the Risorgimento, the Piedmontese were the driving force toward the unification of Italy. They had a dynasty, a trained army, an educated class capable of service, and above all a brilliant leader in Cavour. The kingdom expanded until in 1861 it included all of Italy except Austrian-dominated Venetia (obtained in 1866) and papal Rome and Latium. In 1861, Victor Emmanuel II was proclaimed king of Italy.

With the achievement of unity, the new nation faced many problems; among them was the antagonism between the economically and politically developed North and the underdeveloped South. The average Piedmontese or Tuscan regarded someone from Calabria or Sardinia as his inferior. The agricultural South bore a disproportionate share of taxes and found that in many instances unification had merely substituted one group of exploiters for another. Sardinia remained forgotten.

The leaders of the new nation regarded foreign policy of paramount importance and were determined that Italy become independent of France and Austria, which had ruled much territory now Italian. During the 1870s, the army was reorganized and the navy expanded. Italy temporarily led the world in naval construction. The royal foundries needed great amounts of fuel and looked to the forests of Sardinia to supply charcoal. During this period, Britain and France were colonizing Africa, and Italy attempted, albeit unsuccessfully, to do the same.

These historical events are seen through the eyes of the people of Norbio, a Sardinian village far removed from Rome. Among the older generation are those who still cherish the memory of Mazzini's republicanism over Cavour's constitutional monarchy, and who regard their local senators with indifference. Those who grew up after the unification must reckon with the dislocations and benefits it brings and gain some control over the forces that affect their lives and region. They see the need for change but know that their strength lies in their own traditions and closely knit society. Their children take much of the past for granted and, while deeply attached to their homes and families, they are drawn into the larger orbit of the mainland. Some remain to protect and renew the forests of Norbio.

Part One

The little boy knocked at the small wooden gate, exactly like the one in front of his mother's house on the Vicolo del Carrubo, and then waited in silence. The harsh, booming voice of Don Francesco Fulgheri called out from inside:

"Who's there?"

"Angelo!" the boy shouted back. His voice was thin and high-pitched, and when Don Francesco wanted to tease him he called him an acolyte. Now he pushed at the gate, which creaked as it swung open. His mother had explained that Don Francesco deliberately left it unoiled so that from his study, at the far end of the courtyard, he could hear whenever someone went in or out. Angelo entered with the usual trepidation, crunching the gravel with the hobnails of his shoes, which alone would have warned Don Francesco of his presence. And indeed, the old man signified his awareness by clearing his throat and coughing from the depths of the cavelike room where, like an owl, he was lurking. Actually he had sent for the boy through Comare Verdiana, his neighbor, who always appeared in answer to his call wearing a blouse and petticoat, with a yellow kerchief tied around her head, grumbling that he never let her get on with her work. "I was sieving some flour," or: "I was weaving on the loom," she would say as an excuse for her incomplete dress.

Don Francesco frequently sent for Angelo—to go get him

meat for soup stock, bread, or spaghetti, to feed his horse Zurito, to dust his study, or simply to keep him company. Sometimes he took him into the fields; at others he made him perch on a high-backed chair, like a blackbird on a fence. In the pasture, the horse recognized the boy from far off; he pawed the ground or whinnied, as if to greet him or to hasten the arrival of his ration of beans or fodder. He was a big, bulky, white horse, somewhat spoiled because he got so little work. The herdsman, Gerolamo Sanna, who had been in Don Francesco's service all during the long years since he had been released, by an amnesty, from prison, would have liked to hitch him to a wagon or plow, but Don Francesco defended his idleness. Until recent years, he had ridden Zurito to inspect the cultivation of the fields. He rode in style, on a fine English saddle, and said he liked to feel a live horse, not a wooden one, between his legs. "That's your business!" retorted the herdsman sarcastically. Sanna was a stunt rider at all the festivities of Parte d'Ispi, but he could not put up with the white horse's caprices. He couldn't have galloped, raising himself erect, half out of the saddle, on a horse that was capable of shying at the sight of a passing swallow's shadow. Fulgheri, the lawyer, on the other hand, appreciated Zurito's high spirits; when he rode, straight in the saddle with a long gun over his shoulder, he was, and knew that he was, still a fine figure of a man. Angelo, too, rode Zurito without fear when he took him to the watering trough; like all the boys of Norbio he rode bareback, with a halter in place of a bridle. He would lead the horse alongside some doorsteps or a guardrail and then, gripping the mane in his left hand, would leap onto his back. The horse threw his head, lashed the air with his tail, and softly whinnied; the warmth of his body, as it came through the boy's worn trousers, was reassuring.

Now, too, when Zurito became aware of Angelo's presence, he stretched his long neck over the door of the stall and shook his head, displaying a set of yellow teeth. He knew that the boy always brought something with him, a piece of bread, a handful of beans, or a lump of sugar. Now, sure enough, he pulled a slice of white bread out of his pocket, broke it, and let Zurito take the crumbs from his hand, feeling the tough, short hairs of the horse's lips scratch the extended palm. Zurito let Angelo stroke his neck and head while he was eating, and whinnied as if he wanted to whisper something into his ear. In the study, Don Francesco cleared his throat impatiently, although he knew perfectly well what was causing the boy's delay. He liked the idea that the boy and the horse were friends—it fitted in with his ideal picture of the world, which had little counterpart in reality —but he was an intolerant and impatient man, above all when he was kept waiting. Finally, when the boy's figure appeared, like the black silhouette of a daguerreotype, in the lighted doorway, he bent again over the sheet of paper in front of him and went on writing with the white, barely sharpened goose-quill pen that had been given him by Angelo's mother. The quill stuck up over his right shoulder and grazed the long, black hairs of his beard, which framed his swarthy face with no-longer fashionable side-whiskers. His dress, too, was old-fashioned, although his ideas were so up-to-date as to be considered dangerously revolutionary by the Island's government officials, the men around the viceroy, the head of the Lawyers' Guild and, above all, by the two most conspicuous men of Norbio, the senator, Antioco Loru, and Professor Antonio Todde, who each occupied chairs, of Roman Law and Economics, respectively, at the University of Cagliari.

"So there you are," said Don Francesco loudly. "Come here!"

The boy came up to the desk and let the old man chuck his chin with a cold, horny hand, redolent of ink and tobacco.

"Sit down and wait a minute," said Don Francesco, pointing to the usual high-backed chair between the window and the bookcases. Angelo sat with his legs tucked beneath him, in a position which his mother had repeatedly told him was unsuitable but to which he knew Don Francesco would make no objection. Soon his legs were aching.

"Do you want me to feed the horse?" he asked, searching for an excuse to go run around outside.

"If we'd waited for you, we'd have been out of luck, both the horse and I. I've already given him his beans; I even had to grind them. What made you so late? I sent Verdiana for you over two hours ago."

Angelo unwound his legs and blew his nose into the clean handkerchief his mother had put into his pocket.

"I had to cut the grass for the rabbits, and then my mother sent me to buy spaghetti."

"You've always got an excuse on the tip of your tongue," Don Francesco muttered.

"I'm telling you the truth," said the boy, somewhat plaintively.

"What's that you set down on the floor?"

Angelo's legs were prickly, and he was happy to get off the hard chair. He picked up the basket from beside the desk and held it out to Don Francesco, who took the handle with the little finger of his left hand and, raising it to his face, sniffed it.

"Gooseberries!" he exclaimed with satisfaction.

"From my mother, and she said to apologize for the lateness."

"The lateness doesn't matter, boy. I don't want her to go to trouble."

Almost every time the boy went to Don Francesco's Sofia sent something—new vegetables or fruit, a bowl of hot soup prepared the way he liked it, or a pot of *migiurato* or *gioddu,* a sort of yogurt very popular in the Parte d'Ispi region.

"Oh," said Angelo, parroting his mother's instructions, "it's no trouble. You're the one who goes to trouble for us, Don Francesco."

The lawyer snorted with annoyance. His upper lip curled back, revealing teeth as long and yellow as those of Zurito.

"That's enough!" he said abruptly. "Just tell your mother what I said."

The boy stared at his thick, wiry eyebrows, arched in displeasure. "Ugly, you'd have to call him," he thought to himself, but he wasn't afraid, at least no more so than he had been at a wake, where he was left alone for a minute with the dead body and was dismayed by its stillness. Just as at the wake, he could hear a deathwatch beetle gnawing in the corner table.

"Can I water the horse?" he asked, for something to say.

"He'll drink when we go by the trough," the old man answered abruptly.

Whenever they went together to Balanotti, Don Francesco stopped to let Zurito drink at Lacuneddas. He drove him up to the watering trough, and Angelo jumped down and slipped the bit out of his mouth so that the horse could drink more easily. Then he put it in again and jumped back up on the gig. Every time they went into the country together, Don Francesco gave Angelo a coin which, because there was always a hole in his trouser pockets, the boy would clutch in his fist until he could take it home, where his mother stored it in a special box. Sometimes, on holidays, the lawyer gave him as much as a silver crown. Not in return for small services—it was too much for that—but, as the old man had often told Sofia, out of friendship and in order to help the boy build up some savings. Angelo's father, Giuseppe Uras, was dead, and no one but Don Francesco ever gave him a present. In fact, relatives had tried to cheat him of the little left by his father—a house at Norbio and a few acres of land in the area called Acquacotta which contained a spring of mineral water. Only Don Francesco's legal intervention had saved the inheritance, and he had not only refused to accept any compensation but had even defrayed the costs. As a consequence, Sofia looked on him as a guardian angel and did what she could to pay him back. "A guardian, yes, but no angel," they said at Norbio. Indeed, there had been considerable gossip about Don Francesco Fulgheri's friendship with Widow Uras, but eventually it died down because everyone saw that it was without foundation. The only two persons to keep it going were his two enemies, the professors Loru and Todde, and what they said was discounted because everyone knew they had a grudge against him. Besides, it was well known at Norbio that Francesco Fulgheri had more than once represented the very poor, without any fee, and even meeting the expenses out of his own pocket. This was what happened when the shepherds rebelled against the law that abolished community cultivation of the land, and Mummia and Tincone were arrested and put on trial. Pantaleo Mummia was from Norbio and Valerio Tincone from Nuoro, but Francesco Fulgheri, faithful to his principles, assumed the defense of them both. The new law gave property rights to anyone who threw a hedge, or wall, or other enclosure around his land. As a result, monied men became landowners, while shepherds, who owned nothing but their hungry sheep, had to go into debt in order to pay the exorbitant rent demanded for pastures. From the start, Fulgheri had taken the shepherds' side; he had written and spoken with authority, although unsuccessfully, against the new law, which overturned an Island custom that went back for centuries. Theretofore, land had been parceled out every year, free, to farmers and shepherds, according to the need of the individual, and there was a yearly rotation between sowing and pasturing. "But fortune is not always on the side of justice," Fulgheri himself would say, or, "God is never with the just and the poor" —a statement that drew down upon him the epithet of revolutionary and blasphemer. In support of which axiom, the two arrested shepherds were sentenced and hanged on the public squares of their respective villages, Tincone at Nuoro and Mummia at Norbio, the last two executions to take place on the Island before the abolition of the death penalty. Indignation was aroused by the fact that the poor fellows—known to be good family men—were punished for a crime committed some forty years before, when the enclosure law went into effect in 1820. Popular protest had endured, intermittently, throughout the interval, keeping alive fear and hatred of the new landowners, whom the king was unwilling to antagonize. And so it was that, upon the advice of a committee of eminent jurists, Victor Emmanuel rejected Fulgheri's petition for clemency. Many people at Norbio, Sofia among them, remembered the lugubrious ceremony of the hanging of Pantaleo Mummia. The scaffold was set up in the usual place on the Piazza Frontera, in front of the monastery of the Mercedari Fathers. Mummia had arrived from Cagliari the evening before, on a wagon flanked by a whole squadron of light cavalry. At eight o'clock the next morning, he was brought from the prison, where he had spent the night, to the square in an oxcart, and soldiers with drawn swords were once more at his side. Close to the cart four drummers, wearing white gaiters, rolled their drums so that everyone in the town, even as far away as the Sant'Antonio section, knew what was going on. Actually, the execution had been announced the day before by a herald on horseback who, upon the governor's order, invited the whole population to come witness the rebel's punishment. But nobody came. Some people went out into the fields; the rest shut themselves up behind locked doors and barred windows. Norbio seemed a ghost town; when the drums fell silent the only sounds were the creaking of the cart's wheels and the pounding of the horses' hoofs on the pavement. Just before the noose was slipped over Mummia's head, the prior of the Mercedari Fathers offered to confess him, but Mummia held to the silence of his townsmen, merely shaking his head and grunting like a boar.

"Repent! Repent!" called out the prior, in an increasingly loud voice, but Mummia only grunted. The monk's repeated admonishment and the victim's repeated grunt resounded in the silence. After Mummia had been led up to the platform with the rope around his neck, there was another sound, the desperate outcry of his wife, the only person on the square. She fainted away and was taken home in the same cart in which her husband had traveled a few minutes before. The cavalry squadron returned immediately to Cagliari, and a host of small boys came out with baskets and gathered up the horse dung, which they threw over the market-garden wall along the Fluminera River. But poor Mummia, as the sentence ordained, was left hanging for three days, so everyone saw him, the men coming back from the fields, the women going to the fountain for water, and the children returning from school. They made the sign of the cross, all of them, and mumbled a requiem for his honest and stubborn soul. Fulgheri, who was not given to prayer, went to the square and stood, bareheaded, at the foot of the scaffold as if to apologize for having failed to prevent the execution. His lips moved, as if he were praying, so that an old woman went up to him and asked:

"What's this, Don Francesco? Have you been converted? I see that you are praying."

"I don't know how to pray," he said, with irritation, "but you can pray in my stead. This man died for us all."

"A shame!" the old woman exclaimed. "He was a good fellow, and fine-looking as well."

The lawyer nodded gravely.

"Christ was a fine-looking fellow, too," he said.

At which the old woman ran away as if she had heard a blasphemy.

Fulgheri continued to talk and write against the law of enclosure and to fight against abuses and injustice, thus confirming the opinion that he was a dangerous agitator. He founded and edited a paper devoted to discussion of the agricultural and economic problems of the Island, and of Parte d'Ispi in particular. Because of his attacks on the governor and the magistrates of the Royal Court, he was warned, and finally prosecuted and sentenced to a brief detention in the Buoncammino Prison at Cagliari. No sooner was he released than he resumed his futile struggle. The unification of the kingdom of Italy had been proclaimed in 1861 while he was in prison, but he maintained that only the bureaucracies of the various Italian states had been amalgamated, whereas true unity, the ideal for which so many men had sacrificed their lives, could be achieved only through a federation. The execution of Mummia and Tincone seemed to him one of the last excesses of the old Piedmontese regime and a sample of what was to be expected from the hybrid and rudderless government of the new nation.

Don Francesco belonged to a patrician family of long standing, that of the Counts of Nepomuceno, but he ran counter to family tradition by opposing the House of Savoy, first because he was a convinced republican and second because of his abhorrence of its flagrant misrule of the Island.

The long goose-quill pen stuck up over Don Francesco's right shoulder, and Angelo tried to synchronize the quiver of the white feather with the scratching sound of the point on the unseen rough yellow paper. He was used to perching for hours on the high-backed chair behind the lawyer, but on this particular day the old man stopped writing earlier than usual. He laid the pen down with care after stroking the feather with the thumb and forefinger of his left hand, tugged at his side-whiskers, and stretched his whole body. At just this moment the gate creaked loudly, and Angelo ran to see who was there, although actually he knew. He recognized the step of Gerolamo Sanna, the herdsman, a gaunt man over six feet tall, wearing spurred boots and an odd black cap on the top of his head. Sanna had a mustache and eyebrows as white as the goose quill; his hair, too, was white and feathery, while his face was as red and shiny as the rind of a roasted pig. He looked after Don Francesco's three hundred head of cattle, which were put to graze in the mountains at this season before they were brought down to spend the winter on the plains. Several other cowherds worked under his direction, and once a week he came down to the village to report to his employer and to lay in provisions— bread, pasta, brandy, and tobacco.

Now, without saying a word, he raised his chin, mutely asking whether Don Francesco was at home. In reply, Angelo pointed with his thumb over his shoulder. The herdsman winked at him as if he were an adult and then, jingling his spurs, walked toward the study.

"Here I am," he proclaimed, "if there's anything I can do. . . ."

Don Francesco raised his eyes.

"If you have time, hitch the horse to the puddle-jumper" (this was what he called the gig).

"Yessir," said the herdsman, giving a mock military salute before he backed down the steps and set off for the stable. Don Francesco heard him start to harness the horse, whistling as he did so. The herdsman's whistle was the sound of the silence into which he withdrew, like a wild creature, after his brief exchanges with other men. Meanwhile, Angelo looked on as Gerolamo brought out the gig, then put a halter on Zurito, led him out of his stall, brushed some bits of straw out of his mane and tail, slipped on the harness with its yellow felt pads and brass studs, and finally put him to the gig with its narrow, curved shafts. Only then, under Gerolamo's scornful gaze, did the boy try to lend a hand. With his small, unpracticed hands, he tightened a strap and fastened a buckle, but even standing tiptoe he was unable to pass the reins back through the rings of the saddle.

"Leave them alone, midget," said Gerolamo, in a voice as hostile as his expression. "Hitching up a horse is no job for the likes of you. You didn't give him anything to drink, did you?" he added, putting a statement into interrogative form. When it came to the horse, Gerolamo Sanna knew everything, without need of questions.

"I can go get the bucket," said the boy.

"The bucket?" asked Gerolamo jeeringly. "Why not bring him a glass; it might suit him better. . . . You may as well wait until you get to the watering trough. But remember to slip out the bit. He's a high-strung horse and won't drink with the bit in his mouth. Understand?"

"Yes, I understand," said Angelo, who resented the herdsman's manner.

When he went back to the study, he found Don Francesco loading his gun. He scattered some black powder on the palm of his hand, poured it into the long barrel, and added a piece of tow, which he rammed down with a rod. Angelo heard the click of the lead bullet, then watched Don Francesco load his two saddle pistols in the same way. The old lawyer never went out unarmed, saying that no one was going to take him by surprise. Who might such a one be? Didn't he have more friends than enemies? He shrugged his shoulders and grimaced. A man may have a hundred friends but they are powerless to defend him against a single enemy. One enemy is enough, and in this case the enemy might be Gerolamo Sanna, who went freely in and out of his house. Many years before, Don Francesco had been responsible, because of a few words at the opportune moment to the judge and to the medical expert (who happened to be his own younger brother, Tommaso), for Gerolamo's going to jail. Gerolamo had married Teresa Contu, daughter of a prosperous land and livestock owner, who was found one day strung up from the ceiling of a cottage which he owned in the country. The first reaction was that he had committed suicide; both the police magistrate and Tommaso Fulgheri, the medical expert, agreed on this point and were about to turn the body over to family for burial when Don Francesco arrived upon the scene. After a quick look at the dead man's underwear, he gave a brief lesson in legal medicine, quoting texts that his two hearers had read but forgotten.

"But he died of strangulation," Tommaso Fulgheri insisted.

"He was strangled, yes, but not by hanging. The body was strung up after he was already dead."

They came around to his view, and, after listening to the testimony of several witnesses who had seen Gerolamo leave his house at a certain hour, the magistrate issued a warrant for his arrest. Gerolamo had been anxious to lay hands on the money his wife was to inherit from her father, and the old man was too slow in dying. In court he confessed to the murder, but swore that he would settle accounts with Don Francesco Fulgheri as soon as he got out of prison. Because of an amnesty, he was released while he was still a young man and, to general astonishment, the lawyer took him into his service. "It's better to have your enemy close by where you can keep track of him," he explained and, knowing that Gerolamo would seize the first chance for revenge, he went around with two pistols and a loaded gun. When he went to hunt partridges, he shot off the bullet against a tree and reloaded the gun with buckshot. But on every other occasion, he was prepared for a human target; over and over again Angelo had seen him change from bullet to buckshot and vice versa. He carried, too, a horn-handled cane whose secret—a concealed twelve-inch blade—the boy also knew. This sword-cane had been given him by Sir H. P., the Englishman who had come to Norbio for years during the hunting season and, with his hounds and gun, had all but exterminated the deer and wild sheep in the forests of Parte d'Ispi. The identity of the donor is of little consequence; the important fact is that Don Francesco always carried the cane, just as his ancestors had carried a sword, especially when he went in the evening to play cards with his old friend, Giacinto Spano, the tax-collector.

now he took off the old-fashioned black coat that he wore in the village and put on a loose corduroy hunting jacket, stuck the pistols into his belt, slung the rifle over his shoulder, and gave the hunting bag to Angelo to carry. Together man and boy walked out of the study. Gerolamo had calculated their moves to the second; he had opened the gate, wheeled the gig up to the foot of the steps, and now stood there, holding the horse's bridle and motioning to them to climb in. His own horse, on which he had ridden down from the mountains, was still tied up outside the gate with the saddle pouches empty. After Don Francesco had settled himself comfortably on the leather seat, he took a coin from his pocket and threw it, nodding, to the herdsman, who caught it on the palm of his left hand, which was no less agile than the right.

"Buy what you need and go back without waiting for me," said the lawyer.

Gerolamo shook his head, impassively.

"It's not enough," he said, continuing to extend his hand for a moment before tucking the coin into the small pocket of his goatskin vest. Without arguing, Don Francesco threw him another coin just like the first, which the herdsman caught and pocketed in the same manner, nodding assent. Then he stepped back to let Don Francesco drive the gig through the narrow gate. Don Francesco turned to the right and the horse broke into a fast, swinging trot up the hill.

"Where are we going?" Angelo asked him timidly.

"To tell your mother to have some soup ready for our return."

At the juncture of the Vicolo del Carrubo and the main street, Don Francesco leaned back and pulled in the reins, bringing the gig to an abrupt stop, then he wheeled the horse around so that he was not under stress on the steep slope. Angelo jumped down and ran to call his mother. There was no question of driving the gig into the narrow, stony alley, although ox-drawn wagons loaded with wood, grapes, and sheaves of wheat did manage to enter, leaving grease marks from the hubs of their wheels on the brick walls on either side.

Through the bars of the wooden gate, Angelo saw his mother

sweeping the area around the woodpile. She was wearing a bodice, a petticoat, and a pair of slippers, and rips in the petticoat revealed the white panties below. "She's quite capable of going out onto the the main street just that way," the boy thought to himself. Although Sofia respected and even feared public opinion in Norbio, she was also aware of its injustice, and at times she ignored conventions out of a certain independence of spirit. Angelo shrugged his shoulders, threw a stone at the gate, and pointed silently to the street where Don Francesco was waiting. Sofia understood immediately and ran to change her clothes. Angelo pushed open the gate and went into the house, where he found his mother putting on a skirt, kicking off her worn slippers, and replacing them with a pair of shiny black, imitation-leather sandals. She took her son by the hand and, without asking for further explanation, ran with him to the gig, where Don Francesco waited impatiently, cracking the whip.

"I want to ask you for a favor, Comare Sofia," he said, barely glancing at her as she finished pinning her shawl. Sofia met his look with a pair of sharp, still youthful and sparkling black eyes.

"At your orders," she said gravely.

"I'm going to Balanotti to see what those lazy fellows have done, and taking Angelo with me. I'd like you to go put my house in order and have some soup ready for us when we return."

Angelo was sharpening a stick with his penknife. There were mingled tenderness and gratitude in his mother's eyes. She was happy, to the point of tears, over the old man's interest in her son, and nodded a ready assent to his command.

"If you dust my study, don't touch the papers on my work-table. Leave them just the way they are."

"Of course," she answered, shaking her head. "You've told me that before. I know that I'm not supposed to touch your papers. Don't worry. And I'll make a soup with fennel and fresh cheese."

Angelo raised his head and licked his lips. And Don Francesco leaned forward and nodded.

"That good soup!" he exclaimed. "Perfect! We'll be back before the Angelus."

"If you're going as far as Balanotti, you'll need more time

than that. But when the Angelus rings your soup will be ready."

Don Francesco turned the horse's head toward the upward slope and touched his back with the whip. Zurito set out at the same brisk trot as before. When Angelo glanced back, a moment later, the street was already empty. Sofia had looked after them for an instant and then darted back into her house, pulling her shadow with her the way a mouse pulls its tail. She thought of Don Francesco as a man under constant threat and in constant danger and didn't want Angelo to share his fate. Now she made a sign of the cross and recommended her son and his protector to the care of the Blessed Virgin. She didn't want anything bad to happen to Don Francesco any more than to Angelo. And on this particular day, she thought she had noticed something out of the ordinary in his facial expression. Nor did she like the extended trot of Zurito. Ever since the death of her husband, Don Francesco had been her adviser, and she did nothing without asking his opinion. Only when she had sent Angelo to the seminary at Ales had she failed to consult him. On that occasion, she had followed the advice of the parish priest, knowing that Don Francesco would oppose it.

"To enter the priesthood you must have a vocation," Don Francesco told her when he found out. And Angelo didn't have a vocation. He ran away from the seminary, in his shirtsleeves and with bare feet, and came home. It was then that Don Francesco started to take an interest in him, going so far as to say that he would assume the expenses of the boy's schooling if he showed any inclination for learning. Meanwhile, he took him along when he drove about the countryside, or had him sit for hours in his study.

"Here's hoping nothing happens!" Sofia said to herself as she shooed a hen that was trying to get into the house back toward the chicken coop where she belonged.

€very now and then, the horse broke out of his trot into a gallop, to the joy of Angelo, who clung with one hand to the armrest and with the other to Don Francesco's hunting jacket.

They drove through the Piazza Frontera, where the usual idlers sat talking and smoking on the stone steps, near the former site of the gallows. The memory of the hanging caused Don Francesco to urge Zurito forward and drive him into the Via delle Tre Marie. Two old men had barely time to get out of the way by flattening themselves against the wall of the house of Giacinto Spano, the red-bearded tax-collector, who almost certainly recognized the sound of Don Francesco's gig and raised his green eyes from the contemplation of the papers before him. Don Francesco imagined this reaction as vividly as if he could see through the walls, and barely heard the two old men's imprecation: "Break your neck; it would serve you right!" Without turning around, he brought the horse back to a trot, talking to him in order to calm him down. He started to whip him up again as they approached the watering trough, but then thought better of it.

"We'd best let him drink," he said aloud; "he has quite a way to go." And he added, to himself: "That will quiet him." Zurito was overly excited and the road to Balanotti called for prudence. As he drove up to the trough, he saw a man squatting on his heels and sharpening a stick. It was Gerolamo Sanna, the herdsman; his horse was tethered to a nearby tree, with the saddle pouches weighed down by the purchases his master had made in the town.

"Greetings!" said Gerolamo, standing up on his long legs.

"Shall we follow the road together?" asked Don Francesco, without looking him in the face.

"I'm waiting for a friend," Gerolamo answered, walking up to Zurito and starting to take the bit out of his mouth so that he could drink. The horse eagerly sucked in the dark, clear water, while Gerolamo stroked his neck.

"He's in a lather," he exclaimed, looking at Don Francesco out of half-closed eyes.

"He trotted all the way," Don Francesco retorted. The herdsman claimed to know everything about horses, but Don Francesco would take no advice or interference. He tugged at the reins in such a way as to almost pull the bit out of Gerolamo's hands. Something seemed to give way, and Don Francesco lashed out with the whip at the horse's ears. Zurito shied to the left and tore off down the road to Balanotti. Angelo scarcely had time to grasp the armrest and swallow his saliva. As for Gerolamo Sanna, he did nothing to prevent the abrupt departure and threw the stick that he had been sharpening away. He made a cutting motion with his hand in the direction of Balanotti and shouted out: "Good luck!" The horse's shoes and the wheels of the gig raised sparks from the granite pavement, and when one hubcap grazed the guardrail, the gig heeled dangerously to one side but did not turn over. In Gerolamo's mind was the certainty that at some point of the dangerous road there would be an accident. Don Francesco Fulgheri, the man who had sent him to prison, would reap the reward he deserved. He was sorry about the boy, who was not to blame. But he was the son of Giuseppe Uras and Sofia Curreli, who had testified against him. So let the boy perish as well!

Zurito was galloping along the downhill road that ran between ten-foot-high banks of clay. The road had been dug out by the passage of thousands of carts and wagons, and there were several inches of reddish dust on the surface, which impeded the horse's gallop. But every now and then the gig skidded against a rock and would have turned over if the road had not been so tightly squeezed between the clay banks with their stone filling. The right fender, the one on Don Francesco's side, was torn loose and hung down over the wheel, clanking against it. Don Francesco pulled on the reins with all his might, wondering how the horse's mouth could be so insensitive, as he galloped on with his head and neck stretched forward.

"The wretch never put the bit back into his mouth!" he muttered to himself. He remembered that when Angelo had started to climb down from the gig to make sure that the bit had been adjusted, Gerolamo had shot him a ferocious glance. Don Francesco had laid his bent hand on the boy's shoulder to prevent him from moving. And now Angelo, still clutching the armrest, raised his eyes to those of the old man, who smiled down at him, aware that he was not really to blame.

"I shouldn't have let the wretch have anything to do with the horse; I should have got down myself!"

But it was too late for recriminations. Don Francesco saw in his mind's eye the granite basins of the watering trough, set out on a slope so that the water ran from one to another, remaining crystal clear. Bits of straw floated on the surface, following the current. Don Francesco reflected for a moment that life has inexorable laws to which men, like so many straws, are subject. But this wasn't really his way of thinking; he had always fought against fate rather than drifting with the current. He looked around, hoping to find a way to save the boy. Should he throw him out of the gig? No, the clay walls and the protruding rocks made this too risky. Perhaps it would be possible farther down, in the valley, where the road, as he recalled, was bordered by meadows. Meanwhile, the loose fender was making an infernal noise. Don Francesco extracted a monkey wrench from the door pocket and, transferring the reins to his left hand, he leaned over and unscrewed the nuts that held the fender to the body of the gig. The twisted wooden fender fell onto the dusty road, and the noise stopped, giving way to the rhythmic beat of the horse's feet, dulled by the dust that rose up in a red cloud behind. The canyon formation gradually disappeared; now the road ran between low walls, with olive trees, haystacks, and piles of stones behind them. Once more Don Francesco thought of throwing Angelo out, but he realized that it would be the next thing to murder. At the bottom of the hill, before the curve, he saw an ox-drawn wagon; he waved his arms and shouted to the driver to place himself across the road and block the passage of the runaway horse. Out of the corner of one eye, Angelo saw the wall on his side rush by at a dizzy speed, and he clenched his teeth in order not to bite his tongue at every bump. Perhaps the end was near; perhaps the Blessed Virgin had listened to the prayers which he had addressed to her since the beginning of the mad race.

"Save us, Blessed Mother, save us, and I promise I'll go back to the seminary and become a priest! Only bring us home safely!"

He moved his lips as he prayed, because they had taught him in the seminary that prayers must be said, not just thought. But although he spoke in a mere murmur, which should have been drowned by the clattering wheels and hoofbeats, Don Francesco overheard and turned furiously upon him.

"Confound you!" he shouted with what voice he could muster. "To become a priest when you haven't a vocation is worse than death, and it's a sin as well. My will is in the top drawer of the chest, and your mother and you are my heirs, but if you go back to the seminary, you'll not have a penny!"

The wagoner had heard the rattling of the gig and Don Francesco's cry, but instead of putting the wagon across the road, he cautiously moved it over to the right side in order to leave free passage. Zurito galloped by at a mad speed, but Angelo had time to see a black hole in the wagoner's mouth where two teeth were missing.

"Idiot!" shouted Don Francesco, waving his whip. A moment later, he threw it away and took one of the pistols out of his belt. Angelo imagined that he was going to shoot the wagoner, who looked after them with a stupidly vacant expression. The road was flat now, running between the carefully tended olive groves of Balanotti. Don Francesco braced himself against the back of the seat, with his feet firmly planted on the floor, took a cartridge out of his pocket, inserted it into the barrel of the pistol, stretched out his arm and aimed it at an area no bigger than a coin between the ears of Zurito.

"Hold fast!" he shouted to Angelo. An instant later Angelo heard the pistol go off, but nothing happened, and Don Francesco threw it away. The horse only quickened his pace; he rounded a curve so fast that the gig keeled over onto one wheel, but without capsizing. Five hundred yards ahead a man was standing, with his legs far apart, in the middle of the road, looking as if he were determined to stop the horse; he took off his jacket and waved it. As they drew rapidly nearer to him, they saw every detail of his face: the bristling beard and the heavy eyebrows that formed a single line across his forehead. At a certain moment, he bent his knees as if to step aside, but when the gig was upon him he failed to move; the right shaft struck his chest and knocked him down, and the wheel went over his body. There was a dull thud and then a cry. Turning around, Angelo saw him prostrate on the ground, his face covered with blood, and thought there was something familiar about him.

Don Francesco, swearing between his teeth, was loading the other pistol. He aimed carefully, spreading his legs and digging his feet into the floor. He was not a good shot, and he knew it, as did Angelo, who looked on with bated breath. Gerolamo, who made bets on hitting a coin he threw up into the air, would have had a better chance, but perhaps even he could not have put a bullet into the horse's moving neck. From the swaying seat Don Francesco fired his second shot, then, just as before, threw the precious pistol over his right shoulder. Once more the horse's pace quickened. The road narrowed, the gray walls looked as if they would converge, like the sides of a wedge. The olive trees arched overhead. A low branch lifted the hat from Don Francesco's head and, with a strange gesture, he raised his hand to tear off a handful of leaves, then released them one by one between his fingers, into the wind. The boy smiled at him, holding up his arms to protect his face from the scraping branches. Don Francesco loaded his rifle and prepared to make his last shot.

"Hold on tight!" he shouted to Angelo as he deliberately took aim. The shot rang out, reverberating in the adjacent valley; the bullet grazed the horse's back and neck, and the sting of it, together with the noise of the detonation, caused him to gallop even harder. The gig swayed from side to side, threatening to turn over. Don Francesco threw the rifle at the horse's head; it slid to the ground and a wheel went over it. Don Francesco leaned back, holding his head between his hands, but the bouncing gig threw his body from one side to another. Brusquely he hugged the boy, then lifted him up by his armpits.

"Grab one of the branches and hang onto it," he shouted, "and I'll try to follow."

The boy raised his hands, caught a branch and hung from it, ten feet above the ground, while the gig lurched on down the now more level road. Don Francesco turned around to look at him, waving his long, skinny arms, and Angelo shook his legs in response. The old man shouted something, but the boy could not hear. Below him he saw the dusty road; perhaps Don

Francesco was signaling to him to let go and drop down, trusting in the dust to break the impact of his fall. He released the branch and fell, with a bunch of leaves in his fist, onto the thick, warm dust, which rose up in a cloud around him. The gig, smaller and smaller in the distance, continued on its zigzag way, raising a curtain of reddish dust, like a morning mist, behind it.

Foam had formed under the horse's harness, reddened by blood from the open wound on his back. The blood had spurted onto Don Francesco's face; the warm, sweet taste of it was on his lips. He wiped his face with one hand and spat onto the ground. Out of his pocket he took a switchblade knife, opened it, and knelt down to cut one of the traces. Why hadn't he thought of it before? The trace was made of several strips of leather sewn together and he had difficulty cutting through, but finally he succeeded. The horse, partially freed, surged forward, but the trace on the other side kept him attached to the gig. "I should have cut them both at the same time," Don Francesco thought to himself. At just this moment, the gig veered to the right and rolled over into the dry stream-bed at one side of the road. Don Francesco was thrown into the air and then fell onto the stones.

Angelo lay in the middle of the dusty road. He could hear the clatter of the gig and the hoofbeats die away. In his mind's eye, he saw the yellow gig, the waving arms of Don Francesco, and the bloody line of the wound on Zurito's back, and on his lips he tasted the spurting blood. He sat up, with the clatter of the wheels still in his ears. Suddenly there was a loud crash, and the clatter ceased. In the distance he saw the gig rise up and then fall on one side, and even the tiny black figure of Don Francesco, suspended for a moment over the shattered frame of the gig, which entangled the horse's white body. After that he heard and saw nothing. The empty road stretched out toward the horizon, and the cloud of dust was gradually laid. Angelo shut his eyes and sank into an exhausted sleep in the sudden silence of high noon.

He woke up in the late afternoon, when the rays of the sun, setting over Monte Magno, came through the olive branches and struck his face. He rubbed his eyes, remembered Zurito's wild gallop, and, looking down the road, saw again the gig's last leap and Don Francesco's body projected into the air with the arms and legs askew. He got up, shook himself, and ran toward the distant curve where the gig must have turned over onto the dry stream. But fifty yards along the way, he stopped and looked around. He was in front of the gate of Don Francesco's little farm; he could see the house and the clump of reeds in front of the spring. Suddenly he had an urgent desire to drink; even while he had slept, thirst had tormented him. He pushed open the half-unhinged iron gate and leaned over in order to see as far as possible under the leafy branches of the olive trees, which very nearly touched the stony ground, then he went up to the house and walked around it. The door and the single window were closed. The farm workers who were supposed to clear the ground around the trees in view of the harvest had already gone away. Why had they failed to find him stretched out in the middle of the road? Perhaps, when they went back to Norbio, they had taken the shortcut through the woods. This was the most likely answer, for it was strange that no one should have passed by on the road in the course of so many hours. Smitten with self-pity, he took off his jacket, hung it on a peg stuck into the wall, and went to drink from the spring. He carefully washed his face and hands, dried them with the clean hand-kerchief his mother had put in his pocket, and used a stick to beat the dust out of his jacket and trousers. Feeling revived, he set out again toward the curve farther along the dusty road. He could see quite clearly the marks left by the horse's hoofs and the wheels of the gig. He had seen Don Francesco precipi-tated into the air as if the gig had exploded. Now he walked slowly, with the dust coming over his heavy shoes up to the ankles, the dust that had saved him when he had deliberately fallen from the tree. Near the curve he heard a weak whinny. He broke into a run and soon saw Zurito standing on the stony stream-bed, with blood on his neck and back and the remains of the harness hanging between his legs. Angelo searched his pockets and found some lumps of sugar, which he held out on the palm of his hand. The horse put a foot forward, stretched out his neck and took the sugar between his rough lips. Turning around, Angelo suddenly saw Don Francesco lying a few steps away under the wreckage of the gig, his eyes staring and his mouth hanging open in a macabre grin, the yellow teeth covered with a veil of blood, and a gash across his forehead. The boy stepped back and stood as motionless as if he had turned into stone. He had seen other dead bodies, but never so unexpectedly or belonging to someone to whom he felt so close. Nothing could have prepared him for such a sight, for in his child's mind Don Francesco was a protector, a strong man who could never succumb to any threat or danger.

With an effort, he made the sign of the cross, approached the body, knelt down on a stone, and said the prayer for the dead. He knew that he should close the dead man's eyes, but he hadn't the courage. From the wound on the forehead, blood had oozed onto a tiny holm oak pushing up from under the rock against which the corpse was leaning. Angelo went back to the horse and patted his blood-flecked, trembling body.

"We were scared," he murmured. "That's why he shot at you."

With difficulty, he loosened the tugs to which splinters of the shaft were still attached, and loosened the girth, causing the horse to give a sigh of relief. He put the bit in his mouth and fastened the strap, as Gerolamo should have done, rolled up the long reins and, holding the bridle, led the horse, like a child, up over the edge of the stream. Zurito followed him, quite docilely, drew up to the wall and seemed almost to bend down in order to let Angelo jump onto his back. The boy grasped his mane and swung himself up. The coil of reins was cumbersome, so he took his knife, cut them and threw the extra length onto the stream-bed, near the gig. From the road he had a last glimpse of Don Francesco and his staring eyes. So they would remain forever. Zurito was usually ready, at the least provocation, to break into a gallop, but now he proceeded at a slow trot, or the smooth, singlefoot gait characteristic of the horses of Parte d'Ispi. It was at this ambling pace that boy and horse went back over the road that they had followed in a mad gallop a few hours before.

Angelo interrupted his ride only twice, to pick up the two pistols, which lay, half buried in dust, where they had fallen. He cleaned them off as best he could and stuck them into his pockets, pulling one out every now and then to examine it. There were few people along the way, most of them men coming back from work, whom he passed with only a brief greeting in order to stave off any questions. Someone must have seen the runaway horse, and someone must have picked up the body of the man who had been run over, which had disappeared, as had Don Francesco's rifle. With difficulty, he raised and released the hammers of the pistols, which made a clicking sound. If he had had the necessary things—gunpowder, tow, and matches—he would have been able to load them. Some day he might be a marksman.

When they came to the watering trough, Zurito slowed down and craned his neck to drink. Angelo had a start when he heard the voice of Gerolamo Sanna:

"A horse can't drink well with the bit in his mouth. You have to take it out."

The herdsman was right beside him, already stretching out his hand to unbuckle the bit. Angelo pulled a pistol out of his pocket and leaned it, unostentatiously, against the horse's withers.

"Let him alone," he said, "he's drinking."

Zurito had plunged his muzzle into the trough and was sucking in the dark, clear water. Gerolamo made a gesture of annoyance, as if to brush off a fly, and stepped back just far enough not to look into the pistol barrel. The men around him laughed, and Angelo shuddered. Did they know that Don Francesco was dead, was this the reason for their laughter? "People are hard and bad," he thought to himself. Zurito once more broke into a singlefoot gait, and glided, with barely audible hoofbeats, down the dark, empty road. Every now and then he almost grazed a shadowy human form. It was doubtless someone who knew exactly what had happened, or else knew nothing and imagined that the horse had been taken to drink and was on his way home with a bellyful of water whose gurgling sound was superimposed upon that of the hoofbeats. The Angelus was ringing when boy and horse arrived at Don Francesco's house. The gate was open and there was a light in the kitchen. Sofia appeared at the door, like a tiny black cricket.

"*Mammai, Mammai!*" the boy shouted reassuringly as he leaped down, his hobnailed shoes crunching the gravel. He ran to his mother, hugged her, and breathlessly told her the whole story.

"I knew it, I could feel it in my bones," she said, beating her clenched fists against the wall. "I knew I shouldn't let you go, today of all days."

She stuffed her convulsive hand into her mouth to stop the flow of words and fell down on her knees before the already prepared table.

"Holy Mother of God, I thank you for having saved the life of my son. Have mercy on the soul of that poor sinner!"

If she had been in her own house, she would have lit the votive lamps before the images of her patron saints. But here in the house of Don Francesco there were neither lamps nor images.

"Come here; I haven't yet had a good look at you," she said to the boy, catching hold of his arm and holding him a little way off. There was no change, except that his face was dirty and his sweaty, dusty hair hung over the left side of his forehead.

"Did you fall?" she asked, touching him with her hand.

"I only fell asleep in the warm dust in the middle of the road."

Once more she hugged him.

"Don Francesco saved your life," she said, "by getting you to catch hold of the branch of an olive tree."

"I know that," he said, shuddering. "Otherwise I'd be keeping him company this very minute."

Sofia cried aloud and hugged him again.

"God protected you, and the Blessed Virgin had mercy."

Don Francesco's house, like the others belonging to his family, was among the few at Norbio with its own water pump and a bathroom, even if the only tub was a round vat of the kind used in the Parte d'Ispi region for pressing grapes. Every time that Don Francesco drove out into the country he told Sofia or

Verdiana to ready a tubful of hot water for his return, and this was now waiting for him. Without saying a word, Sofia led Angleo into the bathroom and started to undress him. In her impatience she almost tore off his clothes, anxious to feel his narrow back and shoulders, his flat belly, and the whole of his miraculously preserved body, as warm and soft as that of a rabbit. He let her pick him up and plunge him into the hot water.

"What about these?" she asked in alarm, taking the heavy pistols out of his jacket pockets and laying them on the seat of the toilet.

"Don't worry, they're not loaded. I couldn't leave them on the road; it would be too bad to lose them."

"They're of no use to us," said his mother, shaking her head emphatically.

"We'll keep them as mementos," said Angelo, with apparent docility, but to himself he thought: "They might come in handy some day, who knows? It would be better to load them."

He was covered with lather and had to hold his eyes tightly shut to keep the soap from getting into them when he said:

"Listen, mother; before Don Francesco told me to hang on to the branch of a tree he said . . ."

"He said what?"

"That he was leaving everything he had to you and me, to the two of us."

Sofia felt a lump in her throat. She was not a grasping woman, and her affection for the old lawyer was not based on self-interest. She knew that he had intended to leave something —not "everything," as the boy had ingenuously said—to her son, perhaps the farm at Balanotti, perhaps Lugheria. But the confirmation of what she had taken for a vague and casual promise filled her with joy. The soap slid out of her hand and struck the mirror.

"Ridiculous!" she exclaimed, groping for the cake of soap on the floor.

"His will is in the top drawer of the chest," the boy gravely insisted.

His mother rinsed her hands, dried them on her apron, and

went like a sleepwalker to look in the drawer. Angelo plunged his head into the water and, when he raised it, she was standing before him with a sealed paper in her hands.

"Here it's written . . ." she said. "Read out to me what it says. . . ."

It was written: "To be opened after my death; a copy is with the notary Pietro Pintus of Norbio."

Angelo plunged his head into the water again. Poor Don Francesco, all alone in the countryside by night! He could never have imagined dying this way, with only the foxes and owls of Balanotti at his wake.

"We must go for Don Francesco," he said, bursting into tears. "We can't leave him like that."

As if to lend weight to his words, a fox barked in the night air. The same fox barked every night, shortly after the Angelus, and stole goats from around Castangias and then hid on the slopes of the Monte del Carmine, where the goats' bones were later to be found. For years, the goatherds had been unable to catch him with either traps or dogs. Now the sharp sound quivered in the air like the beating of a bat's wings or the inarticulate lament of a hired mourner. Angelo held out his arms, and his mother lifted him bodily out of the tub and wrapped him in a warm towel. Then she sat down and held him on her knees, as when he was a baby. But she, too, was crying, out of tenderness for her son and herself and the naked soul of Don Francesco. This last thought caused her to murmur silently the prayer for the dead. He had been good to them in life, the grouchy, eccentric, old man, and he would continue to protect them after his death. Mother and son cried together, in each other's arms. Then she helped him dress while he told her again how he had found the old man's body on the stream-bed, under the shattered gig, with a gash across the forehead which, before it stopped bleeding, had trickled blood onto a tiny plant pushing up from under a rock.

"A fern?" she asked, drying her eyes.

"No, a holm oak," Angelo answered, as if the difference were essential. Then she told him, in a subdued voice, of the local belief that a dead person's soul, after floating for a while through the countryside, like the fragrance from herb or flower, chooses a young tree and takes refuge in it until it pleases God to summon it to share his glory.

"Then Don Francesco's soul may be in the holm oak," Angelo said. "We'll dig it up and bring it home, won't we, mother? And so Don Francesco will be always with us."

Sofia nodded in quiet agreement, and Angelo, in his turn, dried his eyes. His mother's story was consoling, and Don Francesco no longer seemed so irretrievably lost and dead. Hand in hand, they went down the wooden stairs, leaving the darkened rooms of the upper floor behind them. Sofia felt the importance of the boy's presence, the comfort and strength she drew from it. Without him, she would not have dared to take a step or linger for more than a minute in the dead man's empty house, where mysterious creaking and rustling sounds broke the silence. But with the boy's rough, warm hand in hers, she fearlessly scrutinized the darkness and serenely contemplated the future. With her child she was not alone.

"Now let's eat the soup that Don Francesco ordered," she said when they reached the kitchen; "we can't very well throw it away."

Angelo nodded, and she set the candle on an overturned pot in the middle of the table and ladled out the fennel-and-cheese soup. Mother and son made the sign of the cross and fell to.

"So all trees shelter souls, do they? And what about flowers?"

"Flowers shelter the souls of dead children."

"Once I saw a woman giving her milk to a flower."

"What do you mean?"

"She sprayed her milk into the flowerpot."

"Perhaps she had lost a child."

"Tomorrow morning we must go fetch Don Francesco," said Angelo, coming back to reality.

"Yes, early tomorrow morning."

"We must be the first to get there."

Sofia nodded gravely. From the stable Zurito gave a gentle whinny.

"I must take him his fodder," said Angelo, nodding in the direction of the stable. "I completely forgot it."

"Give him oats, and plenty of them. Don't bother to grind the beans; it's too late."

Angelo crossed the dark courtyard, took some oats from the storeroom, stopped to pick up half a sack of straw, and then went to the stable. He stroked the horse and spoke to him in his usual manner, then ducked under his neck to clean the trough, fill it with fresh straw and pour out the oats, which gave off a dusty smell. The horse snorted and rubbed his face against the boy's shoulder.

"You'll have beans tomorrow," Angelo reassured him.

With a pitchfork, he spread straw on the floor, then patted the horse's shoulder and left him. His mother was holding a kerosene lamp over the gate to light the way.

"Did he drink?" she asked.

"Yes, he drank."

As they went away, Sofia locked the gate with the rough wooden key and then strung it on her belt. She had a feeling that, from now on, this was to be her home.

During the five years since she had been left a widow, Sofia had slept alone. Angelo's cot was in the next room, and when she lay awake, she heard his regular breathing. Sometimes, in the dead of winter, she wrapped him in a shawl and carried him to her bed in order that she might finally go to sleep, but this did not happen very often.

"Aren't you sleeping, mother?" Angelo now asked, hearing her toss on the mattress.

"Yes, I'm sleeping," she said plaintively.

A few moments later, she heard the patter of footsteps on the brick floor, and raised the sheet to make room for him. He snuggled up against her and she hugged him contentedly. His feet were hard, smooth, and icy. A mysterious feeling of guilt caused her to resist the temptation of having him in her bed, but when she was worried only his physical presence could calm her. On this particular night, the thought of Don Francesco troubled her. She saw his face when she had said good-by, only a few hours before, in the afternoon, marked with what seemed like a premonition. She recalled his impatient gesture with the whip. Now he was lying on the gravel of the dry stream, among the dust-covered oleanders. She remembered another local superstition: when someone dies, spirits visit his house and the houses of his relatives to pick up the bits and pieces of his soul which, like tufts of wool, are stuck to household objects and to women's hair. The sleeping Angelo's regular breathing kept her company, and she pulled the sheet up over her head. At this hour, the spirits must be in Don Francesco's house, looking for what he had left of himself among the things he loved. She imagined drawers opened by invisible hands, linen thrown onto the floor, books hanging open in mid-air, guns and pistols aimed at nonexistent targets, then replaced in the rack, mattresses turned over, pictures detached from the walls, and the papers on the desk, of which he was so jealous, scattered as if by a gust of wind. "Don't touch a thing!" he told her whenever she went to clean his study. The papers were covered with dust but he didn't want her to move them.

Angelo was asleep with his head on her arm. His sleep was contagious, and as her eyes closed the thought of the spirits took concrete form. A white cloud passed under closed doors and through the cracks of the second-storey floor, invading the entire house of Don Francesco Fulgheri, and through its white, milky substance, she could see objects in the rooms. In the bedroom, the unmade bed; in the bathroom, a tub full of soapy water, with dirty towels piled up in one corner. The two pistols she had taken from the pockets of Angelo's jacket lay as she had left them on the crowded toilet table and one of her hairpins was on the floor. Surrounded by the white cloud which opened up to afford her passage, she withdrew cautiously, in order not to see herself in the mirror, and glided down the stairs, without touching either steps or railing. Don Francesco sat at the kitchen table, over his soup. With a feeling of relief, she went toward him. His lips barely touched the spoon. "The soup's cold; I'll heat it for you," she said, stretching out her hand toward the tureen. Don Francesco shook his thin, crooked finger in refusal. "It's good," he murmured, with a smile; then he took the sealed will out of his pocket and held it out to her. Timidly, she took it. Don Francesco made a gesture of impatience. "Can't I trust even you?" he asked, suddenly smiling again. She tucked the will into her blouse. "Yes, you can trust me. But what can I do for you? In the name of the Father and of the Son and of the Holy Ghost, tell me what I can do!" Don Francesco shrugged his shoulders and opened wide his gray eyes. Looking at her just as he had done when he was alive, he said, quite clearly: "See to it that my last wishes are respected. It's all explained in the will." Then he crumpled up on his chair, and invisible hands carried him out of the kitchen, feet first, as a corpse is carried. She flew away like a flash, followed by a train of white smoke and a murmur of voices like the rustling of dry leaves. But in her flight, she grazed the stony ground. She flew up the street, turned into the Vicolo del Carrubo, and entered her own house, closing the door behind her. Beyond the closed door, she could hear the murmur of voices, like the buzz of dying flies.

From her bed she listened to the buzzing sound, holding the child in her arms. He tossed in his sleep as if he too were aware of danger, and she shivered. It wasn't exactly cold, but summer had gone and there was a presentiment of winter in the long night. She slipped her arm out from under the child's head, stole out of bed and fetched a blanket from the chest. It was a blanket of heavy wool, carded and woven by one of her great-grandmothers, one of those indestructible objects that pass from generation to generation and, by their durable quality, make one aware of the precariousness of human life. She thought of the people who had been warmed by the blanket during long winter nights, all of them now turned to dust, people she had never known but for whom, since she was blood of their blood, she never failed to pray. The votive lamp on the chest of drawers flickeringly lit up the holy pictures. As if in a dream Sofia got up, went over and knelt down, with her hands gripping the worm-eaten top of the chest. She bowed her head, made the sign of the cross, said a prayer, bowed her head, crossed herself again, and then went back to lie under the warm blanket. She drifted off to sleep, but her dream returned to haunt her. Now the house was surrounded by the white cloud, which no longer floated in the air but had taken the shape of a swarming procession, which filled the courtyard, the alley, and the street. The procession was made up of all the people of Norbio transformed into white wraiths: men and women, children holding their parents' hands. There were dogs and horses, two ox-drawn wagons, and the priest, Don Aldo Masala, clad in black-and-gold funeral vestments and riding a horse. They were going, all of them, to fetch the body of Don Francesco and that of the man who had been knocked down and killed by the runaway Zurito. She and Angelo were riding him, forming another wraith in the crowd. She was sitting on a folded horse-blanket, in her Sunday dress, with a black silk veil over her head and her right arm around the waist of Angelo, who sat proudly upright in the saddle. From the height of the horse's back, they could see the procession of white shadows, bending before the least breeze. The big bell of Saint Barbara's was tolling, but the village was as empty as when Pantaleo Mummia had been hanged, the streets deserted and the doors barred. When the head of the procession reached the Piazza Frontera, the silence was broken by a clap of thunder. With a start, Sofia woke up.

The real noise was that made by Comare Verdiana knocking at the door. The sexton had sent her, upon orders from Don Aldo Masala, to find out whether a room was ready to receive Don Francesco's body. Sofia got dressed hastily and, with the sun barely above the horizon, the two women ran to the old man's house. In the study, they pushed the desk against the wall and set up a cot, barely in time, because the wagon bringing the dead body was already in the courtyard. Zurito whinnied and pawed at the door of his stall, while the house quickly filled up with people. All the Fulgheri relatives, old and young, were present, from Don Francesco's ninety-year-old uncle and aunt,

Giovannantonio and Fernanda, to his nieces and nephew—Margherita, Carmela, and Franceschino—children of his brother, Dr. Tommaso, all of them as stiff and proud as though they were wearing the family coat-of-arms and the right to a title on their chests. The body was laid out on the cot, but nobody was pleased with this arrangement, some saying that it should be in his bedroom, others holding out for the dining room. Finally, Don Aldo Masala declared that it was quite all right where it lay and chased everyone, including the relatives, away, after settling the hours at which they should keep watch. Sofia was told to help the women of the family and Comare Verdiana to dress the corpse, but, after a brief examination, Dr. Tommaso decreed that it had already become too stiff to allow a change of clothes. The women brushed off and straightened out his suit, shined his shoes, wiped his face with a wet sponge, and combed his hair. Then Sofia stretched a clean sheet over the body. When she was left alone, she turned this back and slipped a blessed rosary and a metal cross between his fingers. Then, at last, kneeling beside the bed, she gave way to tears. It was all very sad—the old suit in which he was to be buried, and the tearless indifference of the relatives. She painfully remembered the melancholy look in his eyes; although he had plenty of money, there was no one to love him, and this was why he had become so attached to Angelo and herself.

Now Angelo, with the priest holding him by the hand, was walking unwillingly in the direction of the church, where the priest wanted to question him. Three shots had been heard during Zurito's wild race, and rumor had it that Don Francesco had killed himself. The priest was a tall, stout, sixty-year-old man who, even when he was in a good humor, inspired respect and fear in old and young alike. When they arrived at the sacristy, he patted the boy's head affectionately, tousled his hair, then sat down on a shabby armchair, upholstered in red velvet, and motioned to Angelo to kneel on the hard, unpainted wooden prayer stool.

"You must tell me the whole truth," he admonished. "Remember that there's no forgiveness for liars; they go straight to Hell."

34

"I haven't done anything wrong," said the boy, thinking of the sins that Don Masala usually investigated.

"I'm not concerned with you," said the priest, laying a hand on his shoulder, "although you haven't been to confession for some time and yesterday you were in danger of death."

"I haven't committed any sins since my last confession."

"You've told no lies?"

"No, Father."

"You've committed no impure acts?"

"No, Father."

"Am I to think you're innocent as an angel and that, if you'd died yesterday, you'd have gone straight to Heaven?"

"I didn't say that, Father."

"You have only to give an honest answer to my questions. You used to go to that sinner's house."

"Don Francesco—God rest his soul!—was no sinner. He was a good man, one that helped the poor."

"Did you ever see him pray?"

"No, I never did. But he said that doing good was a kind of prayer. And he did good all around him."

"How do you know? You have only to answer my questions."

"Very well, Father," said Angelo, bowing his head and waiting.

"Yesterday Don Francesco shot off a pistol three times."

"Two pistol shots and one shot with a rifle."

"When was the first shot?"

"Halfway down the hill just before Balanotti."

"And who or what was the target?"

"The horse."

"To scare him?" asked the priest maliciously. If Don Francesco had meant to scare the horse, it was plain that his intentions were suicidal. In this case, the priest would have had a right to deny him a religious funeral and to insist that he be buried outside consecrated ground.

"No, to stop him. The horse had lost his head and was out of control."

"What about the other two shots?"

"He was still trying to stop him," said Angelo, almost shouting.

"What did he aim at?"

"At the horse's head. But it was difficult to hit it."

"Couldn't he have jumped out of the gig?

"No, he couldn't."

"But you managed to jump out, somehow."

The boy explained how his old friend had saved his life by telling him to hang on to the branch of an olive tree. But the priest went on with his questions.

"So Don Francesco finally shot himself, did he?"

"He wasn't crazy like the horse, Father, and he didn't want to die."

"Are you sure of that, son?"

"Yes, Father, I'm sure," said Angelo, looking the priest in the eye.

"How can you know?"

"He had told my mother to make the soup with fennel and freshly grated cheese that he particularly liked."

"But what do you know of his intentions?"

Angelo raised his innocent eyes to meet the priest's scrutiny.

"Are you really certain that he didn't kill himself? That he didn't do anything to promote or hasten his death?"

"I'm absolutely certain."

They were both silent for a minute, and then Don Masala asked:

"How did it happen that the horse cut loose and couldn't be stopped?"

"Is this a confession?" Angelo asked very seriously. "Will everything I say remain a secret?"

Instead of being angry, as Angelo expected, the priest blanched, but remained quite calm.

"Yes," he said; "everything you say here is in strict secrecy."

"Gerolamo Sanna took the bit out of the horse's mouth and never replaced it."

"Say no more," said the priest, raising his hand. "You musn't name names."

"But this is a confession, isn't it?"

"Exactly."

"Well, that's why Don Francesco couldn't stop the horse."

"I see," said the priest thoughtfully. "Say the act of contrition and promise that you won't spread any gossip."

He held out the tip of his embroidered stole and its black cross for the boy to kiss and then raised his hand:

"*Ego te absolvo. . . .*"

Angelo backed timorously out of the sacristy, turning his eyes away from the life-size figure of Christ nailed to a wooden cross over the door. Ever since he had seen it for the first time, this giant crucifix had struck fear into his heart.

Giovannino Caddia, the carpenter, with the aid of one of his apprentices, had already brought the rough wooden coffin, which gave out the fragrance of freshly cut poplar. At first sight, it seemed too small. A folded horse-blanket was laid on the bottom, with one end rolled up in such a way as to form a pillow, and Don Francesco's body was placed on it. While Giovannino attached the top with greased brass screws, relatives, old and young, filed by, murmuring prayers or exorcisms.

The whole town took part in the funeral, except for the two professors, Todde and Loru. But the latter sent his coachman, Fideli, with his landau to bring Don Giovannantonio and Donna Fernanda home. The coffin was carried, according to custom, on the mourners' shoulders and set down at intervals on an unsteady trestle, where Don Masala, who had consented to receive the body of "the great sinner" within the sacred precincts of the church, sprinkled holy water upon it. Beneath their merely conventional grief, all those present must have known that the eccentric Don Francesco would be missed in the town. The wooden coffin, with rope marks upon it, was finally lowered into the damp ground, and it fell to Angelo to throw the first handful of earth into the open grave.

Later the family installed a marble slab, with the dates of birth and death, the university honors, and the count's crown and coat-of-arms of the Fulgheri di San Giovanni Nepomuceno.

But Angelo and his mother remembered Don Francesco as he was in life, first with his foot in the stirrup, and then leaning over from the saddle to stroke his horse's neck while the horse shook his mane and flailed the air with his tail. Some of the townspeople remembered him as he was when he went for the last time to see the shepherd Mummia and to beg pardon for having failed to save him from the gallows.

A few days after the funeral Pintus, the notary, called the presumptive heirs together to hear the reading of the will. No one pressed him to do so, but he wanted to settle the matter and forget about it. He foresaw that the relatives would raise strong objections and yet, as executor, it was his duty to carry out the dead man's wishes in spite of any obstacles that might stand in the way. Because his office was not large enough, he asked Sofia to permit the meeting to take place in Don Francesco's study.

"Why don't you ask to go to one of the relatives' houses?" she countered brusquely. "What business is it of mine?"

Quietly the notary held up his hand.

"If I come to you, it's for good reason."

"As you please," she said more calmly.

She came to the meeting in her everyday clothes, with the addition of a black veil on her head. For the occasion she had carefully combed Angelo's hair. When mother and son arrived, the Fulgheris were already sitting in line. Their attire indicated that they did not credit the ceremony with great importance: Donna Fernanda wore a beige lace veil, a heavy gold necklace, and a silk fan on a chain, but Don Giovannantonio's boots were dusty and the silk lapels of his French-style jacket were moth-eaten. Sofia and Angelo sat down together near the door, after making signs of recognition and greeting to which the Fulgheris responded only by dropping their eyes. Present also, upon the notary's request that they serve as witnesses, were Barbara Muscas, a fifty-year-old woman who had long been in the service of Donna Fernanda, Gerolamo Sanna, and Comare Verdiana. The notary himself was sitting at Don Francesco's desk. He got up, looked at those present, one by one, and examined the sealed paper, raising his eyebrows as if the contents were as much of a surprise to him as to them. Before starting to read, he cleared his throat, but his voice remained as harsh and nasal as before. In the notary's language and through the notary's voice, so different from his own, which had been deep and vibrating, Don Francesco Fulgheri made known, from beyond the grave, his last wishes. Yet the unfamiliar, legalistic language was intelligible to all, including children and illiterates, and caused a look of astonishment to come over their faces. Little Angelo Uras was named as the sole heir, thus acquiring one of the largest fortunes of Parte d'Ispi. The dead man's possessions were listed in detail, so that there could be no misunderstanding: the house, with everything in it; the annexes, that is, the storerooms, the stable, the horse, and the agricultural tools; the olive groves at Balanotti, with the cottage and its contents; the orchards at Lugheria, the cottages that went with them, the water mills, and the agricultural machinery; and the fields at Saboddus and Acquacotta. Of Don Francesco's relatives the will made no mention, as if they did not exist and there was no need to justify their exclusion. The relatives remained impassive without so much as looking at little Angelo or his mother, Sofia Curreli. Only when the notary had finished reading the will did old Don Giovannantonio get up and say that he would contest it, that even if it cost him everything he had, he would defend the interests of his great-nieces and great-nephew, Margherita, Carmela, and Franceschino. It was utterly wrong, he said, that the wealth acquired by their ancestors should fall into the hands of a peasant boy who was not even of an age to take care of it. At this point, Angelo raised his eyes to look at his mother and saw that she was staring at the tips of her shoes and gravely nodding her head. The notary answered Don Giovannantonio on her behalf. The will had been legally drawn, he said, and to contest it would only be a waste of time and money. Then he adjourned the meeting, took Sofia aside and told her that, after the execution of certain formalities, she would receive the money and properties, the will having specified that she should be her son's guardian until he came of age. Sofia made a sort of bow and went away, dragging Angelo after her lest he dash upstairs after Don Francesco's pistols and watch, the new possessions which he most treasured. She could not, however, prevent him from taking Zurito to the watering trough. Quietly, under the family's gaze, he led the horse out of the stable, brushed him, and then mounted on his back. Gerolamo Sanna looked at him with a satisfied air and gave him a wink, but Angelo's face betrayed no emotion. "Good luck!" said the herdsman and slapped the horse's rump, causing him to quicken his pace, as he went by. Angelo reined him in. As he rode through the gate, which his mother was holding open, he leaned over to hear what she had to say.

"You're taking the horse to our house, I suppose," she observed.

"Why should I? This house is ours, too, isn't it?"

"Don't be in such a hurry," she said calmly. "For the present we live on the alley and it will be easier to feed and water him there."

Angelo conceded that, as usual, his mother was right and, in order to win her approval, he continued to hold the horse with a tight rein. Turning around, a few minutes later, he saw the street filled with the Fulgheri family. First the two little girls, in silk dresses, with their hair tumbling over their shoulders, holding onto the hands of their great-aunt and great-uncle; then Franceschino, straddling a cane, as if he, too, were astride a horse. The boy was the deceased's namesake, and yet Don Francesco had left him nothing. This, Angelo thought to himself, as he stroked his real horse's neck, was unfair. All of a sudden he remembered the sentence that Don Francesco had shouted into his ear not long before he died: "If you go back to the seminary, you'll not have a penny!" There had been no such clause, he now remembered, to his surprise, in the will. Perhaps the old man had made a prior will. Angelo was almost sorry that the clause was not there. If it had been, then to accept or turn down the bequest would have been up to him, just as it had been up to him to lead Zurito out of the stable and ride him up the alley. Instead, as things were, he had no responsibility; he was simply the object of Don Francesco's generosity and the relatives' resentment. He was sorry, in the last resort, for little Francesco Fulgheri, sorry to see him riding his hobbyhorse while he, Angelo, had suddenly become one of the richest landowners of the community. He was sorry, too, for Margherita and Carmela. Even if they were a bit snobbish, they were pretty little girls, with their bright eyes and the chestnut hair falling over their shoulders. The two old people were indifferent to him; they were ugly and mean, and Don Francesco had done well to disinherit them. The best of the lot was his brother, Tommaso, the doctor. For him Angelo had genuine affection, not only because he was the father of the three children, but also because he was, like them, young and innocent; because, too, with his black beard and black hair Don Tommaso resembled the murdered American president Abraham Lincoln, whom Don Francesco had deeply admired. Indeed, Don Francesco had given a book about Abraham Lincoln to him, Angelo, after he had run away from the seminary.

Sofia walked home alone. She had waited impatiently, during the preceding days, for the reading of the will. Certainly she would have been disappointed if Don Francesco had not kept his promise, but now that she had the assurance that her son would be a rich man she was less happy than she had expected to be; indeed, she felt depressed, as if she had heard bad news rather than good. At the same time she felt somehow guilty, as if she were responsible for what had happened. She quickened her pace and, with a brief nod of greeting, overtook and passed the members of the Fulgheri family, who were walking slowly and solemnly down the street, occupying its whole width and wearing a more funereal look than on the day when they had followed Don Francesco's body to the graveyard. She couldn't blame them for that, but at the same time she remembered that at the time of the burial they knew nothing of the terms of the will. Unless, she reflected, there was a family secret of which they were all aware. "The old man must have had a reason for disinheriting them and leaving everything to Angelo,"

41

she said to herself. "And they must have had some reason not to love him, too. But these things are none of my business, and I don't really care." And she shut the gate to her house on the alley behind her.

For the whole week since the accident, she had left her housework undone. She had not even baked bread, but asked for some from Comare Verdiana. Now she put away her black silk veil, tied her everyday yellow kerchief around her head, went to get half a sack of wheat from the granary, washed it, and spread it out to dry in two baskets in the courtyard, in front of the kitchen door. When Angelo arrived with the horse, she told him to watch out that the chickens didn't eat the wheat or dirty it. He sat down in a low chair between the two baskets, with a stick in his hand and a slightly worried look on his face. Something—he did not know exactly what—was awry. In the course of their conversations, he and his mother had come close to the matter which was on both of their minds, but they had never quite put it into words. And yet he had guessed at her feelings and she at his.

"I'm going out to buy some salt," she said; "wait here for me."

She leaned over and ran her hands through the still wet wheat.

"If the sun would come out," she added, "it would dry in a minute. The weather's out of kilter. In other years by the middle of October, we'd already have had rain. This year there's neither rain nor sun."

"It will rain; you'll see," said the boy.

"Of course, it will rain eventually, and the rain is nearer today than it was yesterday. But meanwhile we have to wait for it to come; we can't sow, and we can't even pick the prickly pears. They're not good for you if you eat them before the first rains."

"Can't they be put to soak in water?"

"No. They have to drink up fresh rain."

"Look here, *Mammai*," the boy said all of a sudden, grasping his mother's hand and looking up at her. "Let's give Acquacotta and Saboddus back to the Fulgheris and keep only Balanotti."

42

He spoke as if he were asking for a favor, but he knew quite well that his mother had the same thing on her mind. She smiled, as if a weight had been lifted from her shoulders, and ran her hand through his hair.

"Balanotti, the house here in the village, and Zurito, that's all we can accept," she agreed.

"And the pistols and the English saddle."

"Yes. Let them keep the rest; that way we can live in peace, without quarrels or resentment."

Sofia didn't really need salt, but it was an excuse for going to the square. She went to get her shawl and then stepped out into the alley. At this hour, the main street was deserted. The gray sky stood high as on a winter day, after rain, and the mountains, clothed in underbrush, were profiled, clear and dark, against the horizon.

Swarms of crows and sparrows flew from the roof of the Archbishopric to the bell tower of Santa Barbara. Sofia walked quickly and lightly, as happy as if she had already carried out her decision, because she knew exactly what had to be done. Now, at last, the inheritance seemed to her a good thing and a lucky one. The few passers-by were not surprised to see her happy face and springy step, since news of the bequest had rapidly spread through the village, but they could not know the real reason why she looked like a girl on the way to a dance or a lovers' meeting. As she reached the square, the bell in the church tower rang out noon. She made the sign of the cross, darted into the salt-and-tobacco shop, and then started for home, clutching the blue parcel of salt to her breast.

The north wind, sweeping down the street, carried the sound of the bells after her. As for the street, it was as clean as if a team of sweepers had just passed over it. Sofia stiffened her back against the wind that was pushing her down the hill. The doors and windows of the houses along the way were closed, but there was a noise of slamming shutters. Resisting the wind, Sofia came to a stop. She felt as if, from behind the doors, from dormer windows and woodsheds, people were spying on her. As they peered through peepholes and slits between the shutters, at a woman with a shawl tied under her chin and a parcel of salt clutched in her hands, who could tell what they were thinking? Perhaps, just because the day was so windy and people had stayed home, news of the inheritance had not made the rounds after all and would not circulate until the morrow, when the women would go to fill their pitchers at the public fountain. Suddenly she remembered the wheat she had left in the baskets; she broke into a run and was carried by the wind, as if in a dream, the rest of the way to her house. In the alley, she felt protected from the blast; and regained her balance. Angelo was trying to drag one of the heavy baskets inside. Together they picked it up, forced it through the narrow door and deposited it in the kitchen. Just as they hauled in the other basket, a torrential rain began to fall.

The heavy drops fell like hailstones on the roofs of the barn and woodshed, where the sparrows had sought shelter. A red hen, taken by surprise, scurried across the courtyard, stretching her neck and flapping her wings. There was a knock at the gate, and, immediately after, the voice of Comare Verdiana. Sofia made a gesture of annoyance and muttered something under her breath.

After the will had been duly registered and an agreement signed between Sofia Curreli on behalf of Angelo Uras, a minor, and Giovannantonio, Fernanda, and Tommaso Fulgheri, the widow and her son took possession of their inheritance. The villagers' comments were numerous and contradictory. Some praised Sofia for giving up the bulk of the legacy and thus avoiding a long, costly, and uncertain legal battle. Others called her ingenuous and stupid because she had let a fortune slip through her fingers. On all sides, people said that the reason was to disprove the gossip about the relationship between herself and Don Francesco Fulgheri.

"Gossip has nothing to do with it," Sofia said to Comare Verdiana. "I've never paid any attention to that. But I don't want to throw money away on lawyers."

Comare Verdiana had come for the usual cup of coffee.

"The olive trees at Balanotti and the house here in the village are quite enough for me," said Sofia.

"But what about Angelo? Have you looked after his interests the way you should? Perhaps some day he'll blame you for giving up without a fight. . . . And you told me yourself that the old man made you promise not to let his relatives get the better of you."

"Don't worry; they haven't wronged me. I've done what was best for myself and for Angelo as well. He's content to have the horse, the harness, the English saddle, and the pistols."

"Of course; he's only a child. But when he grows up he may think differently."

"I couldn't do other than what I did," said Sofia, pouring another cup of coffee for her friend. "Before, I'd never needed any legal advice because Don Francesco looked after our affairs. Now, I'd have had to go to Cagliari and look for a lawyer. And how could I have found one, when I don't know a soul there in the city? The Fulgheri family had put the case into the hands of Senator Loru and Professor Todde. It might have dragged on for years, and meanwhile I'd have had to borrow money, to mortgage property that I couldn't be sure was really mine. No. . . I did the right thing, and I have my peace of mind."

"But you would have had almost two hundred acres of land at Saboddus, with the richest soil anywhere in Parte d'Ispi, another hundred and fifty acres next to the few you already own at Acquacotta, and the orchards of Lugheria. . . ."

"I'm afraid of money, Comare Verdiana. I've told you that, over and over."

"And I'm afraid of being poor," Verdiana retorted.

Angelo listened distractedly to this exchange, which he had heard so many times that he knew the terms of it by heart. He was on the side of his mother, but he took no part in the discussion because he felt that, coming from him, his mother's arguments would not have the same weight. He was quite content to have the cottage at Balanotti and the olive trees, which he knew one by one, from the slender saplings to the gnarled trunks which six pairs of arms could not encompass. The nearby river kept the wells filled with water, even in summer, so that

45

both the orchard and the vegetable garden could always be irrigated. The wound on Zurito's back had healed so that Angelo no longer had to chase the flies away with a myrtle branch. A scar had formed over the wound under the mane, but the area was still so sensitive that the horse shook his head violently when the hairs were parted and the scar tissue seemed to be detached from the flesh and to move independently of the muscles that should have controlled it.

Old Raimondo Collu, who had been over thirty years in Don Francesco's service, came out to greet his new masters. Although he was almost seventy years old, he went every day on foot from Norbio to Balanotti and back to Norbio. He was healthy and strong, but because all his elders had died in their sleep, he was sure that he would die in the same way and wanted to be sure that it was in his own bed. What he couldn't endure was the idea that his dead body might be brought back over the road that he had traveled on foot all his life long. His children teased him affectionately whenever he brought up the subject, but he insisted that death was drawing closer and one morning they would find its cobwebs in his nostrils.

"Welcome!" he said now, bending unaccustomedly over Sofia's hand as if to kiss it. She drew back, grasped his bowed head in both hands and kissed the white hair.

"May God preserve you another hundred years, Zio Raimondo!"

"That's too many!" exclaimed the old man, running his hand over the place she had kissed. "I've been a long time in this world, and the cord is worn thin. One day the bucket will fall into the well."

Sofia stood with folded arms and laughter in her youthful eyes.

"There's time, plenty of time," she said in a mocking but affectionate singsong voice. "You'll bury the lot of us, Zio Raimondo."

"I've seen too many young men die," said Zio Raimondo,

waving his arms. Then, turning to Angelo: "Now that you're a landowner, my boy, you must be a real countryman as well. Tell me, do you know how to build a fire? That's one of the first things a countryman must know: how to build a fire and how to put it out."

Angelo piled up some dry branches against an already blackened portion of one wall of the house and applied a lighted match to a wad of paper. Immediately the fire took and the flames crackled. The old man's pouch was hanging from a nail and from it he took a loaf of bread wrapped in a linen napkin. With his leaf-shaped knife he cut three big slices, one of which he speared with a forked twig and held over the flames. When the bread was a rich, golden brown he picked a handful of black olives from the nearest tree and squeezed their bitter, dark juice over it. After he had toasted and doused all three slices expertly, he sat down with his back against the wall and began to eat.

"To your good appetite, my lady," he said, with his mouth full of bread.

"Don't call me 'my lady,' Zio Raimondo," said Sofia.

"What else should I call you? I belong to you, like these trees, and the rabbits and foxes that have their lairs in this land."

He got up, cut some sticks, and made a small fence around the holm oak, the tree which he knew was important to Angelo because he associated it with the death of Don Francesco.

"What fine weather for a visit to the country, Sofia Curreli! Did you know that your father and I were born on the same day?"

"No, I didn't know," she answered.

"Yes, I could have been your father, and have taught you what you learned at your father's knee. Because if an old man doesn't want to forget all he knows, he must teach it to the young."

Meanwhile, Sofia had washed the anchovies she had brought with her and put them in a bowl with vinegar at the bottom. The old man watered the young holm oak with the water left in his bucket.

"I'm going along," he said. "I must close an opening that

they've cut over near the river. Otherwise, when the grapes are ripe, they'll steal them off the first two rows of vines."

He put the packsaddle on the donkey, loaded on a scythe, a pick, and a hoe and waddled off. He was so bowlegged that there were holes in the outer sides of his shoes, revealing the dirt-gray skin beneath them.

"We must buy him a new pair of shoes," Angelo whispered to his mother, nodding in the old man's direction.

"For the feast of All Saints," said Sofia.

Angelo unhitched Zurito from the cart, wiped the sweat from his back with a handful of dry hay, and led him to the shed behind the house. He cleaned out the stall, filled it with fresh straw, and gave the horse the ration of ground beans that he had brought from Norbio. Zurito, with his ears erect, followed every movement and, at the end, rubbed his head against the boy's shoulder. Sofia put the basket full of linen to be washed on top of her head and started toward the river, which was actually only a mountain stream that filled up with water after a heavy rain.

As for Angelo, he went off to one of the three wells, known as the "Weasel," which particularly fascinated him because of the olive trees around it. They were the largest of the whole Parte d'Ispi region, grafted on smaller specimens, so Zio Raimondo said, three hundred years before, and looking like great elephants, with their enormous, gnarled trunks. Above the trunk, at the place where, according to Zio Raimondo, the graft had been made, there was a slender tuft of branches with a circumference no larger than that of a man's wrist. Twelve of them, Angelo counted. Who could know whether the well had been dug because of the olive trees or the trees planted on account of the proximity of the well? After giving the matter some thought, Angelo inclined toward the second solution.

He was tired and bored, and sorry not to have brought along one of Don Francesco's pistols and ammunition. He remembered the pocketknife that he had taken out of the drawer of Don Francesco's desk, which was now his, like the pistols, the rifle, the horse, and all the rest. The olive trees belonged to him also, but this idea was somehow distasteful, as if they were human

48

beings in the times when serfs were bound to the land and were bought or inherited along with it. He took the knife out of his pocket, opened the blade, and felt its solidity and balance in his hand. Turning around abruptly, he started to run, turned back, balanced the knife, and threw it at the biggest of the olive trees. The knife shot through the air and hit the exact part of the tree at which he had aimed, proving that he knew how to throw a knife, from both near and far, and how to make it a weapon no less killing than a pistol. He walked slowly up to the tree, extracted the knife from the wrinkled gray bark and threw it, with equal success, at another trunk. Then he folded the knife and put it back in his pocket.

The will, as the notary had read it, said that the olive trees of Balanotti were one thousand fifty-seven in number. Perhaps he should count them. The number didn't matter, but he was curious as to whether Don Francesco had calculated it correctly. The will gave an exact count of the apple, pear, and almond trees as well. Raimondo Collu, a seventy-year-old peasant, had faithfully served the owner of Balanotti for thirty years, the will continued, and for this reason the heir, Angelo Uras, should keep him on until his death. These words impressed him now just as deeply as when the notary had read them aloud, in a voice which had seemed to him as threatening as that of Don Francesco in person. Yes, Don Francesco had spoken from the grave in order to make sure that no one disobeyed his last wishes. Yet he and his mother had disobeyed them by giving up the rich lands of Saboddus and Acquacotta. Standing alone amid the olive trees, Angelo felt guilty for having made the suggestion. They had signed away Saboddus and Acquacotta and the livestock that went with them and, in return, the Fulgheri family had not opposed their taking over the cottage and land at Balanotti. The dead man's wishes had not been respected, but at least his favorite property had fallen into the right hands.

As Angelo walked through the silent olive grove, he counted the trees. From the road they all looked alike, but now, for the first time, he saw that they were very different; each one, like a human being, had a physiognomy of its own. From a distance, the people in a crowded square or in an approaching procession

49

seem all the same, but if you mingle with them you realize that they are alike, yes, but that there is diversity in this likeness. So it was now with the trees. He was aware of their silence, not as the silence of inanimate things but as the silence of people who keep quiet because they are thinking. His thoughts about the last wishes and will of Don Francesco were shared by the trees, or, rather, by the souls which, according to the local belief transmitted to him by his mother, inhabited them. He remembered that whenever Don Francesco had anything on his mind he would order his horse to be saddled and would ride, not to Saboddus or Acquacotta, but to Balanotti, where he would walk for hours, as he himself was now doing, among the olive trees.

He had counted a hundred and forty-three of them, in a part of the grove where the straight, smooth trunks indicated that they had been grafted no more than ten years before, when, through the leaves, he heard his mother's voice, like that of an invisible bird, calling to him. Making his hands into a funnel he called back, in the direction of the cottage, just visible among the leaves: "I'm cooooooming!" Among the branches above him, he caught a glimpse of the clear blue autumnal sky. Before going, he marked the place where he had stopped counting with a pile of stones. "If not, I'll forget," he said to himself, but he realized that by now it didn't much matter. He imprinted the number on his mind, and also the physiognomy of a gnarled old tree, which seemed to have eyes, a nose, and a mouth, and to be grinning ironically at him. Then he walked toward the cottage, with Sofia's voice as a guide and companion.

"I must get myself a dog," he thought to himself, "for the times when I come here alone." He had always wanted a dog as well as a horse, and he had an idea that now his mother would let him have one.

Several weeks had gone by since the signing of the agreement with the Fulgheri family, but Sofia was still living in her little house on the alley. Almost every day she went to "Don Francesco's" to air the rooms or water the vegetable garden. But she couldn't make up her mind to move; it still seemed to her impossible that she should live in such a fine house, even if it was now hers and she gave it such proprietary care. It had been easier to accept Balanotti, with its rustic cottage, fields, and olive groves. Only in the autumn did she decide to occupy the house at Norbio, after consultation not with Angelo but with Zio Raimondo.

"I'm thinking of moving into Don Francesco's house in town —God rest his soul," she said one morning.

The old man's tanned, wrinkled face lit up and his big teeth parted in a smile. Sofia felt reassured, but she added:

"What do you say to that, Zio Raimondo?"

The old man sat back on his heels and ran a finger through the dirt without looking up at her.

"I've been wondering what held you back," he answered.

Angelo, who was there with them, rubbed his hands, then went off with a handful of sugar to Zurito. Sofia put sugar into a cup of coffee and then placed the cup on the palm of Zio Raimondo's hand, which was wide as the chestnut-wood shovel that the women of Norbio use to separate bran from flour. He stretched out his lips and drank the coffee noisily, then continued to hold the hot cup in his wrinkled hand.

"It's as God wills it," said Sofia, rising to her feet. The old man stood up, too, his joints crackling like dry branches.

"Tell me, Zio Raimondo," Sofia added, pouring him some brandy, "would you help me move my belongings into the new house?"

"Of course," the old man replied.

"Can we do it in a single day?" Sofia asked, peering into the smoky kitchen.

"That depends on how much stuff you are moving."

"Just kitchenware and linen."

"Then half a day will do."

A week later, to the general surprise, she actually made the move. She had spent so many hours putting Don Francesco's house in order and knew every corner of it so well that she loved it with a jealous passion. The day before, she began early in the morning to wash the floors, dust the furniture, and hang the pictures of her patron saints on the walls. Angelo chose a room opening on the top landing. Everything was left the way it had been before: a metal bedstead, a chest of drawers, a cupboard, a table in front of the window, and a couple of chairs. Sofia hung a crucifix over the head of the bed. The general effect was that of a student's quarters. In a recess near the table there were bookshelves containing paperback translations of French novels, agricultural manuals, several years of the *Eco dei Comuni*, the periodical founded and almost entirely written by Don Francesco Fulgheri, a dictionary, and the famous *Enciclopedia Universale*, from which Angelo had learned all he knew of history. What he liked best was the window from which, beyond the Fluminera and the red housetops, he could see the bare slopes of Mount Volpe and Mount Homo.

When the bells of Sant'Antonio and Santa Barbara began to ring noon, the house was all clean and shining, and Sofia lit a fire in the kitchen stove. Angelo washed his face and hands at the pump of the well and then came to sit down across from his mother. The wine in the carafe was so cold that the glass was clouded. Sofia filled the tumblers. After the hard work and confusion of moving, she was happy to sit in the kitchen, alone with her son. This was the beginning of a new life, and she was half afraid, because an ancestral wisdom told her that life comes out of death. Suddenly, and for the first time since she had started unloading her belongings, she thought of Don Francesco Fulgheri and saw him, as he had appeared to her in a dream on the night of his death, sitting at the table over his fennel-and-cheese soup. She was aware of his protective presence and silently thanked him for it.

"Aren't we going to ask Zio Raimondo to eat with us?" asked Angelo, starting up.

Sofia nodded, but at the same time she calmly stretched out her arm to hold him back. She wanted to be alone with him at the table a little longer, to prolong the moment in which the two of them were taking possession of Don Francesco's house. Unfamiliar voices and sounds came from nearby houses, but gradually they would lose their strangeness. Angelo took a piece of chicken and bit into it. She liked to see him eat, and from habit watched him before picking up her glass and drinking long swallows of wine. Then she stood, set another place at the table, and said to Angelo:

"Now go call Zio Raimondo."

After the rains, Zio Raimondo proposed to sow wheat on the land that Sofia had inherited from her husband near the mineral springs of Acquacotta, and Angelo was to go with him. Sofia told the old man to sow no more than three bushels; she was unwilling to venture more, especially as the land hadn't been prepared during the summer. One Monday morning Zio Raimondo came to fetch Angelo. He hitched Zurito to the cart, loaded two half bags of wheat, some fertilizer, the heavy iron plow, the lunch basket and a bottle of wine, and off they went. Their journey took them through the village of Leni where the road ran past the foundry. The foundry, which had lain idle, had been reactivated some time before and was spewing out into the autumn sky smoke and soot that drifted onto the vegetable gardens of Leni. When they came to Acquacotta, Angelo recognized the mineral spring at the foot of a low, bare hill, and pointed out the boundaries of his mother's terrain: the spring and a wild pear tree on the east, and on the west, two boundary stones of the kind commonly used at Norbio, which the boy himself had whitewashed the year before to make them visible from a distance.

The old man mentally calculated the measurements involved and picked out the area he would sow that day. Then he hung a canvas sack full of seeds around his neck and, walking with long, regular steps, threw them out with a broad, rotating motion of his arm. The assurance of his gesture lent him a misleading air of age-old wisdom and experience. The seeds bounced off the hard earth and disappeared among tufts of dried grass. Near the white horse, Zio Raimondo fancied he could see the angry ghost of Don Francesco, who would never have allowed him to sow in this old-fashioned and inefficient manner. But then Don Francesco had tried to change many ways in Norbio and now he was dead. Zio Raimondo was sure that the seed would take hold and sprout just as well this way as any other. When the sack was empty, he shrugged his shoulders and spat into the distance. Then he hitched the horse to the plow and stuck the plowshare into the ground to turn the earth over and cover the seeds. Zurito walked in a straight line, with no need of guidance or encouragement; obviously he was accustomed to this work.

Angelo sat by the cart, munching a piece of bread and looking on. Plowing looked fun, even easy, and he wanted to try his hand. But his head was no higher than the handles and he could only hang on and be carried along. Zio Raimondo laughed, displaying his strong, white teeth, and set him aside. At the edge of the field, he effortlessly lifted the heavy plow, pulled the gleaming plowshare from the dark earth, and put it in again to cut another parallel furrow. Every now and then, someone passed by on the road, stopped to look on, and asked: "Plowing, are you, Zio Raimondo? Go ahead and plow, and may God be with you!" To which he replied: "Plowing, yes. I'm plowing the land of Sofia Curreli and this one here." He pointed to Angelo, who turned away blushing, feeling embarrassed, although he did not know why. Perhaps he shouldn't allow the wheat to be sown in the old-fashioned way when Don Francesco had told him many times that the land must be readied long before the actual sowing. Or perhaps he was ashamed to sit there doing nothing, while an old man with the bowed legs wearied himself behind the plow. The sun shone wanly out of the gray sky and the few parched trees around the steaming spring cast no shadows, but the boy knew, all the same, when it was noon. He saw the old man stop, look at his watch, then detach the horse from the plow. At the same time, he heard the bells gaily ringing in Norbio, although the village was no more than a light patch at the foot of the bare mountains.

"You did well to light the fire," said Zio Raimondo as he drew near. He bent over to wash his hands in the hot water, which ran, steaming, among the reeds and ferns. "Eggs can cook in this water," he added, taking them out of the basket. He set one egg on a flat stone and twirled it between his fingers, then touched it lightly to stop it. But he had no sooner withdrawn his hand than the egg slowly described another half circle.

"There's a trick you didn't know, did you?" said the old man, laughing.

"No, I didn't," said Angelo, but he did not ask for an explanation. He had understood immediately that a raw egg keeps on turning, while a cooked one doesn't. He gave a knowing smile and winked at Zio Raimondo. The old man was disappointed; in his time, he hadn't caught on so quickly. While Angelo gave the horse his fodder, Zio Raimondo slipped the eggs into the steaming water and looked at the second hand of his watch.

"How do you want your eggs?" he asked.

"Medium," the boy answered.

They ate, and Zio Raimondo poured wine from the bottle directly into his mouth, without letting his lips touch it, then handed it to Angelo. It was then that the dog went by, running so close to the fire that its passage raised a small cloud of ashes. The dog was young, with tawny hair and black stripes that emphasized the thinness of the body. The head and tail were like those of a greyhound. It was running at desperate speed toward the road, but some fifteen yards away came to an abrupt stop and looked around at the two human figures behind it.

"Pup!" Angelo called out. The dog lowered its head, twisted its body, and wagged its tail furiously. It even bared its sharp slender teeth as if to smile. Angelo held out a piece of bread. Only then did the dog advance, cautiously. Angelo threw the bread and the dog caught it in mid-air and noisily devoured it, salivating and trembling all over. It was a female.

"Let her go! She's just a mutt," said the old man. "I know dogs, and this one makes too many faces to be any good."

Angelo looked at him apprehensively. One sudden move and she'd run away.

"She's trying too hard to please," said Zio Raimondo, looking intently at his companion. "She's untrustworthy, for sure, and probably a thief in the bargain."

But when he saw the look on Angelo's face, he cut another

piece of bread from the loaf and tossed it to the dog, which once more caught and gobbled it.

"She's ashamed because she doesn't know us and because she's hungry."

"If you're honest, there's no shame in being hungry," said the old men sententiously. If he had bent over and pretended to pick up a stone that would have been the end of it. But he didn't move. It would be up to Sofia to say no and send the animal packing. Angelo was thinking the same thing. Who could tell why the dog had run in their direction and then stopped to look back at them? Had she smelled the bread or had she caught the smell of him, Angelo? In any case, the decision was hers; she had chosen him. He had long wanted a dog, and this was the way to get one. You find a dog on the street or in the fields, all alone and hungry; you call out: "Pup!" and that's it; you're friends for keeps. Perhaps the dog would be a friend to Zurito also.

Zio Raimondo went back to his plowing. In the late afternoon light, the field had taken on a darker hue; it was a large rectangle of brown earth, different from the land extending as far as the eye could see around it. Suddenly the old man shouted and waved his arms. A hare dashed by, leaping through the air so fast that Angelo had hardly time to see its long ears, arched back, and white belly. Zurito shied, pricked up his ears, and turned to look. Zio Raimondo muttered to himself, as if he were repeating his outcry of a moment before when the hare had escaped from between the horse's legs. He stepped back and aimed the long whip, like a gun, at the hare, which, after its high jump, had squatted in a furrow and stared at him out of eyes as round and dark as the seeds of black grapes. With an unexpected but characteristic lightning-swift gesture, he shot the thong of the whip at the hare. But he missed his aim, and the hare, leaping again into the air, escaped westward, to safety. Once more Angelo saw its small dark body outlined against the sky like a bird about to land.

"If only I'd brought my gun!" the old man exclaimed.

He clapped his hand on his thigh and bore down on the plow as a signal to Zurito to move ahead. When the dog heard his first shout, she instinctively froze, her tail sticking straight out in line with her back, the corners of her ears upraised, and her muzzle quivering. And when the hare escaped the stroke of the whip and took flight, she, too, went into lightning motion. She circled the old man and the plow, sniffing the furrow where the hare had squatted, picked up the scent, and followed.

"Tomorrow!" the old man shouted mockingly after her.

At intervals, the dog barked in the distance and the white tip of the hare's tail could be spotted in the tall grass as it pursued its zigzag flight through the fields.

"It's late," said Angelo, silently overtaking Zio Raimondo.

The old man pointed to a black cloud, as dense as the smoke thrown off by a charcoal pit, which seemed to be coming out of the summit of Mount Homo.

"Tomorrow there'll be rain again, and there's no telling how long it will go on raining. I've no more than a strip left to plow, and I'd better get it done."

Two or three times man and horse traveled the length of the field. Then Zio Raimondo detached the plow, loaded it onto the cart, and took a sip of wine from the bottle. Angelo was fitting the shafts of the cart into Zurito's harness when he saw the dog come back. First he heard her panting, and a minute later she was at his feet. He hadn't dare to hope that she would perform so well. "Carignosa" (this was the name he had already decided to give her) had brought back the hare, and Zio Raimondo proceeded at once to cut it open.

"You're better than I thought," he said to the dog, as he threw the entrails into the bushes. And he added, to Angelo: "There's a real hunting dog for you! Even if she's half-starved, she doesn't touch the guts. I'd never have believed it."

Angelo leaned over to pat the dog and to press her slender head to his chest. When he got up, he waved his hand and she jumped gracefully onto the cart. Zurito needed no encouragement to start for home. The harness bells tinkled like far-away chimes in the twilight.

Part Two

The rain came that night and lasted for days without stopping, just as Zio Raimondo had predicted. When the earth was drenched, a thousand rivulets ran down from the mountains and joined together to form rushing streams that carried away soil, stones, twigs, bushes, even whole trees, that obstructed or channeled the violence of their course. This was especially true of the river into which all the others ran, the Fluminera, whose course through the whole countryside, from the mountains to the valley, had never been regulated. It raged against its banks and undermined the foundations of houses. More than once over the years, the rushing stream had borne away whole houses and taken a toll of human lives. This time no disaster occurred. After six days, the rain stopped and Angelo saw the skies were clear.

The real crisis came years later. Angelo was now a young man. He had begun making frequent visits to Comare Verdiana's house next door where, from the porch, he could gaze un-observed—as he couldn't from his own premises—upon the nearby house of the oil miller Manno. There Valentina Manno, a brown-haired girl of seventeen, lived with her father and six sisters. That year in Norbio no rain had fallen for months. The people waited. They carried the statue of Saint Roch in proces-sion. Finally, as it often happens after a long drought, the sluices of the sky opened. For a whole week, a monotonous dense rain fell that seemed muddy before it ever touched the ground. The Fluminera thundered and foamed against the banks, carrying ever more dirt and stones with it. Wherever there was a bend, the waste piled up in a sort of natural dam; behind this, the water rose until it overflowed the banks on either side and poured down the village streets. Mindful of previous floods, people gathered in the Piazza Frontera, women with bare feet and skirts rolled up as when they washed clothes in the river, and men on horseback, wrapped in coarse woolen capes with the points of their hoods pulled down over their eyes. Among them Angelo, wearing the cape that had belonged to his father, watched gloomily. The river had cut the village in two and Valentina was on the other side. People stared, fascinated by the rushing water, and looking as sad and desolate as the houses that the rain had pounded for so long.

"Let's pray to Saint Roch," said a woman. "Saint Roch sent the rain, and Saint Roch. . . ."

"Saint Roch, you don't say!" a man broke in derisively.

"Float Saint Roch down the river!" said another. The women crossed themselves.

Standing on a table in front of the glass door of the post office, a tall, husky man with a reddish beard was talking and gesticulating like a Lenten preacher. Everyone turned toward him, but not many could tell what he said. Had he spoken in Spanish, many of those present, both old and young, would have understood, but he was a Piedmontese and he was talking Italian. Among the few that could follow was Angelo, and he sensed the importance of the stranger's words. The speaker was the engineer Antonio Ferraris, and he was calling for volunteers to stave up the riverbanks so the village would not be flooded. Angelo pushed his horse through the crowd right up to the table where the engineer stood. Turning to face the people, Angelo rose in his stirrups, raised a hand to enjoin quiet, and started speaking in a strong, clear voice that impressed the crowd and commanded silence.

"Let him talk," shouted the women. "He's the son of Sofia Curreli, and he's trying to explain what the monk is after."

"That's no monk," called out Feliciano De Murtas from his

black horse. "That's Antonio Ferraris of the Royal Mining Engineers."

At the mention of this name, a shudder ran through the compact and suddenly silent crowd, then there were sharp whistles and a threatening murmur.

Antonio Ferraris had been sent to Norbio to obtain twenty-five tons of wood for the Royal Foundries of the area; he had been chosen for the task because he was strong-willed and authoritative. He had gotten wood from the town council before by threatening to requisition horses, oxen, and wagons, and to have the forests cut down by the convicts who worked, under his supervision, in the mines of Iglesiente.

The government's demand for wood went back over a whole century. In 1740, the king had conceded to a Swedish nobleman, Carl Gustav Mandell, the right to exploit all the mines in the region of Parte d'Ispi in return for a small percentage of the profits from the smelted iron and other metals; and also to take the peat and wood necessary for the foundries from the surrounding forests. The forests were laid waste and the villagers had had to undertake the hard job of logging in the bargain. The destruction had continued after the Swede's thirty-year contract expired, when the mines and foundaries had reverted to government control. Indeed, the situation had worsened, because the demand for fuel had become more pressing and peremptory than before.

Now the crowd was certain that the engineer's proposal had a catch to it. Actually he wanted only to help, and with Angelo as interpreter he was trying to give directions. The ignorant mountaineers could not conceive that the tough, authoritarian Ferraris was one of the few educated Piedmontese concerned about deforestation. Several times he had proposed to the government authorities that the foundries be fired with the peat that was available in the same mineral basin of the Sulcis region. But the king, greedy for the meager two-percent allotted to him from the value of the smelted lead and silver, would not hear of any experiments that might slow production even temporarily. For his efforts to save the woodlands of Parte d'Ispi, Ferraris risked being branded as a Jacobin and a subversive by government functionaries, while the common people viewed him as the tool of a greedy and tyrannical administration. And indeed, when he demanded the wood, he was inflexible. Now, similarly, he expected his orders to be obeyed. But as he stood there on the Piazza Frontera, he realized that there was a misunderstanding. Speaking again through Angelo, he made it quite clear that he wasn't interested, at the moment, in coal or wood. He heard his words echo strangely, in another man's voice, through the square. Without renewing his call for volunteers to help, he jumped down from the table, took off his jacket, walked into the raging water up to his waist, and, with his bare hands, started to remove the debris whose accumulation threatened to make it spread even more widely.

Moved by his action rather than by his words, twenty or thirty men turned their horses and capes over to the women and followed his example. Picks, shovels, hoes, ropes, and hooks were collected from nearby houses, and within a few minutes the artificial dam was eliminated and the water flowed freely. Still the volume of it was such that the river could not be forded, and the village remained cut in two. On the two opposite banks, from the high and dry Piazza Frontera on the one side and the flooded Piazza Cadoni on the other, crowds observed the unexpected sight of a stranger, accustomed to command, who exerted himself like a workman in water up to his chest. But the flood continued to sweep tree trunks and branches, bushes and bunches of grass, and the dead bodies of drowned cows, sheep, and pigs along with it, so that soon an obstruction had formed again and the water rose ever higher. Ferraris, red in the face, was shouting out orders, which came across in gestures rather than in words. Angelo craned his neck to see, along with the others, thinking all the while of Valentina and her sisters. Who could tell how long they and the other residents of the right bank would be cut off? With his black cape drawn around him, he brooded. To be unable to get to the church for Mass didn't bother him. But to see Valentina only from across a raging torrent, that struck home. Besides, the engineer, who was splashing about in the water, unable to make himself understood, obviously needed assistance. He pulled his black cape tightly around him, adjusted his feet in the stirrups, and rode toward the river. On foot he could never have got through the crowd or have braved the flood.

"What are you trying to do, boy?" people protested. "Where are you going with your horse?" But they stepped back and gave him passage, patting Zurito's neck as he went by.

Zurito walked right into the water, and Angelo found himself beside the engineer, who smiled up at him. Ferraris was attracted by the boy's intelligent face and was glad to have him once more close by. In battle he had often taken heart when he came across a soldier to whom he could talk. There was something strange and at the same time familiar in this young man who had been able to translate his technical terms into the local dialect, with its Latin derivations, and to make everyone understand them. Because, obviously, people did listen to his words, did understand and heed them. Ferraris had met a fellow of the same kind at Bezzecca, in 1866, when he fought with Garibaldi against the Austrians, a man from Pisa who had enlisted in the army a fortnight before. They had taken an immediate liking to each other and, in the heat of the battle, when the roar of the cannons made it impossible to hear a human voice, they had only to exchange glances to communicate.

"If only we could make a bridge of stones!" said Angelo, pointing first to the river and then to the crowd on the opposite bank. "Those people need to cross over."

"Quite right," the engineer assented, "but it would take big rocks."

"And boards," Angelo added, "or tree trunks."

So it was decided to build the wooden bridge, which not only made for the resumption of normal life at Norbio at the time of the flood but also established the site of the present-day iron bridge named for Ferraris, a stranger who, instead of exploiting the townspeople, used his skill to help them. On previous occasions he had been harsh and tough in his dealings, and even now he had come with a firm resolve to obtain the wood that they were supposed to supply. But the sight of the swollen Fluminera flooding a village at the foot of mountains which he himself was responsible for having deforested brought about a change of heart. He remembered the woods of an earlier day and knew that they would have blocked the torrential streams pouring down from the mountain slopes and saved the goatherds' shacks at Castangias, swept away by a landslide that very morning. The people watching him haul boards and logs through water up to his chest and anchor them to the riverbed could not guess at his motivation. He had a feeling of guilt when he looked into the faces of these men and women who had, all unwittingly, become "Italians" and yet were still vassals as before.

Angelo, astride his white horse, continued to translate the engineer's orders. Rolling up their capes, some of the men went upstream along the river; others fanned out from the square. The crowd opened to let them pass and then closed after them like water in the wake of a boat. Everyone lent a hand, if only to point out the places where material for the construction could be found. The volunteers came back in their shirtsleeves, through the rain, carrying poplar and eucalyptus trunks on their shoulders. It took two or three men to carry a single trunk, steadying it with their hands and using their knees to guide their horses. With the trunks balanced on their shoulders, they rode down the stony river banks, where the horses might easily have stumbled. A hum rose from the crowd and mingled with the roar of the swollen stream. Women's shrill voices sounded above everything else as they called to their children to come home; names winged their way, like birds, through the air in spite of the curtain of mud-colored rain.

There were two sonic backgrounds, two different but super-imposed images. One, almost tragic in character, had touched the heart of Ferraris and impelled him to brave the waters in order to stem their flow. The other, gay and colorful, recalled Norbio as it used to be and could be again if its mountains were reforested. Within a few hours, the pontoon bridge was finished, and the oldest of the old women walked gingerly over it in order to test its strength. Now anyone could cross the flooded stream. Children crossed in play, and dogs, sniffing the air and looking for their masters, and finally the parish priest, who was looking for the engineer in order to thank him in the name of the whole community.

"In another hour, the Piazza Cadoni will be dry," said Ferraris. He had had an idea, one inspired by a method that he had successfully tried out in Piedmont. He called Angelo to him, borrowed a horse and, at the head of a group of men, rode up along the Fluminera to the point where the river broadened and seemed uncertain as to whether to pass to the right or the left of the promontory where the priests of the last Jesuit mission had planted a rough, wooden cross. The water passed to the left, but it could be seen from the lay of the land that if it passed to the right, the volume of water now flooding the village would be reduced. Ferraris ordered several men to get picks and shovels. Angelo was to carry out a special mission. Angelo set off downhill at a gallop, for Zurito was sure-footed even if the road was steep and uneven. Soon he came to the Piazza Cadoni, where the water was about to flood the first floor of the Granary and destroy all the local grain stored there. He went at once to the house of the Cadoni family, where Ferraris was a guest. Riding into the courtyard, he threw off his cape, leaped down from the saddle, and looked for the mistress of the house. Instead, he ran into Antioco, the lawyer's son, an alert youth of his own age and a good friend. He had the key to Ferraris's trunk, which the engineer had entrusted to him. Together the two boys ran to the engineer's bedroom on the second floor. The trunk had shiny brass corners and a brass padlock. Angelo leaned over to open it. When the top was raised, a fragrance of eau de cologne pervaded the room. Angelo removed shirts, starched collars, a silk dressing-gown, then dug in on the left side. There he found a bunch of dynamite sticks wrapped in an oily yellow paper. On the right was a roll of wick, from which he cut off several yards and stuffed it into his pocket. The dynamite he wrapped in a woolen undershirt and tucked under his arm. Before leaving the courtyard, he embraced Antioco and whispered into his ear:

"Don't worry when you hear an explosion. I'm pretty sure we shall save the grain. You'll see."

"I'm glad of that. Good luck!"

Angelo led Zurito over to the mounting platform, threw his leg over the saddle, and rode away, holding the bundle of dynamite sticks tightly under his cape. The relentless rain dripped down from the hood into his eyes, practically blinding him, but Zurito found his way and soon, from under the hood, Angelo glimpsed the Mission cross in the distance.

During his absence, the engineer had made preparations for the dynamiting. Now he rammed the sticks of explosive into a hole drilled in the rock and filled the hole with twigs, stones, and earth, leaving a good fifteen inches of wick suspended outside. Lighting a cigar, he motioned to the men to mount their horses and move some distance away. With the burning cigar he lit the wick and hurried down the hill on foot. At a certain point he grabbed Zurito's bridle. A moment later, the dynamite exploded and Zurito broke loose and reared up. Angelo saw flames rise and great clumps of earth and shattered rock fall into the valley. Soon, as the engineer had foreseen, the divided flow of the river abated. The water in the Piazza Cadoni, which had threatened the Granary, trickled away among the bare feet of the women.

After the flood, Ferraris insisted that the town council provide the wood. He was reluctant, so hard on the heels of a calamity, to insist, but where professional duty was concerned, he put his personal feelings aside. One day he explained the problem to Angelo. This year, because of the prolonged rain, peat was in short supply, but five tons of wood could be had from the forest of Escolca, beyond the already exploited Mazzanni region. The Royal Foundries were willing to accept this amount as an initial installment of the entire quota. However, it would take time to cut and transport it to the collection depot, the big square in front of the foundry at Leni, from where wagons could carry it to Monteponi, its final destination.

"Green wood?" exclaimed Angelo who, from listening to the engineer's conversation, had acquired some idea as to how the foundries functioned.

"Yes, green wood," said Ferraris, biting his mustache. "It's not the ideal, but they'll have to be satisfied. And you people can only gain, because green wood is much heavier."

But Angelo was thinking of the splendid forest of Escolca, with its recently regenerated growth, which would be destroyed just to keep the Royal Foundries going.

Ferraris was a passionate mountain-climber. In Parte d'Ispi, however, for want of peaks to scale, he had to content himself with long walks through the hills. Every now and then the village people saw him set out on foot, with a satchel containing writing and drawing material slung over one shoulder, a stout stick, and a pair of field glasses. To them it was almost inconceivable that he should go into the country without a gun for self-protection and for the pleasure of hunting. If he had taken an occasional shot, if he had come back with a snipe hanging from his belt or a hare in his satchel, then his walking would appear to have some purpose. But as it was, he was viewed with a certain suspicion, like a man who eats no meat and seems not to care for women.

He was preparing now, in customary fashion, to go to the forest of Escolca, via Balanotti and Mazzanni, a trip which, on foot, would take a whole day. Angelo would have preferred to ride, but he had to content himself with taking Carignosa. They went up along the Leni River, crossing and recrossing the old narrow-gauge railway which had formerly carried freight to the foundry at the bottom of the valley. One of the purposes of the trip was to examine the railway's condition and see if it was worthwhile to reactivate it. Walking beside the old rails, they found them in better shape than the engineer had expected. Angelo noticed that, as they walked along, he muttered something to himself and stopped every now and then to jot down a number in a worn notebook. Only, as far as Angelo could make out, a number. Then he realized that Ferraris was noting the ties that needed replacement. To bring wood down from the mountains by horse- or ox-drawn wagons was impractical because of the time and money that would have to be spent on repair of the road. And so the rails, running from Escolca straight to the foundry of Leni, offered the best means of transportation. The freight cars still existed and needed few repairs, and so did the engine. The only disadvantage was the consumption of fuel, fuel that would have to be taken out of that delivered to the foundry. And more fuel meant more destruction. Angelo flinched with pain, as if the intended victims were human. He loved trees too much to give in on this point, and racked his brains for another answer.

As he pondered the problem, he hit upon a solution that a child playing with a toy train would have recognized—to pull the empty train up and then let it slide down with its load. The forest of Escolca was two thousand feet above sea level and the wood had to be brought down to the valley. Angelo gestured to the engineer, who sat down to listen. He knew the young man well enough by now to have confidence in him. As for Angelo, he stretched out on the ground, leaning on his elbows, as he had so often done with Don Francesco Fulgheri. His words came as easily as if he were, indeed, describing a game, and the engineer smiled with satisfaction, blowing cigar smoke into the air.

"Good boy!" he exclaimed.

The plan was quite simple. The empty freight cars could be towed up the mountain by three pairs of mules, the Piedmontese mules whose praises the engineer was always singing, although no one on the Island had ever seen them.

"There will have to be a special car to bring the mules down, along with the wood. For them to tow the train up will be no problem."

It was as a result of Angelo's suggestion that the engineer offered him a job.

That year the olives of Balanotti were taken to Manno's mill. No other mill could extract as much oil out of them. Manno, moreover, undertook to bottle and sell the oil. He left the olive husks with the grower, either to be used for fuel or to be sold, in which case he himself was the buyer. By his ability he had won over clients from all his competitors. But that year there was business enough for everybody. The olive harvest was so abundant that even the oldest mills had work to do and took turns staying open at night. These were primitive affairs, where a blindered horse walked in a circle around the crusher, turning the granite wheel in the hopper, and where the screw presses were operated by hand. The work force consisted of four men at the presses and one who mixed the paste in the hopper, stoked the fires, spooned the oil out of the tubs, filled the wicker baskets when the paste was ready, and stacked them up on the presses' round bases. It was hard, tiring work, and there were frequent changes of shift, with each shift undertaking no more than four millings a day. And, of course, the horse, too, had to be relieved. Besides the men, there were two or three women who brought water from the public fountain or well and performed other light duties. At Manno's mill things were different, for he had a steam engine that ran both the crusher and the hydraulic presses. His squads were composed of three men and two women each, and the work was done neatly and with dispatch.

That afternoon oil from the olives of Sofia and Angelo Uras was being poured from the decanting tubs into the earthenware jars set up in rows in the storehouse of the mill. Manno had warned his clients and friends that the quality of the oil would not be as high as in previous years, because of the olive flies, which had come down from the northern part of the Island as far as Campidano. There was no cure for this plague. From year to year, as Manno knew from experience, the olives would deteriorate progressively. He took one into his big fingers, opened it with a nail, and showed Angelo and Sofia the tiny white worm which had eaten away the pulp under the skin. Sofia was close to tears.

"Is it possible that there's no remedy?" she sighed. "First the worm devours the pulp, and then it comes out of the olive as a tiny fly which lays eggs by the thousand. We'd have to destroy millions of these flies. Only God could do that, and, instead, He has sent the flies to punish us for our sins." And she made the sign of the cross.

Manno shrugged his shoulders and made as if to wave her away, but she detained him.

"You've found a remedy by changing your occupation," she said.

"Yes," he admitted, wiping with a handkerchief the steel-rimmed glasses that left a red mark, almost like a scar, on the bridge of his nose. "I've tried to forget that I own thousands of olive trees, and I've gone into business. It wasn't easy at first, but now I'm used to it. How many trees do you have at Balanotti, Sofia Curreli?"

"A thousand," she told him.

"Well, I had, and still have, three thousand, but the olives aren't worth picking. Unless the cursed fly can be destroyed . . . Do you know what I'll do with my trees one day? I'll cut them down, let them harden, and then sell them for wood!"

"Oh, no! I'd never do a thing like that," put in Angelo, unwilling to believe the merchant's words. But Manno insisted. There was nothing to do but to abandon the olive groves or cut down the trees.

Sofia went to seek comfort from Comare Verdiana; she wept, as if for a death, over the trees of Balanotti, the trees to which her existence and that of her son were now so closely bound. All of a sudden this certainty was gone. Thinking of Balanotti she no longer saw the trees with their precious fruit, but the white worms inside, worms that were eating away her modest resources. In vain Comare Verdiana tried to cheer her up; she wept silently and without hope. That evening, at supper, Angelo spoke to her of the engineer's offer. Mastering the tears that still welled up within her, she listened to him without emotion. The offer, she said, seemed to her a good one and he should accept it, even if it entailed some sacrifice on his part. For she knew that he would prefer not to work for an outsider. They talked on, after supper, but with no mention of the invasion of flies and the fact that they could no longer count on the olives of Balanotti. Sofia spoke only of the loss of the wheat crop. The rains had come so soon after the sowing that there had been no time for the wheat to sprout.

"There's no counting on the land," she concluded, "especially when you have as little as we do. You'd best accept the engineer's offer. It doesn't mean committing yourself for a lifetime; when you've had enough you can quit."

Angelo was reluctant to work for the Mining Consortium that was responsible for the destruction of the forests, but Sofia continued to urge him.

"The damage is done, and even if you don't accept, you can't repair it. Already you've made yourself useful to the engineer. Perhaps you can prevent further damage, and do so more effectively by working from the inside. The job has been offered you because you suggested how to make use of the railway; it's a reward to which you're entitled."

Angelo had to admit that his mother was right. Eighty liras a month weren't to be scorned; they came to almost a thousand liras a year, a larger sum of money than had ever passed through his hands. The next time he saw Ferraris, he told him that he would take the job.

Manno's olive mill was working full time. His daughter, Valentina, had to leave her loom and shuttle and watch the gauges of the hydraulic presses. It was here that Angelo found her one Saturday when he brought olives to the mill. Through the smoke which filled the enormous room he saw her sitting on a high stool beside the gauge of the farthest press. Her feet, clad in green velvet slippers, were tucked up under her and resting on a rung of the stool and her eyes were fixed upon the white face of the gauge and the quivering needle. With every stroke of the piston, it seemed as if the needle would reach the red dot marking the danger point. But before this could happen Valentina stretched out her hand and opened the safety valve. She was unaware of Angelo's arrival, although the men had greeted him in loud voices and the hobnails of his boots rang out on the gray stone floor. Her father had told her repeatedly that if the needle passed the danger mark the tubes of the press would explode like a bomb, so she watched the gauge with narrowed eyes and clenched lips, as if the safety of the world depended upon it. At her feet, with one knee on the floor, an old man, Vincenzo Usula, known as Zio Vissente, spooned the oil into a zinc pitcher held by a woman crouching beside him. She greeted Angelo by batting her eyelashes but Valentina continued to stare at the gauge, oblivious. Just as Angelo was about to touch her arm, the needle reached the red dot, and she jumped so violently that one of her green slippers fell off her foot and would have slipped into the tub full of olive paste had not Zio Vissente, quick as a cat, caught it in its fall. When Valentina opened the safety valve, a stream of oily water, mixed with steam, shot up, whistling, and struck the black wall. Zio Vissente and his assistant drew back, holding up their hands to protect their faces and laughing at Valentina's discomfiture. Angelo started to laugh too, but restrained himself because of the girl's serious expression. Zio Vissente held the slipper hesitatingly, then wiped his hand as best he could on his trousers, gently fitted it onto her foot, and bent over to blow the dirt off the yellow silk tassel.

"Oh!" Valentina exclaimed, suddenly aware of Angelo's presence. "Have you been here long?"

"I saw the whole thing," said the young man, winking.

"What whole thing?" she asked, lowering her legs.

"Everything!" he said, with innocent malice. "Why were you so scared?"

"If I hadn't turned the tap of the valve, we'd all have exploded. . . . It's like a bomb, I tell you!"

"Have you ever seen a bomb?"

"I've seen the mines at the quarries."

Zio Vissente laughed, stroking his gray beard. Angelo approached Valentina, looking into her gray-green eyes. She drew her face back and leaped down from the high stool, ignoring the hand that he held out to help her. Then, laughing, she started toward the entrance to the storehouse and also to her father's office. Without looking back, she waved her hand over her shoulder, beckoning to Angelo to follow. She walked rapidly and lightly, on tiptoe, so that her heels came out of her slippers, and every step was almost a jump. This mannerism, which Angelo had observed in her since childhood was, to him, one of her great charms, along with her green eyes, the half-open lips that revealed her upper front teeth, her husky, subdued voice, her small, strong hands, and the whole of her harmonious person. She appeared to him as a bird perched on a branch, ready to take flight. As he overtook her, he caught a whiff of verbena scent.

"I've brought my olives," he said, raising his chin in the direction of the small window giving onto the courtyard. Through the dusty clouded glass, they could see the figures of the men unloading the wagons that had just arrived from Balanotti.

"How many sacks in all?" asked Valentina, opening the door with the long iron key that she wore on her belt. She struck a sulphur match, lighting the kerosene lamp on the crowded office desk. Angelo was happy to be so close, to see her light, springy walk, and to follow her footsteps. In his heavy boots, he had followed carefully close behind, anticipating her every motion as she moved through space like a dancer; he felt her presence in the fragrance of the verbena, which cut them both off from the sharp, heavy smell of the mill. A few months before, in the house of Comare Verdiana, he had been in the same room with her—so close to her that he had been able to see the gold flecks in the dark irises of her eyes. It was then, for the first time, that he had breathed in her perfume and really *seen* her.

Now she pushed open the door to the storehouse, a large, high-ceilinged room lit by acetylene lamps and exuding cold, damp air like that of a well, filled with the bitter odor of the mass of olives, which occupied the entire floor and came up almost to the narrow, swinging platform from which newly arrived sacks were still being unloaded. The men came from the courtyard, with a sack on one shoulder, while they held out the other arm as tightrope dancers do, in order to keep their balance on the platform, which seemed to give under their weight. They advanced slowly and cautiously, at a distance of five or six yards one from the other, to the end of the platform. There, breaking the reed tied around the neck of the sack with their teeth, they spilled out the olives onto the mounting pile. Then they folded the empty sack lengthwise, threw it over one shoulder and gingerly retraced their steps, taking care not to bump into their fellows who were advancing in the opposite direction. Angelo breathed deeply the bitter smell of the olives, but at moments he caught a whiff, above it, of the perfume of Valentina. Standing beside him, Valentina looked on in silence at the scene. Suddenly, Giulia Nonnis appeared in the courtyard doorway. She was wearing her usual patched burlap skirt, but she had coquettishly bound up her hair in a white woolen scarf with a colorful embroidered border, though her rebellious black hair defied constriction. Her dazzlingly white blouse was slightly open over her breast. At the very moment Angelo recognized her, Giulia raised her hand and shouted a familiar "Hello!"

"Who's that?" Valentina asked in a low voice.

"An olive-picker, who works on contract at Balanotti," answered Angelo, briefly acknowledging Giulia's greeting.

"How many sacks are there in all?" he called out to her.

"Fifty-nine," Giulia shouted back, in a voice almost as deep and loud as his, holding up first the five fingers of one hand and then nine fingers of both pulp-blackened hands together.

"Just in case we hadn't understood," Valentina said, laughing. "A pretty girl, though. . . ." In her turn, she waved her hand and called out "Good-by!" as she turned around and walked back, followed by Angelo, to the office. The voices of Giulia and the men echoed from the storehouse behind them. With speed and assurance Valentina took in hand the account book and wrote with a heavy pencil the date and the number of sacks from Balanotti.

Soon after, the work on the railway began, and Angelo helped Ferraris to supervise it. Although he was used to overseeing the work on his own farms, this was a different matter. On his land, where the men were hoeing he hoed, where they were scything he scythed in competition with them, where they were breaking the earth to plant a vine he took a pick and joined in. Here, instead, according to the orders of Ferraris, orders he was paid to execute, he had to ride continually up and down the line, without taking part in the work. He had only to make sure, occasionally getting off his horse in order to do so, that the ties were securely attached to the rails and to see to it that the men didn't slack off. The workers, most of whom were from Norbio, greeted him by his first name, and were surprised when he told them not to idle on the job. There were certain old men with bowlegs and holes in their shoes, like Zio Raimondo, who moved about with difficulty, and Angelo would gladly have let them sit down to rest for hours on a pile of stones. Instead, it was his duty to urge them on and, if necessary, to shout at them; he was paid for this and, what was more important, he was determined to justify the engineer's confidence in him. This confidence filled him with joy and pride, but at the same time, it mortified him to be on the side of those who gave orders. Sometimes he was so ashamed that he could not meet the old men's eyes when they stared at him, leaning their chins on the handle of their pick or shovel. Nevertheless the work went well.

On Saturday, when the engineer arrived with the payroll in his pouch, he congratulated Angelo. No one, he said, had ever got so much work out of these men, who were known for their laziness and inefficiency. Angelo felt even more mortified. He knew that the men had done their best because they cared for him and wanted to see him cut a good figure; they had worked alongside his father and danced folk-dances with his mother on the church green. He would have liked to explain to Ferraris that the merit was not his but of these misjudged Sardinians, who, in spite of their undeservedly bad reputation, were loyal and generous friends. But it was too difficult to explain, just as it was too difficult to give up the engineer's confidence and praise. Angelo was not rich, but neither could he call himself poor. More money had passed through his hands than through those of any other boy in Norbio. And yet when the engineer gave him his pay envelope, he felt that the eighty liras—twice the pay of the workers—was an enormous sum. He put the envelope into his pocket and got ready to go home, as impatient to turn the money over to his mother as when Don Francesco

Fulgheri had given him a silver crown and he was afraid it would slip out of the hole in his pocket.

One day, in the early hours of the afternoon, when everyone who could afford it took a nap, there was a rumbling noise like that of a distant thunderstorm, which seemed to be carried by the wind, because at moments it rose and then fell, as if the earth had absorbed it. Even Angelo did not understand at first what it might be, and shrugged his shoulders when Sofia raised her eyes and looked questioningly at him. Then he clapped his hand to his forehead. But of course! It was the train, loaded with timber, and with the mules imported by the engineer from Piedmont, as Angelo had suggested, in the last car. He was surprised that the engineer had not called him to witness the tryout but was pleased that all seemed to be going well, judging from the regularity of the noise. He saddled his horse, called Carignosa, waved good-by to his mother, and galloped off to the foundry. When he got there, men were making piles of the timber that had been spilled out haphazardly alongside the tracks in the great open space in front of the foundry. Ferraris was there with Giuseppe Antola, the foreman, Giulio Morelli, manager of the foundry who was known as "Captain" because he had held this rank with the Engineer Corps of the Piedmontese Army, the brakemen of the train, and the workers from Norbio. The trial run had been successful, except for one detail. The mules had taken fright during the descent and had bitten the trainmen severely. These two men now were cleaning themselves in the icy water of the well, swearing that never again would they ride in that last car of the train. For two and a half francs a day, they weren't going to let the mules rip their clothes to pieces and bite them.

"I'll ride with the mules myself, next time," said Ferraris, cutting them short. "We'll fix them so they can't bite."

He signaled Angelo and, with his help, made certain measurements. Then he ordered the harness-maker to fashion a half dozen halters with iron rings. He also ordered strong rope with which to secure the mules to the sidewall of the freight car.

It was decided to test the new system the next day. Ferraris and Angelo rode together to the foundry and, when the three pairs of mules had been hitched up to the first freight car, Angelo picked up the long reins and cracked the whip. The train got off to an easy start. The mules pulled it along without undue strain, proceeding at a slow walk up the slope. In each car was a trainman ready to pull the brake if the slope proved so steep that the little convoy was in danger of sliding back downhill. It took two and a half hours to reach the plateau.

The ancient forest of Escolca was in ruins, a collection of massive stumps and trunks and piles of trimmed branches, ready to be loaded on the train. The train stopped in front of a low red-roofed building, headquarters of the employees of the Mining Consortium, the woodmen who had done the logging. They started at once loading the cars, while the shackled mules grazed in a nearby field. When the loading was done, the mules were led to a drinking trough and then to the ramp set against the last car of the train. Mindful of the preceding trip, the mules balked. But patted, soothed, and blindfolded, they were finally persuaded to enter one by one. Ferraris and Angelo went with them and, a moment later, upon the engineer's order, the wedges were removed from the wheels. The heavily loaded train, with brakes grinding, started downhill.

The Escolca plateau, like other such formations, falls away abruptly at the top. The original railway builders had chosen the least precipitous slope, and had further eased the grade by a succession of curves. Nevertheless, the drop was steep and the ride alarming, not so much for the blindfolded mules as for the human passengers, who found themselves more than once at the edge of a sheer drop hanging over the valley. Later, Ferraris admitted to Angelo that he had not been as frightened since he had crossed the Alps as a young man, from Switzerland to Lombardy in a balloon. He shouted orders to brake, and braked his own car as the train rounded one curve after another. The brakes had to be applied at the beginning of each curve, otherwise the speed built up in between would have snapped the last cars over the edge. With the brakes in use, however, the train took the curves safely, and even slowly enough for the passengers to distinguish individual oaks and the olive trees—young and slender, or old and gnarled—in the gap below.

At curve after curve, they saw flocks of sheep or goats grazing on the reddish soil or huddled around a bush. Occasional herdsmen, wrapped in long, sleeveless goatskin garments, guns slung over their shoulders and rough crooks in hand, followed the animals or sat a short distance away. Once, a reed flute sounded above the grinding wheels and Angelo, looking down, glimpsed the player beside a spring, which appeared from a distance as a dark spot on the ground.

When the train reached the base of the steep slope, it seemed to stop on the apparently flat terrain covered with tall trees whose small stiff leaves rustled in the still air. Ferraris and Angelo prepared to jump out when, as if by magic, the train jerkily resumed its course along a line where the descent continued, like a current in the middle of an apparently motionless river. The track had been laid in such a way as to take advantage of every dip, almost as if the builders had foreseen the day when the train would carry its cargo from the heights of Escolca down to the foundry merely by coasting. Now the train wound its way up and down like a roller coaster, passing in front of the rustic church of San Giuseppe and almost grazing the wall around San Sisinnio. It aimed directly at the church, as if it were going to ram it, then, at the last minute, abruptly swung around the wall and proceeded in a straight line toward the foundry, which appeared at the end of the course with its reddish, smoke-blackened walls and the sharp profile of its tall chimney. The engineer raised his arm to signal a halt, like a cavalry officer at the head of his squadron. With loudly screeching brakes, the little train slowed down, slid into the courtyard, and came to a stop beside the enclosing wall.

For some time, the engineer had not asked Angelo to go with him into the forest, but Angelo was too proud and too discreet to show his hurt feelings. The engineer's walking companion was now a stranger who had contracted with the Mining Consortium at a special price for the logging rights. The situation was again what it had been before, and the local people saw the remains of their woods gobbled up by the insatiable foundry furnaces. Angelo didn't want to believe it, because Ferraris had promised that the woodlands would be respected and the furnaces fired with peat and lignite. It seemed to him impossible that the engineer should have deceived him; when he had persuaded him to become his assistant he had repeated the promise and voiced his conviction that the forests must be saved.

One day he vented his misgivings to Manno and Antioco Cadoni, the fiancé of Manno's daughter Olivia. Olivia, Valentina, Barbara, and Manno's other daughters were sitting around the table after supper, listening with dismay to Angelo who heatedly cursed the Piedmontese and their methods of government. Manno calmly fingered his glass of old Malvasia wine, holding it up to admire the amber color, while Antioco, sitting beside the blond Olivia, twisted his mustache with a slender white hand. Valentina sat across from Angelo, and now she touched his knee with the tip of her shoe, grimaced, and shook her head.

"Don't forget the old saying: 'Your Piedmontese is false and fair-speaking,'" said the master of the house, genially lighting his pipe. And he added, blowing a ring of smoke into the air: "Forests are made to be cut, after all, and wood to be burned."

Angelo was thinking of all that Don Francesco had taught him: that trees improve the climate and feed the springs, that they can be cut down, but with certain limitations. Words welled up in his throat, but he held them back. Valentina again nudged his knee with her foot and, with a nod of her head, signified that he should follow her. The two of them got up and went out on the porch, shutting the door behind them. They embraced in the darkness. As Angelo held her, he could feel the strength that underlay the apparent fragility of her body.

"What are you thinking?" she whispered into his ear.

"I'm thinking of Don Francesco," he said, drawing her to

81

him more closely. She seemed to understand, for she asked him nothing more.

Angelo felt frustrated at having been unable to state his cause clearly and calmly, as Don Francesco would have liked it. But Valentina's caresses soothed him and her tender, warm kisses were more persuasive than any discourse. He responded to her kisses and pressed her to him so tightly that she was almost stifled. They remained in this embrace until the powerful and authoritative voice of Manno called out:

"What are you doing out there in the cold? Come back in!"

At the same time the door half opened, and Barbara's bare arm held out a woolen shawl to Valentina. They recognized the coral bracelet and an amethyst ring which gleamed in the light from the room. Valentina trembled all over and withdrew a little from Angelo's embrace. The door banged shut, and they remained suspended, as if in mid-air, barely touching each other with their lips and the tips of their fingers. Then their bodies and lips met. After a long, sweet kiss, Angelo laid a hand on her shoulder and said:

"I have to go now. Say good-by to the others for me."

"Yes," said Valentina docilely, wrapping herself in the soft shawl; "that's the wise thing to do. But I'm going to walk with you as far as the bridge."

With her right hand she caught his left and gripped it so hard that it hurt. Angelo had never imagined that her slender hand could be so strong, and he stood for a moment in a happy daze. With her free hand Valentina opened the door a crack and called out in her musical voice: "I'm coming right away." After she had shut the door, they went silently down the steps, leaning against each other. It was pitch black, but she led him as if she could see the way.

"Perhaps she really does see in the dark," Angelo thought pleasurably to himself. And in this happy state of mind, with her perfume mingled with the damp night air in his nostrils, he told her that he loved and would always love her and wanted her for his wife. Valentina, still holding his hand, said yes; then she drew him to her and lightly bit his lips with her tiny, sharp white teeth. They had no thought of their parents, who might or might not approve, or of any other obstacle that might stand in the way. It seemed to them that the promise they had just exchanged had always been part of their inner lives and would remain immutable. They could hear the subdued murmur of the Fluminera and the crunching gravel beneath their feet. The outlines of the Fulgheri houses and that of Verdiana stood out against the dark blue sky. The smoke from their squat chimneys mingled with the mist-laden air. On the dark walls, darker than the night, the windows were marked by narrow strips of light. Standing on the improvised wooden bridge, the lovers kissed for the last time before they separated. Valentina whirled around, held the shawl tightly over her chest and ran toward home.

"Take it easy! Be careful!" Angelo called out after her, seeking to distinguish the white shawl and the clicking of her heels in the darkness. He stood quite still until the door opened and he glimpsed her figure framed by the light from the room inside. The festive voices that greeted her return convinced him that everyone suspected what had happened. Well, they might guess —the father, the sisters, and Antioco—but they didn't know for sure. He was glad that the promise he and Valentina had exchanged only a few yards away from them, in the damp, dark night, should for a while remain a secret.

He went into his own garden by the wooden gate at the back of the house. Immediately the cold, wet nose of Carignosa rubbed the back of his hand. The dog turned around and around with sheer joy, and her thin tail lashed his legs. His mother had stayed up waiting for him; she was sewing by the light of an oil lamp on the table.

"I've told you a hundred times not to sew in that light," said Angelo, by way of greeting. "You'll strain your eyes." And he shoved the tip of his boot against the tip of her shoe, which stuck out like a mouse's face from under the hem of her long, pleated skirt.

Sofia stuck her needle into the cloth and raised her eyes to look at her son, pressing her pale, wrinkled lips close together. Angelo could never look at her prematurely aged mouth without a tender feeling. Her bright, black eyes were as eloquent and mischievous as when she was a young woman.

"When you sew, you should light the acetylene lamp, you know that!"

"I don't know how to light it, and besides, it scares me, because it's always popping," she said teasingly. Angelo felt sorry to have left her alone all evening.

"At least you could have lit the kerosene lamp," he said, just for the sake of having the last word and also in order to stave off a subject that was much more important and more difficult to put into words. But his mother's eyes read his thoughts and he knew that they would have to talk seriously together. Sofia had been waiting from one day to the next for Angelo and Valentina to announce their intentions. But she wanted him to tell her about it of his own volition, in the climate of trust that had always existed between them and that there was no reason for this new love to destroy. She looked around, sighed, picked up the needle, wet the thread between her lips, and said:

"Well, did you tell her?"

Angelo nodded, looking up from under his half-closed eyelids at her suddenly smiling face. He knew that his mother liked Valentina and approved his choice. Her only reservation might have been that he was so very young. But with her peasant wisdom and the experience she had acquired from grappling alone with problems large and small, she recognized the advantage of marriage to a girl with the qualities of Valentina.

"And what did she answer?" she asked, not without anxiety.

"She said yes," replied Angelo, leaning over to pat the dog, which lay wriggling at his feet. "So, *Mammai,* if you're happy, you can ask her father for her hand. If you like the girl, the next step is up to you."

"I do like Valentina," said Sofia simply. "I believe that she'll be a good wife to you and that we'll get along together. I'll speak up before Christmas, and so this year's festivities will be especially happy."

She got up, put her sewing away in a basket, then kissed the blue vein on Angelo's forehead, as she had used to do when he was a child. Mother and son did not often kiss. As country folk they were not given to external signs of affection. But every now and then, when she thought of her own faraway childhood or the more recent childhood of Angelo, when she remembered him as a small orphan boy, a feeling of tenderness overcame her and she gave him a hug and kissed him on the forehead.

Angelo had grown up without any friends except, in spite of the difference in their ages, Don Francesco. The only boy with whom he had been at all friendly was Antioco Cadoni, the son of Giuseppe Antonio, a rich owner of lands and livestock. Now Antioco was studying law in Turin and came to Norbio only for the holidays. He was an obedient son, but he did not share his family's class consciousness. Even as a child he had sought out, whenever he could, the companionship of the boys who played on the square in front of his father's house and whom his family called "street urchins." This square, later given the Cadoni name, was then just a sort of playground for the village children. Their games followed a strict schedule, according to the season. In summer, they played the "bell game" and the "clock game"; in the spring and fall, there were long and highly complicated competitions—real tournaments—of top-spinning, with different categories of competitors according to the type and quality of the top and the kind of wood from which it was made. In the fall, there were marbles, made of iron, earthenware, or glass; these last, made from crushed bottles of soda (the only non-alcoholic drink obtainable in Norbio's smoky taverns) were the most highly prized. And the "button game," in which bone or metal buttons were pushed by the players' thumbs into a hole. On rainy days, the boys played cards on the roofed porch of All Souls' Oratory or under the arcade of the Granary. Or else they played heads-and-tails, tossing copper coins into the air or against a wall. At Norbio, there was very little small change in circulation, and yet every boy had in his pocket enough pennies to play heads-and-tails, just as every old woman had enough to buy a few ounces of coffee or snuff. Little boys and old women gathered kindling wood in the forest, sold it for a lira a bundle, then changed the lira into smaller coins and spent or gambled them away. There were other games that knew no season, such as the "war game," which took the players far from the Piazza Cadoni, through the narrow village alleys, along the rocky bed of the Fluminera, on the dusty road to Acquapiana, or through the surrounding woods and fields. But in the evening, when sparrows gathered in the cypresses around All Souls' Oratory, their deafening chirping was like a mysterious signal that brought the boys streaming back into the square. The sparrows' chirping and the boys' shouts were the first signs of oncoming night, followed by the Angelus, rung out by the bells of Santa Barbara.

When Antioco's parents sent him to the seminary at Ales, their purpose was not to make him into a priest but to get him away from the "street urchins." It was there that Antioco and Angelo met, but they did not become close friends until after their adventurous flight from the seminary and their return to Norbio. They did not run away together, although Angelo gave the idea to Antioco, who later followed the same route, through San Silvano and Ruinalta. Like his mentor, he put on a shirt and trousers, wrapped and tied up his cassock and threw it onto the lavoratory roof, and took with him a blanket, hidden in the woodshed, as protection against the cold. The two boys had planned the flight in detail, even if, at the last moment, Antioco withdrew. Angelo himself had been tempted to give it up. That he went ahead was partly due to the difficulty of recovering his cassock, which he had already thrown onto the roof, and partly because he wanted to win the esteem of Antioco. At that time Angelo's feeling for Antioco was not friendship but admiration, not for his intelligence and other gifts but for his wealth and social position. Antioco, for his part, had been so humiliated by his own timidity that he did run away, a month later, all alone.

After his short stay at Ales, Antioco went to school in Cagliari, where he lived with members of his mother's family. But whenever he came to Norbio, he looked up his old friend and ally. As for Angelo, he envied Antioco his handsome appearance, stylish clothes, and money, but at the same time he was ashamed of his envy. Actually, he both liked and envied Antioco for the same reasons. He wanted to be in his company and please him, and he was jealous of Antioco's acquaintance with other boys such as the nephew of Senator Loru. He would have liked to claim Antioco as a relative. For this reason he was glad when he saw that Antioco was courting Olivia Manno, that Olivia encouraged him, and that her family looked on him with favor. If they both married Manno girls, then they would, indeed, be related. But even this feeling of satisfaction contained an element of envy. Antioco, a university student and of good family, was treated as an official fiancé, whereas he, Angelo, was considered just an old playtime companion. Antioco called twice a week on Olivia, and her older sister Barbara played the part of chaperone, to the discomfort of the engaged couple. But the father insisted, and when Barbara was busy, one of the other sisters took her place. Most often this was Dolores who, out of an excess of zeal and boredom, stood very close to Olivia and insisted upon over-hearing what she and Antioco had to say.

Angelo would have been happy with his work had he not felt guilty about collaborating with the Mining Consortium's destruction of the forests. At the beginning, when he accepted the job, he had thought that, with the engineer's support, he could prevent the rape of what remained of the forests of Escolca and Mazzanni—some two thousand acres on which the inhabitants of Norbio exercised their age-old rights of pasturage and wood-gathering. At Norbio there was no such extreme poverty as in other villages of Parte d'Ispi; even the poorest man had at least a pig, which could be fed on nuts and prickly pears, and if he had more than one, he took the lot of them to feed in the forest, where he had also a right to gather dry twigs and branches and dead or fallen tree trunks. On win-ter nights, in even the crudest mud hut, there were always a fire and a bowl of hot soup with bacon in it. Now, as the ovens of the Royal Foundry of Leni devoured the trees, springs had dried up, and there was an ever-greater danger that flood water would pour down from the bare mountains. Antonio Ferraris had persuaded Angelo to take a job as his assistant by holding out the prospect that in the future the foundry would burn pit coal and lignite from the mines of Iglesiente instead of wood and charcoal from the forests. But this project had been turned down, or at least postponed, because of transportation costs and the necessity of remodeling the ovens. With apologies and the promise that he would try again, the engineer had explained things to Angelo and made arrangements for a Tuscan contractor, Giuseppe Antola, to supply the foundry with wood or charcoal at the current price. Antola and his men were to cut the forest of Mazzanni, with the obligation to take precautions that would ensure the forest's renewal. Angelo had no choice but to accede, and he accepted the job of supervising the logging, to make sure that the least possible damage was done. He was reassured by the engineer's promise that this cutting would be the last.

One morning, from the courtyard, Sofia pointed out a column of black smoke rising behind the summit of Mount Homo. She and all the other inhabitants of Norbio knew that it was smoke from a charcoal pit, and that the wood was from the forest of Escolca. Angelo read a mute reproach in their eyes, as if the fault were his, since he was a paid employee of the Consortium. He saddled his horse and took with him not only his lunch basket, but a gun and a hunting pouch as well. He rode first through the Piazza Frontera, with the gun slung over his shoulder. Fortunately he had obtained a permit to carry firearms only a few days before. Zurito arched his tail, shook his mane, and proceeded at a trot; Carignosa went ahead, with her tail erect, heedless of the other dogs which came to run along beside her. Men in black capes leaning against the wall next to the tavern smiled under their thick mustaches and waved their hands when Angelo raised two fingers to his cap to greet them. As he turned Zurito down the Via delle Tre Marie, he wondered where Ferraris might be at this hour. Perhaps he had already gone to the forest, and he could talk to him there.

As he posted to the horse's gait, he thought about the forest of Escolca and Mount Homo. Now they were cutting not only the age-old trees, but also the arbutuses, the mastics, the willows, and even the olives. And this slaughter was taking place against the wishes of the people of Norbio, contrary to the law, and in violation of the explicit promise made by the Mining Consortium through the engineer. The column of smoke was still rising from behind the Punta del Vischio, the highest peak of Mount Homo. Angelo was sure that if he could find and talk to the engineer the slaughter would cease. He could not get this idea out of his mind.

Carignosa had come to a halt a couple of hundred feet ahead, among the bushes. She had caught the scent of game. Angelo reined in Zurito, leaned the butt of his gun against his left foot, held it upright with his knee, and loaded it. The dog froze, her narrow head with its long, flapping ears thrust out, one forepaw upraised, and her tail sticking straight out in line with her head and body. She quivered all over as she waited to lunge forward in pursuit of the prey. Angelo slipped out of the saddle and stood near her, preparing to shoot. The dog turned her head to look at her master and make sure that he was ready, then she took off. At almost the same moment the woodcock rose out of the bushes and flew in a zigzag diagonal up over the treetops. Angelo took aim and fired. The woodcock, struck by a hail of shot, rolled and plummeted to the ground. Carignosa knew exactly where to retrieve the bird, and soon came back with the body. Angelo held it for a moment by the legs, then put it into his pouch. He took the blackened cartridge out of the gun-barrel and remounted his horse. Although he was not particularly tall, he had grown in recent months, as he was aware because of the ease with which he could slip his left foot into the stirrup and swing himself into the saddle. The most insignificant things often make a man happy. To have shot down a woodcock on the wing, with an old-fashioned, breech-loading shotgun was a feat whose accomplishment drove all the worries out of his mind. For the moment, he was self-confident and in high spirits. His heart was pounding and his ears still rang from the shot's detonation. He urged Zurito forward, keeping his eyes on the dog, which paused at intervals with upraised paw to look questioningly at him.

"You're the one that should know if there's other game in the vicinity," Angelo said aloud, as if the dog could understand.

Nearby he could hear the sharp blows of the axes and the voices of the men who were cutting down the trees. But the woodcock in his hunting pouch was a talisman against anger or melancholy. Soon he would be face to face with the woodcutters, and perhaps with Ferraris or Giuseppe Antola. The ax blows, louder and louder, acquired a feverishly rapid rhythm. Every now and then this rhythm was interrupted by a sort of roar, a sound of crackling branches and voices shouting in unfamiliar accents as an ancient tree, its base chipped away, hit the ground.

To Angelo, every sound evoked a picture. Soon enough he saw through the bushes the fallen trees and the great stumps that gave out the unmistakable odor of freshly cut 'wood. The woodcutters wore Tuscan-style black cotton shirts and bright-colored sashes around their waists. They worked individually or in groups, hacking away with billhooks and pruning knives at the young shoots that grew around the stumps, and leaving them no chance to grow up and replace the felled trees. Angelo stopped in a clearing and called out:

"Hello there!"

"*Salud!*"

Some of the men returned his greeting without pausing in their work, others made no reply. Angelo dismounted, removed the bit from the horse's mouth, and led him over to the edge of the clearing where green grass was growing. Carignosa sniffed at the bundles containing food that the woodcutters had left on the ground and under the bushes. A tall, gaunt man was wielding an ax alone at the base of a big holm oak. With every stroke he let out a throaty *Achhh!*, and the tree trembled from top to bottom.

"Who's in charge here?" Angelo asked.

The man scrutinized him at length, then spit into his calloused hands and once more raised the ax above his head.

"When Signor Antola's not about, I am."

He came out with another *Achhh!*, and white chips flew around him.

"We're making charcoal, too," he said in a laconic but calm manner.

"So I see. . . . But there are rules and regulations. You're supposed to cut only one tree out of ten, and none that isn't full-grown. . . . What's your name?"

"Renato . . . Renato Graneri. I'm the foreman. And who are you? The mayor?"

"I'm Angelo Uras, and I'm supervising the logging operation on behalf of the Consortium. Is Ferraris, the engineer, anywhere around?"

"I work for Signor Antola. I don't know about any engineer."

"I'll have to register a complaint. The way you're doing things the forest will never come back. It's a great loss, and against the law, besides."

"The forest should never have been sold in the first place," said the foreman. "I see your point, but it's no use lodging a complaint with me. You'd better talk to Signor Antola. . . . Meanwhile, just step aside; the tree's about to fall."

The tree, with its base very nearly cut through, was leaning to one side, and a push was enough to tumble it over. Angelo leaped aside, while the woodcutters, all together, emitted a long, tuneful cry. There was a rustling and tearing sound and finally a crash. Then the men threw themselves at the trunk with axes, billhooks and pruning knives, as if they enjoyed the destruction. A bevy of wild pigeons passed, with rustling wings, over their heads, skimming the treetops. Before Renato's watchful and somewhat incredulous eyes, Angelo loaded his gun.

"Don't tell me you can shoot a pigeon on the wing," Renato said, laughing.

"I can always try," said Angelo, unafraid of the other's mocking look.

They were at the edge of the wood, and there was an expanse of level ground between them and the moor where Carignosa was running and jumping, now visible, now invisible, among the tobacco-colored rock-rose bushes. Her concern, however, was not with the doves but with a hare. The hare leaped out of the bushes, almost in the direction of the two men, then veered to the left. Angelo calmly loaded his long gun, ran his thumb over the sight, took aim, following the progress of the hare, and fired. The hare seemed to stumble, was catapulted into the air, then fell down and disappeared in the grass.

"Good shot!" the Tuscan exclaimed, spitting out the blade of grass that he had been holding between his lips. Carignosa ran after the hare, retrieved it, and ran to lay it at Angelo's feet and receive his caresses.

"Lucky fellow!" the Tuscan added.

Angelo waved his hand in farewell, and started to ride downhill. The pouch weighed agreeably on his hip. Perhaps the foreman was right. He was a lucky fellow, and aware of his luck. He was trotting along beside the railway track when he heard a roar behind him. He reined Zurito to one side, and a minute later, with a clanking of iron and the sound of loud voices, the train passed close by, loaded with wood, sacks of charcoal, mules, and men. The mules, in the last car, held their ears erect, stiff with terror. From the head of the train, the loggers waved their caps and shouted a greeting. The train snaked its way up and down the steep terrain, now appearing and now disappearing from view, and was soon out of sight, leaving the countryside more silent and deserted than before. In the silence, the rustling of the trees seemed to Angelo as deep-toned and complex as the anxious bustling of a crowd.

So you're getting married," said the engineer, standing motionless at Angelo's back and looking over his head at the bell-tower clock. Angelo started, but did not turn around. His hands were stuck into the chest pockets of his coarse wool jacket and his fingers were playing with some nuts, still in their rough shells. He had gathered the nuts several days before in the forest of Mazzanni to make tops for Valentina and her sisters, especially Dolores, who was still a child. He made the tops under the girls' attentive eyes, seated at the rustic dining table, using his sharp pocketknife. He cut a nut in two, then gave each piece four sides, on every one of which he printed a capital letter. After he had stuck half a toothpick into one end for whirling, everything was ready for the game, played with roasted almonds for chips, which was popular in Parte d'Ispi among children and engaged couples. The almonds had been provided by Sofia, who three days before had asked Manno for his daughter Valentina's hand. On the table there were also freshly picked oranges and tangerines, and bottles of aged Malvasia wine from Bosa and of sparkling Vermentino from Tempio. Comare Verdiana and Manno joined the chorus of shouts that greeted every winning spin. In every house in the village, the same game was being played and there was the same festive air, the same sharp odor of peeled tangerines and brandy. Peasants and rich "notables" vied with one another in loud shouting; they could be heard all the way from the main street as they sat eating, drinking, and playing by the light of an oil or kerosene lamp whose wick had to be periodically trimmed.

"So you're getting married. . . ."

The deep but muffled voice of Ferraris rang in Angelo's ear like the fatherly voice of Don Francesco Fulgheri. For some months they had had no friendly talk, only business discussions. Angelo made his reports and then it was up to the engineer to set the fine and force Giuseppe Antola to respect the regulations. But on this score, the engineer, usually so upright and energetic, was inactive. Angelo had accused him, to his face, of weakness, and accosted Antola, threateningly, on the street, where their arguments often took an openly quarrelsome turn. In spite of all this, Angelo still esteemed and liked the engineer and had not lost hope of changing his apparently negative attitude. At times he thought it must be his own fault that he had not kept after him in friendly fashion and brought him around. Now, when he heard him speak in the same tone of voice as earlier in their acquaintance, he was deeply distressed, and felt suddenly guilty because he had never spoken to him of Valentina Manno or asked him to the engagement party. The accumulated resentment of the last few months melted away, giving place to warmheartedness and hope. No, Antonio Ferraris wasn't like all the others, set only on his own selfish purposes, chiefly money-making. He, Angelo, had believed his

93

promises, and now he believed again. A few words were enough, and the hand laid on his shoulder. Perhaps it wasn't too late to ask Ferraris to the party. He said nothing and did not even turn around.

"You're angry with me," the engineer stated calmly. Angelo thought of Valentina and her sisters, sitting around the big, square table, and couldn't imagine the engineer in their light-hearted company. It would be better to ask him to dinner or for a glass of the Malvasia wine from Bosa, which Manno kept in his cellar. Then they could talk of important things, of mines, foundries, and forests, and of the Island's relinquishment of its old independence.

"We're having a family party at the house of my future father-in-law," he said at last, "and I thought it would bore you. But I'd like you to meet my fiancée, Valentina. . . ."

"Valentina?" the engineer repeated half to himself, adding aloud: "But I met her just today! Your father-in-law asked me to visit the oil mill, and afterward to have a drink. The mill's a model of its kind, as up-to-date as anything on the mainland. As for girls, there were so many of them. . . ."

"Well, she's the most beautiful of the lot," said Angelo, trying not to show his feelings.

"They're all beauties," said Ferraris, laughing, and shaking Angelo's shoulder until finally the young man turned around. "So which one is yours?"

"The third. First there's Barbara . . ."

Ferraris took him by the arm and stamped his feet on the ground to warm them.

"Let's move," he said; "it's getting cold."

Passing over the wooden bridge built during the flood, they walked toward the Piazza Cadoni. At a certain point the engineer halted and squeezed Angelo's arm.

"I think you've made a good choice," he said.

"How can you know, if you don't really remember her among the seven sisters?"

"I may not remember her exactly, but I was able to size up the whole family."

They started to walk again, with the bridge echoing their

footsteps. There was a moment of silence as they stepped aside to make way for a group of girls with pitchers balanced on their heads. For a moment, the two men were enveloped by their chatter. After the girls had gone by Angelo said:

"If you were to be my witness at the wedding, my best man, it would establish a special relationship between us, something even closer than family."

The engineer blew a ring of cigar smoke into the air. An outburst of voices came from the Cadoni house.

" 'Best man,' " he said. "Is it more than being a friend?"

"No, not more, but just as much."

"Then I'll be your 'best man'!"

"I appreciate it. Thank you. One of these evenings you must come to supper with us. You promised me you would a long time ago."

"I promised, yes, but you forgot to invite me!" said Ferraris jokingly, throwing away the butt of his cigar, which described a luminous curve before falling into the stream.

They had reached the tavern, which had a sign reading "Bar and Stable" over the door. From the still crowded ground floor there came the smell of the licorice used to flavor the local spirits, a wave of warm air from the drinkers' bodies, and loud voices. The two men hastened their step, each of them resolving, for his own reasons, not to go in. The stars seemed larger than usual in the transparently clear dark blue sky, and the familiar profile of the mountains stood out against it.

Angelo shook the engineer's hand emphatically, and the latter watched him walk away before plunging into the suffocating air of the tavern, which he had to go through in order to reach the narrow stairway leading to the second floor. As he went by, Giovanni poured him a glass of brandy, so full that the brandy spilled onto the zinc bar. Ferraris took the glass, hardly larger than a thimble, between his thumb and forefinger and, under the eyes of all those present, swallowed the contents with a single gulp, peasant style. The stares bothered him, as did the heavy air, sodden with alcohol. Although he enjoyed the company of his fellows and considered it his duty to spend some time among them, he had every now and then an irresistible urge to be alone. This was one such moment, and he wished that, instead of coming in, he had walked farther with Angelo. With a hasty greeting, he went out again into the cold night air.

Antonio Ferraris had always loved the mountains, and all the hardships involved in mountain-climbing—the glaciers, the almost impassable paths along the edge of a precipice, the rude shelters. The Alps, of course, were *his* mountains, the ones he had crossed so many times to go to France or Savoy. The mountains of Parte d'Ispi, with their gently curved, almost human shapes, were very different, but still they conditioned the life of their inhabitants and had so even more when they were covered with dense forests. The people of Norbio, although they had little in common with the people of Piedmont and Savoy, were none the less "mountaineers"; on them there was the smell of burning wood, and grass drenched by the long autumnal rains. Suddenly he felt guilty in their regard, for not having kept his promise to Angelo, which was not only a promise but his duty as well. He had neglected an obligation and broken his word in the bargain.

Standing on the deserted street, he breathed in the pure night air, listening distractedly to the raucous, slightly drunken voices still coming out of the tavern, among which he could easily distinguish those of the Tuscans brought in by Antola, a dozen or so strapping young fellows, very different from the men of Norbio and from the Islanders in general. The difference in their speech and ways reminded him of the war, or rather the wars, in which he, like so many others, had taken part "in order to create a united Italy," which remained, however, simply an aggrandizement of the kingdom of the House of Savoy. As usual, this thought made him feel unfulfilled and despondent, as if he had somehow missed fire and wasted a good part of his life for a mistaken cause. The real Italy was not the one of which he and so many other young men had dreamed, it was the Italy making an uproar in the tavern, divided as it had been before and even more so, since its "unity" was only the bureaucratic unification of the inefficient bureaucracies of the multitude of Italian states. These noisy, impoverished Sardinians had no ties with the peoples of Florence, Venice, Milan, and Turin, all of whom looked upon the Island as an overseas possession or a penal colony. Even the mainland Italians had nothing in common but an abstract and rhetorical nationalistic idea, couched in vague terms by half-baked philosophers and second-rate poets. The idea of liberty, as incarnate in the French Revolution, had not been fulfilled by Mazzini and Garibaldi who, each in his way, had betrayed the cause for which they had demanded the sacrifice of so many young lives.

A man was walking, with heavy steps, on the empty street in his direction, and Ferraris recognized him immediately as Giuseppe Antola. Up to now, although the engineer had been aware of Antola's transgressions, he had avoided a confrontation. But this evening, as soon as Antola was in hearing distance, he called out to him by name: "Signor Antola!"

"Shall we have a drink?" said the Tuscan, encouraged by his cordial tone of voice.

"Later, later," said the engineer, turning his face toward the mountains. "First, let's talk."

"It's too miserably cold," said Antola, stamping with his heavy boots on the ground.

"Just for a few minutes."

Walking along, they reached the point where the road turns to the left and skirts the foothills; then they turned around, walked back to the bridge, and all around the Piazza Cadoni. For the first time, they thrashed out the procedures involved in the logging. Ferraris accused Antola of being rough and careless, and Antola rejected the accusation.

"You're taking the word of Angelo Uras against mine," he said, raising his voice. "You've never come to the forest to see with your own eyes how we're going about it, and you've swallowed the story of that good-for-nothing boy."

"Signor Antola, you're trying to make all the money you can, but you'd have an ample margin of profit even if you respected the conditions of our contract."

Angelo had told the truth, and besides, the people of Norbio were on the verge of staging a protest. Not only had Antola failed to carry out the job according to specifications, but his men were preventing the peasants from bringing their pigs to forage in the areas marked for cutting.

"The boy's told you a pack of lies!" Antola shouted angrily, slapping his hand on his hip.

"Easy, there," said the engineer calmly. "Uras isn't the only one. The whole population is up in arms. Just a few days ago they took their complaint to the town hall. That day you didn't show your face, and the *carabinieri* sergeant couldn't find you."

"Let's put our cards on the table. We're talking now not about logging procedures but about pigs and goats and grazing."

"These people live from the little they can make out of their livestock, and if we take that away from them . . ."

"I contracted to supply the Royal Foundry at Leni with a certain amount of fuel. I shouldn't have to remind you of my obligation."

"Come, come! You know perfectly well what I mean. Your contract is one thing, but you have another obligation no less important—to spare the forest. You have a right to cut down only a certain percentage of the trees; you're not supposed to touch the olive trees or the young saplings or the underbrush. . . ."

Antola stopped and stood with his legs braced, looking at the engineer defiantly. Their voices resounded in the clear, cold night.

"But where you and your men have passed . . ." Ferraris continued, "the forest of Escolca has been razed to the ground, and Orida and Mazzanni are going the same way."

"That's a lie!"

"What did you say?" exclaimed Ferraris, stopping in his turn and sticking out his red-bearded chin.

"You've been misinformed. You're passing on what's been told you. It's because you put too much trust in that lazy, lying protégé of yours, who comes up the mountain every now and then to shoot pigeons."

In the darkness, the engineer turned pale.

"It's not just Uras," he said, folding his arms and looking Antola straight in the eye. "Everyone at Norbio says the same thing."

"A bunch of swineherds!" shouted Antola, running his hand over the butt of the pistol he carried on his belt. "I won't let them lay hands on me!" And he shook the thick oak stick that he carried as if it were a cane.

"If I were you, I wouldn't face a crowd of Sardinian swineherds with your gun and stick," said the engineer. "You and your men had better take care not to provoke them. What's more, I'm in no mood to tolerate any more of your irregularities."

"You're on their side, I know that," said Antola, tapping with his stick on the ground.

The engineer puffed at his pipe and let the angry words fade into the air along with the pale blue smoke.

"I'm on the side of the law, which, for once, is on the side of justice. You know that as well as I do, only you don't want to admit it."

"Just remember this," Antola retorted. "Only once I was late in delivering the wood, and you were the one to tell me that if it ever happened again, my contract wouldn't be renewed."

"I remember. But now I'm putting it to you just as strongly that you have to observe the regulations. You do your duty, and I'll do mine."

Ferraris went back alone to the tavern. A group of peasants standing at the door drew back respectfully to let him go by. They had overheard the discussion and wanted to assure him of their backing. The engineer walked quickly through the tavern and climbed the wooden stairs to the upper floor. He regretted the bitterness of the argument with Antola, but felt he had done right and was resolved to exact respect for the law. He leaned out of the window, looking at the mountains, while he finished his pipe, and then went to bed.

That year, for the feast day of Saint Barbara, patron saint of the village, the organizing committee had planned both fireworks and horse races. These were to take place on the main street that recently had been renamed "Via Roma," by a unanimous vote of the town council, in honor of the removal of the capital of Italy from Florence to "the Eternal City" in June, 1871. The significance of the change of name was not very clear to the local people who innately distrusted anything new, especially when it came from "above," but they looked forward to the festivities.

Men, women, and old people, dressed in their Sunday best, waited in double lines on both sides of the street. They were so closely crowded together that the children, to see anything, had to slip between their elders' legs. All eyes were turned toward Funtanedda, the lowest section of the village, from where the horses were to race up into the square. Six pairs of horses, mounted by three riders from Norbio and three from Ghilarza —a village famous both for its fine horses and beautiful women —were to compete. As far back as any living person could remember, the races had always been uphill: the riders chose to have it this way so that the horses, launched at a gallop, would not get out of control. Actually, the event was not a race as much as a competition in horsemanship and acrobatic skill.

The onlookers laughed lightheartedly and there was a gleam of anticipation in their eyes as they turned, at frequent intervals, to look down at the curve at the foot of the hill, where the first two pairs of horses would appear, greeted by loud shouts and acclamations. There were people at the windows, on balconies and rooftops, who tried, occasionally, to quiet the crowd below, as though the hum of voices on the street were responsible for the horses' delayed arrival. Occasionally, one of the crowd thrust a leg out toward the middle of the street, trying to detach himself from the others and have a better view, but rough hands soon pulled him back and angry voices reproached him.

"It's dangerous out there," they told him.

From the balcony of Comare Verdiana's house on the Via Roma, there was a view all the way to the curve where, sure enough, preceded by a sudden clamor, the first horses now came into sight. Valentina Manno, at a window above the balcony, was looking through the binoculars lent to her by Angelo, which her sisters were trying to snatch away. With her body as stiff as a tree trunk, she was leaning so far out that she would have fallen had not Barbara and Olivia held on to her, while Lisetta, Annamaria, and Martina tried to seize the binoculars, leaning dangerously far out themselves and spanking her in fun.

"What a bottom!" Annamaria shouted teasingly, in a voice so loud that it might have been heard on the street.

Valentina wheeled around and gave her a slap which made such a noise that Sofia, on the balcony below, raised her head and, perceiving how far out and how dangerously she was hanging from the window, rushed upstairs to restore order. Valentina, holding tightly on to the binoculars, struck out with her heels to push her sisters away. Her idea was to climb the ladder leading to the attic and from there to get to the roof, where it would take Sofia and her sisters some time to overtake her and she could enjoy the race undisturbed.

For a minute, the room was filled with a whirlwind of arms, legs, skirts, and petticoats. This was the sight that greeted Sofia's eyes when she emerged from the top of the stairs and called out: "Girls, girls!" Valentina flattened herself out on the floor and half slid, half leaped between and over her sisters' legs to the ladder. With the black binoculars swinging from a long leather strap around her neck, she climbed up as nimbly as a cat. Sofia took a long, leaping step forward, groping with outstretched arms in an attempt to catch her. But she was left with her nose in the air while Valentina passed, as if snatched up into heaven, through the trap door. The sisters gave out "Ahs!" and "Ohs!" of astonishment as they saw her long, bare legs disappear and the trap door slam shut.

"Shame!" shouted little Dolores, fingering the thick black braids that fell over her chest. "Lucky there were no men around!" exclaimed Annamaria, her cheeks crimson.

"Men or no men," said Sofia, in a singsong voice, "that girl isn't afraid of anybody!"

"But to go up on the rooftops on a windy day like this! . . ." Annamaria continued.

They laughed in chorus, and the girls, attracted by the increasing noise on the street, went back to the window. Valentina tiptoed along the edge of the roof, against the wind, her dress clinging to her slender body. She felt as if she had taken wing and were scraping the clouds in her flight. Down below she saw other roofs, walls, trees, courtyards, and a mass of dark figures converging from all over the village. Shivering in the north wind, she leaned for a moment against the chimney, gathering her long skirt around her legs. She had a sensation of total freedom and a strange, silent happiness. Lifting the strap from around her neck she pointed the binoculars toward the far end of the street. At this very moment, three horses and their riders emerged from the crowd, galloping flat-out, side by side. The crowd had fallen back against the walls of the houses in order to widen a passageway which, even so, seemed almost too narrow. Above the general hullabaloo, the shrill cries of little boys sounded like whistles. The middle horse was ridden by a man wearing the black garb of Norbio.

With the binoculars, Valentina could make out every detail and she recognized him as Mariano Spada. Mariano leaned his hands on his horse's withers and, slipping his feet out of the stirrups, skillfully drew his legs up on the saddle. Then, looking straight ahead and biting his lower lip, he stood upright in the stirrups and leaned slightly forward, holding the reins loosely in his hands. The street was dry and hard, echoing the regular hammer blows of the hoofbeats of the three leading horses.

Valentina looked for a while longer through the binoculars. Suddenly she thought of Angelo and remembered that she hadn't seen him all day. Stepping gingerly in order not to break the roof tiles or slip on them, she retraced her steps, in a straight line, with the wind blowing as if it would carry her away. She suddenly felt lost and alone. She opened the trap door and went down the ladder as carefully as if she were still at the edge of the roof, wishing that she could be invisible and her return unobserved. No more noise rose from the street; the race was over and, so it seemed, was the festive excitement. In all the village there was no more than a vague rustle. Her sisters, who were still in the room where she had left them, barely raised their eyes, as if they were excluding her from their company.

"What's the matter?" she asked, wrinkling her nose impatiently, "did something go wrong?"

They burst into laughter and gave her a hug.

A pause followed the acrobatic display, before the festivities resumed. Some people disappeared down the side streets; many went home to rest and wash up. The long wait, the nervous tension, the almost physical participation in the race had turned the late autumn afternoon into a stifling holdover from summer; even the northwesterly wind seemed like a sirocco. But soon afterward, people drifted back to the center of town, crowding around the vendors of nougat from Tonara and sherbets from Aritzo. In the Piazza del Municipio and along the wall of the old convent, the scaffolding was ready for the fireworks which, after supper, would mark the end of the celebration. Wherever there was space, in front of houses or at the foot of the wall, there were round baskets containing round cakes with a hole in the middle, like doughnuts. Knife-sellers from faraway Pattada displayed their wares on outspread black capes. There were knives with horn handles and leaf-shaped blades varying in size from a hand's breadth to that of a baby's little finger. Everyone in Norbio either already had or wanted to have one, to use for cutting bread or slitting the throat of a young lamb, for both attack and self-defense. People commented on the race, each one picking his own winner and waiting for the judges' announcement. But at a certain point, the hum of the crowd grew louder, like that of a beehive in a state of alert. Nobody knew who had brought the news, but it came to the square and penetrated the houses and even the church.

The news was of a death. Some hearers concealed their satisfaction; others said openly, "Serves him right!"; while still others deplored the event as casting a shadow over the entire village. Giuseppe Antola had been found dead, with two bullets in his chest, on the front car of the logging train. He had insisted on keeping his men at work even on the holiday; the train had been loaded as usual in the forest of Escolca and started punctually downhill with its cargo of logs, mules, and men.

The brakemen were under Antola's orders, and he sat on the first car. At a certain point, just before the church of San Sisinnio, as the Tuscans told the story, they heard gunfire, but they didn't dream that their boss, sitting motionless in his place, was the target. Wild pigeons were flying overhead at just that moment, and they thought the shot came from a hunter. Only when the train came to a stop on the square in front of the foundry did they realize that Antola was dead, his feet in a puddle of blood, one hand on the brake lever and the other in the wide pocket of his corduroy jacket.

Whispers, exclamations, unfinished sentences. All that was known for sure was that Giuseppe Antola had been killed and that Dr. Fulgheri, together with the police magistrate and the sergeant of the *carabinieri,* had gone to the foundry at Leni to take legal note of his death. The body was to be brought to Norbio and laid in the cemetery chapel, which served as a morgue. But soon this sparse news was enriched by a number of details, and the people of the town felt as if they had seen with their own eyes the stiffened corpse on the first car of the train, with the two holes in the chest and the checked wool shirt soaked in blood. They expressed little pity, but all of them had a sensation of guilt, mingled with hidden fear, as if they were afraid of finding themselves somehow involved.

In the past, Island laws had held the whole community responsible for a crime. But the present fear did not stem from this long-since-lost collective responsibility; it reflected simply mistrust of the machinery of justice.

Everyone asked, of course, who had shot Giuseppe Antola. For no particular reason a name came to the fore, the name of Angelo Uras. It was as if people had seen him lurking behind a tree until the train went by, shooting off his old-fashioned gun and then disappearing into the woods. No one thought that Angelo Uras was capable of murder and yet, at this particular moment, everyone found him guilty, without any proof to bolster this conviction other than the notoriously tense relationship between him and Antola. Several times, on the Piazza Frontera, Angelo had called Antola a thief and said that one day he would be sorry for the harm he had done to Norbio. Just a few days before they had almost come to blows; and Angelo had been called to the barracks of the *carabinieri* and severely reprimanded by the sergeant.

Angelo had risen early on the feast day, saddled his horse, and picked up his hunting equipment. Sofia tried in vain to hold him back, remarking that work in the forest should be suspended. But Angelo was not making one of his customary inspections; he was going to shoot wild pigeons. So much the better, he explained, if there was nobody around. He was thinking of the valleys of the Leni and the Narti, of the holiday emptiness of the woods and of the silence of all growing things, interrupted only by the rustle of pigeon wings and the trampling feet of mountain goats, or of a hog that had lost its fellows.

"It's Saint Barbara's Day!" Sofia insisted.

"Saint Barbara is to be honored by shooting off a gun," said Angelo, putting his foot in the stirrup.

"When will you be back? Did you take something to eat?"

Angelo shook his head, and Sofia ran into the house, returning with a linen bag into which she had put some black bread, cheese, pickled olives, and a bottle of wine. She stuffed this into the pouch of the saddle bag and then went to open the gate.

"I'll be late to Mass if I don't hurry. . . . Don't pick a fight with those Tuscans if you run across them in the woods! . . . God be with you!" she murmured as she closed the gate behind him.

Angelo had a glimpse of her as she traced the sign of the cross and, leaning over his horse's neck, he followed her example. He took a deep breath as if he could already smell the fragrance of the trees. He had no wish to pick a fight with the Tuscans;

indeed, he hoped not to see a living soul on his way. He trotted, first downhill, thinking to follow the foundry road as it ran parallel to the river, across from the line of the narrow-gauge railway. The village was awake but there were few people on the streets, mostly old men and women going to early Mass, with their wrinkled, cork-colored faces and their hands like dried-up roots, but all of them in their Sunday best—the men wearing clean shirts and the women gold buttons and rosaries hanging from their belts. Young people went to the High Mass, later on; the only ones now on the streets were disheveled girls going to draw water at the fountain. Those who had a private well stayed at home, washed themselves from a bucket, and combed their hair behind closed windows. Angelo let his thoughts wander idly to the many aspects of the village's life. He knew who lived in every house, and although he had few friends and rarely, if ever, went to the taverns, he was aware of the conflicts of interest and differences of opinion among the inhabitants. Scattered words and sentences that he had heard a long time ago returned to his memory and fell into place. The only people with whom he stopped to talk were old men, toward whom he harbored a feeling of pity and respect, adding up to a sincere affection which they appreciated and returned. He genuinely enjoyed talking to them and questioning them about their youth. When he met such an old man, he usually offered him a lift in his cart or behind him on the horse. But on this particular morning he rode fast and alone, happy to leave the village and its familiar sounds behind him and anticipating the pleasure of the day of solitude that lay ahead. For quite a way old Zurito proceeded at his customary fast walking gait. Near the bridge, in sight of the foundry chimney, Angelo heard a sudden outburst of angry voices above the pounding hammers and the screeching saw. From the middle of the bridge, he paused for a moment to look down at the foundry. The train had left for the mountain, just as on an ordinary day, and the foundry workers from Norbio were pushing their creaking wheelbarrows as usual. Angelo guided his horse down the steep path leading off the bridge and once more took the narrow road going upstream on the shore opposite to that of the rail-way.

The roadbed, winding its way among tall bushes, was soft and restful; Zurito broke again into his fast walk, and soon silence enveloped the scene except for his hoofbeats and the rustle of the leaves. Carignosa trotted in diagonal lines, always at the same distance ahead. Occasionally she strayed among the oleanders that formed a hedge on either side of the road, only to reappear almost immediately. She looked up at her master, shook her head and long, droopy ears as if she were just coming out of the water, and resumed the line she had been following.

Angelo was expecting to find a woodcock. But perhaps an-other hunter had passed by before him, or else Carignosa simply didn't want to linger. She might even have read his mind, for he, too, had no wish to tarry. Suddenly he heard the hoofbeats of another horse behind him. The rider was a tall fellow; he rode with his legs widespread and long stirrups. Angelo pulled over to one side in order to let him pass. As he went by, the man slung around his neck the long-barreled rifle which he had been carrying across his saddlebow; he grunted and waved his hand by way of a greeting. A young woman sat behind him, her arm around his waist. The man did not so much as turn his head, but the young woman looked sideways and smiled. They were not from Norbio, and it was unusual to find strangers on this road, especially on a holiday. But Angelo knew that the hog-owners of Norbio were selling off their animals because of the cutting-down of the forest and the lack of pastures, and a holiday wouldn't interfere with any such transaction. The stranger rode ahead of Angelo at the distance of a rifle shot. At a certain point, he slackened his horse's pace, turned to the right, and disappeared among the oleanders. There was no road in the direction he had now taken, only a clearing where riders often halted.

Angelo made an about-face, but instead of retracing his steps, he whistled to Carignosa and urged Zurito up the hillside. All around, the countryside was empty and silent. A young hawk perched on a bare tree; a magpie flew, chattering, across the river. Angelo turned in the saddle and saw it disappear among the gray olive trees on the opposite shore. Zurito stepped through a gap in a rough stone wall and went toward a tall, leafy walnut tree, where he had stopped before. Not far from the round, smooth trunk was a small spring. Angelo jumped to the ground, knelt down, and drank; then he loosened the girth, took off the bridle, put hobbles on the horse's feet, and, with a slap on the rump, sent him off to graze on the abundant grass nearby. Zurito ate greedily, jumping every now and then on his forefeet. Angelo found a long stick leaning against the walnut tree and with it he knocked down some nuts. He cracked the shell between two stones, extracted the nut as if it were an oyster, separated its parts, and, with the worn pocketknife he had had since childhood, carefully peeled the bitter, yellowish skin. He ate the firm but tender nut with obvious enjoyment, crunching it between his teeth.

Walnuts were one of his favorite treats, and now his enjoyment reminded him of his mother and Valentina. There was a big walnut tree in Manno's garden and, on Sunday afternoons when they were not in church, his mother and Valentina picked the nuts. Little Dolores claimed the job of shelling them and serving them on an earthenware plate from the sideboard. Everyone peeled off the inner skin for himself, except for Angelo; Valentina did it for him with her long, slender fingers which knew no other work than that of the embroidery frame and the loom. As for Dolores, her hands were blackened by the juice of the shell; her father and Barbara scolded her, and Valentina took up her defense. Now Angelo's hands were black, and they would not come clean in the cold water of the spring. Finally he gave up washing them and lay down, with his hands clasped behind his neck, in the tall grass. High in the sky above, a transparent cloud dissolved in the autumnal sky like smoke in the wind. Perhaps up there a high wind was blowing, so remote from the earth that it would never cause a single leaf to tremble. A leaf did fall, however, from the top of the walnut tree, and came to rest on his chest. The cloud had evaporated, perhaps by the same process as that by which the ice on a lake melts in springtime. Angelo had never seen a lake except in book illustrations, but these had fed his fancy, and now he had an even clearer perception. He felt as if he were a stone at the bottom of a small Alpine lake which he had seen on a map in Don Francesco's atlas. And yet his mind was primarily focused on the face of Valentina, as she bit into a freshly shelled nut, and on Dolores's stained hands. Suddenly he realized that he had been sleeping. He glanced at his watch, which had slipped out of his vest pocket, and started. Half-past twelve already, and he had not fired a shot. Carignosa was sleeping with her head against his foot; Zurito was moving about as best he could at the edge of the field. The silence of the countryside was less intense than before, as if others who, like himself, had slept away the lazy autumn morning, had also come suddenly awake. He patted the dog's wet black nose and went for Zurito. After taking off the hobbles and rubbing the backs of the horse's ankles with a handful of fresh grass, he picked up the rest of the nuts to take to Valentina. It was time for lunch, but the nuts had cut his appetite. In a few moments, he was back on the narrow road at the point where he had left it, where he had seen the stranger with the long gun and the beautiful girl disappear among the oleanders. Nothing untoward had happened, but the unscheduled sleep had left him feeling vaguely discontented. Carignosa stopped at the exact spot where she had been when the stranger's black horse made the right turn, and now, as then, she looked up at Angelo as if asking for an explanation. At just this moment, a gaunt old man stepped out of the bushes down the road and stood there with his chin and hands resting on a long stick. Carignosa jumped back, barked in surprise, and pawed the ground. Angelo recognized him from a distance as the pig-farmer Sisinnio Casti. As a young man and an ardent hunter, he had made a mistake in measuring gunpowder, and his rifle had gone off in his face, blinding him. Angelo gave Zurito a gentle kick, and the horse walked on. The old man was waiting with his face uplifted.

"Jesus Christ be praised!" he exclaimed in the old-fashioned manner when the horse stopped in front of him.

"For ever and ever!" Angelo answered.

The clearing was now filled with people, ox-drawn wagons with men and women, pigs and their herdsmen, and the stranger with the beautiful young woman sitting behind him on the black horse.

"Can you tell me what time it is?" the old man asked, turning his disfigured face.

Angelo opened his watchcase and shut it again before giving a reply. He couldn't believe that a half hour had gone by since he had looked at it before, on the hillside, that day time was passing by without his noticing it. The old man moved his lips in a toothless smile, as if he were mocking Angelo's thoughts, as if he alone knew the secret of time. Turning his back on Angelo, he raised his forefinger and proclaimed the hour.

"One o'clock," he said, in a sarcastic, mocking tone of voice.

Carignosa was sniffing his faded tan cotton trousers. Carmela, the widow of Sisinnio's eldest son, leaped down from the wagon and offered Angelo something to drink. Because he had not yet lunched, Angelo was reluctant to accept. If he were to tell them, they would insist that he stop and share their meal, and he had a nagging sensation that time was going by all too fast.

"It's just our own little wine," said the old man, smiling to himself. "No need to worry; even if you haven't eaten, it will do you no harm."

Angelo stretched out his hand and drained the glass.

"Some more!" said the old man imperiously, as if he could see him.

The daughter-in-law refilled Angelo's glass. She wore the black kerchief symbolic of a widow's perpetual mourning, just as the old man wore a black band on his sleeve. The loss of his son, as Angelo well knew, was a greater source of sorrow than his blindness. If only the boy had not died so far away, across the seas! If only he himself, with his groping hands, had been able to lay him out in his coffin! He never forgave the king for having taken his son away, for having seized him as a horse or a brace of oxen are seized for unpaid taxes. For this boy was the best of all, not only the best of his sons, but the best of all the young men of the village; he was eyes and hands to his father. Angelo could read the old man's inconsolable grief on his face; it was as if his empty eyes and scarred flesh came not from a gun but from the letter from the Minister of War brought to him by the sergeant of the *carabinieri*.

Zio Sisinnio Casti and his two surviving sons were among the major pig-farmers of Norbio and had considerable vineyards and wheat fields as well. Angelo drank his second glass of wine slowly, in order not to be obliged to accept a third. The old man raised his sightless eyes to the sky and held up his forefinger to ascertain the direction of the wind. He was listening to a sound that none of the others, except Angelo, detected. In Angelo's ears, it had definite connotations; it was like a rumble of thunder, muffled and absorbed by the earth. Eventually, however, the others recognized it as the mule-train coming down the mountain with its load of timber. Beyond the dried-up riverbed, the invisible rails vibrated among the blackberry and oleander bushes. Every second the noise grew in ear-splitting intensity. The women jumped down from the wagons with their babies in their arms. The stranger, who had never heard just such a sound, tried to calm his horse and looked questioningly around him. Zio Sisinnio raised his hand and nodded reassuringly, and the stranger turned to speak to the young woman who was clinging to his side. Masses of terrorized wild pigeons flew low over the open space, heading straight toward the rumble, as if in a frenzy of self-destruction. At the moment the sound reached a climax, a rifle shot rang out above it. Everyone turned to look, but there was only a tiny cloud of blue smoke and the bitter smell of burned gunpowder. The noise of the train faded away as rapidly as it had come.

"If you shoot into a mass of birds like that, you may bring down half a dozen of them," the stranger observed.

"Yes," said the old man, calmly, "but only if your gun is loaded with buckshot. What we just heard was a gun loaded with a regular cartridge or, rather, two cartridges."

"How do you know?" asked the stranger's girl.

"For me, it's as recognizable as a chord struck on a guitar," the old man tossed back at her.

Before going on, Angelo loaded his gun.

"Buckshot, eh?" asked the old man, as he heard it going into the barrel.

"I came after pigeons," said Angelo, ramming the tow down with the rod. Then he wheeled his horse around and whistled to Carignosa.

"God be with you!" the old man murmured.

Valentina came down to the second floor, where Sofia and Verdiana had closed the balcony shutters. She reopened them and stood looking down upon the street where people were standing or walking about in little clusters. Children shouted as they played tag, but over everything she could hear the chatter of the women, who started and made the sign of the cross when the men leaned over to whisper something into their ears. The whispered word, repeated over and over, was "murder"; once she had heard it, she could read it on the women's lips as well, and she saw glances shot at the closed shutters of Angelo's house. Finally, she left the balcony and hurried down to the street. The women were chattering uninterruptedly, in low voices, but upon her approach they fell silent and looked away. She caught hold of one of the boys playing tag and pushed him against the wall.

"Who's been murdered?" she asked. "Tell me who."

"Signor Antola," the boy gasped. "With two bullets here in the chest."

Valentina pushed him aside and ran toward the house of Sofia Curreli. Although Sofia had remained with Verdiana, the front door was unlocked. The kitchen door and the windows giving onto the courtyard were shut, and Zurito's stall was empty. Sofia had told her that Angelo had gone pigeon-shooting early in the morning, and, of course, she knew that he was at odds with Antola. A terrible thought crossed her mind.

"God, don't let it be true!" she prayed aloud.

She threw open the back door and ran down the alley to the wooden bridge over the Fluminera and her father's house. She beat with her fists on the door. Barbara had been the last to go out and she had locked it. But perhaps the key was in the geranium pot.

"If the key's there, it means that nothing's happened, that it isn't true," she said to herself.

She moved slowly toward the pot, then, breathlessly and with her heart pounding, stuck in her hand. The key was there.

"God, I thank you," she murmured. Then she kissed the key and entered the dark, empty house. She knew that Angelo was incapable of killing, but she knew also that seemingly impossible things can happen. Now she went first to the kitchen, where she poured a glass of water from the pitcher and gulped it down, then up to her own room, where she took off her light dress shoes and put on a pair of heavy ones, better suited to the long walk she had in mind. She wanted to see Angelo as soon as possible, to run to meet him, to hear him say that the horrible thing she had imagined wasn't true. A few minutes before, in her simple way, she had felt suddenly aged and disheartened, but the discovery of the key was like a reassuring message. She knew now that Angelo was innocent, but she wanted, none the less, to hear the words from his own mouth. She'd have to hurry if she wanted to set off before her father and sisters came home. She finished lacing her shoes, went out, closed the door, and put the key back in the flowerpot.

The days were growing noticeably shorter, and she could count on no more than an hour or so of light. She crossed the vegetable garden almost at a run, went along the wall, and finally leaped over it. Beyond the wall, she followed a path shaded by tall elder bushes. She would have to walk, in part, by night, but she hoped for a full moon. By now she had reached the road to the foundry, and from there she would go to Balanotti. She knew the way well, having taken it on horseback with Angelo and on foot with Sofia. She couldn't have known that this was the road Angelo had traveled early in the morning, but she hoped, and indeed was almost certain, that he would take it on the way back, and this certainty quickened her pace. Walking along the edge of the road, she felt as free as she had felt on the rooftop. The few people she met greeted her, the men with a nod and an unintelligible murmur, the women with the ritual *"Ave Maria,"* to which, without slackening her pace, she answered *"Gratia plena."*

When she came to the bridge over the Leni, she saw a crowd gathered in front of the foundry, not only inside the fence but also beyond the surrounding wall. Many of them must have traveled the same road as herself, although she had not noticed them. Suddenly she lost her self-confidence. The sight of this crowd of people who had come to see the dead body was oppressive. She still had the binoculars around her neck, but she did not give in to the temptation to look through them. Two *carabinieri* stood one at either side of the door to the office, which was lit by the flickering yellow flames of candles. The crowd moved steadily around the bier where the body had been laid. There were moments when she could have seen it with her own eyes, but when there was an opening in the ranks she turned her eyes away. From the foundry there rose a muffled murmur of prayers. She made a sign of the cross, recited a *requiem,* then went down the steep path leading to the narrow road.

Valentina walked faster. By now it was nearly night; the mountains melded into the darkening blue sky and the moon, setting over their summits, was a frail crescent rather than a source of light. But Valentina recognized the bends in the road she had rounded by day so many times before; she recognized even the shapes of the bushes and the sharp smell of the mint and other aromatic herbs that grew in the dried bed of the river. Once, when they had halted for lunch, Angelo told her that an underground stream continued to flow even in the season of drought. Suddenly she heard the dull hoofbeats of an approaching horse. As she stopped to let it go by, she recognized the rider as Gavino Macis, one of the workers at her father's mill. Perhaps her father had seen her go and had sent him after her. This thought was passing through her mind when the man said:

"What are you doing here at this hour? Did you come to see the dead man?"

"No, I didn't," Valentina answered, with a lump in her throat, as he drew closer.

"What shall I say to your father if he asks about you?"

"Did he send you after me, Gavino?"

"Nobody sent me. I was here, I saw you, and I followed."

"Are you going back to Norbio?"

"No. I'm coming with you. It's not that I'm curious. But I think I can imagine where you're going, and I can't leave you alone at night. You'd better get up behind me."

"Very well," said Valentina, resignedly.

Gavino guided his horse over to a big rock. Valentina jumped up behind him and put her arm around his waist just as she was accustomed to doing with Angelo. He had on him an odor of smoke and olive pulp, the familiar and reassuring smell of the mill.

"It'll take us about an hour to go where I imagine you want to go," he said, turning his bearded face. On his breath there was the smell of garlic and tobacco. "It's Balanotti, isn't it?" he added dryly.

"Yes, Balanotti," she assented. "But tell me the truth, Gavino: didn't my father send you after me?"

"No, I came on my own because I wanted to see the dead body. When I saw you, I was on my way back to the main road. You were on the bridge, but then you walked down the path and in the direction of the mountains. I knew where you were going, and I came after you. Everyone in Norbio's saying that he did it, but I don't believe it. The Tuscans insist that they saw him in this neighborhood this morning, but that doesn't mean he was the one to shoot. Unfortunately, that's the idea people have got into their heads. He must be told to go into hiding, because if he comes home, they'll arrest him. The *carabinieri* are searching for him already. But eventually the truth will come out: Angelo Uras is innocent."

"Thank you," said Valentina, holding back her tears.

Gavino felt her shudder.

"We're coming to a stretch of good road, and we must make time while we can. Afterward there's a long climb. Hold on tight, and if you're afraid let me know."

"I'm not afraid."

Gavino touched the horse with his heels, and the horse broke first into a trot and then a canter. Holding tightly to Gavino, Valentina felt a new surge of confidence, as when she had found the key in the geranium pot. Soon she would see Angelo.

"Now we're starting to climb," said Gavino, spurring the horse up the steep hill.

Valentina had faith in Gavino and Gavino had faith in his horse. Ahead, they heard a fox barking. Then the bark moved off to the left while they continued in a straight line. The slope grew steeper. In the distance, they heard a succession of explosions.

"They're starting the fireworks," said Gavino. He scraped the tip of a match on the seam of his trousers, lit a cigar, looked at his watch, and said: "Half-past eight."

A flare, wavering in the darkness, rose toward the slender moon, then burst into an umbrella, lighting up the summits of Mount Homo, Punta del Vischio, and Mount Volpe. Valentina recognized where she was and caught a glimpse of the cottage at Balanotti. As the fireworks continued to crackle, she fancied she could hear the muffled roar of a crowd.

"We're nearly there," said Gavino.

The horse walked gingerly downhill, digging his forefeet into the ground. A dog barked, and the dog was Carignosa.

A ngelo had not wanted to go back to the village until the festivities were over, and therefore had stopped at Balanotti. He was sitting by the fire when Carignosa began to bark and to throw herself against the closed door. When he let her out, she dashed into the darkness, still barking, but in a welcoming manner. He heard the iron gate creak and a horse's hoofs pound the ground. Instinctively, he took his gun down from the nail where it was hanging and shot it off into the air just outside the door. This, too, was a token of welcome, but also a warning that he was armed. He slipped another bullet into his gun and started down the path to the gate. Now he could hear voices.

"Who's there?"

"Friends," said a man's familiar voice, but one which he could not immediately identify.

The slowly advancing horse almost knocked him down. He

stepped aside and at just this moment heard a muffled laugh and smelled a familiar perfume.

From the village, beyond the hill, they could hear fireworks exploding. Flares lit up the olive trees, the cottage, and the haystacks with a forked pole in the center. At regular intervals, a Roman candle went off high in the sky, opening out into a fan of many-colored lights. After a moment of silence and darkness, there came the last sensational event: a very loud explosion with no illumination.

Angelo took Valentina into his arms and she kissed him.

"Is something wrong?" he asked, pulling away from her.

"Why didn't you come back earlier in the evening?" she said, taking his hand.

Hand in hand, they walked toward the cottage. The doorway was lit by the fire blazing inside. The rider on the horse followed them without speaking, then dismounted, and tied his horse to the iron ring in the wall. They invited him to come in.

"Just for a minute," he told them.

"Thank you for coming," said Angelo, lighting the oil lamp that hung from a projection of the chimney.

"I only did my duty."

Valentina was holding Angelo's arm. He raised his chin in her direction, looking at Gavino.

"She told me about Antola," he said.

"And did she tell you the rest?"

"What rest?"

"That people are saying you shot him."

Valentina hugged Angelo and burst into tears. Gently he freed himself from her embrace and laid a hand on her shoulder.

"Are people saying that? Do they really believe it? When, exactly, did it happen?"

"I don't know what people actually believe," said Gavino gravely. "But the *carabinieri* are looking for you. You had a row with Antola and threatened him. That's all they need to know. The magistrate has signed a warrant for your arrest. You were seen this morning, passing in front of the foundry after the train had gone. You were carrying a gun. . . ."

"I always carry a gun. I was going pigeon-shooting."

"I don't need any explanation . . . Your mother is very afraid. She's spoken to Lawyer Cadoni."

"And my mother, does she . . . ?"

"She doesn't believe you did it, but her belief and ours don't matter. You need proof. And meanwhile, the lawyer says, you'd do well to stay in hiding."

"I'm innocent, and I'm going to give myself up. If I hide or run away, it means that I'm afraid, that I'm guilty. . . ."

"No!" cried Valentina, hugging him again. "No, no!"

"That's what your mother said, but the lawyer insisted that you hide out. . . ."

"Like a bandit? Like Lorenzo Gamurra, who hid out for twenty years?"

"If you have the nerve, do like Gamurra!"

"But I'm no bandit. I'm going back home and turn myself over to the sergeant."

Valentina hugged him tightly and wept.

"I've done my duty. It's up to you to decide. What message shall I give to the lawyer?"

"That I'd like to talk to him, or to his grandson, Antioco."

"Very well."

"Meanwhile, I'll wait here."

"Very well," echoed Gavino. "But we must go right now. It's late."

" 'We'?" said Valentina, relinquishing her embrace. "I'm staying here. Tell my father that I wouldn't go back with you. Tell him whatever you like."

Gavino looked surprised.

"Valentina Manno, I can't believe my ears!"

"Believe them! Believe them!" said the girl, boldly but with a certain embarrassment.

"Well, it's your business," Gavino tossed back from the door.

Angelo locked it behind him. They heard the horse's hoofbeats and then the creak of the gate, opening and shutting. They embraced. The air was fragrant with the smell of wheat and apples. But Angelo was aware only of the intimate, secret, disturbing scent of verbena.

It might have been planned that way, and yet it wasn't. They were alone together at night for the first time, out in the country. . . . Valentina thought of how at her house they must be sitting silently over their dinner, wondering where she had disappeared to, and Angelo thought of Sofia. He offered Valentina olives, cheese, and bread toasted on the fire, and she ate without saying a word. Zurito whinnied and pawed the ground outside. As for Carignosa, she lay down on an empty sack near the fireplace and yawned.

They undressed in the darkness and slipped into bed where they lay in each other's arms, afraid but happy to be together. He kissed her mouth gently and she opened her lips to return his kiss. She had come to find and protect him, and then, on the spur of the moment, she had decided to stay. Perhaps, she thought, this was the only wedding night she could hope for. Fear, pain, and joy overtook her in quick succession and mingled together. The love-making of this night was not so much a pleasure as it was an act of trust, sorrow, and dedication.

Outside, the trees rustled in the wind. Several times they imagined that they heard footsteps and voices. Finally, the wind fell, the leaves were silent, and they heard the song of the nightingale.

Carignosa was snoring; every now and then she yelped in her sleep as if she were dreaming of hares, partridges, or woodcock in erratic flight. They did not know which one of them was the first to fall asleep, each imagining that he or she had kept watch over the other by the reflected light of the kitchen fire. Actually, Valentina stayed awake longer. She felt Angelo slide, unconsciously, out of her arms, listened for a while to the snoring dog, and watched the shadows, projected by the fire, dance on the wall. For a moment she felt alone and afraid, but then the sight of the sleeping man at her side evoked in her a determination to protect him with all her strength. She pushed back a lock of hair from his forehead, murmured a prayer, and went to sleep in her turn.

Valentina was the first to awake as well. She felt as if she had slept for only a few minutes, but she was rested, happy, and clear-headed. She got dressed, put on her shoes, fed and watered the horse like a countryman's wife, washed herself in cold water from the well, came back into the cottage, lit the fire, and made coffee. In the musty kitchen cupboard, she found pots, pans, plates, tableware, oil, vinegar, salt and pepper. In one corner there was a coal bucket; she threw a handful of coal on the fire, transferred the embers to the oven, threw on more coal, and blew on it with the bellows, raising a shower of sparks. Turning around, with her arm over her eyes, she caught a glimpse of Angelo, standing by the chimney. They embraced and looked silently into each other's eyes.

"I must go home," said Valentina, "and you can't stay here. The olive pickers and the men with the wagons will be along soon, and after them the *carabinieri*."

Angelo looked at her while he blew on his boiling-hot coffee. Between one swallow and another, they talked together. There was a cave in the side of the hill and, at the first alarm, he would hide there. Valentina or his mother or Raimondo Collu, if they came from the village, would leave provisions inside the cottage.

"Don't forget gunpowder and bullets!"

Valentina was to take Zurito, leaving Angelo without transportation. He saddled the horse, buckled the girth with special care, and adjusted the bit and bridle. Valentina rode astride, tucking her skirt around her knees. He went with her to the gate and slapping Zurito on the rump, sent him off at a gallop. Suddenly, Angelo found himself alone and wished he hadn't let her go home so soon. For the first time he felt lost. He walked about holding on to Carignosa's collar. Passing in front of the cottage, he picked up his gun, and the dog, imagining that they were off hunting, jumped up and down, barking happily. The gun was loaded with bullets, and Angelo wanted to shoot it off into the air and reload it with buckshot, but Valentina would have heard and been afraid. For the moment it was wiser not to shoot. Who knew how long he would have to stay in hiding? Lorenzo Gamurra had turned into an old man in the forest of Escolca before they managed to capture him. They had shot at him and had wounded one of his legs, and he had had no choice but to give himself up. Yet in the end it turned out that he spent all those years as a fugitive needlessly, because at the trial he was found innocent.

Zio Raimondo stood with his shoulders against the door-post, half inside, half out, smoking his clay pipe with the long cane stem. Angelo had lit a cigarette and every now and then he made an answer to the few intelligible phrases that emerged from the old man's usual mumble. Neither of them seemed to attach much importance to what the other was saying; they might have been talking in their sleep. At intervals, there was a drizzle of rain.

"It's going to rain like this all day," the old man said, pointing with the stem of his pipe to the sky.

Angelo looked up at the gray heavens and the sooty clouds that a strong wind was pushing, at a great height, from the mountains toward the plains. A different wind, at a lower level, was pushing another mass of clouds in the opposite direction. This stratification was a meteorological phenomenon not usually perceptible to the naked eye, and one which confirmed Zio Raimondo's forecast. The sight of the clouds, moving like vast herds against one another, gave the old man a strange sensation of security. He felt himself to be knowing and invested with a responsibility that devolved upon him not so much from his venerable age as from his vigorous, faraway youth. The presence in the kitchen of the chattering girls who had gathered to pick the olives but were afraid to go out in the rain annoyed him. He directed a stream of yellowish spit at the mounting-block, then turned around and said scoldingly:

"You've taken your quinine and drunk your brandy and dried yourselves off, haven't you? What are you waiting for? The sun isn't coming out today, that's for sure. You'll have to make do with the weather as it is. If you've dried yourselves off, you'll get wet again, of course, and then you can come back to dry. But if you stand around toasting your backsides at the fire, you'll waste the whole day and soak yourselves to no purpose when you go home."

He spat again, then went into the smoke-filled kitchen, waving his arms as if he were chasing chickens.

"Out! Out! Take your sacks and baskets, and go do your work! I want you out of the way."

The words and the tone of voice were angry, but there was a smile on his face, the smile of a man incapable of malice or unkindness. He looked at the girls with satisfaction as they streamed outside, winked at the surprised Angelo, and went to lean again against the doorpost, puffing at his pipe. The girls scattered among the dripping olive trees, continuing to chatter in little groups as they worked. They were talking of the festivities of the day before and the killing of Antola, and wondering why Angelo was waiting for the *carabinieri* at Balanotti instead of going to hide in a safer place, farther away. Zio Raimondo was still mumbling half to himself.

"If I were you," he said, "I wouldn't wait here for them to come get me."

Angelo started, aware once more of the reality of the situation.

"Do you think they're really looking for me?"

The old man looked at him with astonishment.

"Of course they are, and the minute they find you they'll put you under arrest. Almost everyone believes you were the one who killed Antola."

"Do you believe it?"

"What does it matter? No, I don't believe it, and there are others that feel the same way. But many people are against you. You were seen riding by the foundry yesterday morning. And a shot was heard just before the train arrived with Antola's dead body."

"I was pigeon-shooting."

"I believe you. But you have to convince the sergeant and the investigating magistrate. They'll arrest you and question you and then you'll be tried."

"I'll go to Norbio and turn myself in."

Zio Raimondo did not give an immediate reply. He relit his pipe, drew on it and then said that even if to turn himself in might seem to bear out his innocence it wasn't a wise thing to do.

"You need proof, and during the investigation you'll be better able to serve your own cause if you are free."

He had no confidence in justice; a man in Angelo's situation had to rely on his wits.

"You can't tell how long the investigation and the trial will drag on," he said. "Cooling your heels in jail without being pronounced innocent or guilty is no joke. Take my advice: hide out, and don't let them catch you."

"I was thinking of holing up here at Balanotti," said Angelo. "There's always the cave. . . ."

"Nonsense! That's the first place where they'd expect to find you. I'm surprised they haven't searched it already."

"So where should I hide?" said Angelo, shivering.

"You're not the kind of fellow to take to the woods. You should hide in town."

"In town?"

"Yes, but not in your own house, of course. The best place would be the house of Cadoni, who'll be serving as your lawyer. If Senator Loru weren't a son of a bitch, he could shelter you with impunity. But he's not to be trusted . . . I'm talking too much . . . I've given you my opinion, but you should get your mother's advice, and Manno's. Manno's an honest man and an intelligent one; he should be a great help."

"He'll be put out by the whole affair," said Angelo, coughing with embarrassment.

"I don't think so. We're going to get you out of this mess, you'll marry Valentina, and all will be well."

The old man looked up at the clouds scudding in opposite directions at different levels overhead. He felt as sure of himself as he had a few minutes before, when he had predicted more rain. Angelo was thinking of Valentina. She must have been drenched by intermittent showers along the way. Perhaps her sisters had put her to bed and were clustered around her to hear her story. . . .

In spite of his optimism, Angelo knew that he couldn't sidestep a direct confrontation with his future father-in-law. With this thought in mind, he took leave of Zio Raimondo, who had finally sat down by the fire and pulled off his boots. Taking his gun and his hunting pouch, he started to walk, under a light drizzle, in the direction of Norbio. Following the old man's advice, he took the unfrequented shortcut through the woods, pausing at intervals to adjust the shoulder flap of his rough woolen cape and the gun strap. In certain spots he could distinguish Zurito's hoofprints, and he felt as if Valentina were hovering nearby, invisible but watchful. Comforted by this feeling, he walked faster.

He met no one on the road as it wound its way around the base of Mount Homo and Mount Carmelo. The atmosphere was that of a holiday, yet the silence of the countryside was different from what it had been the day before. When Angelo paused to listen, he could make out a multitude of small sounds, like bubbles in a glass of spring water: creaking wagon wheels, the blow of an ax or the scraping of a hoe, the rhythmical rasp of a saw, and muffled voices, all indicative of unseen human presences, masked by the rustle of the rain. At one point the scattered voices fused, as if they belonged to the walkers in a barefoot procession. Then, around a curve, he saw the tiled rooftops of Norbio. The rounded top of the bell tower, with the iron cross and the lightning conductor, stood out against the gray sky. Voices rang out more clearly in the damp air, and he could hear the continuous dull sound of the turning millstones with which every one of the twenty-five hundred houses of Norbio was provided.*

Angelo skirted the watering trough and made his way through vegetable gardens, jumping over walls, crossing courtyards, slipping through secret passageways and hiding, for minutes at a time, behind woodpiles, wondering all the while what the people whose voices he barely heard from inside the houses were thinking about him. After twenty-four hours, did they still think he was the killer of Antola? Not all of them, at any rate.

* To this day the millstones used in the Parte d'Ispi region retain the shape of those stones used in the construction of the "nuraghi" towers, structures dating from the sixth century B.C. and still visible and numerous. The millstones are turned by blindfolded donkeys to grind the wheat.

124

He was eager for the company of trusted friends to whom he could talk freely.

Coming out of a courtyard, he inadvertently bumped into Zia Marietta Serra, an old peasant woman who bore the ancient and aristocratic name of the judges of Arborea * and who enjoyed general respect for her wisdom, kindliness, and her mysteriously acquired family connection. She looked at him from under the reddened lids of her small gray eyes and made a mimicking gesture peculiar to the old women of the village. With her emaciated hand, she administered three or four mock blows to the top of the head that he had bent before her. This gesture, which seemed to be a threat, was, in reality, an affectionate absolution. It was as if she were saying: "Yes, you're a bad boy, but this time you're not to blame; they're accusing you wrongly." Angelo could have hoped for nothing more; her verdict meant more to him than that of all the judges in the kingdom. With a grateful heart, he seized and kissed her hand, then raced away, through another courtyard, over a wall into a vegetable garden, and through a labyrinth of more courtyards and gardens, where the red top of the bell tower was his only guide. In this manner, he passed through half the village, followed by an echoing train of dogs' barking. Carignosa trailed him at every leap, like a shadow, but without making a sound. Finally, he waded into the Fluminera, swollen by the rain. The churning, muddy water came up to his thighs and his wet trousers hindered his passage. He went back to the shore, leaned his gun against a wall and rolled up his trouser legs. In order to reach his own house, he would have to wade downstream for at least a quarter of a mile, whereas the house of Antioco Cadoni was closer and in plain view, and it was there that he meant to go for advice and help. For a moment he was torn between the desire to see his mother and Valentina and the urge to get in touch with his friend. He chose the latter course and plunged back into the water, making his way upstream. Soon he was at the Cadoni woodshed, which overhung the river. The courtyard wall had collapsed during the last flood and had never been rebuilt.

* Eleventh-century rulers of the region.

Still followed by the dog, he climbed the bank up to the woodshed and thence to the barn, where the oxen stood side by side chewing their cud before the feed troughs. It was unlikely that Antioco would be coming to the barn. For a moment, Angelo thought he might have done better to go home and send someone to call him, since he could go from one place to another without arousing suspicion. But here he was, and he had no wish to go back to the cold stream. He took off his water-logged shoes and then his trousers, which he wrung out and laid on the warm back of an ox. All he had to do was to be patient until they were dry; the only danger was that someone might come along and find him there almost naked. He wrapped himself in his rough woolen cape, which he had carried through the water on his shoulders, and leaned up against another ox while he waited. Without turning its head, the ox looked at him out of one shiny black, convex eye, in which Angelo saw his own reflection as if in the lens of a binocular. He tried to wriggle his ears as he had done to amuse his classmates at the seminary, but without success. He had lost the trick without even being aware of it. Suddenly he realized his situation and its gravity. Only the evening before, with Valentina in his arms, he had been strong and happy; now he saw himself as the most miserable and ridiculous creature.

The worst thing wasn't that he should be unjustly accused of a crime which he hadn't committed; it was that, under these circumstances, he had compromised Valentina. For he was sure that everyone in the village knew that Valentina had slept with him the night before in the narrow cot at Balanotti. In this supposition, he was not far from the truth. The people of Norbio had a collective perception of certain facts, all the sharper for being the mysterious sum of individual perceptions, which pile up and are matched one with another, only to break down again into individual insights and opinions. Thus, from that moment on the day before when Angelo's name had been bandied about as the murderer of Antola, everyone, as if with a single mind, had imagined and "seen" his every movement. Likewise, from minute clues and unfinished sentences, they had guessed that Valentina had run away from home and joined him at Balanotti. In a village like Norbio, even the most reserved person cannot long keep a secret. So it was with the workers in the olive mill, with Comare Verdiana, with Sofia, who had left a lamp lit all night long, and also with Valentina's sisters, who woke up with their eyes red from crying. It served no purpose that Valentina had stolen back home through the village by secret paths that not even she herself could have retraced. She lost her courage only when she heard the mill machinery and had seen, under the black smoke coming out of the chimney, the roof of her father's house and the wide-open windows framed in ivy. She rode, still "invisible," into the courtyard in front of the house. No sooner had she dismounted than, unexpectedly, her skirt fell to the ground. She swept it up with one hand, removed the cloth that she had rolled, like a turban, around her head, and walked deliberately toward the front door.

Her father, who was standing at the sideboard in the dining room while he drank a cup of coffee, said no word of greeting. Like the others, he knew everything and, in her half-undressed condition, she felt naked before him. He set down his cup and pointed to the door which she had just closed behind her. Without saying a word, he abruptly nodded his head. She felt as if her legs would give way, but she summoned the strength to turn around and go out. Intuitively, she realized that if she went without protest or any attempt at self-justification, "everything would turn out all right in the end."

From where she had left him in the courtyard, Zurito greeted her reappearance with a whinny. Valentina strode toward him, but at the last moment she turned aside and went in the direction of the wooden bridge and Sofia's house. She had to see someone who would not reject her, who would welcome her with open arms and let her cry. As she went away she heard a strange sound, one she had never heard before. Later, her sisters told her that it was her father, who had broken into loud sobs, leaning his elbows on the sideboard. They came down from the floor above but hesitated at the dining-room door. When Barbara finally went in, he was no longer sobbing. He had wiped the tears off his face with a handkerchief and was sipping his cold coffee.

"Make me a fresh cup," he said, as if asking for forgiveness. Barbara nodded to Olivia and, exchanging an understanding look, they went, both of them, to the kitchen. They had seen Valentina ride up to the house, go in and out again, and run in the direction of Sofia's, and they had immediately grasped the situation.

Soon the house was pervaded by the aroma of the fresh brew. Manno followed it into the kitchen. The other girls trooped in, noisily blowing their noses before helping themselves to some coffee. Then, barefooted as they were, they started out to fetch Valentina home. She must get married at once, their father had said. Little Dolores imagined her as already having the swollen belly that she had seen on many girls of Norbio before their wedding day. That day she did indeed see a swollen Valentina, because Sofia had wrapped her in shawls and blankets and put her to bed, with a cup of hot milk flavored with sugar and brandy. Valentina lay like a newly delivered mother, with flaming cheeks, in the big double bed which Sofia meant to give to her and Angelo. Comare Verdiana was bustling about the house, happy to be helpful.

Carignosa was bored with staying in the barn. Angelo was so absorbed in his thoughts that he paid no attention to her, but she looked at him expectantly, waiting for him to move on. She had sniffed at all the corners, discovering everywhere, above the many other smells, the familiar one of her master, who stood motionless, chewing at a wisp of straw. Suddenly a new odor assailed her nostrils, pricking her memory and also her appetite, for she had eaten no more than a crust of bread all day. She crouched for a moment on the straw, with her nose quivering, then advanced slowly on the trail of the smell, which led her out of the barn, through the courtyard and to the kitchen door of the Cadoni's house. Inside the kitchen, the smell had a concrete form and a human face.

"Go away, dog!" called out one of the women inside.

Carignosa paused on the doorstep, with an imploring look in her wet, dark eyes.

"Go away!" the woman repeated.

"Leave the creature be," put in her companion. "She belongs to Angelo Uras."

"You don't say so!" said the first woman with sudden interest.

On the kitchen table there was a pile of sliced meat. The more indulgent of the two women was cutting every slice in two and making a second pile. Now she took a slice between her fingers and threw it to Carignosa. The dog didn't catch it on the fly, as she had expected, but let it fall onto the stone step where she sniffed at it somewhat disdainfully before taking it into her mouth.

"She can't be very hungry!"

"Hungry? I should say not! Angelo Uras wouldn't let her go hungry."

"She's thin though; you can count her ribs."

"Thin, yes. Because she has worries."

And both women broke into laughter.

A bell on the kitchen wall rang loudly. Someone was calling from the dining room. The younger of the two women grumbled, because the call meant that she had to bring in the coffee. Another slice of meat traveled through the air, and this time Carignosa caught it. A few minutes later, while he was enjoying his cup of coffee, Antioco was told that Carignosa was in the kitchen, which meant that Angelo couldn't be far away. Perhaps he was on his way back to the village and the dog had arrived a few minutes before him. Or else Angelo was already there and he had sent her. Antioco went to look for his friend in the barn and found him there in his underwear, with his woolen cape wrapped around him. After a hurried embrace, he led Angelo to the house. He took him first to a storeroom filled with flour sacks and old papers, where in a corner he found a chipped candlestick containing the stump of a tallow candle. He offered Angelo a cigarette and said that he himself would prepare the guest room, the one that Ferraris had occupied at the beginning of his stay in Norbio. Angelo begged forgiveness for causing any disturbance, but said he had nowhere else to turn.

"We'll get you out of this," Antioco assured him. "You never killed that filthy Tuscan."

"I never killed him, for sure. But I wish I had. I'm in just as much trouble as if it were true."

"If you listen to us and do what we tell you, you won't get into any trouble."

" 'Us' . . . what do you mean by 'us'?"

"My grandfather and myself. My grandfather's a first-rate lawyer, and he's obtained the release of other innocent people."

"Well, I'm innocent," said Angelo, with a certain embarrassment. He had little confidence in old Cadoni, who had the reputation of being an outstanding criminal lawyer but also a man of little character.

"Neither my grandfather nor I has the slightest doubt of your innocence," Antioco continued. "But you were seen passing in front of the foundry shortly before the train arrived with Antola's dead body. These are facts, and we need other facts with which to contradict them. Most of all, what we lawyers call an alibi. Exactly where were you when Antola was shot? Dr. Fulgheri has been able to establish the exact time of his death."

"One o'clock, isn't that it?" said Angelo.

Antioco stared at him with amazement, and Angelo couldn't help smiling. Then he told of his meeting with the blind Sisinnio Casti, leaving out no detail, not even the old man's answer to the pretty wife of the merchant of Acquapiana when she had asked: "How do you know it was a gun loaded with two cartridges?" and he had answered: "For me it's like recognizing a chord struck on a guitar."

Antioco's eyes widened with astonishment.

"Incredible!" he exclaimed, clapping his hands. "What a story! The perfect alibi, as it might be dreamed up by a great criminal lawyer!"

Angelo shrugged his shoulders and laughed, as if he were not directly concerned, but inside he felt relieved. He visualized the scene quite clearly, even more clearly than on the spot. He saw himself raise the glass of wine to his lips while the blind old man listened to the rumble of the train and started at the shot. Those minutes passed through his mind like the ticking of his big silver pocket watch.

"Do you think those people will testify on your behalf?" Antioco asked him.

"I can't say," said Angelo, looking at the yellowed face of the watch, where the minute hand turned like an agile black bug. It was seven minutes past one, one o'clock of the day after. . . .

"Let's make a tally," said Antioco, scribbling on the first sheet of paper that came to hand. "Old Sisinnio Casti, the widow of his son Piero, Giovanni and Giuseppe Casti and their wives, the merchant from Acquapiana and his wife, the two farmhands, Luigino Onida and Pietro Madao . . . ten persons in all, who were with you and can confirm your alibi, that is, unless you have any reason to think they're hostile to you. . . ."

"Hostile? Why should they be hostile? They're all friendly enough, it seems to me. We drank together. . . ."

"Don't be naive! You know how people are. . . ."

"Well, I think I can trust them."

"We have to be sure. If they testify for you during the investigatory trial, my grandfather will ask for and obtain your immediate acquittal, and you'll be a free man."

"How can you be sure that your grandfather will want to defend me? He's a well-known lawyer and has a right to large fees."

Antioco beat his clenched fists against his forehead as if to signify: "Are you mad?" Aloud, he said: "Just leave it to me. I'll take care of my grandfather."

Angelo shrugged and looked up at the ceiling. "It's easy enough to say," he thought to himself, mindful of the time when Antioco had held back at the last minute from their joint flight from the seminary. He was shivering from cold, but Antioco didn't dare invite him into the dining room, where a fire was blazing. First he had to talk to his family and, above all, to his grandfather. Angelo understood this. He felt a certain mistrust of the Cadonis. They were a family of peasants who had raised themselves to the rank of landowners and, as a result, they envied aristocrats, even when these were decadent and impoverished, and they kept away from the common people for fear of being identified with them. Former peasants were in constant danger of returning to the status from which they had come, of falling into the same poverty as that of their ancestors. He, Angelo Uras, who until forty-eight hours before had been counted a prosperous landowner, was now a beggar wanting to warm himself at another man's fire and fill his empty stomach with a bowl of hot soup.

The Cadonis, like everyone else in Norbio, had talked of little else but Angelo during the last two days. Antioco, without any basis of fact, had maintained that his friend was not guilty. Now he told of Angelo's meeting with the swineherd and his companions. He said he had heard the story but he didn't say how.

"If that's so, then your friend is safe," said the old lawyer.

Antioco had a hunch that it was wiser not to reveal to the assembled family that Angelo was at that moment in the storeroom. He told only his grandfather, when they were alone together, and the old man, perhaps because he liked the idea of putting a trick over on the womenfolk, gave his approval.

"Bring him to my study after I've had my nap," he said.

After the usual heavy lunch, he was accustomed to sleep well into the afternoon, but on this day he got up earlier than usual, sent for old Sisinnio Casti and had from him confirmation of Angelo's story.

"That's the truth, sir. My children and farmhands can only tell you the same thing. They're honest people, all of them. So is Angelo Uras, and he deserves our help."

Before the afternoon was over, old man Cadoni had decided to take on Angelo's defense. He relished in advance the effects of his oratory and the certainty of a new legal triumph. When announcing this decision to his wife, daughter-in-law, and grandson, he added that he proposed to shelter Angelo under his roof for the duration of the investigation. After this, he summoned Angelo to his study. The young man's clothes were dry, but covered with caked mud, and he sat timidly on the edge of his chair, as if he were facing the prosecutor. The lawyer did put some tricky questions to him, but afterward he offered him a glass of brandy and said that he was taking on his defense, without any fee. Leaning over his dusty desktop and pointing a gnarled finger at Angelo, he specified:

"You'll pay only for the costs of the trial—notarizations, tips to courthouse employees, and, later, presents to witnesses. Then, when the hunting season comes around again, you can bring me a few hares and woodcocks."

But he laid down one binding condition: Angelo was to do whatever he told him. And, first of all, he was not to stir from the guest room, except to come down for meals or to answer a summons from the study.

"What about my mother?" Angelo asked. He wanted to add the name of Valentina, but Antioco motioned to him to keep quiet.

"Your mother can come to see you after dusk, without making herself conspicuous." Upon which he signified that the conversation was over, got up, and walked out of the study.

Antioco threw an arm around his friend's shoulders and, with lowered heads, they, too, left the room. There was in it an odor of dust, ink, and tobacco that reminded Angelo of Don Francesco Fulgheri.

That same evening, after dark, Sofia came to see him. After the lawyer's words had reassured her, she went back to her house taking Carignosa with her, tugging the dog by a rope because she was unwilling to leave her master.

While Angelo remained shut up in his room, the sergeant of the *carabinieri* continued to look for him. He had nothing personal against the young man but, as a Piedmontese, he looked down upon all Sardinians as belonging to an inferior race, as being unworthy of the civil rights the king had bestowed upon them. Angelo Uras did not fit into his preconceived ideas, but for this very reason the sergeant was impelled to take advantage of the first occasion to persecute him. He looked forward to leading him, handcuffed, through the square and shutting him up in the jail behind the former Archbishop's Palace.

From his hiding place, Angelo watched the comings and goings and, heedless of danger, slipped out repeatedly to see Valentina. Under cover of darkness, he left the Cadonj house by the rear door, which gave onto the Fluminera. The stream was no longer in flood and there was a strip of dry sand on which he could walk; even his hobnailed boots did not prevent him from running swiftly and silently. He was familiar, one by one, with the bark of the dogs, the creaking millstones, and the shape of the woodsheds whose supporting beams came all the way to the water. When he paused to rest, he could hear beyond the rustling stream the village's nighttime noises, could detect the smell of the barns and the smoke from wood fires fitfully blown by the breeze; over the walls there drifted a woman's high-pitched voice or the wailing of a child or an old man's cough. Soon he was near Valentina's home, aware of it less from its appearance than from the familiar warmth and from the odor of freshly milled flour and freshly crushed olives that seemed to envelop it in the night air. Every time he arrived at this point, he hesitated as to whether he should go see his mother or Valentina first, for he never left his hideout with any preconceived plan. He knew, of course, that he was the object of a search, that *carabinieri* were posted among the elder trees, and that the moon might come out from among the clouds any minute. But he was not afraid, and nothing ever happened. He knew what time it was even without looking at his big pocket watch. Valentina, who had the same instinctive perception of time as he and whose blood flowed with the same rhythm as his own, was waiting for him behind the storehouse door. She would have waited even longer before going back upstairs to her sisters, silent accomplices of her long vigils and absences and of the meetings with her lover. Even the innocent little Dolores understood from the whisperings of her older sisters that a child was to be born.

Stealthily, Angelo crossed the open space in front of the house, skirted one side, and came to the wooden door, draped with ivy, whose hinges creaked like the voice of a woman. There she was, her warm body enveloped in the red woolen shawl, which even in the dark he recognized by touch, like a blind man. Valentina's womanly fullness and beauty, the fact that she neither laughed him off nor held anything back, but gave herself to him as freely as she had the first time, made Angelo feel cleansed of every sin and shame, as if God loved him.

"Why don't you grease the hinges of that door?" he asked her.

"It's not that I forget," she answered. "But I'm embarrassed to come here by daylight with a bottle of oil."

It was hard for them to break away, and to Valentina it seemed that their long kiss lasted on in the darkness even after he had gone. She heard only the creaking of his boots and the low whistle with which he signified to Sofia that she should open her back door.

Angelo thought that his mother was none too happy to see him, certainly not as happy as Valentina. Actually Sofia was happy, but with an underlying sadness, which, in spite of her perspicacity and common sense, she could not explain. She was sorry that her son had shot up so fast, so that he was taller than his father and she could no longer kiss the vein on his forehead, the only thing which recalled his childhood to her. And then she was worried because he risked capture by leaving his hiding place. She guessed, of course, that he had gone first to see Valentina, and her concern for his safety was mingled with unconscious jealousy.

Between wet days and dry ones, Christmas was well on the way. For Valentina it should have been the happiest Christmas of her life. But she had sinned. The priest to whom she had made her confession had told her so, and had treated her like a sinner, chastising her in blunt terms and forbidding her to see Angelo again. She told him that they had planned to be married at Christmas and that, meanwhile, she had reason to believe she was pregnant.

"You should have thought of that before!" he whispered

through the grating of the confessional, his bad breath assailing her nostrils.

"I didn't have time to think," Valentina sobbed. "It all happened on that unlucky day. . . ."

"And how can you propose to marry this bandit? If he shows up at the church, they'll arrest him."

"They can't arrest him; he's an innocent man," said Valentina tearfully when she heard.

The priest's opposition to the marriage nearly caused her to lose all hope, but she continued to insist and in the end he gave in.

"Very well," he said in a churlish manner. "I'll marry you on Christmas Eve, that is, if they don't come after him at the foot of the altar. Meanwhile, you must say forty *Our Fathers* and three hundred *Hail Marys* before the statue of Saint Agnes, Virgin and Martyr."

Valentina's knees ached on the hard wood of the prayer stool, but all of a sudden she felt elated. She had a particular devotion for Saint Agnes and had frequently brought her bunches of flowers from the garden.

"Thank you, thank you!" she said, her voice still choked with emotion.

Actually, neither Sofia nor the Manno sisters had interrupted their preparations for the marriage, even when its celebration seemed the most unlikely.

"We're going ahead quite blindly," sighed Barbara, who was a mother to Valentina, as to the rest of the sisters, and she sat up late at night working on the contents of the marriage chest, feeling, somehow, that her efforts were not in vain. After all, her father had seen her at work and had not discouraged her. The elder Cadoni had, indeed, told Manno that Angelo would be declared innocent after the investigatory trial and that on Christmas Eve he would be free to go to the church and marry Valentina. For the time being no public announcement would be made; when he walked out of the house, the *carabinieri* would not arrest him and the declaration of his innocence would come later.

Old man Cadoni had an exaggerated idea of his own intelligence, because within the narrow limits of Norbio he knew everyone and everything that was going on. He was endowed with a prodigious memory; he was familiar with the lives and minds of his fellow townsmen. When anyone sought his professional aid, a few details of the case enabled him to reconstruct the whole story. He was a great reader and an admirer of Manzoni, but his real idols were Spanish and, above all, French writers. In his dusty, smoke-filled study, Balzac, Chateaubriand, Diderot, and Voltaire were given places of honor on his shelves. His esoteric, scholarly tastes isolated him. As the years went by, he felt an increasing scorn for everyone around him, including lawyers, judges, and politicians, all of whom he considered petty and narrow-minded. Quite understandably, he put a passionate enthusiasm into his cases and prepared them with meticulous care. He was a brilliant orator, perhaps because he had just missed being a writer and sought, in the ephemeral glory of the courtroom, a compensation for the literary fame that was denied him. Tyrannical with his womenfolk and with the servants who catered to his whims, he was wont to shut himself up for days at a time, letting his imagination play over every detail of a case and reconstructing the reality which his fearful and mistrustful clients had sought to conceal from him. Ever since he had been convinced of the validity of Angelo's alibi, he had gloated inwardly over the effect he would produce when he summed up the defense. Because of the multitude of proofs of guilt assembled by the prosecutor, his final harangue, in which they were all overturned, would be all the more startling.

After talking first to the blind Sisinnio Casti, he questioned all those who had been present on Saint Barbara's Day in the clearing among the oleanders. Upon every one of them he enjoined secrecy, for he wanted no rumors to get around the village. One day, Sofia Curreli incurred his wrath by saying to him:

"I hope Angelo will be declared innocent at the investigatory hearing. . . ."

"Are you trying to teach me my job, woman?" he shouted at her, bringing his fist down on his cluttered, dusty desk.

He had not reckoned with the fact that in Norbio nothing

can stay secret very long and, in spite of his injunctions, the story of Angelo's alibi gradually made the rounds. It came even to the ears of the examining magistrate and the sergeant of the *carabinieri*. The latter questioned the witnesses and had to admit, unwillingly, that Angelo was not guilty. Before definitely giving in, he insisted upon testing Sisinnio Casti's ability to determine how a rifle was loaded by hearing it shot off. The test took place in the valley of Castangias, not far from the village, in the presence of very few witnesses. The blind man guessed right every time, and was able to distinguish the caliber of the gun as well.

"So what was the caliber of the gun you heard that day?" the sergeant asked him.

"Twelve millimeters," said the old man, holding up his hand to signify that he was willing to swear to it.

As everyone knew, Angelo Uras' gun was one of the few sixteen-millimeters in the village. And the bullets which the coroner had found in the dead man's body were twelves. At this point, there could be no doubt of Angelo's innocence.

Old Cadoni realized, with bitter disappointment, that his carefully planned closing harangue would not ring out in the Cagliari courthouse, flooring the prosecutor with the brilliance of its argumentation, because the trial would never take place.

And so the murderer of Giuseppe Antola remained unknown.

On Christmas Eve, the sergeant ordered his four men to put on their dress uniforms, with red-and-blue feathers on the tricorn hat and the special musket slung over one shoulder. He himself went half an hour early to the church to mount guard over the doll that had been placed in the Manger.

This Infant Jesus was already blackened by the smoke of the sexton Zio Antoneddu's big, smelly cigar, which he blew from behind the scenes through special tubes that ended in the nostrils of the ox and the ass. The bluish vapor was a good facsimile of the breath of two well-fed animals on a winter night.

The bride, already dressed, had gone down to the dining room, where Manno, with his hat on his head, was sitting at the table. At Norbio, as in many countries the world over, custom willed that the bride and groom should not see each other before the wedding ceremony.

Not only had Valentina not seen Angelo, but she had also, for some time, lacked news of him. All they had told her was that there would be a surprise. This secret was kept, and it was only at the last minute, in front of the Cadoni house, where servants stood with upraised candles, that she saw Angelo dressed, not as she had expected in the local costume, but in "French" style, with a white shirt and stiff collar, a dark suit, a pearl-gray silk tie and a top hat, like that of a gentleman.

Her joy was inexplicably mingled with dismay, but when he took off his hat and opened his arms, she pushed Barbara and Sofia aside and threw herself into them, heedless of everyone waiting on the street. Her father had driven her this far in a carriage, but now they all walked to the church, treading on the already deep snow. It had been snowing since morning, and the mountains were white, almost gleaming, in the dark.

It was nearly midnight. The organ sounded from the church, now high, now low and gloomy, in accompaniment to the Christmas hymns. Sofia held Angelo's arm, Valentina her father's. Comare Verdiana had put on the local woman's costume: a white shirtwaist, a four-ply gold necklace, and a flowered bodice decked with heavy buttons of different sizes. The engineer politely offered her his arm, which she took with alacrity, and they led the procession. The bride and groom came next, then the whole Cadoni family, and finally the guests, who included even the Fulgheris, Senator Loru, and Professor Todde.

The whole village had come to celebrate. The church was full, and many voices joined those of the choir, the women's from one side, the men's from the other, since in church the sexes were separated, as in olden times.

Valentina stood near the holy-water font, at a level with the Manger, still on her father's arm. She listened distractedly to the voices, letting her eyes wander over the persons around her. Her sisters, together with Sofia and Angelo, were all kneeling together near the statue of Saint Cecilia, immersed in prayer. Valentina was lost in her thoughts and could not pray. In her mind she went back to the way her father had received her when she came back from Balanotti. She had thought he would scold and perhaps beat her; instead, he had remained silent and then broken into sobs. He had not scolded, to be sure, but neither had he received her with any affection, and she had need of a warm, human touch and of verbal comforting. That was why she had gone straightaway to Sofia and let herself be put to bed. From that morning on, she had made no decisions but simply let things take their course. Everything that had happened and was still happening seemed to her unreal. She didn't know the words of the marriage rite, but she knew that it was going to take place. She and Angelo would walk out of the church husband and wife and that night, while it continued to snow outside, they would sleep together in the big bed that Sofia had made up with lace-bordered sheets and pillowcases. Never again would she share the little room at the top of the stairs in her own house with her sister Barbara. She was saying good-by to her father's house, to her father and sisters. She tried to imagine the new life that lay ahead, but she could not yet see herself as living in the house of Sofia Curreli, although already she called her *Mammai*. She had always thought that the moment of her wedding would bring great happiness; now that it was here she was happy, yes, but not in the way that she had imagined. She glanced at the severe face of her father, met the gaze of his nut-brown eyes and, to her surprise, saw his smile, which seemed to signify some sort of secret understanding. With her mind quite vacant, she responded to his smile, then lowering her eyes, she knelt on the prayer stool that someone had slipped in front of her. The priest was holding the Host above his bald head, which gleamed in the light of the candles, and as the voices fell silent the church was filled with vibrant organ music. When Valentina raised her eyes, the priest was still holding up the Host, and she made the sign of the cross, holding the silver cross of her mother-of-pearl rosary in her fingers. The prayer stool was hard, but she was obliged to remain kneeling. In spite of her vacant mind, she remembered the words that the priest had spoken a short—or was it a long?—time before. Unconsciously she repeated them: "Almighty and merciful Lord, hear our prayer. . . ."

Now he was reading the Epistle:

"Wives, submit yourselves unto your own husbands as unto the Lord; for the husband is the head of the wife, even as Christ is the head of the church: and he is the savior of the body. . . ."

Valentina's knees were already aching. She recognized the priest's voice as she had heard it so often from behind the grating of the confessional, but it was louder now, authoritarian and almost terrifying as it pronounced these absurd words. Why should she submit herself to Angelo? She loved him and had slept with him; she would do the cooking and wash and iron his shirts, but these things did not signify submission. They would submit reciprocally, one to the other. But this the priest could not understand. He was repeating words that had always been said and always would be said when two people got married. And after that, he, the priest, would continue to look on; from his dark confessional he would pry into the life of the married couple but understand no more than did their next-door neighbors. The real truth of their married life he would never penetrate; perhaps it did not even interest him.

"Your husband," the priest was saying, "will be like a fruitful grapevine; your children will be like olive shoots around the table. . . ."

Valentina was no longer listening to his flow of words. Led by her father she approached the altar, where she found herself standing beside Angelo. She squeezed his hand and held it in hers, almost furtively, as if to warm it.

The rings lay on a silver plate. The priest blessed them and then went on talking, addressing himself, now, directly to the bride and groom, and calling them by name:

"You, Valentina Manno, and you, Angelo Uras. . . ."

He asked them if they wished to be joined in marriage, then called upon the God of Abraham, Isaac, and Jacob, asking the Almighty's blessing on their offspring to the third and fourth generation. He spoke of calamities, of death and life eternal and, without leaving them any time to take in the meaning of his words, gave them communion, spoke again, and blessed the rings. Valentina held out her hand so that Angelo could slip the ring on her finger. At this point she saw out of the corner of one eye that the *carabinieri* were saluting Senator Loru.

The pavement of the church was covered with a slimy mixture of mud and snow. The congregation hurried out through the main door, which Zio Antoneddu had thrown open. The married pair and the wedding guests followed them into the clear cold air. Many people crowded around to offer their congratulations and Christmas wishes, but Manno, who was holding an open umbrella over Valentina's head, was anxious to get her to the house, where a wedding supper was waiting, fearing that, in her silk dress and flimsy shoes, she might catch cold. Sofia threw a woolen shawl around her shoulders, and Donna Luisa Loru, taking the lantern held by the old coachman who for years had driven her and her husband, held it up in order to better see Valentina's face. She kissed her on both cheeks, and embarked on a string of compliments, but Manno abruptly said that it was time to go. Donna Luisa offered to take the bride and groom in her landau, and would not accept no for an answer. Valentina tried to hold back, but she was carried away almost by sheer force. She held on to Angelo's hand, and he too was swept into the landau, which set off at a fast clip, swaying frighteningly from side to side down the unevenly surfaced Via Roma.

In front of Manno's house, Donna Luisa discharged her passengers as summarily as she had acquired them, and they were left standing in the middle of the street in the snow until Manno, in his modest carriage, drove up behind them. He had to pull over quickly to one side in order not to be hit by the landau, whose black bulk, standing out against the white snow, disappeared between the rows of low houses that flanked the street.

Manno cursed under his breath as the landau drove away. He cursed also in order to stave off bad luck, for the rattling black landau, so like a hearse, seemed to him to be an evil omen.

"May you burn in hell, you old trollop!" he shouted, with one arm sawing the air.

Valentina and Angelo started to run, holding each other by

142

the hand, and he followed, his gloved hands impeding his efforts to re-open the umbrella. No inhabitant of Norbio would ever have dared show disrespect of Donna Luisa Loru. Only Manno, as an outsider and a man of means, could allow himself certain liberties. He could disregard everyone and everything. Not even the bandits dared attack him when he was traveling with wagons full of goods between Bosa and Cagliari.

Now, as master of the house, he received his chilled but light-hearted guests at the door. In the kitchen, his workers Gavino and Visente were carving the kids and piglets roasted in the furnace of the mill. A hand-woven cloth was spread over the table, and on it was the silver service given as a wedding present by the engineer, contrasting with the rustic plates and platters. The guests ate heartily, and the girls' faces were flushed with joy. They all shouted in order to be heard from one end of the table to the other.

"This snowstorm is a piece of luck," said Manno, in his deep, musical voice, filling the glass of Zio Raimondo Collu. The old peasant made a vague sign of disbelief.

"If it doesn't last too long," he said, shaking his head.

"The more snow the better," Manno insisted authoritatively.

Valentina asked why.

"Because snow kills the olive flies. There won't be any for several years to come. The olives will be intact and the oil of superior quality. You'll see. All to your advantage, Comare Sofia," he concluded, looking over at his daughter's mother-in-law.

"To everyone's advantage," said Sofia, half ashamed, as if her advantage might detract from that of others.

"Well," said Manno, "the ceremony in the town hall is set for tomorrow. The mayor's expecting us at eleven o'clock."

"Yes, of course," said Don Tommaso Fulgheri. "If you don't go before the mayor, this evening's ceremony has no validity."

A murmur of protest arose around the table.

"No *civil* validity, I mean," the doctor added, stroking his short black beard.

Valentina's feet were cold and she had a vague feeling of nausea. She got up and left the room, saying that she would return immediately. Barbara ran after her and found her changing her shoes.

"Are you sick?" she asked, leaning over to help.

"No," said Valentina, shaking her head. "My shoes got soaking wet, and my feet are freezing."

Barbara persuaded her to take off her stockings as well, and put on some soft woolen ones. Most of Valentina's clothes were still at home, and only in the course of the next few days would she transport them, little by little, to Angelo's house. The hem of her wedding dress was wet, also, and Barbara wanted her to change that too, but Valentina refused. If she took off her dress, she said, she'd be tempted to go straightaway to bed, there, in her room. The idea of leaving home forever saddened her, and Don Tommaso had put her out of sorts when he said that a church wedding was invalid from a civil point of view. She had felt that she was Angelo's wife ever since the night when they had slept together at Balanotti. Since they *were* already husband and wife, why did she have to go this particular night to sleep with him again? Looking into the distance, with her hands folded on her lap, she thought this over, without reaching a decision. She might as well let custom have its way, since that was what everyone expected. Before standing up, she smiled at Barbara and glanced about her childhood room. A new life had now begun. Barbara brushed against her shoulder as they went down the stairs to the ground floor, where there was a confused sound of voices.

As she came into the dining room, Valentina caught Angelo's eye and signaled to him that all was well before she sat down. The first guests to leave were the Fulgheris, followed by the engineer and Antioco Cadoni, who had managed to pursue Olivia into the kitchen, give her a furtive kiss, and whisper into her ear that next Christmas it would be their turn. Sofia, too, was getting ready to leave, and nodded at Valentina. The time had come. Valentina had another twinge of nausea. In a low voice she said:

"I'll come tomorrow."

Sofia paid no attention and Angelo did not hear. Manno, however, heard distinctly, and deep down inside he did not disapprove. Just as he had understood and forgiven the impulse that had driven Valentina to go to Angelo at Balanotti, so now he understood the pain she felt in leaving him and her sisters and all the beloved objects among which she had grown up. He was reluctant to let her go and for a moment inwardly took her part. Then he grasped her bony shoulder and drew her to him.

"You're no longer a little girl; you're a married woman."

And he looked pointedly over toward Angelo. As for Valentina, she already repented of her moment of weakness.

"Just now I was very silly," she admitted.

Her father gave her an affectionate hug. He cupped her chin in one hand, constraining her to look up at him.

"Do you still love him?" he asked. "If not, you can stay here, not just tonight but forever."

She loved Angelo, but she loved her father as well. With him she had a feeling of safety such as her young husband could not give her. Angelo was not so protective as he was in need of tenderness and protection. This—now she saw quite clearly —was the bond between them, not the submission of which the priest had spoken, but rather tenderness.

"Papa," she said, leaning her head against his shoulder, "I love Angelo, and I believe I'll be a good wife to him. But it's hard to leave home."

Manno looked down affectionately at the white part in her dark hair and her frail, narrow shoulders. He hugged her again and kissed her on the forehead.

"I must go," said Valentina; "they're waiting for me."

"Go, go!" he said, pushing her, almost roughly, away in order to hide his emotion and then lingering to watch her sisters make her ready. Although Angelo's house was only two hundred yards distant they seemed to be preparing her for a long journey. Indeed, they were the ones to build up the anxiety that goes with leaving a familiar place for one far away and thus to increase Valentina's inner turmoil.

"I'll live half here and half in Angelo's house," she told herself, "and every night I'll sleep with him and hold him in my arms. . . ." Then, brusquely, she said aloud: "That's enough, now; let me go!" She pushed them aside, swung a bag, in which

Dolores had put her nightclothes, over one shoulder, took Angelo's arm, and left the house. The deep snow made it hard to walk. Superstitiously, Valentina did not want to tread in other people's footsteps; she insisted on walking on untrodden snow, pulling Angelo along with her.

The village houses were still lighted up and so, of course, was Sofia's, where Comare Verdiana was waiting. Valentina resented this intrusion, even if she expected it. Comare Verdiana, she knew, would be always underfoot, listening to what she and Angelo had to say and guessing at what they were thinking. Suddenly she was nostalgic for the cottage at Balanotti, for the first night of love, the awakening to the patter of raindrops among the olive trees, the freedom to speak out loud. No, she must submit to no one, not even to Sofia, who was always ready to help, to make things easy, too easy. . . .

A fire was lit in the kitchen, and Comare Verdiana turned her narrow, brown face to greet them.

"The bed's already warm," she said, winking broadly at Valentina. The wink was characteristic. Comare Verdiana had a way of seeming to create a tacit understanding and then saying or doing something that destroyed any element of secrecy or intimacy.

"It's late, and you'd better go to bed," said Sofia, raising her finger as the clock of Sant'Antonio struck three o'clock in the morning. Angelo and Valentina gave her a goodnight kiss. Sofia took her daughter-in-law's head between her hands, kissed her on both cheeks, and murmured the words of an old incantation.

"Thank you, Mother," said Valentina. Then she took Angelo's arm and went with him up the wooden stairway to the upper floor.

In the bedroom, there was a penetrating odor from the orange peels which, according to custom, Comare Verdiana had burned in order to purify the air. Valentina found it slightly overpowering; she closed her eyes, and it turned into the complex odor of the house at Balanotti, made up of thyme, peppermint, dried myrtle, gunpowder, leather, and the smoke of a wood fire.

Angelo's lips brushed hers in a light, chaste kiss. It took her

146

some time to remove her jewelry: an incredible number of pins and catches, and the gold necklace that got caught in the hook of her earrings. She put all these things in a drawer and finally took off her clothes and put on a nightgown with a lace edging that came all the way down to her feet. She rapped the wall with her fist to signal to Angelo to come back from the adjoining room, and slipped into bed. The blankets were heavy and stiff, the sheets, home-woven a hundred years before, were rough, but the mattress was yielding and the bed was agreeably warm.

"Shall I leave the lamp on?" Angelo asked.

"Are you mad? Put it out!" she exclaimed, and blew it out herself.

The odor of the wick followed them under the sheets. They sought and found each other's bodies under their voluminous nightclothes and came together in an embrace. Their love-making was smooth and easy; they heard themselves sigh and groan; then, weary and satisfied, they relaxed in sleep.

When they woke up the next morning, the room was flooded with light reflected from the snow. They exchanged a hasty kiss. Angelo jumped out of bed, pulled on his trousers under his nightshirt, then peeled the nightshirt over his head and was left bare down to the waist. His skin was smooth and white, but there was thick hair on his chest. He had always shrunk from cold water, and his mother had spoiled him by bringing a pitcher of hot water to his room. But this morning he put on his boots and went to wash under the pump of the well. Valentina, when she found herself alone, went to look out the window. The first thing she saw was her father's house, covered with snow, the shutters still closed. The olive mill was buried under a white blanket, and the village houses were distinguishable only by the dark holes formed by the windows and the horizontal lines of the roof ledges. Trees were twisted and frozen like the drawings which a child traces with a lump of coal on a newly whitewashed wall. The few persons moving around in the courtyards and alleyways were like so many puppets.

In all her life Valentina had never seen such a snowfall. Indeed, snow seldom falls at Norbio or anywhere else on the Island, except in the Barbagia mountains. And so now people were moving about clumsily, bundled up in old coats, shawls, scarves and caps pulled down over their ears. Sounds and voices carried through the icy air. Valentina felt the cold bite her face. She was about to close the window when she saw her father open the door of his house. She lingered, looking at him; soon he saw her, smiled, and waved his hand. His cheeks were red, and his white teeth were visible under his thick black mustache.

"Did you sleep well?" he asked, without shouting, as if he were only a few steps away. It was strange to hear his voice, in spite of the distance, more clearly than she could see his eyes and mustache and coat buttons.

"Slept, slept," she said, echoing his words. She swayed slightly, half closing her eyes and feeling happy. Happiness, like the snow, was something new; she had heard about it, but now she experienced it.

The town hall ceremony was brief. Valentina preferred it to the religious ceremony of the previous evening. Even the articles of the law, which the mayor read aloud, seemed to her to express the mutual consent she and Angelo felt toward one another. She was so moved by the proceedings that when it was time for her to sign the register, her tears of happiness fell upon the page and she had to pause, blushing with embarrassment, to wipe her eyes. She laid down the silver pen like a schoolchild caught making a mistake, but after Angelo, too, had signed, the mayor cleaned the steel point with a cloth, wrapped the pen in tissue paper, and put it in a white leather box with silk lining which he handed to her, bowing and asking her to accept "this small token" from the administration. Then the mayor vigorously shook Angelo's hand and wished him well.

When the newly married pair came out of the town hall, women were waiting to throw wheat and salt over them, according to the custom of Parte d'Ispi. Snow had begun to fall so heavily that only the gray profile of the bell tower was visible. Manno hurried to the waiting carriage and quickly raised the hood, which whistled softly as it opened above the broad seat. Only then did Valentina realize that this was her father's wedding present; she hugged him and planted a kiss on his mustache.

A long time ago, he had said that he would give her a horse for her marriage, but they had never spoken of it since; now here was a horse and a cabriolet as well. Suddenly, she felt herself plucked off the ground as when she was a child and deposited on the soft seat. Her eyes searched for Angelo and just managed to glimpse his astonished face under the cap with the ridiculous ear-flaps that he was wearing. Her father handed her the reins and slapped the rump of the horse, which responded smartly, as if aware of being on display. Angelo jumped up beside his wife, but left her the reins. The horse's hoofs kicked up the snow and the wheels slid over it, creaking agreeably. Valentina drove the cabriolet into a narrow street on the left. The horse nearly slipped and fell, but Valentina steadied it with the hands of a good driver.

They were on the Via delle Tre Marie. The paving stones were icy and the wheels threatened to skid. Valentina handed the reins over to Angelo and adjusted the veil on her head. They drove, under admiring eyes, across the Piazza Frontera. For a moment, Valentina felt uneasy. She sensed envy as well as admiration in those stares and remembered the story of the little child that took sick because she was too beautiful, a tale she had heard many times among the superstitious people of Norbio.

"A penny for your thoughts," said Angelo.

"I was thinking that I don't know my horse's name!"

"First of all, it's a mare . . . the name's ugly but you can't change it. You must never change a horse's name, or a dog's either, or else the animal will die. She's called Zelinda and some day, please God, she'll give you a little colt."

"That way I'll have two horses," said Valentina gleefully, giving him a playful kick in the shins.

Zelinda had broken into a trot, and the cabriolet slid smoothly over the snow, making a slight rustling sound.

"How long will you wear that suit?" Valentina asked, making a face.

"I can't wait to change back into my wool jacket. But sometimes I shall dress like a gentleman, and you'll wear your silk gown. The gentry will invite us to their homes. . . ."

They drove down the steep, winding street that led to the

Manno house. Coffee and cakes were waiting on the dining-room table. Margherita Fulgheri, who had not come to the preceding night's supper, was present. In her proud, reserved manner, she apologized for her absence and presented her gift of a dozen extra-fine linen napkins. Her silk dress, passed down from Donna Fernanda, was not unlike Valentina's wedding gown, and at the neck she wore a diamond pin. At twenty years of age, she was slightly taller than Valentina, but had none of the latter's good looks. She was aware of being narrow-hipped and shallow-breasted; what she did not know was that her thin, bony body had a certain charm and her eyes a tender expression that counteracted her stiff manners and rigid posture.

The new life of a married couple is commonly supposed to date from a single moment, from a certain day, but in reality this is not so. Their new life is built up hour by hour, minute by minute; the apparently most insignificant things have a meaning that is revealed only with the passage of time.

It was quite marvelous, for both of them, to grow accustomed to sleeping in the same bed and, for Angelo, to wake up in the morning while Valentina was still asleep. He lay there, motionless, looking at his wife's childlike profile outlined against the rough, white wall—her half-open lips, gently rounded forehead, and the long, curling eyelashes which suddenly quivered just before she woke up. She opened her eyes, shot him a lazy look, stretched, and held out her open hands, rolling over toward him in order to exchange the first kiss of the day. He brushed her breasts with his fingers, and she slipped agilely away, laughing. Sometimes she told what she had dreamed and wanted to know whether it was "good" or "bad." She and her sisters were accustomed to interpreting dreams in accord with the superstitions of Norbio. In these interpretations, happenings were less important than things; water meant tears; clouds, sorrow; fire, gaiety. Angelo gave little importance to such matters, but Valentina, if she had a "bad" dream, could not free herself from a feeling of discomfort.

She was the one, now, to prepare Angelo's lunch when he rode to Balanotti or to supervise the work in the forest. She went out of the house, opened and shut the gate, and watched him ride down the main street. She would have liked to go with him, but she had to stay home and lend a hand to her mother-in-law, although Sofia tried to do everything on her own and forbade her to undertake any heavy task, just as she had forbidden her to ride a horse until after the baby was born. At first, the coming of a baby was most incredible to Valentina. She had only occasional attacks of nausea, but Verdiana told her that her breasts were enlarged. Secretly she touched them, and they seemed to her the same as ever. She was aware of nothing new except for the nausea, to which she came to pay little attention. The only real change lay in the courtesy and consideration with which people treated her; perhaps these were exaggerated, but they gave her pleasure. "They must see *something*," she said to herself, and she looked into the mirror, without seeing what everybody else obviously saw. Perhaps it was in her face or eyes. It couldn't be in her body, because she had not had to let out her clothes.

Her married life had grown quite naturally out of her life as a young girl; essentially, nothing had changed. Only she knew now that she was going to have a child, that the name would be Salvatore if it was a boy and Maria Christina if it was a girl. The question of the name had been definitely settled.

At times she caught herself thinking of death, not her own death, but that of others—Sofia, her father, Angelo—and she was deeply distressed, as if by a mysterious presentiment. Death was something she had learned about from the catechism, a passage from life temporal to life eternal. This latter she could not imagine, and so what struck her the most about death was its most obvious feature, the concrete image of absence. She had seen very few dead bodies: at Bosa, her mother's and that of a young man who had drowned in the river; at Norbio, only those of persons unknown and unrelated.

She had a horror of corpses, yet at the same time she was fascinated. Whenever anyone died in the Funtanedda or Sant'Antonio sections, she went to "pay her respects." Actually, she went because she wanted to see the corpse, as if the sight could somehow help her penetrate the mystery of death. She would take her mother-of-pearl rosary, and would say a few *requiems* and *de profundis* like the other women did. Before going away, she would force herself to touch the dead person's forehead and folded hands. Something inside her compelled her to experience the immobility, the stony cold of the body. Never did this enable her to penetrate the mystery; every time made it more dark and discomforting.

Curiously then, it was she who, one late January morning, found old Zio Raimondo dead in the cottage at Balanotti. When she pushed open the half-closed door, she had seen immediately what had happened. The fire was still smoldering, and he lay in front of it on a mat, clutching his long-stemmed pipe in his hand. He had died in his sleep, like his forebears, and as he himself had predicted. None the less Valentina went inside the room, knelt over his body, and made the sign of the cross. A moment or so later, Angelo arrived. There was no need for words between them.

It was one of those dry, cold winter days, good for the land, that the old man so much enjoyed. Carignosa was howling mournfully in the empty stable, and Saverio Spano, the oldest farm laborer, went to fetch her and dragged her to the cabriolet.

Adelaide, Zio Raimondo's only daughter, who lived with him, heard the news at the fountain, just when she was raising a pitcher of water to the top of her head. She gave a loud cry, loosening her grip on the heavy jar. The pitcher fell and shattered at her feet. The old man had lived in perfect health and with all his teeth to an extreme old age, and yet every day Adelaide had expected him to die, especially when he spent the night alone at Balanotti. He himself had often spoken of his death.

Valentina and Angelo went to see him laid out on his iron bedstead in his house in the Castangias section of the town. Sofia went, too, and she and Valentina knelt on the brick floor to pray. Angelo left word at the town hall not to send a pauper's coffin, and ordered Giovannino Caddia, the carpenter, to make one of stout oak. He couldn't believe that the old man was gone. From him he had learned how to sharpen a scythe, how to hold a grafting knife, in what month and on what day to sow wheat; he had learned to recognize a wind that foretold rain, to love animals, and to size up men.

Now the joy was gone out of the journey to Balanotti. Every time he went, he had an almost agonizing feeling of emptiness, as if along with Zio Raimondo he had lost the security inherent in the old man's mumbling and grumbling, in his words aptly spoken or unspoken, in the gestures with which he gave things their meaning and proportion. Wandering among the olive trees, Angelo himself felt suddenly older. His childhood was far away, and he had lived his adolescence in Zio Raimondo's shadow. The old man was not so much a memory as a part of his very being.

After the cold sunny spell in January, there came a period of rain, and finally the slow, almost stealthy, push of spring. "There'll be a rich flowering of almond blossoms," Zio Raimondo had said a few days before his death, and here, too, his prophetic soul had seen clearly. All the almond trees of Balanotti flowered on the same morning. The day before, their twisted gray trunks had seemed frozen and dead, and only an expert eye could have detected the tiny rose-tipped buds. At this time, almond trees were still an exotic importation. Professor Todde, an amateur farmer as well as a highly esteemed economist, had brought them to Norbio. He had little land, but he cared for every bit of it with his own hands whenever he had time left from his studies and travels. In his flower garden he grew Dutch tulips and roses from the Riviera and from Luxembourg; in his fields were orange trees from Sicily and almond trees from the Far East. He had been the one to teach the peasants of Norbio the technique of grafting. Although they had not been friends, Don Francesco Fulgheri had admired his enterprising spirit and asked his advice when he planted the almond grove at Balanotti and the orange grove at Lugheria. Now Professor Todde's al-

mond trees burst into bloom on the same day as those at Balanotti.

Every now and then, Valentina went with Angelo in the
cabriolet to Balanotti. Zelinda, although she was heavier than
before, had the same fast trot, but she was in a sweat by the
time she reached her destination. Under Valentina's attentive
eyes, Saverio rubbed her with a handful of hay or a piece of
burlap.

Valentina enjoyed housekeeping. On the days when she
didn't drive out with Angelo, she helped Sofia with her domestic
tasks and learned things that no one had ever been able to teach
her before. Her mother had died when she was very young, and
the mother's sister, Filomena, who took over her brother-in-law's
house for a while, had married three years later. And so the
Manno girls had been brought up largely by servants; whatever
they knew they had learned on their own, inspired by natural
inclination or ambition. Women neighbors who took an interest
in them had taught them embroidery and lace-making.

Sometimes Valentina strolled in her father's garden, waiting
for him to come home or for Angelo to call for her. Her sisters
were the ones to make the baby's clothes, just as they had put
together her trousseau. On account of her pregnancy, everyone
spoiled her and wanted to satisfy her wishes. But Valentina had
none of the traditional pregnant woman's whims, and this was
considered reassuring. Her only peculiarity was an almost mani-
acal aversion to anything old.

In every house there are old, worn, even broken objects of
no value to which their owners have become attached. Not so
with Valentina; she could not bear a cracked plate or a chipped
bowl; she had to get rid of it, not by just putting it away out
of sight but by throwing it out of the house immediately. This
peculiarity was tolerated and, indeed, seconded by Manno and
his family. No one reproached her for hurling a dish out of the
window, and if her sisters found themselves with a piece of
glassware or china damaged even slightly, they winked and
laughed and let it drop and break. The whole thing was a sort
of game.

Getting rid of old things was less simple in Sofia's household;

she cared for her belongings and would have been very unhappy to see them flying through the window and landing on the heap of shards piled up at the foot of the prickly-pear hedge. Valentina understood, and threw nothing away. At Balanotti, on the other hand, she spared nothing. And every time she went there with Angelo, she carried the purchases she had made the preceding Sunday on the square or in the shops of the Sant'Antonio section of the town. At Balanotti, she could do what she pleased; this was her real home. She bought a new bucket for the well and an earthenware bowl to replace the majolica one which she had always seen on the wooden trestle beside the holm oak of Don Francesco.

After Antola's death, the Mining Consortium decided to handle directly the acquisition of the fuel necessary to run the foundry. Soon the supply accumulated from the forest of Mazzanni would be exhausted and other woods would have to be cut down. The engineer spoke to Angelo about it. He knew that the young man would be distressed, but he had to carry out his job. The important thing was that the forests should not be ruthlessly destroyed, and Angelo had to admit that if the Consortium handled the logging directly there was a better chance of conservation. As he listened to the engineer set forth his problem, he found no immediate solution but did not lose hope of reconciling the needs of the foundry with the saving of the forests.

The old project of using pit coal had long been under consideration by the Consortium's board of directors and, without being rejected, it was postponed from year to year. The Piedmontese government was unconcerned about the conservation of the forests of Sardinia. Despite unification, the Island was still thought of as a colony to be exploited, and its people were relegated to the level of the brigands of Calabria.

One evening toward the middle of February, Manno proposed to Angelo that they go hunting in the region of Aletzi, northwest of Norbio, behind Mount Volpe, where the forests were still intact. The invitation came from Luca Cubeddu, who owned an old-fashioned olive mill and conducted wild boar hunts. He was considered an unscrupulous, violent fellow, and was suspected of having organized the famous sheep-snatching expeditions that had involved bloody actions in the Sulcis region. Perhaps he was innocent, but his appearance and ways were against him. Only five feet tall but broad-shouldered, he was endowed with herculean strength and surprising agility. Since boyhood, he had won the cock-shooting contests that took place the first Sunday of August at Norbio near the church of San Sisinnio, patron saint of witches. A cock was hung by its feet from the branch of an olive tree, and the contestants shot a single bullet from a distance of a hundred and fifty paces. The men and boys of Norbio were famous sharpshooters and hitting the cock was no great feat. But Luca Cubeddu gave it an extra fillip. When the signal was given, he leaped onto a horse's back under the eyes of the assembled crowd, loaded his long gun, settled himself on the saddle, stroked the thick black beard that came down to his belt, took aim and, with a single shot, hit the cock's head and severed it from the body. The crowd shouted its enthusiasm, and Luca jumped down from his horse and went to have a drink with his friends. Perhaps some other one of the contestants could have shot off the cock's head from the same distance, but no one had the nerve to come forward and dispute Luca's claim to the championship.

"It's not so very hard," he used to say. "At this season, the coxcomb is extra red."

Besides being the permanent cock-shooting champion, Luca was "prior" of the Confraternity of All Souls, which had as its rival the Confraternity of Our Lady. On solemn holidays, the two Confraternities alternately had the honor of carrying the saints' statues in procession. This alternation had, over the years, been regulated, but originally it was a cause of violent and sometimes bloody battles. At religious ceremonies the Brothers of All Souls wore red hoods and the Brothers of Our Lady white ones, both with holes for the eyes. And the members of both groups carried a *leppa*, the ten-inch-long Sardinian knife similar to the *machete* used in Latin American countries to cut sugar cane. The Brothers—whichever group they belonged to—were patented thieves and all of them had built up considerable holdings of livestock and land. Legally, they were registered as "mutual aid societies," but everyone knew that they were criminal gangs and that the *carabinieri* and the *barracelli* (a very old, popular militia) were unable to repress them. Their members were bullies and so were their leaders—Luca Cubeddu of the one gang, and Battista Corrias of the other.

Angelo disliked the idea of hunting in such company, and he tried to dissuade his father-in-law from going. But Manno held fast, saying Norbio was a town of witches and gossipy women, where every trifle was blown up out of all proportion. Luca Cubeddu, the bearded sharpshooter, was a fine fellow and a likeable one, Manno insisted. He was going to accept the invitation, and as for Angelo, he was free to stay home if he so desired. Valentina, when she was unable to make her father change his mind, worried about his going alone and begged Angelo to go with him.

On the appointed day, the hunters met at the Piazza Cadoni in front of the Granary. To his surprise, Angelo saw Ferraris among them, carrying a very special French gun, and with a tuft of magpie feathers stuck into his hat. There were some twenty people in all, peasants, shepherds, and minor landowners with their farm laborers who were to act as beaters. Luca Cubeddu was the leader, there could be no doubt of that; he was riding a big three-year-old sorrel horse and, after a quick look around to make sure that everyone was there, he gave the order of departure. All the others fell into single file behind him. They rode up the narrow, pebbled Via dell'Oratorio, to the sound of echoing hoofbeats and the clank of guns, spurs, and the banging of pots and pans by the beaters.

Angelo noticed that all the Brothers of the Confraternity of All Souls were present, probably, he reflected, the very men who had taken part a few weeks before in one of the usual bloody sheep-snatchings. Boar hunts served to keep the gang members in good form and to strengthen their loyalty and discipline. The little procession passed at a fast trot in front of the cross set up by the Seddanus Mission and took the road bordering the lower slopes of Mount Volpe, just below the "Sa Spendula" waterfall that splashes down amid thickets of oleanders, blackberry bushes, and tall poppies. The roar of the waterfall could be heard some distance away, and its spray struck the leaves of the roadside trees and the faces of the hunters. The road narrowed, winding under an arch formed by ancient oaks and ilexes.

"Look around you," Angelo said to the engineer, who was riding beside him. "This is a place the Tuscans never reached. Here the trees are just as they were in the time of Hostus. . . ."

"And who was Hostus?"

"A Sardinian who fought against the Romans. A contemporary of Hannibal, I believe."

"Very good," the engineer mumbled, lighting a cigar and offering one to Angelo, who declined it.

Ferraris had become accustomed to the strong, black Sardinian cigars, which he picked out, one by one, at the tobacconist's. But they were too heavy for Angelo, who smoked only cigarettes, and these sparingly, without inhaling. That day the two men, the older and the younger, were particularly happy. They were happy to be together, to ride through the fragant woods to a part of the country that neither of them knew, rich in trees, water, and game. The Aletzi valley takes its name from a rushing stream, and now, all of a sudden, they came to its rocky banks.

Between the riverbed and the rocky side of the mountain, a narrow road wound its way up the valley. The stream was almost completely hidden by oleander and blackberry bushes and wild pear and olive trees. The rock crevices were filled with vegetation, and the whole valley was traversed by echoes, as if it were a huge shell. After proceeding for some time along the river, the riders arrived at an open, almost flat area where two valleys came together. In the center there rose a conelike hill, covered by oak, holm oak, and mastic trees. Upon closer inspection this hill was seen to join the chain of mountains behind, which opened up into a wide amphitheater. They dismounted, tied their horses, and broke up into groups to eat an early lunch. The engineer spread out a map that he said covered an area of some five hundred acres belonging to the township of Norbio.

"Here there might be a good reserve of wood, even if the

Leni foundry is some distance away and the roads are in bad condition."

Angelo was so afflicted by these words that all his good humor left him. He could not even speak. How could anyone turn from the beauties of the surrounding landscape, with its evocation of past geological eras, and focus his thoughts on fuel for the foundry? The engineer detected his uneasiness and called him over. Angelo had learned to read a map when he had worked at the reconstruction of the narrow-gauge railway, and he recognized at first glance the region of Aletzi, with the two streams flowing through their respective valleys and, between them, as if set down by a god's hand, the conical hill, Mount Mei. But on the yellowish map there were signs that he did not understand.

"That's a quarry," explained the engineer, pointing with his finger, "there's a lime kiln, and there an abandoned mine. And we're right here."

"Then we're close to the mine gallery. Why don't we give it a look?"

They went around a row of willows and elder bushes, climbed over a wall, crossed the stream, walking on the dark rocks that stuck up out of the water, and went through an area covered by ferns into a grove of eucalyptus trees. There they discovered the entrance of the mine almost completely covered by a curtain of ivy.

Ferraris made his way in, picked up some twigs, and made them into a bundle which he lit with a sulphur match and held up to illuminate the interior of the cave. In the light of the flickering flame, the walls seemed to be clothed with precious stones. Angelo stretched out his hand to touch them and felt the cold water dripping from the rock. The twigs crackled as the light of this improvised torch shattered the surrounding darkness. The dripping water formed a rivulet which ran toward the entrance. The two men picked up a couple of rough stones which shone like the walls.

"Lead with streaks of silver?" Angelo asked, as if he did not welcome an affirmative answer. The idea of mines was associated in his mind with foundries and the fuel they required, which entailed the destruction of the forests.

The engineer read his thoughts and burst out laughing.

"Yes, lead, with streaks of silver. But the amount of silver is so small that the mine, as you see, was abandoned."

"How long ago?" Angelo asked.

"At least two hundred years. You can tell from the method of excavation."

The bundle of twigs was almost completely consumed, and the engineer, followed by Angelo, made his way back to the entrance.

"Too bad nothing came of the mine," said Ferraris. "It's no use now except for cooling our wine."

The other hunters were already starting to ride on, and Ferraris and Angelo obeyed Luca's orders to fall in at the end of the line. The hunt was to take place on Mount Mei. Already the beaters and dogs were at the top of the hill and the hunters were to take up their stations at intervals on the sloping sides. At a prearranged signal, the dogs were let loose. The beaters followed them, blowing horns and drumming noisily on the tin pots and pans.

Angelo was sitting under an ilex, with his gun leaning against his knee, watching three paths on which, preceded by the barking of the dogs, the boar might at any moment appear. He heard several guns go off and the dogs' barking rise and fall, then, suddenly the sound of crackling bushes and rolling stones just behind him. Wheeling around, he raised his gun to his shoulder. There was a full-grown male boar, weighing at least a hundred and fifty pounds, surrounded by a pack of dogs, Carignosa among them.

Carignosa was a bird dog, but she had the speed and the courage to tackle a big animal as well. The boar, its legs bloodied, was coming directly toward Angelo. He did not shoot immediately for fear of hitting one of the dogs. The boar, breathing heavily, paused, shook off the dogs, then lowered its head and charged its pursuers. Already two dogs lay with their bellies ripped open a few steps away. Angelo took aim. At just this moment, Carignosa circled the boar and threw herself forward, biting at its left ear. With lightning speed, the boar twisted about, caught her on its tusks, and tossed her onto the grass. Even as he pulled the trigger, Angelo glimpsed Carignosa with her bloody guts pouring out of her belly. The boar's knees gave way, its snout hit the ground, and the other dogs closed in. Angelo did not reload his gun but yanked his long knife out of the sheath, grasped the boar's sinking head in his left hand, and, with the right plunged the knife into its chest all the way to the heart. The animal, though wounded, was still murderously powerful, and Angelo held on to it with the strength of desperation. The knife blade quivered as it struck the pounding heart; then, finally, the boar gave up the struggle and fell lifeless to the ground.

At once Angelo turned to Carignosa. With her hind legs paralyzed and her guts trailing in the dust, she was trying to drag herself toward him. There was death in her eyes, as once there had been shame, humiliation, and joy. He stroked her head, and she licked his hand, her tail feebly wagging. Without even knowing it, Angelo wept.

"By only a second," he was thinking. "If only I had shot a second before!" He examined the wound; dogs with ripped bellies had sometimes been saved. The gut could be replaced, the wound washed with a vinegar solution and sown up. But here in the woods he could do none of these things.

Heedless of the blood that spattered over his jacket and trousers, he lifted the dog, laid her on a bed of dry ferns, gave her water from his canteen in a tin dipper and, holding her head between his hands, watched her die. The beaters arrived, finished off the other wounded dogs, and hoisted the boar onto their shoulders. They complimented Angelo on his prowess, but he heard them distractedly. He was thinking of Carignosa, and his thoughts were tinged with anguish and shame.

There was a banquet that night at Luca's mill, but Manno and Angelo excused themselves and went home. They were disgusted, both of them, with the hunters' rowdiness and vulgarity. As the hours went by, Angelo felt more and more guilty. When Valentina tried to console him, suggesting that they'd get another dog, he turned on her furiously, calling her stupid and incapable of understanding. Deeply hurt, she left the room and went to walk in her father's garden in the dark. She didn't want to see anyone, least of all her sisters.

She went into Zelinda's stable and gave her a handful of sugar lumps, talking aloud. What's love, she asked herself, if when one partner is suffering the other can't find the words with which to console him? Love, she decided, is dumb; that is why we can love even speechless animals. She and Angelo had never spoken very much, either. They had fallen in love and made love for the most part in silence.

Coming out of the stable, she saw him leaning against a corner of the woodshed. Without saying a word, she held out her arms. He told her again how clumsy he had been. If only he had pressed the trigger a second before! . . . She knew what had held him back, but she did not put her understanding into words. They embraced each other and returned to the house, hand in hand. The table was set, and Barbara was about to serve the fennel-and-cheese soup she had learned how to make from Sofia.

Days and months went by. Valentina felt the passage of time flow through her body. She knew that, God willing, the baby would be born in September. Everything was going well; the attacks of nausea had stopped, and, as she grew larger, a sleepy well-being pervaded her body.

When she got up one April morning, she felt the baby move for the first time. It kicked lustily. She reacted not, as she had expected, with tenderness but with resentment. It must be a boy. She loved Angelo, of course, but one man in the house was enough. Men are selfish, and expect to be waited on. She wanted a girl, but her hopes were dampened by the vigor of the kicking. She spoke to Sofia, who, without really knowing why, said yes, it must be a boy. So there would be no Maria Christina, only Salvatore. And yet Valentina had dreamed several times of having a girl. She visualized her quite clearly, imagining the future years with a daughter growing up at her side.

The garden was in flower, the countryside green, the wheat sprouting. But Valentina was obsessed by a strange fear. It went back to the faraway days of her childhood at Bosa, after her mother had died, her fear of night and darkness, and it was connected with death, with her childish idea of nothingness. She never spoke with anyone of this fear, but her sisters—from Barbara to Dolores—knew her secret and didn't laugh at it. Her only defense was prayer. Before her pregnancy, she would hastily, sleepily recite her evening prayers. Now she was so fearful that she prayed at length, saying *requiems* for every person she had seen dead or whose death had been reported to her. The idea of the dead was saddening; she had a more vivid mental picture of eternal darkness than of the light of divine mercy. Light and mercy were abstractions, but darkness, silence, and the unknown were absolute realities, all of them part of death. Once, in the confessional, she voiced her fears to Don Masala. He had become embarrassed and had quickly changed the subject. Valentina concluded that the old priest didn't know what she was talking about. She resolved not to bother him again with embarrassing questions. As a result, she went less frequently to confession.

Before spring was over, in the month of May, Angelo and Valentina took Sofia with them to Balanotti. The olive trees were in bloom and the crop promised to be a good one, barring an unexpected hailstorm or cold wind, or an unusually hot *sirocco* that would make the olives shrivel and fall to the ground.

"If all goes well, this will be a good year," said Sofia. "According to your father, Valentina, there'll be no worms or flies."

As they entered the cottage, Sofia complimented her daughter-in-law on its neatness.

"That's to the credit of Giulia Nonnis," said Valentina, winking at her husband; "she's the one who keeps everything in order."

Sofia stood in the doorway, breathing in the crisp, fragrant air.

"Don't make a fool of yourself with Giulia," she said to her son as he passed by.

"Come, come, Mother!" he tossed over his shoulder.

"No nonsense, my boy!" she insisted. "At *cabidanni*, you'll be a father."

In the Parte d'Ispi region, words, like everything else, have a long life. *Cabidanni* comes straight from the Latin, but it means September. To the ancient inhabitants of Sardinia who spoke the language of their mainland rulers, September was the *caput anni*, or beginning of the year, and, as such, propitious to new beginnings. In the same way, it should be propitious to the birth of a child. All three of them were aware of the fact, and Sofia said, quite naturally:

"With God's help!"

With God's help, spring went by and summer made a brusque arrival. In retrospect, the spring seemed very short, but in reality it was like any other spring, with good days and bad, and occasional storms.

Summer, however, seemed longer than usual. It was, in fact, extremely hot, and there were many forest fires. One mid-August night, a sinister glow reddened the sky behind the summit of Mount Homo. The remains of the Escolca forest were in flames. A boy on horseback arrived with the news that the Tuscan woodcutters were encircled by fire. He knocked at several doors, but no one wanted to hear him. Finally he called Zio Antoneddu, the sexton, and forced him to open the bell tower. Then he swung himself on the rope of the big bell, and gave the alarm. A boy's words may not convince sleeping people to get up in the middle of the night, but a pealing bell will arouse them. And so it was that night. Many of the village men mounted their horses and, with picks and shovels over their shoulders, galloped through the darkness in the direction of the fire. In spite of the resentment they felt toward the Tuscans, there was no question of not going to the rescue. Angelo kissed Valentina, saddled Zurito, and galloped off with the others. As soon as they had ridden around Mount Homo, they found themselves in the red glow of the fire.

An entire mountain was ablaze, and the roar of the flames absorbed all other sounds, producing an effect like a terrifying silence so that the men could not hear one another even if they shouted. Leaves and branches crackled like exploding grenades.

The overwhelming noise had a visual counterpart when whole trees on the mountainside were suddenly twisted, then enveloped in a burst of fire, and finally fell, reduced to a mass of sparks, to the ground. The men, armed with picks, shovels, and axes, or empty-handed and riding bareback, were lined up along the river. Finally a voice overcame the roar and gave orders; Angelo thought he recognized it as belonging to Renato Granieri. By the time the horses had started to ford the river, the water was crimson from the reflection of the flames; as they climbed the opposite bank, their shins and the faces of their riders seemed to be tinged with blood.

A certain number of trees had to be cut down in order to create a break in the growth and prevent the fire from spreading farther. After studying the direction of the wind, the leader indicated which trees these were to be, and the men set to work, as if their own lives depended upon it. The cut trees were stripped of foliage and dragged some distance away, and shovelsful of dirt were heaped on any stray flames. When the Tuscans who had been cut off were rescued, they became the hardest-working of all, distinguishable by their mode of dress, their aggressive, hand-to-hand attack on the fire and, above all, by their salty language. After hours of apparently vain struggle, the wind fell, and the fire diminished. But where one of the the most ancient forests of Parte d'Ispi had once stood, now there was only a vast brazier.

Men and horses cooled off by plunging into the river, then, when the tools had been redistributed, they started back to Norbio. They had come in a group, galloping through the darkness, but they returned wearily, each one on his own, in a long line which wove its way through the dim light of dawn.

There were other fires throughout the summer, caused by spontaneous combustion or by shepherds who wanted to enrich their pasture land with a good scorching. Not only in the Parte d'Ispi region but all over the Island, forests, moors, and fields of grain ready to be harvested and representing the work of a whole year, went up in flames. The air temperature, already affected by the warmth of the earth, vibrated with waves of heat. It was almost unbreathable. And as a final burden, there was an outbreak of malaria that was always more prevalent in summer. To linger late in the fields after a hard day's work was enough to make a healthy man take sick and to make a man previously stricken (as most people had been) grow sicker and perhaps even die.

One evening when Angelo went to buy cigarettes from the tobacconist on the Piazza Frontera, he found Ferraris standing at the counter selecting cigars from a wooden box. He didn't cut his cigars in half as did the parsimonious peasants, but trimmed the tip and smoked them whole, puffing deliberately and taking care not to shake off the white ash, which he said testified to the quality of the tobacco. Giglio, the tobacconist, had left him there alone. Angelo could hear the 'tobacconist's shrill voice alternate with the louder, more sonorous tones of his wife from the rear of the shop. At a certain point, the wife came to the door and peered in. She was a tall girl whose full breasts were barely contained within her blue velvet bodice fastened by tiny pearl buttons. Around her white neck she wore a gold chain with a coral horn hanging from it. When she raised her arm in greeting, the ornament fell between her breasts.

"Giglio will be here right away," she said to Angelo, who, ever since he had stayed in the Cadoni house, had smoked the same smuggled cigarettes as Antioco—cigarettes that Giglio handled at a modest rake-off. Now Giglio emerged from the rear and placed upon the counter a parcel wrapped in paper like that used for packaging sugar.

"Here you are," he said in his falsetto voice. "That's ten liras, plus what you owe me from last time."

Angelo ran over the addition in his mind, put the six packs of cigarettes in his pocket, and paid in silver and copper coins. Then he opened up a pack and offered a cigarette to the engineer.

"You'd do better to smoke cigars," Ferraris told him, turning it down. "They cost less and they're not so unhealthy." He took Angelo by the arm, and they left the shop together. "I want to talk to you," he said. "Come have supper with me at Giovanni's.

This evening he's serving stewed rabbit and polenta. We can sit in the private dining room, where no one will disturb us."

"Why don't you come to our house, instead? We're having the same thing—stewed rabbit and polenta—and my father-in-law's wine is better than Giovanni's!"

"I wouldn't want to disturb your women by being a last-minute guest."

"Don't worry; they'll be delighted."

"Good! But perhaps you have guessed what I want to tell you."

"Something to do with fuel?"

"Yes, that's it, I'm sorry to say, there's a new crisis. If it weren't for that damned fire, we could have gone on a bit longer. Now we'll have to sacrifice another forest."

"Which one?" Angelo asked between clenched teeth.

"The most beautiful of them all. . . ."

"Aletzi?"

"Yes, Aletzi."

Angelo came close to swearing like a Tuscan, but all he said was: "Damnation!"

"I'm sorry, too, believe me, but we can't do without it."

"You could install coal-burning furnaces near the mines and save money. There'd be no transportation expenses."

"Oh, I told them that, you can be sure," said the engineer, throwing away the butt of his cigar. "But they wouldn't give in. For the time being we have to accept it. A contract is to be given for cutting down the trees, and bids will be called for ten days from now."

"These mines have always been the curse of Sardinia. Foreigners are attracted by the hope of making quick money, and our people have no benefit from them. If it weren't for the mines, we'd still have our forests."

"But if the trees were cut with more foresight and intelligence. . . ."

"It's all the same," said Angelo, his voice choked with emotion.

In the darkness, Ferraris could feel Angelo's fierce eyes on him and could imagine the sense of outrage accompanying the quivering voice. He felt guilty, as if he had not done all he might and should have.

Everyone enjoyed the stewed rabbit, which Valentina had cooked according to a family recipe. Supper was at Manno's house, in a festive atmosphere. It wound up with a dessert, Malvasia wine, and some of Barbara's strong coffee. Afterward, the three men sat at the card table near the fireplace, and the conversation soon turned to the forests and the foundry. Manno, like Angelo, deplored the government's failure to stop the destruction, and the engineer had to sympathize with him.

"Citizens must learn how to defend their rights," he concluded, taking the glass of brandy that Manno had meticulously poured for him.

"And in our place, what would you do?" Manno asked him.

"I was talking about that to Angelo, a short time ago. . . ."

"Well, give us your opinion and advice," said Angelo, "since the coal-burning furnaces you proposed seem fated to remain a dream."

"I'll give you my opinion and advice if you'll smoke one of my cigars," the engineer replied with a kindly laugh.

Angelo took the cigar, but the first puff made him cough.

"Easy there," said Ferraris. "New things have to be tried out with care."

Angelo inhaled more slowly. Unintentionally, he blew a ring, which remained suspended, like a halo, in mid-air, then he smoked the rest of the cigar as if he were an old hand, until a cap of white ash piled up at the tip.

"You're lucky with your first cigar," Ferraris continued. But Angelo would not be distracted from his question. Shaking off the ash, he insisted:

"We're waiting for your reply."

Manno had deftly shuffled the playing cards and now he dealt the third round. Ferraris picked up his cards, opened them into a fan, and made a face. This evening he was having a streak of bad luck.

"It's always hard," he said, "to find an honest contractor. They're all like Antola, set on rushing the job and making a lot of money. If we interfere with protests or fines, the only result is to slow down the work. Then the government's angry, because it wants the foundry to work full blast. . . . There's only one chance of improvement, and that's for a local man to win the contract for Aletzi and to do the logging without the greed and haste of the Tuscans."

The last hand was finished and the engineer had lost again. Manno, who had been the winner, did not try to detain him when he got up to leave. Ferraris put on his heavy coat with the fox collar, thanked his host, and asked Angelo to walk down the street with him. The outside air was chilled by the north wind.

"As I was just saying," Ferraris repeated as they went down the Via Roma, "the best thing would be for a local man to get the contract."

"A local man? Who could it be?"

"You, for instance!"

"Me? You must be joking."

"I'm not joking, I'm proposing a piece of serious business."

"But I'd have to put up the money. And where can I find that?"

"The Aletzi contract is bound to yield a profit, even to an honest man."

"I agree. But it takes money to make the bid, and I haven't got it."

"That's what banks are for," said Ferraris, turning his back to the wind. "I'm sure any bank would make you a loan, with your land as collateral. The Mining Consortium would put up part of it and a bank the rest. And when the job is done, you'll have made a profit. The contractor always has."

"But there's a risk involved. A single lighted match, and the forest can go up in smoke. I'd lose everything. . . ."

"I don't say there's no risk. Everything's risky. Every time you ride your horse, you risk breaking your neck. But with the experience you've acquired over the last few years, you ought to be able to handle the job."

"I'll have to think about it."

"Think about it, of course. And talk it over with your wife and your father-in-law. But, after you've heard what they have to say, you'll have to make up your own mind."

When they said goodnight the engineer put his arm affection-ately around the younger man's shoulder.

The engineer's words had fired Angelo's imagination. Always he had identified himself with the Island and its land, with Norbio and the outlying forests. Now the future of Aletzi was called into question. His imagination played over the age-old trees, the rushing streams, the mountains that closed the valley. Could he make this little world his own? Actually his mind was made up. He would ask for a loan and go to the auction where the contract would be awarded. Intuitively, he knew that to succeed in any enterprise one must exercise good timing, patience, and a cool head. Agricultural maps showed that there were fifteen thousand wild olive trees in the Aletzi area. "No one will be bossing me around," he said to himself, "and while the logging is under way, I'll graft the olives. I'll hire some of the Tuscans. Renato Granieri is a good friend, and he'll help me. They're all good boys, for that matter, and hard workers if they get good pay, which I intend to give them." ". . . Yes, *Mammai*," he said aloud, imagining a discussion with his mother and the points that he would make in case of any argument, "above all they're quick, and I'm sure that they can cut down trees and graft olives simultaneously."

"Aletzi will be mine, because I'll make something of it with my own hands. Twenty years from now it will be one big olive grove, and olive trees are untouchable."

At a certain point, he wearied of his own thoughts and felt a need to communicate them. Sofia wasn't tempted by what she called "castles in Spain," and it frightened her to think of borrowing money with Balanotti as collateral. Finally she burst into tears. She'd known too many people who had lost everything because they speculated with money borrowed from a bank.

"We're well enough off, thank the Lord. Why must you gamble everything, just when you're expecting a baby?"

She tried to enlist Valentina in her effort to dissuade Angelo from this venture. But Valentina was on his side. With him she dreamed of Aletzi, of the pipeline with which he proposed to bring in water, and of a new house where they would live, a house all her own.

Angelo asked the advice of his father-in-law. Manno listened to him attentively, made a few reasonable objections, and then declared that the risk was worth taking and that he wanted to participate. He proposed also, if Angelo was willing, to organize the transportation of the wood from the forest to the foundry at a minimum cost. This backing raised Angelo's spirits, which had been dampened by the opposition of his mother. He set great store by Sofia's opinion, knowing at first hand that she was seldom wrong. Now he hoped to enlist his father-in-law's help in bringing her around.

Valentina did not catch malaria; her pregnancy proceeded satisfactorily under the watchful care of Dr. Fulgheri, who predicted a birth without any complications. She was healthy, strong, and confident, or so she appeared. Inwardly, however, she was profoundly melancholy, perhaps because the end of summer was near. Winter was still far away, but day by day it came closer. The leaves were beginning to change color, especially those of the great walnut tree that stood against the wall which she had so often climbed over. She hardly spoke to Sofia, and her silence had something graceless and almost provocative about it. No longer did she drive out with Angelo; her attention was fixed on the premonitory signs of winter. Time seemed to her to be slipping by. When she walked down the steep, narrow, stony alley, she leaned against the wall with one hand like an old woman. She found the fears of her neighbors oppressive. If they hadn't always been staring at her, perhaps she would have run down the alley as she used to, or like Dolores or Solimena, the daughter of one of her father's workers, Costantino. Manno had taken in Solimena to help around the house and also to make up, with her exuberant gaiety, for the absence of Valentina's jokes and laughter. Even to her sisters Valentina now had little to say. She realized that she had left an empty place in the house; her sisters told her so, and she understood it; she knew that it was really so. The days when they had been all together were gone, never to return. She was happy, to be sure, but when she had lived at home with Barbara, Olivia, and the others, there was something to look forward to. Now everything, or almost everything, had come to pass, and the unity of the family was broken. Sometimes they invited her to dinner. This was a festive occasion, when her father never failed to break out a bottle of wine.

"You ought to drink some wine with your meal; it's good for you," he insisted. And she genuinely enjoyed the good Malvasia wine of her native Bosa.

Valentina went often to see Zelinda, who had remained in her father's stable. The mare's belly was swollen and the skin was as shiny and taut as that of a piece of ripe fruit. It didn't take an expert eye to see that she was close to foaling. She pawed the floor of her stall, scattering the straw, and looked at Valentina out of her big eyes as if she were asking her help. Valentina decided to take her home. Angelo cleared a stall next to Zurito's, built a wooden manger, and put fresh straw on the floor. Then he fetched Zelinda, leading her by a roundabout route so that she wouldn't have to climb up the steep alley from the Fluminera. Old Zurito turned one eye to look at the newcomer over the partition. That same night the foal was born.

In the course of the evening, Angelo and Valentina went at intervals with a kerosene lamp, which cast shadows all around, to look in on her. Before going to bed, they covered her with a soft blanket. When they went to bed, they could not go to sleep and lay silently in the darkness, listening to the stillness of the night as it rose up into the starless sky. All of a sudden they heard something like the bass note of a flute. It was the tremulous whinny of a newborn colt.

Together they ran down the stairs and Sofia grabbed the lantern. In its red light they saw the foal, still wet, but miraculously standing on its shaky, spindly legs. Zelinda was working without interruption at licking the foal dry. When it whinnied again, old Zurito whinnied back, peering over the partition between the stalls. Sofia pushed Valentina into the house for fear she catch cold, and Angelo with her.

"Go on back to bed," she insisted. "There's nothing that needs doing. I'll make sure that everything's all right."

After she had gone to sleep, Valentina dreamed of Bosa. From the mouth of the river, which wound its way among orchards and vineyards to the sea, she saw the dark, jagged profile of the Malaspina Castle. She remembered how happy she had been among the fruit trees, or going down the river in a boat, years and years before. Now this happiness was only a dim memory. Angelo was not present in her dream; he had died at war, like the fiancé of Comare Verdiana, and he was no more than a handful of dust, which slipped like sand between her fingers.

She woke up late, to a gray day and an empty place beside her. With considerable effort she sat up, catching a glimpse of her face in the mirror over the chest of drawers and tapping her swollen belly. The nightcap she wore over her unruly hair struck her as slightly ridiculous; she tore it off her head and threw it into a corner. She stuck out her legs and, taking care not to slip, put her feet on the floor. When she felt the wooden planks, she remembered that she had gone downstairs barefoot the night before, something that she had not done in a long time.

The sad mood of her dream persisted, fading, however, as the things around her took shape: the chair with which she rapped the floor as the conventional signal that she was awake, the marble top of the chest of drawers, the sight of her own bare body, which was reflected by the mirror as she peeled off her nightgown. Hurriedly she got dressed lest her mother-in-law come up and find her stark naked. She felt heavy and logy but free of pain and unafraid. Of course, she had been told about labor pains and how they would gradually increase in intensity. Now, all of a sudden, she remembered that the foal had been born during the night, and this seemed to her a good omen, especially because the birth had cost Zelinda no apparent suffering. The discomforting dream of Angelo gave way in her memory to the arrival of the foal. During the morning, all the children of the neighborhood came to peer through the boards of the wooden gate and admire it. Their elders admired it, too, saying that it was a very fine foal and of good pedigree on the side of its sire; the dam, however, was a stunted creature of low degree. Valentina didn't like to hear her mare insulted. "Sheer envy," she said to herself.

A tall, gaunt woman, staring at Valentina's belly, said half-aloud that it was too bad women couldn't give birth without travail. She was Feliciana Spanedda, daughter of Amedeo Spanedda and Lica Piras, a couple so old and wizened that it seemed impossible they should have had so towering an offspring. For this reason gossip had it that she had been abandoned by a tribe of gypsies who had passed through Norbio some fifty years before. She did, indeed, look and rig herself out like a gypsy. Her hair was tied up with strands of brightly colored wool, and she was laden down with rings, bracelets, and necklaces of uncertain origin. She begged for money, in spite of the fact that her parents were well off. Like a gypsy, moreover, she read palms and told fortunes, in competition with the professional witches of the town who had Saint Sisinnio as their patron and protector.

As usual, Feliciana held out her long, yellowish hand and Valentina slipped a coin into it. Feliciana caught hold of the left hand of her benefactress and almost forcibly tried to turn up the palm. Valentina at first resisted, then, with mixed feelings of curiosity and apprehension, gave in.

"The hand of a true lady," Feliciana murmured. "Are you expecting a child?"

Valentina had to laugh. Anyone could see that without being a soothsayer.

"How is it going to go?" she asked, lowering her eyes.

"Very well, miss, very well. You won't feel a thing."

"Will it be a boy or a girl?"

"A boy! A boy!" the "gypsy" said with a gesture of self-assurance.

Valentina gave her another coin. Even if she had secretly wanted a girl, she was glad. Besides, all hope was not lost, for she realized that the "gypsy" was talking nonsense.

"I see happiness," said Feliciana. "You'll be very happy!" And, waving her hand, she practically ran away.

The foal's slender legs were quite straight, and he was attempting a few steps. Zelinda pushed him with her muzzle, but he moved only far enough to be able to shove his head under her teats and suck them, switching his blond tail with pleasure. He was very thin, with a bony head—a sorrel, like his mother. An elongated white star stretched from his forehead all the way to his soft, pink nose and, again like his mother, he had three white feet.

"Three white feet hold a king's seat," said Manno, recalling an old proverb. With two fingers he separated the colt's lips, forcing him to open his mouth. To her amazement, Valentina saw that his white front teeth were already beginning to push up from the gums.

The weather had suddenly turned cold, and in order to protect Zelinda and her colt Angelo nailed wide strips of burlap to the walls and ceiling of the stall. When Valentina went to feed her horse, it was warm enough for her to linger there and caress the foal, which affectionately sucked her fingers while she felt the growing teeth that had so surprised her when her father uncovered them. It was there that she felt the first faint stab of her labor pains. With a last pat on the colt's neck she hurried away, obedient to the doctor's orders that she should go to bed and send word to her family. Angelo was away inspecting the work in the forest, but the minute Valentina appeared at the kitchen door Sofia understood what was up. She led her slowly upstairs, helped her to lie down, and ran to fetch the midwife and the doctor.

Valentina lay flat on her back, momentarily alone. The pains kept coming, with growing intensity. Now she felt as if a knife were ripping through the lower half of her belly. If there had been anyone else in the room, she would have called for help, even though she realized there was not much anyone could do. If Angelo had been there, he could have cheered her by holding her hand. She was tempted to get up, go to the window and call to her sisters, who were close enough to hear, but she decided against it. No one could alleviate her pains; they were the penalty or ransom that had to be paid for the joy of love-making. Dwelling upon this idea afforded her some comfort. As each wave of pain descended upon her, she gathered her thoughts together and folded her hands over her belly. She did not groan or cry out, but lay perfectly still. Finally, she heard hurried footsteps on the stairs; Sofia had returned with Signora Clorinda, the midwife, a bony, red-haired woman highly reputed for her skill. When the next round of pain descended, Valentina at last let herself go. She heard her own shriek as if it came from another person. At the same time, she saw the wrinkled, freckled face of the midwife leaning over her.

"If you yell like that it will hurt you all the more," said the midwife, knowingly. She thrust her big, warm, muscular hands under Valentina's clothes. Somehow the pain about to claw Valentina's insides was arrested. The midwife carefully dried her hands on the linen towel Sofia held out to her. She raised her head triumphantly and looked up at the ceiling, then bent over to undress Valentina, staring at her out of cat-green eyes.

"The worst is yet to come," she said, with a grimace that was meant to be affectionate. "Stay alert and don't let it get you; just push it away."

Sofia helped her with the undressing. For a moment Valentina lay on the bed, naked; then they pulled a sheet over her.

"What a little beauty!" exclaimed the midwife, running her hands over Valentina's back, then over the hips and down the legs all the way to the knees. Valentina felt protected by the warmth of these big hands. The midwife talked very fast, hardly opening her lips, as if she were reading aloud or saying a prayer.

Soon Comare Verdiana appeared. Two black corkscrew curls hung over her temples, and she had knotted a red kerchief around her head. For the first time Valentina noticed that she wore plain gold earrings in her small red ears and that her face was covered with tiny wrinkles. Because she had never seen them before it seemed to her as if Verdiana had grown old all of a sudden.

With a curt, authoritative nod, the midwife imposed silence. Verdiana said not a word as she busied herself bringing blankets, towels, and hot water. As time went by the pain was less aggressive. Valentina heard the outside gate open, Zurito's hoofs crunch the gravel of the courtyard, and Angelo calling his mother. A minute or two later, he was there coming toward her.

"Only for a minute!" the midwife warned him.

Angelo threw himself down on his knees beside the bed, stroked Valentina's hands and face, kissed her cheek, and then the midwife pulled him away and put him out of the room. Valentina thought that he would soon be back, that the baby would come as easily as Zelinda's foal. Instead, her travail went on for hours. Dr. Fulgheri came; she saw above her his bearded face, gold-rimmed glasses, and reassuring smile, and felt the touch of his cold, tentative fingers. Then his hands made a reassuring, almost priestly gesture, and he went away.

The midwife, as if to counteract a spell, thrust her hands under the sheet and retraced the itinerary of the doctor's fingers with her own. Again Valentina felt more confident, more protected. But during this moment of relaxation she was once more gripped by ferocious pain.

"It's the breaking of the waters," said the midwife, her witchlike face broadening into a radiant mannish smile.

Verdiana brought more towels, and sheets that had been warmed at the fireplace. The women changed the bed and lit an acetylene lamp which flooded the room with dazzling white light. Two sheets were rolled up like ropes and fastened to the head and foot of the bed.

"Catch onto them and pull hard when the moment arrives," the midwife told Valentina.

But the moment didn't arrive. Her pain was dormant within her, like a wild beast, weary and hunted down. They covered the lamp so that it would not glare in her eyes and gave her something hot to drink. Valentina drank it in big gulps, feeling it slip down into her stomach. It seemed to her as if the beast lurking inside her were greedily sucking it. She heard a bell, far away and unfamiliar, strike the hour, and she sank back, cradled by the echoes. But the midwife shook her; she had to stay awake and do her job; the baby must be born.

At two o'clock in the morning, Dr. Fulgheri returned.

"If by three hours from now nothing has happened, we'll have to operate," he said. "Keep plenty of hot water on hand." This time he left his surgical instruments behind him.

Sofia and Barbara wept and embraced each other. The midwife insisted that there was no danger, that Valentina would do the job on her own. They heard a long moan and rushed over, all three of them, to the bed. Valentina had grasped the rolled sheets and was trying to sit up. The midwife made her lie down again and thrust a clean handkerchief into her mouth so that she should not bite her tongue. Then she washed her hands in the basin, asked for more water, took hold of Valentina's wrists and enjoined her to summon up all her strength.

"This time you've got to make it," she said, "or else the doctor will have to cut you open. You're young and strong, so get to it!"

Valentina held on to the rolled sheets more tightly, bit the handkerchief in her mouth, and gradually began to feel that something was happening. From under her half-closed eyelids, she saw the faces of Sofia and Verdiana and the red cheeks of the midwife, but, in the same rhythm as that of her breath, the light which flooded the room alternated with darkness. She felt not as if she were giving birth but as if she were being, ever so painfully, born. Another stabbing pain caused her to spit out the handkerchief and give a loud wail like that of a baying dog. Then the pain ceased and she let herself go. In the midwife's hands she saw a bloody object like a freshly skinned rabbit.

They washed her with a towel dipped in warm water, and she felt grateful and happy. She heard a whimper reminiscent of the foal's whinny, except that this one was harsh and gasping, and repeated, like a protest, over and over. The midwife, Sofia, and Verdiana had turned all their attention to the baby, and the whimper came from farther and farther away. Beside the bed stood Barbara, shaken by the sobs that follow upon heavy weeping. She patted her sister's cheeks and wiped away the perspiration. Gradually Valentina felt a sense of well-being. With Barbara's head beside hers, she welcomed the oncoming of sleep as if it were a pervasive good smell, a tangible sign of the contentment that now filled her weary body. A little later, Sofia tiptoed back into the room, put out the lamps, and closed the shutters. Taking care not to wake Valentina, she threw a blanket over Barbara, who had fallen asleep beside her sister.

When Barbara woke up, morning light flooded the room. Valentina seemed to be still sleeping, and Barbara, after a glance at her childlike profile and pale cheeks, merely touched her hair. Valentina's lips were half-open in a smile; she lay perfectly still, as if she were not even breathing, and her immobility was as unreal as her beauty. Barbara had never seen her so beautiful, and she could not resist the temptation to kiss her. But when her lips brushed Valentina's cheek, she found it stone-cold and she recoiled in horror. Lifting up the bedclothes, she saw the pool of blood, and with a loud cry she collapsed on the floor. Sofia and Verdiana rushed into the room, and soon the whole house was filled with shouts and hurrying footsteps. Dr. Fulgheri appeared.

"You didn't notice anything?" he demanded, glaring at the midwife.

"Dear God, if I had noticed. . . ." she said, her voice choked with emotion.

The doctor put on his glasses and took a stethoscope out of his pocket, but he changed his mind and did not use it, or even take the pulse. Instead, he leaned over and kissed Valentina's forehead.

"She's been dead at least two hours," said the doctor.

Angelo's sobs reverberated through the whole house. He retreated to the kitchen. Verdiana, her eyes streaming tears, offered him a cup of coffee. Without a word, he hurled it into the fire.

Valentina had never looked more than eighteen years old; in death she seemed a mere child. They clothed her in her ivory-white wedding gown and laid her out in Don Francesco's study. The hands folded across her breast held her mother-of-pearl rosary.

The funeral took place the next day. Woodcutters carried the lightweight, white coffin. The townspeople who had gathered along the river and in the courtyards of the neighboring houses walked up the stony riverbed, emerged from gateways and alleys, and formed an orderly crowd, moving slowly down the street. On the road between the church and the graveyard, the subdued voices of the women said the *Avemaria*. All through the village and the surrounding fields, the chant rang out, as sweet and sad as a lullaby. A dense crowd paid Valentina a last tribute of affection, and at the same time shared Angelo's despair, in a spirit of silent rebellion and sorrowful protest.

Valentina was laid in the tawny earth which, a few months before, had received the body of Zio Raimondo Collu. But the old journeyman had lived to the natural end of his days like a piece of fruit ripened by the sun and ready to fall from the branch; Valentina had hardly begun to live. So the whole village mourned for her. Angelo felt his own sorrow reflected in theirs; and yet for them, it was all over in a few minutes. Rapidly and efficiently, his mother and sisters-in-law put the house in order, piling up the sheets and towels, making the bed in the room where Valentina had died, while he remained outside, not knowing where to go. A few minutes earlier, half the village had passed before him; he had shaken hundreds of hands and heard hundreds of voices say: "We'll see her again in Heaven," to which he had been able to say nothing. Now that the ceremony was over, his grief no longer found an echo in the sorrow of the neighbors. He was alone.

Among those who came to the house were the Tuscan woodcutters. Renato Granieri, who had tacitly become their head since the death of Antola and the disastrous fire, was, by now, Angelo's good friend. Renato had looked at him with a hard, impassive face, rolled his eyes in the direction of the ceiling, and exclaimed: "God be damned!" The people around him made a hurried sign of the cross. But for once this curse, which they had heard so often on the lips of the blasphemous Tuscans, seemed more appropriate than a pious prayer.

Angelo moved through his days in silence. After his first expressions of grief, he withdrew into himself. He continued to work, but his surroundings, Norbio, the house he had shared with Valentina depressed him. He had never traveled any farther than Cagliari and the seminary at Ales, but now he thought restlessly of going away. And yet he continued to live there, to let the days go by while he remained wrapped in his obsession. With time, his awareness of the desperate reality of his solitude grew upon him. The baby seemed to him ugly and hateful; unconsciously he held her responsible for the death of her mother. One day, when he came into the house, he found the wet nurse feeding her. The sight called to his mind how Valentina's breasts had grown full during her pregnancy. Now all that was left to him was this infant suckling greedily. With a catch in his throat, he left the room.

He indulged in the fantasy of going away. But then he realized that the simplest thing would be to die, without apology or explanation. Suicide was fairly frequent among people of Norbio. A disappointment in love, a bankruptcy, a humiliation, all these were sufficient causes. Most suicides hanged themselves or threw themselves into a well. More infrequently, they slit a vein or shot themselves through the head.

So it was that Angelo cradled this idea and grew familiar with it. One afternoon when his endurance was worn thin, he went swiftly and silently, as if in a dream, to his room, with the certainty that in a single second, with a pistol shot, he could put an end to all his sorrow. He took a pistol from the chest of drawers, ran his fingers over the wooden butt, tested the loading mechanism, which was well oiled and in perfect order, effortlessly raised the cock and lowered it again with his thumb so it wouldn't discharge a blank shot. The old pistol held a place in his affection. It was one that Don Francesco had always carried, and both wood and metal seemed to preserve the memory of his gaunt, powerful hand. Angelo regretted in advance the inevitable fact that the police would seize the suicide weapon. Before loading, it occurred to him that a rifle was more reliable. He put the pistol back in the drawer and took the rifle down from the wall. He examined it carefully, rereading for the hundredth time the name of the French maker and the date, 1810. If a single shot could kill a boar, it should be more than enough to kill a man. With no thinking involved but with the precision born of habit, he measured out a sizable amount of gunpowder and inserted the cartridge. Then he took off his shoes and socks, lay down on the bed, with the gun between his legs and the tip of the barrel, which had a bitter, metallic taste, in his mouth. Retracting his tongue, he held it firmly between his front teeth, then leaned the big toe of his right foot on the trigger, imagining the noise of the shot that would blow his head to bits. Familiar sounds drifted up from outside—the grinding of the grain mill, the creaking of the pump in the well—then, downstairs, a door was opened and shut and Sofia's voice called out:

"Angelo, are you there? Renato's here to see you."

So Renato was in the kitchen. A timely arrival if ever there was one! That way Sofia wouldn't be alone. Sofia called out again, but he made no reply. With his toe he began to press the trigger, all the while feeling the smooth, round barrel against his tongue. He pressed hard, he felt the hammer release, but the shot did not go off. Sofia was still calling, then he heard her footsteps on the stair. He put on his shoes, hung the gun on the wall, and went to meet her at his doorway.

Renato was finishing the cup of coffee.

"Sorry to disturb you at home," he said, "but I have to talk to you. Early tomorrow morning, I'm going back to the forest."

"You're not disturbing me," said Angelo, shaking his hand.

One look at Angelo's face told Sofia that something serious had happened. But he had not confided in her for a long, long time, and she could do nothing but worry about his silence, indifference, and self-imposed isolation. Yet just now something had surely happened; she felt it. When she ventured to pose a question, Angelo said curtly:

"Nothing, nothing at all."

Renato made a gesture to indicate that he wanted to talk outside. Angelo nodded and lit a cigarette. They went out together into the courtyard and down the steep path leading to Manno's orchard and vegetable garden.

"What's happening?" Angelo asked his companion.

"It's about the logging contract. Everyone's talking about it in the village. Some outsiders have arrived—fellows whom I know from Pistoia; we're from the Maremma, as you know. I've heard that you're going to make a bid, and my men and I want to know if it's so. Those fellows from Pistoia are hard dealers. They'll exploit not only the trees but the workers as well. If you obtain the contract, we'd like to work for you. But if it goes to them, we're pulling out."

They went on down the path as far as the garden gate, which was closed by a rectangular piece of wood on the inside. Angelo slipped his hand between the iron bars and pushed it through the two rusty metal rings. He couldn't help smiling at the purely symbolic character of the closing.

"I'm sorry, Granieri, but there's nothing I can tell you. In truth, I'd forgotten all about it."

"I understand. But it would be too bad to let it go," said Renato, pausing for a moment under a pear tree. "Too bad, because it's a good piece of business. The forest would be cut the way you want it, and, as I said before, we'd be happy to work for you. I've acquired a certain experience in this line, and I could help you. All of us stand to profit. My fellows asked me to approach you, so that you'd take the possibility of hiring us into consideration."

"Very good," Angelo murmured, lost in his own thoughts. "Thanks for calling the matter to my attention. I'll remember what you've told me."

There was a moment of silence before they said good-by. To Granieri, Angelo appeared to be sleepwalking. This was how he described him to his companions, adding that, under these circumstances, it wasn't likely that he'd compete for the contract.

Angelo accepted the cup of coffee his mother poured for him and did not draw back when she stroked his cheek and said he ought to shave. He inquired about the baby, suddenly remembering that he hadn't heard her cry all afternoon. Actually, she was in Manno's orchard with Maria Rosario Lampis, the wet nurse, who had fallen asleep in a comfortable cane chair under the walnut tree while little Maria Christina sucked at a breast emerging from her unbuttoned bodice. The breast was white and swollen with milk, and contrasted with the brown color of her face and hands. Maria Christina was in swaddling bands and covered by a loosely knit red shawl which had belonged to Valentina. Angelo was overcome by a feeling of tenderness; he leaned over and gingerly picked her up, feeling the warmth of her tiny body. Holding her for the first time in his arms, he was guiltily aware of his previous neglect. He trod heavily on the white gravel, with all the awkwardness of a man carrying a baby. Suddenly Maria Christina made a face, opened her mouth wide, and began to cry. Angelo went back to the wet nurse and placed the infant in the same position as before. The wet nurse awakened and enfolded the infant in her arms. At once the baby quieted down and reached out blindly for the nipple. Angelo looked on from a short distance away. Tears flooded his face; he did not even bother to wipe them as he strode up and down, with his hands in his pockets, in the alley flanked on either side by sycamore trees. It was long before he finally decided to go home. In the kitchen, his mother was busily preparing supper.

A
fter Valentina's death, the engineer had barely glimpsed Angelo at Manno's. Angelo no longer went there in the evening, unless Dolores came to fetch him. She arrived, tripping briskly along and holding the ends of her long braids in her hands, greeted Sofia and, if Angelo wasn't there, went to look for him. When she had found him, she tapped with her foot on the ground, raised her chin authoritatively, grasped his hand and, without saying a word, dragged him after her. Without a protest, he followed. No one else could free him from his solitude and sorrow. Indeed, when they were alone together, Dolores could even get him to talk, on a child's level. She spoke of Valentina with complete ease, claiming to have seen her in a dream and to have conversed with her.

"If you want to ask her something, just tell me what it is," she proposed. "Tomorrow or the day after I'll give you her reply, because whenever I put my mind to it, I can summon her up in my dreams."

Angelo found relief in these absurd conversations with Dolores; indeed, they became indispensable to him.

The engineer had said nothing more about the contract for logging in the forest of Aletzi, but Angelo was still wondering how best to go about securing it. The Island was economically poor and politically weak. Obtaining a loan would not be easy. The tariff war with France had curtailed the export trade, and various banks had failed. Particularly disturbing were the failures of the Credito Agricolo Industriale Sardo and the Cassa di Risparmio of Cagliari. The first rumors began to circulate in February of 1887 and the newspaper *L'Avvenire di Sardegna* was unable to quiet them. The central offices and outlying branches were mobbed, and a few days later had to close their doors.

Manno was following these events and, on this particular day, he had just come back from Cagliari where the general discontent had made for widespread disorder. He told how, after rocks had been thrown from the fortifications at the soldiers who were trying to seal off the Via della Prefettura, a police official had given orders to fire into the crowd, and a young worker had been wounded. A few days later it came out that he had died of tetanus.

In Manno's house, such things were often discussed, and Dolores listened eagerly. But because no one paid attention to her questions, she took them to Angelo. What, she asked, was an "Istituto di Credito"; what was tetanus? In her innocence she could not understand why soldiers, whose job, she had been taught, was to defend their country, should shoot at their fellow countrymen.

Talking politics was the order of the day. Manno and the engineer led the conversation, and the others listened, including Angelo who, like Dolores, needed considerable explanation. One thing was clear: no loan could be obtained from a bankrupt bank.

One evening there was talk of the Djebel-Ressas mine in

Tunisia. This mine, abandoned for centuries, had been turned over in 1828 to a French engineer who failed to exploit it. In 1868 it had been granted to Baron Giacomo Castelnuovo as a reward for his medical services to the Bey and, later, to King Victor Emmanuel II. For a while, Castelnuovo had reclaimed the slag still rich in metal that lay in the vicinity of the mine. Later, having contracted debts to more than one Sardinian bank, he had surrendered his claim to his creditors, who, in turn, had created the Italian Mining Consortium, for which Ferraris was a highly prized consultant. Ferraris considered the prospects at the Djebel-Ressas mine favorable because there were still seventy thousand tons of slag available for reclamation. Were it to be sold, the debt could be paid and the mine itself could be exploited. Ferraris had developed an intricate plan whereby the mine could be reactivated and, at the same time, as part of the same maneuver, Angelo could obtain the money needed to bid for the logging contract for the forest of Aletzi. One evening as they walked up the Via Roma together, he said:

"I don't suppose you've thought of the Aletzi contract lately . . ."

"As a matter of fact, I have thought of it," Angelo answered, "but the money stops me. In view of the present banking situation . . ."

"What does your mother say?"

"Oh, she approves, but . . ."

"Good! Then I'm quite sure I can secure a loan from the Consortium. Eighty thousand liras will do."

To Angelo, the possibility opened so suddenly and the sum seemed so enormous that he caught his breath nervously.

"Did you think you'd need anything less?"

"No," Angelo said promptly, "but it still seems to me a lot of money."

"Don't let me force your hand," Ferraris said calmly. "But I'm sure it's a good deal. And I'll be close to you and will help you in every way I can."

"I can give it a try."

"Good! That's the spirit!"

They shook hands on it and, when they came to the tavern

186

where Ferraris had been having a room for so many years, they drank to the project's success.

Sofia was convinced that the death of Valentina had erased from Angelo's mind the Aletzi project that she had viewed with such misgiving. Now she would welcome any project, however misbegotten, that could rouse him from his melancholy. When he mentioned the Aletzi forest again, this was the first thing that crossed her mind; nothing else really mattered. Must he use his land as collateral? Very good, as long as he returned to his old self and recaptured his enjoyment of life. This was what she ceaselessly petitioned in her prayers. And so, when Angelo spoke of his talk with the engineer, she assured him at once of her agreement.

The day of the auction was drawing near and Manno offered to put up the money for procedural expenses. Egidio Costa, the local tax collector, was also manager of the branch of the Bank of Naples, and it was through him that the Mining Consortium would convey the eighty thousand liras to Angelo. Soon, then, Angelo was to have an account at the bank, for an amount which, in those days and especially at Norbio, seemed positively princely. Before receiving the loan, he went with the engineer to Cagliari to be interviewed by a prominent banker. He was introduced to the Honorable Ghiani Mameli, who had played an important part in the recent economic crisis and had thrown his weight behind the idea of making a loan to "the courageous young man" recommended by the engineer. Ghiani Mameli knew Norbio and deprecated as strongly as Angelo the irresponsibility with which the Piedmontese had laid waste to its forests.

After Angelo had quietly and sensibly answered Ghiani Mameli's questions, the old financier talked to him about other operations in which he was involved. After years of uncertainty and violent controversy, affairs in Tunisia seemed more promising. Italian businessmen were creating a whole series of Italian enterprises to counter-balance French interests there. Included in this far-reaching plan, he said, looking with his cat's eyes into the innocent gaze of Angelo, were the purchase of the railway between Tunis and La Golette and the exploitation of the Djebel-Ressas mine. Ghiani Mameli himself was promoting the latter, with the support of Pasquale Umana and the Honorable Cocco Ortu, two politicians very close to Francesco Crispi, generally spoken of as "the rising star in Italian politics," who was expected to fill the place left empty by the late, great Camillo Benso di Cavour.

Of this lengthy dissertation, Angelo clearly understood only one thing: that Ferraris had maneuvered with great diplomatic skill, and that from then on the fate of Norbio would be bound up with that of a whole foreign policy, rather than being in the hands of the Prefect and the Royal Supervisor of Finance. The engineer winked at him and, after they had bid the financier farewell, they made their way to the coach station.

A few days later two soberly attired city men came to Norbio to set a value on Angelo's real property. Without departing from their professional reserve, they intimated that, on the basis of their report, the loan would be granted. So a few days later, just before the auction, when the engineer gave Angelo confirmation of the loan and showed him Ghiani Mameli's letter, the younger man did not show as much surprise as the other had expected.

"One would think that getting an eighty-thousand-lira loan at a time like this was to you like rolling off a log!" the engineer said somewhat reproachfully.

The next day they went to the town hall. The auction took place in the Council's meeting room, which was crowded with people. A representative of Antola's company was present, and so was the third bidder, Giuseppe Sanguinetti. The mayor ran through the usual formalities, and the forest of Aletzi was put on the block at an opening price of fifteen thousand liras.

From behind a barrier, the public grumbled, but the mayor rang his bell and threatened to empty the room. Antola's company immediately offered thirty thousand liras. Angelo said nothing, having decided to let the others fight it out between them and then to come in himself only at the right moment.

The engineer looked at him approvingly. He knew that Angelo had never taken part in a public auction and admired the cool-headedness with which he played the game.

"Perhaps he's so cool because he doesn't realize the importance of what's at stake," he thought to himself.

Sanguinetti raised the bid to thirty-five thousand, but Angelo remained silent. The public looked at him impatiently and with a mute question in their eyes. Most of those present were owners or herdsmen of sheep, goats, and swine. Sisinnio Casti, the blind old man, was there, with his fluffy white hair and the scars on his red face. He raised his sightless eyes as if to look at the ceiling, listened to everything that was said, and spoke reassuringly to those around him.

The representative of Antola's company raised the bid to forty-five thousand, triple the amount of the base price, but the mayor was not satisfied. The herdsmen, shifting from one foot to another, approved the fact that he was holding out for more. The air in the room was heavy with their smell and the weight of their expectant silence. Antola's company went up to fifty thousand. The mayor made an impatient gesture. A moment of silence followed, and then Angelo raised his hand.

"Seventy thousand," he said in his clear, manly voice.

At Norbio people don't clap their hands in applause, but something like a shout rose from the little crowd when the mayor said: "Contract awarded!" and closed the land registry book. Angelo went to the mayor's office with the engineer, signed the registry, and started to hurry away.

"You can start work tomorrow, if you want to," the mayor called after him. "You're a sly fox, did you know that?" he added.

"It's a fair price," Angelo retorted.

"Fair enough," echoed the engineer.

And they left the town hall together. That same day Angelo spoke with Renato Granieri and told him he wanted to hire his loggers.

"When do we start?" Granieri asked.

"As soon as your men are ready."

"They're ready today!"

"We must give Manno time to collect wagons in which to take up the tools, the axes, and billhooks and so on."

"To start with, we'll camp out. Then we'll build some sheds and barracks."

"And eventually houses," said Angelo. "Yes, we'll build houses. Simple ones, of course, but good enough to live in. That way you can bring over your families."

"If it weren't for the malaria . . . !" said Renato. "It's worse there than in the Maremma. Our families had better stay home."

Within a few days, preparations for the project were completed, and Renato asked Angelo for instructions.

"You're to chop down one in ten," Angelo told him, "and to spare all young trees, like that one there, and the oaks that are still producing acorns. The main thing is to make sure that there will be rapid reforestation."

"I understand," said Renato.

And so, one morning toward the end of November, the valley echoed with the rapid, rhythmical ring of ax blows. Led by Angelo and Renato, who chose the trees to be cut, two squads of men went to work at the foot of the mountain that divides Aletzi from Ruinalta. Their first task was to clear out the underbrush—not only briars and brambles, but also arbutus which, after the autumn flowering, was loaded with red berries. Every now and then Angelo popped one of them into his mouth, recovering his childish delight in the fresh, bitter taste and granular consistency.

After their long period of forced idleness, the Tuscans worked briskly. Their strong, happy voices sang out as white chips flew, spreading the odor of fresh wood around them. Angelo had recruited a certain number of *carbonai,* or charcoal makers, from Norbio, who could use the underbrush. These fellows, whose pores had been blackened since childhood by coal dust, wandered silently among the rosy-cheeked Tuscans. They did not remain together, yet they had a mute language of their own, a particular slow way of carrying twigs and branches and of preparing the trench of the charcoal pit. They wielded their hoes as if they were dragging them over the ground, and anyone looking at them could see why they had a reputation for being lazy. Actually, they weren't lazy at all. They had their own ways of doing things, passed on from generation to generation in order to ensure their survival, the survival of a desperately poor people, born in a land where time did not exist.

To make a charcoal pit they proceeded as follows: first, in in an area of cleared ground, they dug a trench five feet long, three feet wide, and no more than fifteen inches deep. On the bottom they made a bed of leaves and tiny twigs. On this they laid out larger twigs and branches, building up a pyramidal structure which rose five feet above the level of the ground. The whole structure was then overlaid with dirt and mud, except for an opening at the base, reinforced all around with stones of an appropriate shape which they gathered, with exasperating slowness, from the nearby terrain. Finally vents, like those of a mole's burrow, were pierced in the sides. It was some time before the green wood started to burn and thick, bluish smoke emerged from the vents. At this point, the man in charge sniffed the smoke as if to test its quality, pounded the mud walls with the palm of his hand to make sure they were solid, and finally sat down on the ground, where he wetted the tip of a cigar butt with saliva and proceeded to smoke it. Beside him was a knapsack with a supply of bread and cheese that had to last him for some time. For this reason, he cut and prepared every mouthful with care and munched it slowly. A charcoal pit smoldered for over a week: under the earthen cover the green wood turned into embers, which burned down to become charcoal, as if the branches, all the same length, had undergone a process of fossilization. The man on watch could not move more than a few steps away from his post; every now and then he revived the invisible fire by sticking a long poker into the base opening or one of the vents and sometimes shoving in a handful of dry leaves. Every day, with his knife, he cut a notch in a twenty-inch-long stick as thick as a thumb.

This, then, was the way charcoal was produced in the Parte d'Ispi region. Although made from light wood, it was charcoal of substance, and was much sought after by peasant housewives all over the Island and in the large towns and cities as well. For generations the poorest men of Norbio, those whose only possessions were a billhook, an ax and a pocketknife, had followed this vocation. The craft was in their blood, and the skin of their hands and faces was permeated with impalpable black dust. They sold the charcoal wholesale for four liras a hundred pounds. Or else they went from house to house, with a donkey carrying two sacks swung over either side of its back and a pair of scales, selling at fifteen centimes a pound.

Now the Tuscans were busy chopping down the trees that Angelo and Renato had marked for cutting. The shiny blades of their long-handled axes circled in the air like pinballs, and the first blow, sinking deep into the base, caused the whole tree to quiver. They knew how to make the tree fall just where they wanted it, without hitting the charcoal pits. No sooner had a tree fallen than it was stripped of its leaves and branches, hauled away, and split into logs by means of hammers and wedges. Although, the *carbonai* were slow workers, a number of charcoal pits were smoldering by the end of the morning.

At noon, Angelo gave orders to stop cutting and eat lunch. Suddenly the valley fell into silence, broken only by the occasional harsh cry of a magpie or the whistle of a blackbird darting in a straight, horizontal line through the unfamiliar landscape left by the cut trees and taking refuge among the bushes along the stream. Among the stumps some fifteen wild olive trees were still standing. From his leather tool-pouch Angelo took out a pair of shears and clipped a few branches, as if he were already preparing to graft. Actually it was only for the pleasure of trying out the pair of newly purchased shears, hearing the sharp click of the blades, and seeing the clean cut.

The grafting would take place the following spring.

Part Three

Part Three

Don Francesco Fulgheri had never used the title of Count of Nepomuceno. The title went back to the time of the Crusades, but it had devolved upon the Fulgheris only in the eighteenth century. To possess it legally, the first Fulgheri bearer, Don Faustino, was required to build a village over which he would dispense justice and from which he could supply the king with whatever taxes he could eke out of his tenants. Don Faustino, and his son Lorenzo after him, did build—in the uninhabited region of Oridda that belonged to them—a village with granite houses, streets, a church, and even a bell tower with a clock that struck the hours. When everything was ready, they posted an announcement all over the Parte d'Ispi region, inviting all and sundry to pick out a house at San Giovanni Nepomuceno. Weeks, months, and years went by without any takers. San Giovanni Nepomuceno met the same fate as many a modern "real estate development" built in the same gray stone. Perhaps people suspected a trap, or perhaps, in those days, a maleficent spell, and they stayed away from the new houses, the new church, and the icy-cold fountains. The Fulgheris remained what they had always been: the free and indisputable owners of vast tracts of Oridda, inhabited only by boars, foxes, and rabbits, and characterized by its tall, withered, almost fossilized trees, covered by gray moss, that resembled an underwater forest. The title of "Count of Nepomuceno" had remained as empty as the empty village of San Giovanni Nepomuceno. Don Francesco used to burst into laughter when he was reminded of his title.

He had had a further reason for letting the title fall into disuse—disdain for the Piedmontese monarchy, and its corrupt government. Don Francesco's argumentative, combative liberal spirit had earned for him the name of "sinner" among priests and "revolutionary" among the officials of the Piedmontese government. Although the Piedmontese found it advantageous to give refuge to political exiles from other Italian states, they severely oppressed liberals within their own jurisdiction.

Don Tommaso was twenty years younger than his brother and had not witnessed the same political events. Yet he too forebore the name of "Count" out of spite for the Piedmontese regime. Of a gentle and meditative nature, he dedicated himself to the practice of medicine and to the administration of his vast inheritance. Don Tommaso was family doctor to all of Norbio. His relationship to his patients was his chief concern: it was direct and human and based on genuine feeling. Different as he was from his late brother, Don Tommaso filled the empty place Don Francesco had left behind him. His medical duties permitted him to live unostentatiously among the simple people, who, as a result, felt for him an affection and respect even greater, perhaps, than the regard they had felt for his fiery elder brother. Every one of them cherished Don Tommaso, and the doctor, in his turn, cared for each of them, not only as a patient, but as a person. The village people made a sharp distinction between Don Tommaso and the rest of the "gentry."

Among the "gentry" was Senator Loru, who claimed distant kinship to the Fulgheris, although, like the other Lorus, he was of peasant extraction. Donna Luisa, his wife, a member of the petty nobility of Cagliari, overlooked her husband's peasant antecedents and extolled his Fulgheri connections which, as is often the case in Sardinia, were lost in the far reaches of Island history.

Don Tommaso Fulgheri had deeply loved his wife, Caterina, and had suffered greatly when he found his medical skill powerless to save her life. Although still young when she died, in deference to their children, particularly the two girls Margherita and Carmela, he had never remarried. Now forty-five years old, he was handsome, tall, and slim, with a short black beard and dark hair that turned gray at the temples and which he wore parted on the left side. He dressed simply, with innate good taste, usually appearing in a longish black jacket, light trousers, soft-collared white shirt, bow tie, and a beaver hat with a partridge feather stuck into its silk band that suggested the emblem of some secret society. Actually, he belonged only to a medical group and to the Agrarian Association, founded years before by his father for the purpose of improving farming methods in the Parte d'Ispi region.

Don Tommaso's great passion was not agriculture but hunting. In those days, there was so much game that a man had only to get off his horse on any country road and walk a few steps into the woods to raise partridges or woodcock. And when Don Tommaso went into the country it was usually to shoot. He seldom inspected the work of the fields, entrusting such matters to his peasants and to the advice of Senator Loru.

The senator accompanied him on occasional visits to his outlying farms, sacrificing what Don Tommaso quite seriously called his "precious time." Actually, he did not have a very high opinion of the senator and considered his parliamentary efforts totally useless. Out of courtesy and sheer habit, nevertheless, he listened patiently to Loru's advice, and endured his tedious, even irritating, political disquisitions. Don Tommaso himself was incapable of vehement opinions or great ambition. He wished only to care for the sick and to raise his own children—Francesco, his son, whom they called "Franceschino," and his two daughters—who would someday inherit one of the greatest estates of Parte d'Ispi.

Franceschino had grown up playing on the pebbled banks of the Fluminera with other boys of his own age, barefoot and with holes in his pants. No one would have thought of calling him "Count," especially if they saw him practicing with one of the slingshots, made of a piece of goatskin and two bits of string, that all the boys of Norbio were expert in using. Their favorite target was a vane on one of the chimney flues of the former Archbishop's Palace, which, when hit, would whirl around, screeching so loudly the noise could be heard even inside the Fulgheri mansion. At other times, they aimed at the weathercock on the lightning conductor of the slender bell tower of Santa Barbara, which stood out above the rooftops against the background of Mount Homo, or at the great bell that could be perceived as a black triangle inside the tower. This last was a difficult shot and only a very few of the slingshooters ever achieved it. When they did, the bell rang wildly and the priest ran to register a complaint with the mayor and the sergeant of the *carabinieri*. Usually the shot could not be traced. Once, however, a woman had pointed out the source, and the culprit was discovered to be Franceschino Fulgheri. The sergeant had solemnly admonished the young Count, who promised, with his fingers crossed, never to do it again.

It was his very distant relative by marriage who habitually referred to Franceschino as "the young Count." Donna Luisa Loru, née Boy, relished using titles, chiefly because she, who came from an ambitious family of the petty nobility, had married a self-made man of peasant origin. Years before, as a student, Antioco Loru had been constrained to engage himself, in the Spanish tradition, as a *maiolu*, or servant, in the house of the noble family in the city of Cagliari in order to pay his university fees. The now rich and powerful senator, president and professor of Roman Law at the university he had attended as a student, had worked in a menial capacity for Donna Aldonsa Brondo di Valdaura. Later, he had become an assistant, or, more exactly, a factotum, of the then professor of Roman Law, serving partly as a secretary and partly as a valet, helping him into his coat, handing him his gloves, hat, and cane. And yet despite these lowly positions, Loru had never felt servile, for he was an unpretentious youth, who accepted unquestioningly class distinctions and the social difference between a peasant and a marquis, or a count, or even a university professor.

Once he was himself a professor, he faithfully upheld the established order of society—so faithfully that he was named to the Senate. This advancement thrust him into the ranks, not of the aristocracy, but of the class between it and that of merchants and landowners, a class which enjoyed prestige and authority. It also made possible his marriage to Donna Luisa Boy. For a peasant from Norbio, his was an almost Napoleonic career.

Although when he married he was not yet president of the university and still lacked social polish, Loru was considered a desirable match. Handsome, young, tall for a Sardinian, with bony, dark-skinned face and big hands, he seemed to be sculptured from oak. Donna Luisa had not been reluctant to enter into the prearranged match; indeed, she had promptly fallen in love. As for Antioco Loru, he regarded Donna Luisa as he had viewed other events of his life, with full awareness of the advantages to be drawn from her connections. She, too, had appraised the pros and cons, and had not been disappointed. Then, unexpectedly, she discovered her husband's kinship to the Fulgheri family. Although only remotely related to the new senator, the Fulgheris were true aristocrats, possessed of considerable fortune and with a crown on their coat-of-arms. She had cultivated the friendship of Donna Fernanda and Don Giovannantonio, and, later, had tried to smooth over the differences between Antioco Loru and old Don Francesco. Now that the older generation was gone, she showered her attentions on Don Tommaso's children—Margherita, Franceschino, and Carmela—and did everything she could to fill in the gaps of their motherless upbringing. Moreover, she had exerted herself to dust off and shine the coat-of-arms that the Fulgheris had neglected. In this, her attentions were far from disinterested: she wanted to say and to show that she had married a man who had aristocratic relatives as well as solid personal achievements to his credit. Finally, she aspired to make her home the social center of Norbio and therefore allied herself to Donna Assunta Todde, wife of the professor of Economics who was her husband's rival at the university. Together they introduced to Norbio what today would be called "public relations," and entertained visiting literary lights, shrewdly sharing the expenses.

One Sunday afternoon, Donna Luisa Loru sent her coachman to summon "the young Count." Franceschino was now seventeen years of age. Margherita Fulgheri gave the coachman, Fideli, two silver coins and assured him that her brother would obey Donna Luisa's summons. She was consumed with curiosity to know what Donna Luisa intended, and hoped the handsome tip that she gave would produce some clue from the coachman. He, however, said not a word, but bowed politely and departed. Margherita gave her brother the message and instructed him to change his clothes and comb the unruly lock of hair that stood up, like a coxcomb, on the top of his head.

"My hair won't stay combed," he said, with a gesture of annoyance.

"You can't go to see Donna Luisa looking like a ragamuffin," Margherita insisted. "After all, you're a Count of Nepomuceno!"

Franceschino continued to walk along the pebbly bed of the Fluminera. When it was time for him to go, Margherita summoned him in a harsh voice. She was deeply attached to her family, particularly to her brother, but he and Carmela had always had to defer to her, the eldest, and to obey her without argument. Margherita did not have the temperament of a hardworking housewife; she preferred to give orders and be waited upon.

"Come right now and wash!" she called out. "Donna Luisa's expecting you."

For a moment, Franceschino thought that Donna Luisa had come in person to fetch him, and he considered running away. Margherita, who by now had come down to the river, caught him and held on firmly with her strong little hands.

"It's still early," he protested.

"She's sent Fideli for the second time to tell you to hurry. She has to go to Cagliari with the senator."

Franceschino, feeling very put out, ran ahead of her, slamming the wooden gate behind him, then peeled off his jacket and shirt and washed himself at the well. Margherita picked up the undergarments he had strewn upon the ground and handed him a towel. He watched her walk rapidly, purposively, up the stone steps leading to the kitchen and automatically followed, drying his face and his sunburned, hairless chest. He was in the habit of riding through the countryside naked to the waist, and the sunburn lasted from one summer to another. Margherita could cajole him into doing what she wanted, but he was too headstrong at times. Only the year before, he had challenged her authority by announcing that he wanted to enlist as a volunteer for the African wars. Margherita had refused even to discuss it. She had walked up to him, looked into his eyes, and slapped him on both cheeks with her right hand. He had returned her stare without blinking. Neither one of them said a word. Even the scatterbrained Carmela did not giggle. Later, when Margherita and Franceschino were alone, she said:

"You're not going to Africa! Your place is here with us, with me and Carmela."

Immediately they made peace when Margherita had sworn never to slap him again, and he had promised not to enlist.

Now Franceschino continued to dry his neck and ears, while his sister climbed the steep, slate steps, swishing the silk lining of her long skirt around her legs. She turned at the landing and pushed Franceschino gently into his room, where a freshly pressed shirt, still warm from the iron, lay ready on the bed and his "good" suit was hung over a chair. Franceschino made a face, to which Margherita replied with a peremptory thrust of her chin. She didn't care for Donna Luisa and suspected that she had been the one to give Franceschino the idea of enlisting for Africa. But appearances had to be preserved.

Franceschino dressed carefully, and let Margherita look him over. His "good" suit was cut in French style; he wore a high-buttoned waistcoat and a bow tie. On the Via Roma he glimpsed some of his old school friends, waved hastily, and went his way.

The senator's two-storied house had no distinguishing architectural style, but it stood out among the rustic dwellings built of unmorticed stone that surrounded it, and its simplicity was not without a certain severe elegance. The wide gate opened onto a large courtyard. There the funereal black landau now stood, with the two horses hitched, ready to leave at a moment's notice. It was the only landau in the town, and was respected as a symbol of power and authority. Fideli, the coachman, was sitting on the box; another servant was loading the luggage. As soon as he saw Franceschino, the coachman jumped down without so much as grazing the shafts with the points of his shiny boots, and went to meet him, hat in hand.

The senator's study gave onto a veranda topped by a roof-garden, which one could reach by a narrow granite stairway with wrought-iron railings, painted green. There were French windows and a heavy wooden door. The servant knocked, and immediately the senator's bulky and impressive figure appeared at the door. He leaned over, squinting, and, when he recognized Franceschino, held out a heavy, cold hand by which the young man was propelled into the study. He had hardly time to take off his hat before the senator said to the servant: "Take the Count's hat."

Franceschino had supposed that he was to see Donna Luisa, with whom he had an easy relationship. Now he found himself facing the intimidating senator and didn't know what to say. He swallowed nervously and buttoned up his jacket.

"I'm afraid I've arrived at an inconvenient time."

The senator laughed and answered in his harsh voice:

"You could never arrive at an inconvenient time, my dear boy, because in this house you're at home. My wife asked you to come, I know, although I'd told her we had to be in Cagliari by nine o'clock. We've been invited to dinner with the governor, and we can't be late."

"I quite understand," said Franceschino, delighted by the prospect of going straight back home. "I can just as well come another day."

Antioco Loru tugged at his long, gray whiskers.

"That would be the sensible thing to do," he said, "but my wife is anxious to see you. It's about an old friend of ours who's coming on a visit to Cagliari and will be staying with us . . . General Marini of the Military Academy at Modena. . . ."

Francesco made a slight bow of assent. The senator rubbed his chin and said to the servant standing stiffly at attention: "Take the Count to Donna Luisa."

The coachman, a former *carabiniere,* clicked his heels and threw back his head. He made a half turn, clicked his heels again, and waited. Silently Franceschino got up and followed him. Donna Luisa, obviously very busy, was waiting for him in the drawing room.

She was a short, stoutish woman who combed her hair in the old-fashioned style with a part in the middle. Franceschino Fulgheri found her slightly ridiculous, but agreeable. At all seasons and at every hour of the day, she gave out the fragrance of violet toilet water. She dressed in transparent tulle blouses that revealed the outline of her breasts and shoulders. At home, she wore small, bright-colored aprons that accentuated her narrow waist and broad hips. On her remarkably small feet, she wore custom-made shoes from Cagliari.

Like the other members of the Cagliari nobility, Donna Luisa spoke a very particular Sardinian dialect, quite different from that spoken in the towns and villages of the Island, or, for that matter, from that spoken by ordinary people in the city itself. It was a dialect more intimate and exclusive than any other, not only in its cadence but also in its words and expressions, in its nostalgic references to the days when the "noblemen of the castle" had exacted tribute from faraway subjects and had worn swords at their sides. Donna Luisa had a facile and persuasive way of talking. As she spoke, she held her young "nephew's" hand in hers, occasionally patting his cheek or chin. Francesco, unaccustomed to such sentimental excesses, listened attentively but spoke only when he had to.

"I'd like to speak to you more at leisure," said Donna Luisa, "but we haven't much time and I must do it before we go."

"I can come back another day," said Franceschino, hoping to get away.

Donna Luisa raised her little hand.

"I need to hear what you think before I see a man who will be staying with us in Cagliari over the next few days, General Marini, commander of the Military Academy of Modena. You've heard of that, I suppose. . . ."

Franceschino hadn't heard, but he nodded.

"It's a school to which boys of your age are eligible for admission, and three years later they come out as second lieutenants in the army. I'm sure you'd enjoy wearing the handsome uniform, and the General can make it all very easy. . . ."

Franceschino had never thought of a career as an officer, nor did he aspire to a uniform. In fact, he had never seen an army officer, either at Norbio or at Cagliari where, after the royal family had returned to Turin there were very few military parades. He liked to dress in peasant style; he liked riding his horse, attending country festivals, calf-branding, hunting—in brief, he enjoyed the freedom he had always known.

"They are recruiting officer candidates," Donna Luisa told him, "and you, my child, have many of the qualities that could lead to a successful army career. Besides, you're the Count of Nepomuceno!"

Franceschino was vaguely annoyed, but he said politely:

"May I ask if you have spoken to my father?"

"Oh, we know your father's way of thinking. I'll speak first to the General, and then my husband will talk it over with your father."

"I don't mind if you ask the General, Aunt Luisa. But without my father's permission, I can't make any promises. If I were to go away, who'd take care of the land? My father thinks of nothing but medicine."

"With the little money he makes in this miserable village!" said Donna Luisa, waving her hands.

"He likes being a doctor," said Franceschino calmly.

Donna Luisa whistled between her teeth in disapproval.

"There's no reason for you to sacrifice yourself by staying here, when you have a chance to make a brilliant career somewhere else."

With which she drew him to her, planted a damp kiss on his cheek, and sent him away.

"I must say good-by. Loru is waiting for me."

According to the custom of the time, she called her husband by his last name. While she was hugging Franceschino, she slipped a knit silk purse containing a few coins into his pocket. This was one habit of hers that her young relatives encouraged, though when they got home they usually laughed among themselves at the miserly amount of the money. Now Franceschino thanked her, politely kissed her hand, and left by the kitchen door.

Outside darkness had fallen. Franceschino walked up the crowded Via Roma, enjoying the slow, restful flow of people, after the discomfort he had felt in the house of the senator.

Margherita had waited all afternoon for Franceschino's return, anxious to hear why Donna Luisa had summoned him. She had emptied and restored to order the drawers of the big chest and then gone down to the ground floor. Something simmering in the kitchen gave out a mouth-watering smell, but she had little interest in cooking or eating. She went to the stove, lifted the lid of an earthenware pot, and stirred the contents with a wooden spoon. A surge of steam struck her wrist and left a burning sensation. Hastily she clapped the lid back in place, muttering a protest against the old serving-woman, Maria Giuseppa.

Ever since her mother's death Maria Giuseppa had taken care of the house and, to some extent, of the children. But although she had dedicated the greater part of her life to them, in Margherita's eyes she would always be a servant—the most alert and devoted of servants, but belonging to a different and inferior class. She was fond of her, yes, but only up to a certain point; she was grateful for all that she had done and would do for the family until the day of her death, but what they owed her could be paid in money, without any unnecessary show of feeling. Dr. Fulgheri did not share Margherita's attitude, nor did Franceschino and Carmela. They were cordial and warmhearted toward everyone, especially Franceschino, who played with the village boys of his own age and who admired the rustic charm of the girls he saw around him.

At the moment, Donna Margherita was annoyed not to find her in the kitchen, but Maria Giuseppa was not remiss. She kept her eye on everything, including the work of the other servants. It was a wonder that she did not direct the sowing and harvesting as well as the housework. Twice a month, when the tenant farmer came to town and sat down at the master's dining-table, according to custom, Maria Giuseppa was the one that asked the most pertinent questions and gave the most sensible advice. The other servants, male and female, looked up to her and called her *Zia*. On this particular afternoon she had sent the two girls Giuanna and Efisina to wash clothes in the river, and had shut herself up in the "flour room." There she separated the fine bran from the gross, running a sieve over a flat, smooth chestnut board. She filled the sieve with gross bran, using a wooden spade, grasped it with her deft, strong hands, pulled it toward her, and then pushed it away with a rotary motion. The sieve, seemingly endowed with a life of its own and barely touched by the fingers that kept the original movement going, went rapidly and rhythmically back and forth, whirring like a top until soon it was empty.

Fascinated by the whirring sound and the almost magical motion, the old woman, whose whole life was spent in household tasks, alone now in the half-dark room, burst into song like a young girl. Her clear, powerful voice filled the whole house. Margherita was annoyed; she thought that this betokened a lack of respect, and she knew that even her more easygoing father, who must by now be receiving the last patients of the day, felt the same way as she did. Once he had said to Maria Giuseppa:

"That kind of singing's for the great outdoors."

"I'm going to silence that madwoman," said Margherita. But Carmela grabbed her roughly.

"She's worked all day, and even now she's still working. If she wants to sing, let her do it."

When Francesco returned, the two sisters were in the drawing room.

"Well, what happened?" Margherita asked impatiently.

"Where's Father?" he retorted, with a stern glance. It would appear that Donna Luisa and he had quarreled.

206

"He's still in the consultation room, but he'll be up any moment."

Carmela answered her brother's severe, questioning eyes with her own keen "magic" eyes, as they were called in the family. Francesco cupped her chin in his hand, shook it as if she were a baby, and planted a rapid kiss on one cheek. Carmela smiled, pirouetted on her toes, fluffing out her skirt around her and repeated her sister's query: "What happened?"

With a mock dance step, he answered: "I'm going to the Military Academy of Modena. Zia Luisa Loru knows General Marini, and says she'll pay my tuition. Meanwhile," he added, tossing the silk purse he had brought back into the air, "she's given me this advance. In three years, I'll be a second lieutenant in the infantry or the cavalry, and in twenty years, a general."

As gracefully as a kitten, Carmela caught the purse and tucked it into her pocket. Margherita laughed, but Francesco assured them both that he wasn't joking; it was a serious proposition.

At this point, their father emerged from the consultation room and went, as he always did after a day's work, to change his clothes. The maids who had gone to the river with the washing came home, chattering, with bunches of mint and thyme atop the laundry baskets. Margherita drew herself up to her full height and preceded her sister and brother into the dining room. She'd have liked to slap Carmela for being so happy without reason. She, Margherita, was obsessed with etiquette, not with politeness or good manners, but with the proprieties. The presence of her father, however, dispelled her bad humor.

Don Tommaso, although not punctilious, found it relaxing and agreeably distracting to change his clothes for dinner. And this evening he was in a good mood. For no special reason, he felt satisfied by his day. His patients all seemed to be better, and an old goatherd had told him that the winter was going well; the goats were producing kids and had plenty of milk to give them. Don Tommaso poured and slowly sipped a glass of slightly bitter red wine, then asked his children, one by one, what they had been doing. When Margherita told him of Donna Luisa's proposal, he broke into loud laughter.

"No one but that madwoman could cook up such an idea," he commented, and the two girls echoed his laughter.

"I can't see myself parading with a cap on my head and shiny buttons on my jacket," put in Franceschino.

"She offered to provide the money, and she gave Franceschino two silver coins . . . ." said Carmela.

"For a miser like her, that's quite a sum!" said Don Tommaso with mock seriousness.

"I say that her offer to pay Franceschino's expenses is insulting," Margherita said dryly.

"There's something you ought to know," said Don Tommaso, filling Margherita's glass. "Some sixty years ago, the senator's grandfather robbed us of several acres of land at Sabbodus. The soil isn't fertile, but land is land. This was at the time of the Enclosure Law. Old man Loru took advantage of the confusion to go there with a dozen men and 'enclose' the land with a stone wall. . . ."

"And he got away with it?" said the young people all together.

"My father didn't know until it was too late. Once the wall was erected, there was nothing he could do; the wall had the law on its side. The Lorus, in order to quiet your grandfather's objections, promised some compensation. Actually, they never lived on that land. And Donna Luisa's proposal is obviously a sort of tardy amends. So, my dear Margherita, no insult was intended."

They laughed again, all together.

"I'd be almost willing to accept," the doctor went on, "if I didn't so dislike the idea of a military career."

"I have no heart for it myself," muttered Francesco.

"Nevertheless," put in Margherita, "in three years, and with a minimum of effort, Francesco would obtain a certain position. What will he do if he stays here? He isn't much of a student, and although he might take over the care of the estate he doesn't seem really enthusiastic about it."

"How do you know?" her brother retorted. "I love the country."

"As an army officer, you'd have a chance to travel, to see people, to visit big cities . . ."

"None of those things matter greatly to me," said the doctor. "But let's wait for more news from Donna Luisa and take our time about deciding."

For the moment, they spoke no more of Modena and the Military Academy. But if Don Tommaso appeared to attach little importance to Donna Luisa's proposal, in the days that followed it came back, at intervals, to his mind. His detached outlook allowed him to see things clearly, as if through a magnifying glass. Francesco, he reflected, had great vitality. His view of life was simple, even superficial, but if he did go into the military he could become a good officer and need not end up a rheumatic, soft-headed old general.

One evening as Don Tommaso was pacing up and down the courtyard and whistling through his teeth as he did when left to his own thoughts, Margherita called down to him from the window. Angelo Uras had been there, she said, asking that the doctor visit his house. Even as she gave him this message, Don Tommaso was on his way. He shouted to Margherita to bring him his little black bag, and set forth to make the call.

I'm not the one that's ill," said Angelo, feeling the doctor's quiet, penetrating look go straight through him.

"I know," said Don Tommaso, clapping him on the shoulder.

At that moment Sofia appeared at the kitchen door and asked him to enter.

"Are you the patient?" he asked, his gaze fixed on her worn face.

She touched her right side, and then stepped back to let him pass, smiling and extending her cold hand, which he held at length in his. For him diagnosis began with the handshake and the manner of greeting.

"Have you felt badly for long, Sofia Curreli?"

"A while. The pain is here, under my ribs, and sometimes in my stomach."

Don Tommaso drew near, examining her eyes closely.

"Sounds like liver. I'll have to see. Just go up to your room and get undressed."

"First may I make you a cup of coffee?"

Don Tommaso pointed, frowningly, to the stairs, and she docilely obeyed. Angelo stood beside him with a mute question in his eyes, but the doctor did not speak. A few minutes later, he started up to the second floor. Unhesitatingly he made for the room where Valentina had died three years before. He walked in, laid his bag down on the bedside table, and looked at Sofia.

"I have to examine you," he said, his lips barely moving amid his black beard. She nodded from the pillow where her head was buried. Her hair was thin and her face sallow. The doctor pulled down the blanket and uncovered her as she lay on a rough sheet in a white cotton nightgown with red trimming. He motioned to her to pull up the nightgown and again she obeyed. Her body was as inert as if it were dead.

"Sorry, if my hands are cold," said Don Tommaso, rubbing them together.

He remembered examining her years before and looked down contemplatively at the scrawny, aged body that had once been so shapely.

"Ahhhhh!" she moaned between clenched teeth, hunching her shoulders at his touch.

As the doctor's long, cold fingers pressed down and around her protruding ribs, she let out a shriller sound, almost a shout. Don Tommaso felt the swollen liver and, heedless of Sofia's lament, went on to search for the hard lumps that he had expected to find and did find, one of them larger than the others.

"Does it hurt a lot?" he asked, as gently as if she were a child. "Is this the place?"

Inwardly he was overcome by pity. He had known Sofia when she was young and strong, and now he knew that nothing could arrest the course of the disease that he strongly suspected. She said yes, and added that the pain was sharper at certain times of the day. She couldn't digest her food, she said, and had stomach pains and headaches, which she had never had before. With a stethoscope even colder than his fingers, he listened to her heart. She would have a long time to suffer; the heart was strong. He lingered over its regular, deep beat, that vital sound of life, life which with every beat grows shorter. Reluctantly he put this thought out of his mind, pulled the blanket up over her, and smiled. Sofia smiled, too, as she raised herself into a sitting position. On the bedside table there was a long-stemmed oil lamp that Don Tommaso remembered as having belonged to his brother Francesco. He sat down to write a prescription, while Sofia, with the blanket pulled up under her chin, looked at him with a skeptical smile, as if from beyond the barrier of disease and pain.

"Is there a medicine that can cure me, Don Tommaso?" she asked, her eyes still scrutinizing his face.

Angelo knocked at the door and came in without waiting to be invited. The doctor had been sitting with his pen upraised over a notebook; now he scribbled something, tore out the page, and handed it to Angelo.

"What is it?" asked Sofia, still waiting for a reply to her previous question.

"A pain-killer," he told her.

Sofia's eyes wandered about the room. Don Tommaso wrote another prescription.

"And this one?"

"Something to ease digestion. That way you won't have a headache."

Angelo accompanied Don Tommaso all the way to the gate. For the moment, said the doctor, he had nothing definite to tell, except that it was a matter of the liver. Sofia was to follow a diet and to avoid heavy work. The two men said good-by; Angelo went to the pharmacy and the doctor back home to his supper. That evening he had little appetite and gave curt, noncommittal replies when his daughters asked what was wrong with Sofia Curreli.

now the affliction that Sofia had carried for weeks and months within her, the dull pain that at moments became piercing and caused her to groan, was no longer a secret. When she felt pain, she reached for a glass of water and the drops of laudanum. She poured the laudanum onto a lump of sugar, which at once would start to crumble between her fingers. Dropping the sugar into the palm of her hand, she would lick it up with her tongue as eagerly as little Maria Christina sucked up cookie crumbs. As the days went by, Sofia gradually understood that her illness was irreversible, but she could not yet think of her death; death was still impersonal, general, the lot of all mankind that she was fated someday to share.

At Norbio and in neighboring villages, many people, especially women, died of "the disease that knows no mercy." Local doctors never called it by name, although the name was written in every medical textbook. Surgeons operated, but more often than not the result was to aggravate the disease and cause it to spread. Usually those so afflicted received no medical care. They knew their illness was incurable, accepted it as such, and never referred to it, as if it were a source of shame. In a short time, this mute acceptance set them apart from the rest of the community. Everyone else avoided the subject or mentioned it only in passing, to reassure the sufferer that he would recover. No one contradicted this view and by tacit agreement the sick and the rest of the world, especially their families, maintained it to the end.

Sofia had not yet arrived at the state of awareness that leads to renunciation. When the thought of death entered her mind, she ran to her room and threw herself on her knees beneath the holy pictures hanging over the bed. She prayed, not that she might never die, but that she might not die of "that" disease. Relatives, neighbors, friends, and acquaintances were all vaguely aware of a change in her and were as kindly as they had been to Valentina when they first saw that she was pregnant. She herself felt, at moments, as she had years before when she was carrying Angelo. She picked her way carefully along the streets, as she had then; she feared solitude. She had frequent attacks of nausea and felt perpetually tired. Nevertheless, she continued to rise early in the morning. She would take a sip of barley gruel, and set about her housework. Later she would make coffee, but, in strict compliance with the diet ordered by Don Tommaso, she resisted the temptation to cut a slice of bacon and fry an egg. Because of such vigilence, there were days when she felt relatively well, even entertained the illusion of being cured. On such days she might ask Angelo to drive her, along with Maria Christina, to Balanotti, where the fragrant country air always bolstered her sense of health, until a stab of pain recalled her to reality. At Balanotti, the memory of Valentina was still alive in the cottage she had considered her own and among the olive trees. Sofia and Angelo would call her to mind with the exchange of a look or a smile. One day Angelo even took his mother as far as Aletzi. Good peasant that she was, she had never had an eye for the beauties of nature, but in the Aletzi valley with its abundant trees and flowing streams, she was moved to sudden enthusiasm.

These excursions into the country did her more good than any medicine. They distracted her from the constant awareness of her illness and took her back to her youth, when her husband had hoisted her onto the back of his horse or into a wagon and she had joined the women day laborers who hired themselves out to hoe and weed. She had rejoiced, then, in her youth and strength, in her indifference to wind and weather when, clad only in a rough burlap garment, she had searched for and nibbled wild artichokes. Even now, when she felt able, she went into the fields to look for artichokes and other edible plants and grasses. Either she picked a whole bunch of them and took them home for lunch, or else she cleaned them on the spot with the pocketknife she always carried and ate them as they were, without salt. She offered them sometimes to Maria Christina, who chewed what she could and spat out the rest on the sly so she wouldn't hurt her grandmother's feelings.

"One day you'll poison yourself," Angelo warned her.

"On the contrary," she protested; "wild things have healing powers."

She taught Maria Christina to recognize wild artichokes and

edible thistles, to pick them without pricking herself, and to prepare them for eating. She taught her, also, the names of fruit trees, the month in which they flowered, and the season when they yielded fruit. Maria Christina was barely three years old, but she was quick to learn.

Don Tommaso came every now and then to pay an unsolicited call on Sofia. He was reassured that, even if there could be no improvement in her condition, the disease had not progressed. She had pains, but she endured them without making an excessive use of the laudanum he had prescribed. He was amazed by her docility and endurance and felt admiration for these qualities that he had not expected in a peasant woman. Neither his scientific training nor his rationalism offered an explanation for the physical and spiritual strength he saw in Sofia.

Almost a year after the doctor's first visit, Sofia's condition suddenly began to deteriorate. Her face turned chalky, her eyes yellowish, and her body rapidly wasted. Her pain became unbearable: throughout the night Angelo would hear her moaning. In spite of her courage, during the nighttime hours the fear of death besieged her. But she said nothing to Don Tommaso. Eventually it was Angelo who spoke to him.

The disease was running its inevitable course, said the doctor. If he wanted another opinion it was quite possible to call in Dr. Belgrano of Cagliari, a capable young man who had studied in Rome and Paris. "You can never tell . . ." he concluded.

"But is there any hope?" Angelo asked in a low voice.

Don Tommaso looked at him without saying a word, and Angelo had his answer.

"Then let's do all we can to save her from suffering."

Don Tommaso handed him a prescription. "Morphine," he said. "She'd better have it every evening before the pain gets too strong. I'll give her the injection myself or else send Efisina."

Angelo nodded, turning his head to conceal his tears, and walked hastily away.

At this very moment, Maria Christina came through the small side gate that gave onto the steep alley, dragging behind her, with a piece of old rope, a little wagon loaded with almonds. Like Dolores, she wore her hair in two braids behind her ears and, like Dolores, she tugged at them in moments of uncertainty. She was fond of the doctor, and greeted him with a mischievous smile. No longer tugging at her braids, but with her large, gray eyes fixed upon him she said: "Father's with Grandmother."

She spoke in a clear, correct manner in harmony with her delicate, regular features and graceful carriage. She appeared mature and serious for her years. When she smiled again, Don Tommaso was struck by her extraordinary resemblance to her mother. That death seemed to have occurred a long time ago, but after a rapid mental calculation he realized that only four years had gone by. Once more he felt the sense of guilt of that September morning. If the midwife had been more competent, or if he himself had been present, perhaps Valentina would still be alive, standing beside the little girl whose innocent stare so disturbed him. She turned halfway around, carefully dropped the rope on the cart, then childishly beckoned with one finger to Don Tommaso, ran toward the kitchen and up the stairs, where she stopped to look back. With long, unhurried steps, Don Tommaso followed, pausing at the foot of the stairs and throwing back his head, with half-closed eyes.

"Are you coming?" said the little girl, holding out her hand.

"You come with me," he answered, grasping her chubby hand between two fingers.

She came back down the stairs and followed him docilely, holding his hand and without any questions. He walked awkwardly, leaning toward the child. They went out through the gate and along the wall, he walking in the ditch, she on the edge, her left hand squeezing the fingers of his right, a hand she was not accustomed to but which inspired her with confidence. To walk along the street with a little girl was, to him, slightly embarrassing. He thought of picking her up and carrying her, but realized that this would be even more ridiculous. They arrived thus at the door set in the Fulgheri gate. With his left hand Don Tommaso turned the handle and pushed the door open; then he lifted Maria Christina over the threshold. His practiced hands felt the robust build of her small-boned body. As soon as he set her down she once more grasped his middle and fore-fingers. She had never set foot in this house, but it was very much like the others she knew. The courtyard was as large as her own and the ground was covered with a layer of sand, which made a crunching sound under her shoes. The doors and windows of the ground floor opened onto a porch, and at the entrance to the kitchen stood Efisina, the maid-servant whom everyone called "the doctor girl," because she helped Don Tommaso in the consultation room and went out to give injections. Efisina was sixteen years old. She had a thin, brown, almost Arabic face whose outstanding feature was the perfect arch of the eyebrows over her big, dark eyes.

Now she ran to meet Maria Christina, and the little girl threw her arms around her neck. Except when Efisina was in an un-usual hurry, they always greeted each other this way. After she had put the child down, Maria Christina, without the least self-consciousness, made her way into the dining room, where the table was already set. Here she stopped and looked around her. Margherita was sitting near to the table and Carmela was stand-ing behind her. They were reading a letter. Maria Christina liked Carmela but not Margherita. She had been told that she should call her "Donna," but, instead, she said "Zia." Carmela smiled and beckoned to her to come closer. Margherita merely said "Good evening," hardly raising her eyes.

Maria Christina couldn't know that she had arrived at an inopportune moment. She only knew she felt uncomfortable and her face took on a serious and watchful expression. Instead of responding to Carmela's invitation, she stood her ground. Carmela came over and lifted her up in her arms, pretending to make a great effort.

"What a big girl!" she exclaimed, puffing up her pink cheeks.

Maria Christina's eyes were like those of her Aunt Olivia, and she had tiny, very white teeth. Now she pretended to bite Carmela's neck, and laughed, shaking her two braids, one of them fastened with a green ribbon, one with a red, in order to stave off the evil eye.

Margherita was annoyed to have been called "Zia" and by the very fact that Maria Christina had come into the dining room instead of staying in the kitchen. She didn't like the child, although she had never had anything against Sofia Curreli or Angelo in spite of her uncle's will. Mother and son had behaved well when they voluntarily gave up most of the land which the eccentric old man had left to them. But little Maria Christina was a different story. She didn't like the knowing look in her eyes or the seriousness that was beyond her years. Just then a man's footsteps were heard on the porch steps.

"May I come in?" said Angelo's voice just before he appeared, bowing with his cap in hand, at the door.

"Yes, come in!" said Margherita in a lively and almost happy voice, in contrast with her stiffness of the few minutes before. Maria Christina flew from Carmela's arms to her father.

"I saw her from a distance with Don Tommaso," Angelo explained. "I've come to fetch her."

"Sit down, Angelo Uras," said Margherita, pushing a chair in his direction.

"I don't want to be in the way," he answered, glancing at the table, which was already set for dinner. "There's something I must give the doctor." And he held out a parcel containing the vials he had just bought from the pharmacist.

"Do sit down," Margherita repeated, once more pushing the chair toward him. "My father will be here soon."

Angelo sat down, laying his cap on his knees. Margherita stared unabashedly at his profile while Carmela put long-stemmed crystal glasses on the table, taking them one by one from the sideboard and polishing them with a napkin. Carmela filled one of the glasses and held it out to Angelo, who got up to take it, looking back at Margherita. There was a smile in Margherita's eyes.

Angelo was one of the few common people that Margherita could tolerate. She liked his honest face and the grace of his ways, unusual in a peasant. Now she watched him drink, observing his Adam's apple as it moved up and down in the act of swallowing, his short nose, and sparse mustache. She looked at him appreciatively and with a certain pleasure which she did not stop to analyze.

All her life long, Sofia had gone late to bed and risen early. After supper, when the others went off to their rooms, she lingered to tidy the kitchen or to mend the clothes of her men: her father's, her husband's, and, finally, her son's.

When Angelo was a child, she used to sit beside her bed, working by the light of an oil lamp until her eyes smarted. Then she said evening prayers and held a sort of dialogue with herself, in which she drew up the accounts of the day just past and prepared for the day to come. It was very late by the time she finally went to bed. She extinguished the oil lamp outside the room and got undressed by the light of a candle. In those years, her hours of sleep were few.

Now, she had to go to bed early, as soon as Efisina had given her the injection. She would be overcome by drowsiness even before Maria Rosario tucked in Maria Christina. The little girl knew that her grandmother was ill, but she had no idea of the nature of the disease or its consequences. And yet at times she perceived the sad look in the eyes of her father and her young aunts and noticed the silence with which the subject of the illness was surrounded. Even her encounters with Efisina were not as gay as they once had been. The girl came at the same hour every day, but she barely said hello and, as soon as she had given the injection, she hurried away, seldom stopping to so much as caress Maria Christina. The little girl accepted this change just as she accepted all the limitations imposed by her grandmother's condition: not to make a noise, to talk in a low voice, not to shout out the window to her aunts, to say prayers whose meaning she didn't understand.

Before the injections had begun, her grandmother had sat at the supper table with her father and herself, and supper had been fun. Now Maria Christina had to act more properly; she could no longer wriggle or giggle, but had to behave like a big girl. Loving her grandmother as she did, she slipped away from the table and ran upstairs to hold and pat the old woman's hand. Sofia appreciated this affection and responded to it. Eventually she would shut her eyes, pretending to be asleep, and the little girl would steal away, holding her breath. When left alone,

Sofia blew out the lamp and lost herself in her thoughts, which ranged back to faraway events of her childhood and forward to the day of her death. She tried to imagine what the house would be like without her, and smiled, to herself, almost without apprehension, in the darkness. She was calm and resigned, and allowed herself to drift into sleep just as she imagined she would drift into death. Sometimes she awakened during the night when Maria Christina slipped into her bed against orders. Sofia felt her smooth, cold feet, as once she had felt Angelo's, and the sensation was reassuring. When the light of dawn filtered through the shutters, she could not resist getting up. Early in the morning she felt stronger and, in the cool air of the courtyard, where she went to fetch wood for the kitchen fire, she could almost believe that everything was just as it had been before. Maria Rosario always got up later, and so Sofia still had the pleasure of lighting the stove.

Angelo, too, got up early. One morning toward the end of the winter, he rose even earlier than usual and threw open the bedroom window. Bare to the waist, he lathered his face and shaved, using the windowpane for a mirror. He was wide awake in the morning air, which was slightly humid, like that of Aletzi, and impregnated with the same mingled odors of young trees, fresh greenery, and smoke. The logging was going well, but his enjoyment of the harmony of everything around him was interrupted by the thought of his mother. He had asked Don Tommaso to call in Dr. Belgrano, but the specialist had only confirmed the diagnosis and approved the prescription of morphine. Moreover, he had said, quite definitely, that Sofia had only a few more months to live. "Until autumn," Angelo thought to himself, remembering that his mother herself always said that everything important happened in September. Valentina had died in that month, and now he foresaw another death, one that would once more leave him alone, more alone than before. Lingering on these dismal thoughts, he was acutely aware that the nature around him was beautiful, harmonious, and . . . indifferent. He dried himself, put on a rough, collarless cotton shirt and corduroy jacket, and went down to the ground floor, where he was sure of finding Sofia. As he passed in front of Maria Rosario's door, he heard her snoring. He was tempted to awaken her, but thought better of it. He wanted to be alone with his mother.

On the stairs he smelled the fragrance of freshly made coffee. In the kitchen, Sofia drew him to her and stood on tiptoe to plant the usual kiss on the vein in his forehead. Then she poured a cup of steaming coffee, which he drank very slowly from the saucer. Sofia shrugged her shoulders and smiled at this unconventional gesture.

"Do you know something?" she said, looking up at him from under half-closed eyelids. "I had a dream, and I want to tell it to you. . . ."

"Yes, do, *Mammai*," said Angelo sitting down beside her and putting his arm around her waist. "Was it a good dream or a bad one?"

"Bad, my boy. I saw a big heap of gold, and bags full of coins."

"Well, what's bad about that?" he asked with surprise.

"Don't you know what it means to dream about gold? It means just the opposite—poverty. . . . But," she hastened to add, "dreams don't really mean anything."

"So it seems," said Angelo, "because, contrary to your dream, my business is going well. The wood and charcoal of Aletzi have yielded more than I expected, and there are still plenty of trees to be cut. If things go on this way until the end of the year, I'll have almost enough money to pay off my debt. That's much sooner than I had hoped."

There was a note of happiness in his voice, which belied the anxiety he felt. Sofia understood his satisfaction and asked, as gaily as she could: "What about the wild olives?"

"Three thousand have been grafted over the last few years. This spring we'll graft more. All the credit belongs to Renato. If things continue to go well, Aletzi will be one huge olive grove. Furthermore, I'm going to plant almond trees, and then poplars and eucalyptus by the canals in the valley. And I'll build three houses . . ."

"By God's will," murmured Sofia. "Here's hoping no one

takes Aletzi from us!" She used the word "us" as if she had no notion of what was to come.

"And who could take it?" asked Angelo, leaning his head on her shoulder.

"Oh, one of the sharks here in our own village, or some sharper from outside. One has arrived just recently, the new pharmacist, Michele Tropea. They say he has piles of money."

"I've seen him on the square," said Angelo, "and he was wearing patched trousers. In any case, I shan't let go of Aletzi."

"People are bad, my boy. Promise you won't do anything to make me worry."

Angelo was happy to hear her speak of a worry projected into the far future. It gave him a sudden, absurd hope, one which, for a second, dispelled the overhanging nightmare of death. He sat there, dreamily, while Sofia busied herself about the house.

Outside there was a bright sun.

At the Fulgheris' there was much talk about Francesco and the Military Academy at Modena. Senator Loru did everything he could to bring the doctor around. He was more persuasive than his wife, perhaps because he was more dispassionate and, indeed, spoke rather ironically of the military. Army officers in Italy, he maintained, did not form a caste as they did in Germany; in fact, they differed very little from civilians of a certain social standing. Soldiering was a profession like any other and the Military Academy was less expensive than the university. In three years Francesco would be a second lieutenant. Moreover, he would have been educated in an atmosphere much healthier than that of a big North Italian city. Chiefly he would be away from Norbio and no longer "in the company of peasants and cowherds." He would be able to make a career for himself and "see a bit of the world" in the bargain.

The doctor was almost convinced, yet he wanted Francesco himself to decide, and the boy seemed to have no strong opinion one way or the other. As for the sisters, they took opposite views. Carmela worried about Francesco's being far away and in danger in case of war; Margherita took the side of the Lorus and lost no opportunity, when she was alone with her brother, of defending it. One day she spoke to him more freely and at greater length than ever before. She envied his chance to go to the mainland and to travel, to see the Italy they had heard and read so much about, and she couldn't see why he apparently preferred to stay in Norbio. Francesco made objections, but Margherita's words stirred his imagination and, almost without realizing it, he decided that she was right. The next time the Military Academy was discussed, he declared that, if the family agreed, he was quite ready to go. Don Tommaso accepted the decision in his usual calm way. He immediately consulted the senator and his wife and took the steps necessary to secure Francesco's admission to the Academy. Then he dispatched him to board in the house of Donna Veronica Crespi at Cagliari to be tutored by Father Fortina and prepared for the entrance examinations.

Michele Tropea, the new pharmacist, didn't appear as rich as rumor bespoke. The purchase of the pharmacy evidently left him without funds. He came, so people said, from a village in the Marmilla region, where another pharmacy, which he had acquired with great difficulty after winning his university degree, had burned to the ground. He was still a young man, tall and ruddy-faced, with a mop of reddish hair that seemed to have been singed in the fire and the blue eyes of a northerner, although he was said to be a Neapolitan. He was also said to have a wife who had tired of village life and had gone back to Naples. In Norbio he made his home in the rear of the pharmacy in order, he said, to be ready to answer any call, even night calls, for which, although such a thing had never been done before, he charged an extra ten percent, even to the very poor. He wore a collar and tie, but his suits were so faded and worn as to seem second-hand. Because of his obvious poverty, or "lack of cash" as he explained it to anyone who cared to listen, he could not extend credit to the peasants, who were used to paying their bills only after the harvest was in. Anyone who had the misfortune to fall ill and need medicine had to turn to the two women moneylenders, Potenzia Moro and Attilia Pontilla, who demanded as much as two hundred percent interest on their loans.

Potenzia and Attilia were reputed to be receivers of the money extorted by highway robbers; in their cellar, so rumor had it, there were sacks of gold, silver, and copper coins. Up until a few years before, every village of the Parte d'Ispi region had had its Granary or Grain Depository, where even the poorest peasants could obtain seed on credit, at a very low rate of interest. After the forced creation of private property consequent upon the law of enclosure, and the ensuing decadence of the Grain Depositories, the peasants could only turn to the moneylenders who flourished all over the Island, especially after the bank crisis. Attilia and Potenzia were also *brujas,* that is, witches or sorceresses, a profitable occupation in a backward and superstitious country. They dealt in spells and love potions, gave advice, and predicted future events. They seemed to be informed before anyone else of everything that went on, including the sheep-snatching expeditions that Luca Cubeddu and his companions continued to conduct in areas near and far. In short, Attilia and Potenzia were faithful repositories of all the secrets of Norbio, and were keenly aware that their reputation for trustworthiness and their prestige depended on silence and discretion.

After Michele Tropea had settled into the rear of the pharmacy, he set about improving his appearance: he bought shirts, a suit, and a new pair of shoes, and then made a ceremonial call on every one of the local notables. No pharmacist had made such a gesture before and the recipients—such as old Antioco Cadoni, Professor Todde, and Senator Loru—were flattered. Claudina, the pharmacist's servant-girl, would appear first, asking what day and hour might be most convenient for the proposed call and distributing a calling card—something quite new—with the printed legend: *Michele Tropea, Doctor of Chemistry and Law, Pharmacist.* Why he had a law degree, nobody knew.

Among the persons on whom he called were the moneylenders Attilia Pontilla and Potenzia Moro; indeed, they were the only ones with whom he became friendly, particularly Potenzia. Heedless of the inevitable gossip, he went frequently to her house. He had a definite purpose, which was to discover the ancient recipe of the powerful liquor known locally as *filuferru*. From time immemorial this liquor had been produced in Norbio; every house had its copper still. At one time the finished product had been sold at Cagliari, and had been exorbitantly taxed. But word had gotten around that it was responsible for stomach upsets. Don Salvatore Cappai, the health commissioner, had dispatched experts to check on every single still in the village, and many were seized because they were not up to standard. From then on, *filuferru* was produced clandestinely. At Norbio it was drunk more frequently than wine because everyone was convinced of its medicinal qualities. It was used to disinfect wounds and taken as a preventive of common colds and malaria. When it was poured over a baby's biscuit, the baby stopped crying and slept for hours in his reed cradle. Michele Tropea was determined to learn the formula and to obtain the money for manufacturing it.

Potenzia, in spite of her years of loose living, still had a certain fascination. At first glance, her bulk made it seem unlikely that any man would want to make love to her, but rumor had it that in an intimate relationship she became quite transformed, that she became beautiful and irresistible. During one of his visits, Michele Tropea threw his arms around her and kissed her upon the lips. Potenzia pushed him roughly away and leaped to her feet, overturning the small table with the lamp, tray, carafe of *filuferru,* and liqueur glasses. For a moment, they wrestled. Although she was almost his height and weight, Michele had not dreamed she could be so strong. Her resistance excited him. He was seized by intense desire for her and fought to overpower her. Holding her very tightly, he threw her off balance. Together they tumbled up against the wall onto a couch, whose sheepskin-covered mattress was stuffed with straw. Potenzia cried out; she kicked with all her might, to no avail; at last, groaning, she surrendered. They made love in the dark, and in the dark that miracle Michele had laughed to hear of actually came true: the aging Amazon became as beautiful and graceful as a young woman. Michele was half terrified by her tenderness when, in responding to his desire, she moved beneath him. Thus they sealed the alliance that was to bind them together until death.

Soon after, Michele Tropea obtained the loan and began, quite legally, to manufacture the famous *Acqua Tropeana* that made his name and that of Norbio famous the world over. He gave employment to many people and, through their hard work and his own wiliness, became a rich man.

Angelo was concerned with everything that affected the life of Norbio, and therefore he closely watched the pharmacist's traffickings, his energy and enterprise. Such a man, he concluded, would bring many changes to the village, changes probably for the better.

Sofia, although she rarely left her bed, kept up with all that was going on and the gossip about it. Maria Rosario or Efisina brought her the latest news, and sometimes Angelo sat down beside her and thought out loud. When Comare Verdiana came to see her, she was surprised to find her so well informed. In her old age Verdiana had become tiresome, and sometimes Sofia fell asleep during her chatter. One day Verdiana said that people were talking about the possibility of a marriage between Angelo and Donna Margherita. Sofia shrugged her shoulders.

"That's sheer madness!" she exclaimed, closing her eyes and refusing to listen to anything further.

But behind her closed eyes she reflected. On second thought, it might not be madness, after all; indeed, it would make good sense for Angelo to remarry. Margherita Fulgheri, thorny as she was, was not the ideal wife but, on the other hand, she could bring him a sizable dowry and eventually she might come to care for his little daughter. The main thing was for him to escape from his solitude. As a matter of fact, people *were* talking, and Verdiana had not made up her story. Village people are always planning and plotting marriages. When two young people seem to be "suited to each other," they are discussed, however little is known of their intentions, and sometimes rumor turns into reality. In this case, the talk was justified by the friendliness which existed between the two families in spite of the difference of class, by the absence of any other suitor for the hand of Margherita, and by the necessity, made more obvious by Sofia's illness, of finding a wife for Angelo and a mother for little Maria Christina. Neighbors' attentive eyes could not fail to detect a certain congeniality between the two young people, even if the only outward signs were that Angelo went often to Margherita's house and Margherita, who formerly never went anywhere, made frequent visits to the house of Angelo and Sofia. Angelo occasionally asked Margherita to ride with him into the countryside, and she was seen mounted behind him on his new horse as it trotted through the village. They were a striking couple.

When Angelo's friend, Antioco Cadoni, broached the idea, Angelo said that because he was a peasant and the son of a peasant it was quite beyond him. And yet this "absurd" idea had rooted itself in his subconscious, although he couldn't have said how it had got there. He remembered quite clearly his decision to marry Valentina. With his own eyes, he had seen Valentina grow up; he had fallen in love with her and felt from the start that she was an integral part of his life. That part had subsequently died with her. He couldn't claim to be in love with Margherita, or else his feeling for her was love of a very different kind. But something in her attracted him and appealed to his imagination: the slender strong body, the proud look that sometimes softened, the long, aristocratic fingers, and a certain frailty that seemed to call for his protection.

Margherita had never thought about love; she knew that it existed, but she considered herself immune. The affection of her father, sister, and brother was all that she needed. "Love" was connected, in her mind, with the idea of sin, with animals, with the common people and with the top-rank nobility, say the king and queen, who had to submit to it in order to preserve the dynasty. Amid this confusion of notions and feelings, she had come to have a special liking for Angelo, a man of the people, but one whom she set above his fellows. She didn't seek him out, but she fell into the habit of seeing him and missed him if he didn't have time to call. She mounted behind him on his horse, like a wife or a fiancée, and rode from Sant'Antonio to Seddanus with her slender arms around his waist.

Sitting on the soft wool saddlecloth, cradled by the horse's gentle gait and clinging to Angelo, she felt the warmth of his body and smelled his masculine odor, a composite of leather, tobacco, and woodland grass. Leaning her head against his shoulder, she discovered a happiness she had never known before. People waved to them as they rode by, with a mixture of respect and affectionate approval. Margherita had never spoken with the peasants or gone into their houses, and she had never dreamed that everything could be so easy and even pleasant.

They talked about simple things—sowing and reaping, forests and pastures—and they had, or so it seemed, no secrets from each other. With Angelo, Margherita discovered an unsuspected and beautiful side of the world and, at the same time, she discovered herself. She was no longer lonely; there were moments when she felt protected, safe, in harmony with creation, happy to live and to accept the fate that God had willed for her, in this house and this village, under this sky, where the seasons followed fast upon one another, impelled by the northwest or the southerly wind.

Had she asked herself the question, Sofia could not have told whether this was a day out of her life or the whole of her life, passing through her mind with the slowness of all the years. But of course she didn't ask. The effectiveness of the morphine had worn off, and letting her thoughts wander, and thinking of the dead, she dropped off to sleep. Toward morning she remembered that she had not prayed for Valentina or for Zio Raimondo Collu and, folding her hands, she murmured a prayer for them as the light of dawn filtered into the room. While she prayed, she saw in her imagination a happy and healthy Valentina, in her dove-gray dress and light shawl, coming to meet her through the tall grass of the sheepfold when they had ridden there one day on Zurito. In the distance, at the edge of the thicket, Zio Raimondo was turning over the earth with a short-handled hoe. Overhead, larks were singing.

As usual, the prayers gave her peace of mind. The tops of the poplar trees stood out vividly beyond the window. Now bright light flooded the room. Sofia closed her eyes, but quickly reopened them, fearful of dying in her sleep. She wanted death to find her wide awake. She was weak, and she felt that the time left to her was a great burden from which she longed to be free. And yet she was afraid.

When Angelo came into the room, she summoned up the strength to greet him with a smile. She wanted to speak, but managed only an incomprehensible whisper and a deep sigh. With an expression of powerlessness and despair, he stroked her hand. His mother didn't accept death, as he well knew. Three days earlier, she had asked for and received Extreme Unction, but not in a spirit of resignation. The young priest had been at a loss for words. He, Angelo, would have known what to say, and he was intent upon helping her now. It was not the time to challenge her faith or to demand resignation, but to help her to face death with the same common sense with which she had faced life. This was the lesson which she herself had taught him.

All in the village knew that the priest had been summoned. Many came to say farewell to Sofia. On this morning, word spread quickly. Soon her room was filled with people. Present were the Manno girls, including Olivia, who had long since married Antioco Cadoni and was expecting her second child, Adelaide Collu, Comare Verdiana, and Margherita Fulgheri. Angelo wiped the perspiration from his mother's brow with his handkerchief, then he went to open the window. Sofia was breathing heavily. Through half-closed eyes, she surveyed the people thronging the room and, at the same time, watched Angelo and listened to what he was saying.

"There's too much of a crowd!" he exclaimed, but nobody seemed to hear.

When Sofia realized that he was trying to empty the room, she tugged at his hand until he bent over.

"Let them stay," she managed to whisper.

Their presence did not in the least annoy her; indeed, it was only when she saw their faces that she felt herself to be still alive. Looking around, she saw them all standing there, as if they were waiting for something to happen; they talked to one another in muffled tones; to her, they appeared to be chewing pumpkin or sunflower seeds. She turned her head on the pillow and gave voice to a monotonous lament, as rhythmical as the song of a cuckoo. Suddenly the gaunt figure of Don Tommaso Fulgheri appeared in the doorway. He understood at a glance that Sofia was dying even if, in spite of the heavy doses of morphine, her heart was still beating strongly. She moaned, stiffening her body and clenching her teeth with pain. The usual dose of morphine would have been ineffective, and he ordered one considerably stronger. It could do not harm, because in all probability she would not survive the day.

Efisina glided silently into the room, put the tray down on the chest of drawers, and prepared the injection. Sofia's eyes were closed and her hands hung over the folded-back sheet. When she heard the familiar breakage of the vial, she imagined the deft gesture with which Efisina poured the yellowish liquid into the syringe. Now the girl laid the readied syringe on the tray and went to close the window. Sofia knew exactly what was going on around her. This was the first time that Efisina had given her an injection in broad daylight. Heretofore, in her mind, morphine had been linked to the dark of night and sleep. Outside the windows, the tops of the poplar trees seemed now to be pale green, but every leaf stood out clearly and in detail. The injection took effect, the pain diminished, sleepiness overcame her, and the moans that had followed the rhythm of her breathing subsided. When Angelo saw that she had fallen asleep, he motioned to the others that they should go away. Sofia was lying flat on her back and he sat down near the head of the bed. Looking at her, he found it hard to believe what the doctor had just said. Her lips moved in her sleep, as if she were praying, and her eyelids fluttered over the cavities of her eyes, which had tiny wrinkles all around them. He knelt down on the bedside carpet and instinctively began to pray, noting with dismay that he was saying the prayers for the dead. *Desine fata Deum flecti sperare precando, Hope not by prayer to alter the course of fate . . .* these words which he remembered from school, had rung for the last three days in his head and poisoned his thoughts. No, he could not pray.

He got up, went down to the ground floor, and told Maria Rosario to keep everything as quiet as she could. She took special care in putting down the pot which she was drying, but a heavy wagon rolled noisily on the Via Roma. There was no way of preventing wagons from passing by. Angelo lit a cigarette and stood leaning against the post of the open door. The breeze carried the smoke away. In spite of himself, he was reassured by the fact that his mother was sleeping, and he concentrated his attention on the immediate problem—how to keep the passing wagons from disturbing her sleep—as if her life depended on its solution. He couldn't force the wagoners to take another route, although for a moment he thought of putting up a sign requesting them to do so. Not all of them knew how to read, and even if the sign did cause them to stop it wouldn't be easy to explain in a few words the necessity of silence. Moreover, he couldn't bear to announce publicly that his mother was dying. He lit another cigarette, inhaling the smoke deeply before he blew it out to be carried away by the breeze. A dozen or so wagons had gone by while he was standing there, and each one had made him feel as if he were about to be run down. All of a sudden he had an idea. He threw away his cigarette, went into the courtyard, and called Maria Rosario. Behind the woodshed there were great piles of straw and hay. In obedience to his orders, Maria Rosario took a fork and joined him in tossing straw and hay over the wall. Soon they had exhausted half of the supply, after which they went, sweating, to spread it out over the street in such a way as to form a layer that would muffle the creak of the wagon wheels.

When the wagons came to the unexpected carpet of straw and hay, the drivers stopped short and stared. Maria Rosario was there to explain: "My mistress is very, very ill, and she needs to sleep," adding under her breath: "she's dying . . ." The wagoners looked commiseratingly at the house and drove by slowly, without shouting or cracking their whips. The improvised carpet was more effective than Angelo had imagined in absorbing the sound of the wheels and also of the horses' hoofbeats. The house was surrounded by silence, and Sofia slept on. She woke up, briefly, at intervals, then relapsed into sleep, carrying with her a perception of silence, in which fragmentary memories floated.

Toward evening Don Tommaso came back, and the room filled up again with people. The doctor sent them away and opened the window. Sofia felt the fresh air and opened her eyes. Angelo bent over to ask if it bothered her, and she made repeated signs that it didn't. She wanted to say that people didn't bother her either, that at this moment she wished for nothing more than fresh air and people together. She dimly realized that there was little time left and that without familiar faces around her these last moments were more than ever grim. This was what she wanted to say, but she knew that she would never succeed. It was difficult to dredge up the words from her memory and, before they reached the surface, they were once more submerged, and her swarming thoughts were left unexpressed in the silence. Angelo saw her throat quiver, her dry lips and face contract like a burning leaf. Suddenly her whole body shuddered and then, little by little, every sign of suffering disappeared. A long moment went by before her face, restored to its original beauty, was composed and still.

Angelo was left alone with his little girl and Maria Rosario. After Maria Christina came back from spending several days with her aunts, she wanted to sleep in the same room as her father. Angelo indulged her, and also took her with him around the village and into the countryside. She was a sensible child and gave no one any trouble. By now she was going to school and kept her books and notebooks in order according to her own very personal tastes. She enjoyed writing in some notebooks; others she neglected and even allowed to become spotted and dirty. But Angelo brooded over her being too much alone; she needed a mother and brothers and sisters and a house with some life in it. During the long afternoons of that cold, dark winter, she spent hours watching the donkey turn the millstone. When her father came home, she ran to meet him; he lifted her high in his arms and made her laugh; sometimes he even combed her hair. Occasionally they took long walks together; she trotted along beside him, never stumbling or complaining that she was tired.

The winter dragged monotonously by. Spring and summer followed, new little wild ponies galloped in the highlands, and there was an abundance of wheat. It was the custom, when the wheat was harvested, for the landowner to give a supper in the fields. This year Don Tommaso Fulgheri wanted Angelo as well as his own daughters to be present, and young Francesco came from Modena expressly for the occasion.

Margherita and Carmela sat in Angelo's cabriolet, along with Maria Christina, while Don Tommaso and Francesco rode their horses, sometimes before and sometimes behind them. Carmela would have preferred to go with the group of laughing servants, and when her sister wouldn't hear of it, she planned a joking revenge. When they were only a mile or so away from the threshing-ground, she let the wind blow her straw hat away. She jumped out of the cabriolet to retrieve it, then signaled to her father to draw his horse up to a guardrail from which she mounted behind him. Maria Christina asked to ride with Francesco, and had her wish. Carmela had planned it just this way, so that Margherita and Angelo would arrive, like husband and wife, together. The peasant women, red-faced and perspiring, surrounded the cabriolet and the men shot their guns into the air in celebration. Margherita was furious, but she realized that this was not the time to show it. Without joining in the general gaiety she made herself agreeable, vowing to get even with her sister later. Angelo ate and drank heartily and responded to the toasts, but it was obvious that his thoughts were far away.

"I'm afraid you're not too happy, Angelo Uras."

"I'm happy sitting here beside you, Donna Margherita, but

I'm thinking that, when dinner is over, I must return to my empty house and you go back to yours, where, God be praised, you are not alone."

Carmela, sitting nearby with a bunch of poppies thrust into her hair, shot a bright-eyed, teasing look at the two of them.

"If you're alone," Margherita whispered into Angelo's ear, "you have only yourself to blame."

Angelo started, and stared at her in a way that seemed to Margherita half questioning, half reproachful.

"You're too young to stay a widower," she added, looking away.

Angelo slowly emptied his glass while the women passed around hard candies made of burnt sugar and almonds. The supper was finished, but the festivities went on, even while Don Tommaso prepared to go home, preferring to travel by daylight than to linger until dark at the merry-making of the threshing-ground. Carmela leaped onto her father's horse, and Maria Christina hopefully grasped the hand of Francesco.

The horses trotted briskly along, anxious to return to their cool stalls. Angelo and Margherita were silent, but the jolting of the cabriolet threw them against each other. The silence was embarrassing, and Angelo thought it must be his fault. It was stupid not to find a word to say.

"So you think I ought to remarry," he said abruptly.

"Yes, I do," said Margherita, with her customary gesture of smoothing her skirt over her knees.

Angelo felt her shoulder against his and tried to analyze the feelings and imaginings into which he had fallen. When he spoke, it was from the heart.

"If I were to remarry," he said, without turning his head, "the wife I'd wish for would be you."

Margherita did not pull her shoulder away, but Angelo felt it quiver. He had said what he had to say forthrightly and without hesitation and now he waited patiently for an answer. Margherita gave a deep sigh and once more smoothed the raw-silk skirt over her thin knees.

"There are lots of girls better than me," she murmured, her lips barely moving.

233

This answer might have seemed evasive or hypocritical, but her tone of voice was pathetically sincere.

"I know none better than you," said Angelo decisively.

"Come, come!" she said with a laugh, moving very slightly away. The carriage hit a bump in the road throwing her back against him.

"I realize there's no hope," Angelo continued, lighting a cigarette in order to maintain his nonchalance.

"If that's what you think, Angelo Uras," Margherita said calmly, "you're mistaken. If it's true that you want to marry me, I'll take you at your word."

Angelo's cheeks felt suddenly hot. He wasn't in love, and yet these last words made him feel exceedingly happy.

"But what will your family say?"

"First they have to be told, that is, if you mean what you said. But it's a matter between the two of us, isn't it? Think it over before you make any commitment."

If she had been another girl, Angelo would have taken her into his arms. But he realized that with her this wasn't the thing to do.

"I do mean it," he said, with emotion in his voice. "I'm ready to be married tomorrow."

"Tomorrow's too soon, but if you agree I see no reason for a long engagement."

The horse, dark with sweat, had slowed down to a walk. Angelo urged him on, although by now they had almost reached their destination. With little thought, as he now realized, Angelo had made a very important decision. Certainly he wasn't as happy as the first time he had kissed Valentina, but he was not unhappy either. He jumped down from the cabriolet and helped Margherita to follow. While he held her arm she smiled, and he felt the frailty of her body.

"You'll let me know, then, when I can come speak to your father. . . ."

"Whenever you like . . . later this evening or tomorrow. . . ." She smiled again, nodded in farewell, and walked away, grasping the brim of her big straw hat in one hand.

No, he would not withdraw his suit, he decided as he watched her leave. The horse, surprised to have been left in the middle of the street, turned his head and whinnied. Angelo picked up the reins, which had fallen to the ground, threw them up over the front of the cabriolet, and walked the horse home. When he had opened the gate, Maria Christina ran to meet him and he joyfully hugged her. A sudden doubt crossed his mind: what if Margherita were not a good stepmother to his child? She seemed to suffer from the isolation which her haughtiness and shyness had created around her. But he shook his head and rid himself of any apprehension. For himself, he hoped to find not happiness but a more settled way of life.

The Fulgheris proved to be not only approving but pleased. In spite of her dowry, they had had little hope that Margherita would marry, and now, from one day to the next, without any idle chatter, she had found a husband. They didn't hold it against him that he was a widower and had a little girl, for one of their secret fears had been that Margherita was too delicate ever to have any children. They voiced no such worry and, indeed, appeared delighted, especially Carmela and Francesco.

"If you are married at Christmas," said Francesco, "I can come to the wedding."

"It won't be at Christmas," Angelo said abruptly.

Carmela tugged at her brother's sleeve.

"Don't insist," she told him. And later she whispered into his ear: "Don't you remember that Angelo was married the first time at Christmas?" And when Francesco still didn't get the point she said out loud: "You men are such idiots!"

She didn't really think her brother was stupid; like other men, he was dreamy, not quick-witted and crafty like a woman. Men would do great things, in her opinion, if they had a pinch of women's adroitness. She simply adored Francesco and only wished he weren't her brother so that she could have him for a husband. And she wondered how in the world Margherita had made a "catch" of Angelo Uras who, as men go, was nobody's fool.

Francesco had done brilliantly on the entrance examinations to the Military Academy the autumn before. Within a short time, he had been assigned to a special tutor and had won the right to wear a patch with the royal initials on his jacket which, with its double row of silver buttons, was extremely becoming. He now put on his uniform, much to his sisters' delight, in preparation for a call on Senator Loru. The senator embraced him in front of everybody, and Donna Luisa looked him up and down and then had him escort her to church, on foot, so as to show him off to everyone on the Via Roma and the Piazza Frontera.

Senator Loru slipped his arm into that of Don Tommaso Fulgheri and, as a man of the world, told him that "we Italians keep an army not to make war but to please the women."

That same morning Don Tommaso announced Margherita's engagement to Angelo Uras, and the Lorus conveyed their congratulations and approval. The senator declared that Angelo belonged to "a class that is on its way up." In the Fulgheri house, there was gaiety due to Margherita's engagement and Francesco's arrival. Francesco talked continually about Modena, the military academy, his teachers, classmates, scholastic successes, and, above all, about the pretty, free-and-easy girls he met when he was able to go around the city. Margherita's back stiffened; she looked him straight in the eye and raised an admonishing finger: "Mind you behave like a gentleman!"

Francesco met her gaze, laid his right hand on his heart, and, bowing over his empty plate, said with a half-serious, half-comical air: "I promise!"

A few days later, Francesco returned to his school. His luggage was loaded down with a picnic basket, a ritual gift that served to prolong the farewells.

The departure was painful. The roll of the ship, the noise of the engines, the smell of oil, all combined to make him queasy. He lay awake in his berth, listening to the sounds from the bowels of the ship, the stifled ring of the bells, and the snores of his fellow-travelers. Alone and with the nighttime crossing just begun, he felt despondent, sorry for himself and his people and his Island, for the familiar little world from which every minute he was drawing farther away. His countrymen—shepherds and peasants—were sleeping on the deck or in the passageways, drawn away from their homes by some mirage. They wore the same capes they had worn in the pastures of Mount Linas or Sopramonte and carried the same olivewood sticks and the same worn knapsacks. He felt a brotherly bond between himself and these men in rough woolen leggings, so despised by the "gentry."

Finally he got up, gulped down some *filuferru*, put on his jacket with a short sword at the belt, and left his cabin to stride up and down the deck. The steerage passengers had jumped over the barriers and squatted there with their knapsacks and flasks of wine as if they were at a rustic outdoor banquet. There were groups of men from Nuoro, wearing red vests under their jackets, sitting in circles with their hands on one another's shoulders. They were beating time to the rhythm of the *bore-bore* (accordion), while a "baritone" intoned a song. With the dark sea all around, there was something picturesque yet pathetic in the sight. Francesco halted his restless pacing and paused near the music-makers, tapping his foot in rhythm. When the dance was over, he offered to pay for drinks all around. Everyone— even the women—accepted, and he lingered to drink with them. Late in the night, with his head whirling, he went back to his cabin, undressed in the reddish light of the night lamp, and fell into a deep sleep.

He woke up at the first glow of dawn. Through the porthole he saw green sea below him and above gray sky, looming over the harbor fortifications of Civitavecchia, which had been completed by Michelangelo. Peasants swarmed over the deck; in a corner, one of them was still playing the accordion. The "gentry" were breakfasting in the dining saloon. The crowd of peasants pressing against the barriers in their haste to disembark might have come from some colonial land. The massive sea walls around the sooty, strange city increased their anxiety. As Francesco left the ship, he waved good-by to his fellow Sardinians in a final gesture of solidarity.

Young Francesco's feeling for his Island was based on senti-mental attachment to his family and home. The unification of Italy had been an accomplished fact before he was born. Angelo Uras, however, remembered that Don Francesco Fulgheri had bitterly opposed the House of Savoy. He recalled what his bene-factor had told him about the history of Sardinia's problems and he himself had witnessed some of the effects.

Sardinia had entered the Kingdom of Italy with a low morale and a weak economy. The House of Savoy, which took it over by virtue of the Treaty of London of 1718, continued and, in-deed, intensified a long-standing policy of excessive taxation and exploitation. Twice the Sardinians had sought liberation—in 1794, popular resentment had caused the Piedmontese to leave the Island; and in 1796, Sassari had proclaimed a republic which had been put down by force of arms and bloodshed.

The royal government and the fanatical supporters of the unification of Italy in 1861 had not taken into account the geographical and cultural differences between one region and another when they hastily applied a single political and ad-ministrative system to both the peninsula and the outlying islands.

A law of July 14, 1864, had imposed a five-million-lira in-crease of taxes on the whole country. More than half was laid upon Sardinia, with the result that the Island's taxes had been increased threefold. In many remote villages, the tax-collectors were met with gunfire: if they survived, they went back with empty hands to their offices. More often the collector came with an escort of *carabinieri*. The houses and fields of peasants who refused to pay were put up at auction. There was no one to defend them. Local politicians, whose interests were tied to those of the government, preached resignation. Sardinians came to think of themselves as subjects rather than fellow citizens of the mainland Italians and fell back into their age-long apathy and mistrust of government.

Angelo knew all these things from both the stories of Don Francesco and Ferraris and from his own personal experience. He forgot the exact figures but not the heart of the matter, and in the microcosm of Norbio he recognized the inept government of the whole of Italy. The tax office of the town hall, which overhung the Piazza Frontera like an acropolis, was guilty of flagrant injustice, and, of course, it was the poor who had to suffer. Shepherds were subjected to the seizure of their horses and sheep, peasants lost their wagons and oxen; indeed the courtyard of the town hall was filled with poor people's seized possessions. The seizure was more than anything an act of spite, because the objects had little value, and no one, except for passing strangers, ever attended the auctions of these goods. Actually, the whole of Italy seemed comprised of unfortunates, supernumeraries in a historical drama they could not direct. Once the excitement of the Risorgimento passed, the country was burdened with prefects and generals, with the flour tax and dubious military adventures. Independence, unity, and freedom were so many fine words. In the sterile controversies between Right and Left was foreshadowed the impotency of the ruling class that was to lead the country into the First World War and then into Fascism.

And yet on Sardinia, the "supernumeraries" were, perhaps, the only real men. The notorious Island brigands were more like untutored statesmen trying for a brief period to fill the places of the actor-politicians who shamelessly and hollowly recited roles they had been assigned on the stage of Rome.

At Norbio, the local government's chief activity was tax-collecting and the collector was kept busy by seizures. Even people with no more than a subsistence income, such as the men who worked in the mines of the Iglesiente region, were not exempted from the "hearth," or household, tax and were subject to seizure when they couldn't pay.

When the term of Mayor Ciriaco Spano was about to expire, the *prinzipales,* or big landowners, began to wink at one another. Ciriaco had held office for too long; frequent reelection had gone to his head; he considered his position so secure that he did not defer to them. And yet they had put and kept him in power. The right to vote was limited to those heads of families who paid over a certain amount in taxes. Many of these were *massaius,* or petty landowners, possessing no more than ten acres, a few teams of oxen, and a single flock of sheep. Every one of the *prinzipales* had a group of *massaius* who did what he said, and so they determined the choice of both the mayor and the town Council.

They winked at one another and, one Sunday, after High Mass, they gathered together in the house of old Antioco Cadoni. All of them were there, including Bartolomeo Chia, who was illiterate and had the nickname of Serrasogu, or Shut-eye, because of the way that he half closed his right eye when he was listening intently. Serrasogu didn't always go along with the others, even with such important persons as old Antioco Cadoni and Senator Loru. This time, however, he agreed that Ciriaco had been in office long enough and there should be a new mayor and a new Council.

"We need somebody young!" he said, watching for the effect of his words and running a hand over his shaven head. But no one came up with any proposal.

"Let's think first of the Council," suggested the senator.

Everyone assented except Serrasogu, who maintained that they must first pick a mayor and then good councilmen. By "good," of course, was meant "submissive," men who would be compliant with the *prinzipales'* will.

At just this moment young Antioco appeared at the door, which gave directly onto the courtyard, and hesitated for a moment before coming in. His grandfather waved and beckoned to him to take a seat. The young man was by now the father of two children and entitled not only to vote but also to be a candidate for election. Many of those present thought that his grandfather was going to propose him, but the old lawyer was too wily to do anything so obvious. He let a few minutes go by and, sure enough, the others said that young Antioco should be put up for the Council and perhaps even for mayor. Serrasogu, abruptly opening his right eye and closing the left one, proposed that Angelo Uras should be on the Council and might even, to judge by his efficient management of his own affairs, make an excellent mayor. His word was persuasive, and, having agreed upon the mayoral candidate, they proceeded to the more important and difficult choice of councilmen.

Each one of the *prinzipales* had his own interests and needed a councilman to defend them. If the mayor ever opposed the Council—as was most unlikely—he would find himself in the minority. For this reason, no one of the *prinzipales* had ever wanted to be mayor; they knew that they could pull the strings more effectively if they stayed in the background.

Such were the beginnings at Norbio of the democratic process, with its intrigues and contradictions. But it was a good deal better than when Marquis Crespi Brondo di Valdaura made decisions without having to consult anybody, or when the famous Donna Faustina called the heads of families "in the number of 278" into the Square to hear how they must cultivate the land and what they might and might not grow—"beans and vegetables, but no wheat or other grains."

When the *prinzipales* had left, old man Cadoni explained to his grandson why it was not to his advantage to be mayor and told him that, before the end of the day, he should approach Angelo Uras.

Antioco, a newcomer to the political game, was impressed by the responsibility laid upon him. He asked his wife to go along, and Olivia, who did not find many occasions to accompany her husband, accepted gladly, and went directly after lunch to change her clothes.

Every Sunday young people walked, in groups or couples, up and down the Via Roma. No unmarried girl or young married woman would consider appearing at the promenade in any attire other than her Sunday best. Olivia bathed, put on a new skirt and a tight silk bodice, and stuck a tortoise-shell comb into her blond hair. From a drawer she took her bridal shawl, shook it out, holding one corner between the tips of two fingers, and then gracefully whirled around, bending her knees, so that the shawl, balanced in the air, should fall onto her high hairdress and shoulders. With a pin held between her teeth, she fastened it under her chin, then drew herself up to her full height and scrutinized her reflection in the cupboard mirror. From the courtyard, she heard her husband's familiar whistle. She looked again into the mirror, passed a damp finger over her narrow eyebrows, and ran downstairs.

Antioco was attired in a dark blue suit; his mustache was pomaded and a newly lit cigarette dangled from his lips. They went out onto the street and mingled with the Sunday promenaders. It was not the first time that they had gone to Angelo's house since his second marriage, but it was the first time that they had gone without giving any warning. Margherita was always agreeable but Olivia felt slightly ill at ease in her presence. On this occasion, too, Margherita gave them a warm welcome and asked them to wait in the "drawing room," a rectangular room with a window giving onto the Via Roma and a glass door opening onto a terrace.

Antioco bowed to the young mistress of the house and started immediately to pace up and down, with his hands behind his back. At every step, his gold watch chain bounced on his stomach. In the few years since his marriage, he had gained weight; but even though his face had rounded, he was still a handsome young fellow. Margherita rang for coffee, and asked the servant to tell her husband that he had visitors. But Antioco, unintimidated, said impatiently: "If you don't mind, Donna Margherita," and knocked at the study door.

Angelo shut himself up every Sunday in his study, not to draw up accounts, as his wife imagined, but to read. In the beginning, he thought fiction was a waste of time and read nothing but history. Then he let himself be tempted by his first novel. He was very lucky, because what fell into his hands was Balzac's *Eugénie Grandet,* which he found totally fascinating. Through the descriptions of the wine-grower and the *prinzipales* of a French town, he came to understand many things that neither the historians Cantu' nor Guicciardini had taught him. His new love of books was a secret passion. There was no one to whom he could speak of Félix and Eugénie Grandet as living people, even if he saw Eugénie in every girl of Norbio. Perhaps he could have talked about these things to his mother. And Valentina, too, would have understood what so gripped him when he read.

In the dusty depths of Don Francesco's bookcases he had found other volumes—Balzac's *Human Comedy,* and Victor Hugo's *Les Misérables,* which he devoured in a week during the evening hours, shut up in his study by lamplight like a school-boy reading under the bedcovers. Often when Margherita saw a distracted look on his face, she asked if he had any worries. But worries, fortunately, he had none. He had turned Aletzi into a very productive olive grove and now it was his. The township had sold it to him at a fair price, which he had paid in installments over seven years; he regretted only that Sofia was not there to share his satisfaction. Margherita was pleased for him, but she didn't understand, really. She had inherited wealth and took it for granted, as if it were her due.

Angelo knew he was well thought of in Norbio because of his success with the Aletzi grove, and also because he had married Margherita, a "lady" who had brought him a large dowry. According to the wish of Don Tommaso, they had signed a tradi-tional marriage contract, which established joint ownership of husband's and wife's possessions. Angelo had consented to this arrangement, but it marred his relationship with Margherita. He thought back often to Valentina and to the daily renewal of the love between them. Luckily, Maria Christina enlivened the house with her running and shouting, her love of animals and growing things. "She's an earthquake," said Margherita, trying to curb the child's "undisciplined" spontaneity and taking Angelo to task for spoiling her. Angelo paid no attention to her, and Maria Christina grew and bloomed freely. She was very attached to her father and quick to obey his slightest wish. To Margherita, she responded less readily; she didn't rebel, but her compliance was formal and passive.

Margherita wasn't satisfied with Maria Rosario either, who was by now a household fixture. The girl was too familiar, and she didn't know how to wait on the table. Angelo admitted that this was to some extent true, but when Margherita spoke of letting her go he refused so calmly and decisively that his new wife realized it was no use insisting. She retired to her bedroom and complained of one of the famous headaches from which she was to suffer every time she could not have her way.

On the afternoon when young Antioco Cadoni knocked at the study door, Angelo was absorbed in his reading and lost in the consideration of social injustice. An insistently dangerous thought returned, no matter how many times he rejected it, to haunt his Christian conscience. Were social inequality and injustice determined by a flaw in the divine will? The fate of Fantine in *Les Misérables* seemed to him to symbolize the imperfection of the world and the "inevitable" evil of human nature.

Raising his eyes from his book, he saw Antioco and Margherita in the doorway. His wife's face had a teasing expression and one more beguiling than usual as she raised her slender hand and said: "Antioco's here to see you, but strictly in private!"

Antioco jokingly protested, and even Angelo sought to detain Margherita, but she turned around and, closing the door behind her, walked with her customary short, quick steps to join Olivia at the far end of the shadowy drawing room.

The two young men held a long conversation and Angelo was sorry when Antioco went away, for he would have liked to talk longer. The unexpected proposal had left him puzzled and even incredulous, yet at the same time he was somehow happy deep down inside, as when he had walked out of the town hall with the deed to Aletzi in his pocket. He had no idea what he could accomplish as mayor, but already he imagined the citizens of the town uniting to support him. The job didn't seem too difficult; he would try to please the majority of the people. He did not think of the burdens of being a public figure, constantly subject to observation and criticism.

Unable to go on reading, he replaced the book in the drawer, hastily put the papers on his desk into superficial order, and left the study. He was still in an excitable state when he almost ran into Margherita, who was aware at once that something had happened. When she asked, he had an impulse to make her his confidante. He slipped his arm through hers, very gently because she did not like physical contact, and they walked together on the gravel of the courtyard.

"I didn't want to commit myself without consulting you," he told her.

He was not in the habit of lying; there had been no need of it with his mother and Valentina, but now things were different. Margherita's face lit up with joy.

"And I wanted your father's opinion, too," Angelo continued.

"Surely this is a decision you have to make on your own," said Margherita. "It's no use asking my father, he's sure to say no. He doesn't want to be involved with anything except his medicine."

She smiled in amusement, showing her appealing long teeth, and went on: "You'll have trouble, plenty of it, but I think you ought to take the job, anyhow."

Angelo had expected no such reaction. He hadn't reckoned with the fact that Margherita didn't at all mind being the wife of the mayor.

"So I'll accept," he said gaily.

"You had already accepted," she said, looking him in the eye.

During the period before the election, Angelo went almost daily into the country. In the village he would have had no peace. At Pranu Mesu, men were breaking the ground to plant grapevines; at Acquacotta, they were plowing the fields before sowing; at Balanotti, the olive crop was almost all in. Through Margherita's dowry, the rich lands of Sabbodus, Trunconi, and Pranu Mesu had been added to those he had inherited from Don Francesco; overseeing his holdings kept Angelo so busy that he had little time for worrying about votes.

The electoral campaign took place without meetings or speeches or commotion. The *prinzipales* did meet together several more times, decided on their choice of councilmen, and passed the word on to their dependents by means of handwritten lists on copybook paper. When election day came, a great crowd went to the polls that were set up in the school. The voters neither added nor subtracted any name from the official list, and they did not dream of turning in a blank ballot. Obedience was the best policy, the one that they had always followed. They were freshly shaven and in their best clothes—a dark suit and a collarless white shirt—with the list of preferred candidates in their pocket. Streaming across the Piazza Frontera, they climbed the stairs, taking off their hats when they entered the room. On the walls hung a crucifix and a portrait of the king, with his great mustache. The *carabinieri* were on duty, scowling and wriggling as if they had itching backs. Officiating was the unsmiling town clerk, Cavaliere Luigi Frongia, a fifty-year-old man with white hair and bushy, black eyebrows that formed a straight line over his small, piercing eyes. He had perpetually flushed cheeks and, because his sensitive skin did not allow him to shave very often, the bristly white hairs sticking out of his chin gave him a sickly air. This odd character recited the same instructions to every voter before beckoning him imperiously toward the booth at the far end of the room. At either side of him sat Muroni, the schoolteacher, and Pintus, the registrar, who examined the ballot, instructed the voter to slip it into the ballot box, then required him to sign the list of those who had effectively voted. Voting went on until four o'clock in the afternoon when, in a magistrate's presence, the ballot box was opened and the ballots were counted. As the good people of Norbio were going to bed, the poll-workers were still counting. Since every voter had voted according to instructions, the results could not be such as to prevent them from sleeping.

Part Four

Part Three

One rainy afternoon as he walked to a Council meeting, Angelo was overtaken by Serrasogu behind St. Barbara's where the Fluminera was widest and deepest. Women, standing up to their knees in water, were doing their wash, scrubbing and rubbing it on smooth slabs of dark gray stone. The spot was called the *bau de sa madixedda,* or "Wagtail's Ford," although, at high water, not even a herd of bulls could have crossed it. The women were stiff with cold from the foaming, icy water and their rolled-up skirts were soaking wet.

Serrasogu and Angelo fell into step and walked side by side under a big green oilskin umbrella. The old man owned many horses and oxen and big stores of beans, oats, straw, and hay. His livestock was well fed and cared for. But his well, which had started to dry up after the mountain had been stripped of its trees, no longer gave even enough water for the donkey that turned his mill. At dawn every day, and again in the evening, horses and oxen had to be led to the watering trough of Lacuneddas. It was Serrasogu's dream to have a trough closer to home, and Angelo thought this was a reasonable aspiration. The trough could be built of bricks, granite, or some softer stone, and the cost, Serrasogu explained, counting on his fingers, would be little more than two thousand liras, a very small item in the township's budget. At the Council meeting, Andria Porcu,

Domenico Cara, and Sebastiano Nonnis would propose construction of the trough to the Commissioner of Public Works and, of course, to the mayor. The commissioner, Serrasogu admitted, had already been approached and had promised his support. But without Angelo's approval, the proposal wouldn't go through. And so Serrasogu was asking him not to oppose it.

At this point, Serrasogu was three or four steps ahead of Angelo, beyond the shelter of the umbrella. Angelo felt uneasy and would have liked to avoid any discussion by saying yes, certainly. But something inside him rebelled and he gave a curt "no" for an answer. The women turned their heads to look at the two men as they came down the steep street. Having piled up the wet, clean linen on the pebbly shore, they stood for a moment, motionless under the pelting rain, with their bodies outlined by their soaked clothes. Serrasogu was haranguing the impassive Angelo, who interrupted him only to say:

"I don't want to arrive late at the Council meeting."

"Better you shouldn't go to the meeting at all, Angelo Uras!" said Serrasogu threateningly.

And, as Angelo strode on, he continued to call down thunder and lightning upon him.

"*Lampu!*" he shouted, according to local custom.

Angelo leaped from stone to stone across the Fluminera at a point where it was possible to ford it. Halfway across, he turned to survey the washerwomen, who seemed to be looking at him with ironical approval. Responding to their smiles, he felt as if he were still a young boy crossing the river and managing to arrive, quite dry, on the other side.

In the town hall, the councilmen were waiting. From the outside balcony a soaked Italian flag, put out whenever a Council meeting took place, hung limply. The councilmen sat at their desks, ready to give battle. Angelo took his place among the commissioners. He glanced out a window at the lowering sky, sniffed the wet-dog smell of the room, then rang the bell that called the meeting to order. His feet were icy cold and, in addition to the stench that he had detected before, he sensed hostility in the air. To steady himself, he lit a cigarette and inhaled deeply. Outside it was still raining, and great cloud masses swept in disorderly fashion across the apparently solid gray sky. He decided to open the meeting for discussion to prevent a further build-up of tension.

Frongia, the clerk, looked at him expectantly, his pen poised over a blank sheet of paper. Andria Porcu asked for the floor and Angelo nodded solemnly. Andria was a neighbor of Serrasogu and, like him, an owner of land and livestock. He seemed at first to be talking on behalf of the general public, but soon it became clear that he was pleading for himself and his friend. His subject, of course, was the watering trough which, if it were fed by that of Sant'Antonio, would save their farmhands so much time and trouble. There had been complaints at Norbio for a long time about the lack of public troughs, and now Antioco Cadoni put in a word to indicate that he would give the project his backing. More troughs were definitely needed; why not begin with the one proposed by Andria? The reasoning was the same as that of Serrasogu. And the councilmen seemed to be all of one mind, determined to put Angelo in the minority. If his administration were to be put in a weak position from the start, it would be unable to recover in the future and his aim of reforming the local government would remain an idle dream.

Angelo lit another cigarette and ordered an employee to bring in the big, detailed map that hung in his office. The map was hung up on the wall behind him and, with a stick for a pointer, he called attention to certain sites. Every street, square, church, fountain, house, and watering trough was clearly marked with Roman and Arabic numbers. It was easy to prove that Andria's project would meet the needs of only a limited number of people.

"Then what does the mayor propose?" asked Vincenzo Abis, an independent old beekeeper who liked Angelo and who was a disinterested party since he had no livestock. He stood leaning against the back of his bench; the outspread fingers with which he grasped it were white with strain, and his wet lower lip was quivering. Angelo looked him in the eye and, speaking slowly, set forth his own plan. He was aware, he said, of the difficulty of bringing livestock to water. . . .

"But you have plenty of water in all your houses," Sebastiano Nonnis shouted.

Angelo pretended not to have heard and proceeded warily. With the stick, he pointed to the "Wagtail's Ford" and said that here was the central place that could be most easily reached from all sides. Indeed, the river lent itself to the construction of a whole row of troughs with water running continuously through them. He spoke calmly and firmly, and Abis seconded him. The others were hostile but silent, not daring to insist on an argument that had been discredited. Old Antioco Cadoni broke the silence: the mayor's plan seemed good, but it required reflection; he suggested that the meeting be adjourned until the following week. Angelo was encouraged. If old man Cadoni went along, the respect he inspired would cause the rest to follow. And the Cadonis had plenty of water. Moreover, when news of what had gone on at the meeting got out, the humble people of Norbio would side with the mayor who had defended their interests. It was with a hopeful feeling that he gathered up his papers, rang the bell, and announced: "Meeting adjourned! You'll be notified of the next."

Waving his hand, he left the room with his folders under his arm. He hadn't won the battle, but neither had he lost it. This was the first time that a mayor had ever spoken out against the *prinzipales,* and the village people were happy about it. They knew that any other mayor would have blindly accepted the project of Andria Porcu.

The township of Norbio had no Public Works office and so Angelo gave the job of drafting his project to the engineer Cataldi, who, one evening after supper, began to make sketches by the light of the kerosene lamp in the mayor's study. He worked fast and at the same time kept up a running conversation, answering Angelo's questions. The idea was to build a reservoir upstream, and below it, watering troughs made of cement. This would be the first time cement was used at Norbio, and while Cataldi penciled his sketches, he explained the advantages of the new material, which made for quick construction and durability. Angelo wanted twelve troughs, and the engineer drew them, in a wide semicircle atop a solid base, at the bottom of the cliff below the house of Professor Todde. Angelo decided that the only way to accomplish the project was to start work at once. After the building had already begun, he would obtain telegraphic authorization from the provincial government. But he still had to deal with opposition from the councilmen.

The town crier of Norbio was Gigi Lubranu, who in 1887 had trumpeted the charge against the Ethiopian forces at the battle of Dogali, where he had received the wound that left him a partial invalid for the rest of his life. Every morning at eight o'clock, he blew his horn from the stairway of the town hall, and people gathered to hear what he had to say. Lubranu would clear his throat, spit on the ground, and then announce the daily news in his clear voice. On this certain morning, after the usual preamble—"By order of the Mayor, the following announcement . . ."—he said that construction of the watering troughs was beginning at Wagtail's Ford, and that anyone looking for work should apply at once to the town clerk. Hodcarriers and diggers were quick to volunteer their services, and when they went down to the ford, a crowd of women asesmbled to look on. For the moment, Cataldi was there alone, except for the foreman, Matteo Pidongia; together they were planting iron stakes and measuring distances with bits of string. At ten o'clock, the workers arrived. Most of them were unemployed miners, because of a strike at the Bugerru mine. No one at Norbio had ever seen pickaxes wielded so fast or with such skill. They swung like rotating wheels, cutting through earth and stone and throwing sparks and chips into the air. Soon the work was well underway. Angelo went down to the ford two or three times a day. One morning he ran into Zia Marietta Serra, who invited him for a cup of coffee at her house. The old woman's dull, dark eyes were so pleading that he could not bring himself to refuse.

"I've just had my morning coffee, Zia Marietta," he said, "but I'll take a glass of cold water from your well."

Marietta Serra's well was famous in the locality, and many members of the "gentry" stopped to drink. It was at the center of a large, square courtyard, covered by a pergola so overgrown that the sun barely shone through. Clusters of ripe grapes hung down among the leaves.

"I have to talk to you," said Zia Marietta, slipping her hand under his arm and propelling him toward the kitchen. "And don't tell me to come tomorrow to your office. It's too far away."

"Very well," said Angelo, sitting down on a stool.

"After all the years I've lived, I'm an old woman," she said. "At my age all of us have rheumatism. Just look . . ." And she held out her twisted fingers.

Angelo knew that most of the old women of Norbio had the same affliction. Brusquely Zia Marietta drew back her hands and hid them under her crossed arms. Now, leaning forward, she added:

"All our lives long, we've wanted one thing: to be able to do our laundry with a roof over our heads and our feet on dry land. You ought to understand the way we feel. I see that you're doing a big job down on the river. And if you're building watering troughs for the livestock owners, you can surely build a washhouse as well. It seems like a good moment."

"I've thought about such a thing over the years," Angelo told her, "ever since I saw my mother come home soaking wet from the Fluminera."

"God bless you!" the old woman exclaimed, touching his forehead with the tips of her fingers.

"It won't be easy," Angelo reflected, "but I'll do my best."

She went to draw some water from the well and brought him back a tall glass. He sipped slowly, thinking all the while of what she had told him. Perhaps indeed this was the time to install a washhouse. He left and walked rapidly to the ford. He was anxious to consult the engineer. Cataldi was there, but the ring of the pickaxes prevented serious discussion of a matter that required thought and figuring. Angelo invited him to his house, where they could talk quietly in the study.

After lunch they sat down together at a worktable. Cataldi quickly produced a sketch: an ornate roof supported by six cast-iron columns ornamented with scrolls and cones, a dozen basins with taps and tubes, and a reservoir like that of the watering troughs. Angelo looked with amazement at the magical pencil as it traced the lines of this essentially homely construction. Every now and then, Cataldi paused to jot down columns of numbers in the margin, and Angelo pointed with his cigar at some of the ornamentation and asked if it couldn't be eliminated. Cataldi stripped it down to essentials and lowered his estimate of the cost accordingly.

Cataldi promised to make, within the week, a blueprint that could be presented to the Council. Except for the iron columns, most of the necessary material was already on the site, including a certain quantity of lead tubing, so that to carry out the two projects simultaneously would actually save money. But, as Angelo feared, the councilmen voted the washhouse down. The *prinzipales* had instructed them to block Angelo's plans, and so they pleaded an insufficiency of funds in the treasury.

Meanwhile, the miners had sounded the alarm. They were the most sophisticated of the workers, accustomed to fighting their employers and strengthened by the success their organization had won in the Sulcis mining basin. Together with the peasants, the women, and the old men, they decided to take steps to ensure that the new mayor's program should not be deflected. For the first time since the end of communal land ownership, the inhabitants of Norbio held a meeting on a threshing ground, and some of them spoke. They said that Angelo Uras was a peasant's son, that he had worked the land with his own hands, that he was a good mayor and deserved their support.

"Yes, but how are we to support him?" asked Marietta Serra, who had as much authority as if she were an old man.

"We have no money," put in Sante Follesa, a miner who had worked in the region of Iglesiente, "but we have strong arms, and some of us have wagons. If we stand behind the mayor, we can bring down the costs of the washhouse to practically nothing and build it, no matter what the *prinzipales* may say."

All those present applauded.

"You go speak to the mayor," someone shouted.

"Let's name a committee," said Follesa, who was used to the procedures of the Workers' Leagues. But he soon realized that most of his townsmen didn't know what he was talking about. He nodded to Salvatore Erbi, a peasant more commonly known as "Whistler," and to two other miners. And, walking away, he called out: "So we all agree?"

"Yes!" the others called back.

Follesa was a ruddy-complexioned young fellow. Although he had worked for some years in the mines, he had a well developed chest and narrow hips, and around the latter he wore a broad red wool sash with a knife stuck into it. He now set off at such a fast clip that the others had trouble keeping up with him. They went first to the town hall, but no one was there except the clerk; then they walked to the ford in search of Angelo, and finally to his house where they found him. The door was open and they walked right in. Angelo stepped forward, as if he had been expecting them, and when they had told him the purpose of their visit, he shook hands gratefully with everyone.

"We see eye to eye with you, Angelo Uras," they told him. "If we could bring others around to our way of thinking, together we'd make Norbio over and there'd be abundance for all."

Whistler, the peasant, fell into a sentimental mood and drank one glass after another of the red wine that Maria Rosario served on a lacquer tray. But he and his companions listened carefully to everything Angelo and Sante Follesa were saying. Sante said that the volunteer washhouse builders could start work that very afternoon. To obtain building material, they would set off a few sticks of dynamite in the township's granite quarry, and transport the granite in their own wagons to the ford.

Angelo drank with them and, for the first time in several days, lit up a cigar. Suddenly he felt as happy as when he had supervised the reactivation of the narrow-gauge railway that brought timber down from the great forests. He felt sure that both the watering troughs and the washhouse would be successes. When the impromptu committee went away, the men waved their hands as if in confirmation of a mutual pledge.

Angelo was walking rapidly back from a call on Senator Loru, whom he had persuaded to support his plans. He was thinking with satisfaction that within a few days he could call the Council together and obtain approval. There would be no need for discussion, because the councilmen would have their orders and vote accordingly.

As soon as he had opened the gate, which creaked the way it always had, he heard the voice of Filippo, the little boy born to him and Margherita two years before. The child ran to meet him, and Angelo swept him up in his arms. In his imperfect speech, Filippo tried to tell him that a man had come to the house and had waited in a chair, there, by the dahlia bed. Filippo was slender and delicate and looked extraordinarily like his mother. He shook his head as he chattered, frustrated by the fact that his father took so little interest in the news. Angelo sat down and took him onto his knees.

"Who's been at the house?" he asked Maria Christina, who stood in the kitchen doorway, beating two eggs in a bowl with a fork. Maria Christina was by now a girl of fifteen, with a well-developed figure and narrow, sensual lips. She was not as pretty as Valentina, yet her looks did echo those of her mother. Her eyes, like Valentina's, were big and golden-brown and were fringed by long lashes.

"Michele Tropea, the pharmacist," she answered. She stopped short, with an imperceptible smile, and nodded in the direction of the Fulgheri house before she continued: "Francesco's here, Father, did you know?"

Filippo made a face at his half-sister and ran away, with the dogs behind him. Angelo got up and went to look for Margherita, who was putting away household linen. She turned around and smiled. Ever since she had become pregnant for the second time there was a pale, timid smile on her thin face. She stood still, leaning her back against the chest of drawers, and laid her hands on Angelo's shoulders. He didn't know whether she wanted to push him away or, in her own awkward way, to express her affection. He patted her arm, and she looked away, but without drawing back.

"Michele Tropea was here," she told him.

"What did he want?"

"To speak to you about the washhouse. It seems it's the talk of the town. He said it was a good thing and ought to be built."

"Good! I'm glad to hear it."

"So you'll manage to give old Marietta Serra her heart's desire, after all!" said Margherita with a kindly laugh. And, starting to move away, she added: "Franceschino's here on leave. They're sending him to Massawa on the Red Sea."

Shortly afterward Angelo went to the house of Don Tommaso. Francesco had arrived a few hours before. He stood in the courtyard, examining a colt that his father had bought at the fair of Sant'Antine, a handsome, gray three-year-old with a fine head and a white star on the forehead reaching down to the soft, damp nose. Francesco was wearing the uniform of an infantry lieutenant, with blue buckskin breeches that displayed his short, shapely legs. He greeted Angelo affectionately and Angelo returned his embrace warmly.

"Is it true that you're going to Africa?" he asked him.

Francesco attached a shank to the colt's halter before answering.

"It's not sure. If I don't insist, I'll be left where I am with the 28th Regiment at Parma."

"Did you ask to go?"

"Yes, I did. I don't want to remain a glorified policeman."

"I understand," said Angelo gravely, "but I hope you don't go so far away."

Carmela, wearing a lace-trimmed apron, was happily occupied in the kitchen.

"Hello, you two!" she called from the window. "Don't you want some freshly made coffee?"

She was lively and charming as ever. A few days later she was to marry Alfonso Pizzuto, the young doctor who had come to Norbio as an assistant to her father, who was now on the verge of retirement. In recent months, every time that Angelo saw Carmela he couldn't help comparing her to Margherita and thinking how different his life would be had he married her rather than her sister. But then he thought the choice had been decided for him as if by fate.

Francesco felt happy in the big kitchen, with its lava-stone floor and shiny tile walls, the big chestnut-wood table, the low chairs with painted flowers, the ample cupboards, the rustic jugs of drinking water lined up on a shelf, and the busy women, their sleeves rolled up over their red arms and their faces flushed by the blazing fire. Norbio was full of florid girls, and Francesco didn't conceal that he found them pretty and desirable.

Efisina came in from the doctor's laboratory, bringing with her the odor of disinfectants. She washed her hands at the sink, then, holding a basin of water in her left hand, began to sprinkle the floor of the porch. Sticking two fingers into the water, she made a rhythmical scattering movement, creating a continuous jet which fell just ahead of her feet and made strange arabesques on the paved floor. In summer all the women of the house—mistresses and servants—carried out this sprinkling, which actually looked like some sort of a game. Only Margherita, who never did anything that wasn't strictly necessary and sensible, failed to participate.

Francesco went back to the courtyard and patted the colt. He examined its teeth and raised its feet one by one to inspect the horseshoes. They didn't satisfy him and he made a disapproving grimace, to which Efisina responded with a michievous smile.

"A fine animal!" he said to Carmela, who had followed him out. "When did you buy him?"

"A couple of months ago," she said, holding out some peas on the palm of her hand.

"I'd say he had some English thoroughbred blood," said Francesco with a knowing air. The colt looked at him, with large, dark eyes and cocked its slender, velvety ears. Francesco walked all around him and then asked Carmela:

"Have you ridden him?"

"He's a demon," she answered. "I don't want to die like Uncle Francesco. He's too wild even for a circus rider."

Francesco was unimpressed.

"I want to try him," he said.

When the colt saw the bridle, saddle, and saddle pad, he trembled, shied, and started to rear.

"He's frightened," said Francesco and then, to the colt: "Come on, handsome one! With me it's going to be different; we'll be friends."

With a brush he removed some bits of straw from the colt's mane and long tail, then he slipped the yellow pad and the saddle on its back and adjusted the stirrups. His precise quiet manner reassured the colt. After putting on his spurs, he took the bridle from the admiring Efisina's hands and led the colt around. Angelo Uras, who had been sitting silently on the porch, came over to give advice.

"You'd better mount him out on the street," he said, pointing to the zinc-covered wires strung up between the columns of the porch and the woodshed. Efisina ran and threw the gate wide open. Francesco slipped on his jacket, smoothed it out with both hands over his chest, planted a kiss on Carmela's cheek, and walked the horse out. No sooner had he leaped onto its back than the animal reared up on its hind legs, wheeling around and pawing the air like a bronco. But Francesco was a skilled rider and kept his seat. There were women standing against the wall holding their children by the hand, some with pitchers of water on their heads, and Francesco looked apprehensively at their thin, bare feet, still bronzed by the summer sun. The colt, plunging wildly, nearly grazed the pitchers with his forelegs, and backed erratically within inches of the women's feet. But the women, who were used to horses, stood motionless. Maria Christina gripped the iron rail of the fence and blinked in fright. From his fingertips, Francesco blew her a kiss and she returned it with equal bravado, but then, terrified for him, she wet her middle finger and ran it over her bare throat. Francesco, exhilarated by her attention and concern, turned the colt toward the steeply sloping street, deserted at this hour, and spurred him to a gallop.

"Take care!" called out a voice carried by the wind.

Francesco, bending over the colt's withers, looked back and caught sight of Maria Christina, who appeared very small and tense. She still held one hand pressed to her throat, whose tremulous, tiny blue veins he imagined as vividly as if she were still only a few feet away. The colt sped past the senator's house, past the flower-covered villa of Professor Todde, but Francesco managed to rein him in before arriving at the Piazza Frontera, which they crossed at a slow trot. They proceeded toward the Piazza Cadoni, slowing to a walk in front of the church, where the priest was standing at the door. Just as Francesco raised his fingers to his cap in salute, the great bell of the Pisan tower rang out over the silent village. The colt, startled, reared up again. Francesco struck his flanks with a crop and drove him forward into a gallop.

By now there were more people on the streets. Ahead, the street was blocked by a procession of chanting worshippers headed by the curate and a choirboy carrying the processional cross. Francesco struggled with the colt while the little group of cautious villagers split in two and flattened themselves against the walls on either side of the street. The curate and the choirboy, however, remained standing in the middle. Some of the villagers made the sign of the cross, some called on the names of Jesus and Mary. As for Francesco, his first instinct to pull the horse up was followed by a different and more perilous plan. He spurred and whipped the colt forward and then, within a stride of the curate and choirboy, checked and then released him. The colt responded, jumped, and landed beyond them. Then he came to a stop. Francesco turned, lifted his cap apologetically to the astonished curate, touched his spurs to the trembling colt, and they trotted along the main street toward home.

Angelo Uras was sitting in the kitchen over a cup of coffee, in the company of a young man with a carefully trimmed blond mustache. Without pausing to greet them, Francesco strode to the wine jug, filled a glass, and thirstily gulped it down. It was the light, semi-sparkling wine that he knew well.

"To your good health!" said the young man sitting beside Angelo with his elbows on the table.

"Francesco, meet Dr. Alfonso Pizzuto, Carmela's fiancé," Angelo said.

The two younger men shook hands. Pizzuto's hand was flabby and limp in Francesco's grasp.

"I'm your father's assistant," he explained.

"And you're hoping to take over his practice when he retires, I suppose," said Francesco, his face darkening at the thought of his father's imminent retirement.

"The later the better," Pizzuto answered earnestly.

"So I say, too," said Francesco, smiling. He winked at Carmela, who was standing behind her fiancé and, with apparent nonchalance, was smoothing his hair.

Alfonso was extraordinarily like his name, with rosy cheeks, blond hair parted in the middle, and upturned mustache. His hands were small and manicured, his mouth sensual, and his build betrayed a tendency toward stoutness despite his youth. Francesco found it hard to believe that Carmela was actually going to marry him, that she had chosen, or at least had accepted, him for a husband.

"Excuse me," said Angelo, emptying his glass and rising to his feet, "I must go." Before actually leaving, he invited all those present to dinner or rather, as they say in Parte d'Ispi, to supper. "You, too, Doctor, of course," he said, clapping Pizzuto on the shoulder.

"You honor me, Mr. Mayor!"

Francesco disliked the idea of Carmela married to the stoutish doctor, but he decided that probably she'd be happy and have the numerous children that she'd always said she wanted. He put his arm around her waist, gave her an affectionate spank, and went to look for Maria Christina.

Just outside the gate, he found Angelo talking to Sante Follesa. Francesco had known Sante as one of his childhood playmates on the dried bed of the Fluminera and had kept up the friendship to the extent that occasionally they went hunting together. But Sante could not forget that Francesco was Count Tommaso Fulgheri's son. Just now, Sante was saying that he must be off to Buggerru.

"What's that?" Angelo exclaimed. "Are you leaving your work on the washhouse? I thought there was still a strike at the mine."

"A strike takes pushing," said Sante. "And I've been made a member of the committee that's to negotiate with the 'Turk.'"

"Who's the 'Turk'?" Francesco asked as Sante walked away.

"His real name is Georgiades. He came originally from Constantinople. He's the manager of the mine, and a tough one, I can tell you."

From the house Maria Christina saw her father and Francesco, and ran out to greet them.

"I'm going down to inspect the work at the ford," said Angelo. "If you two want to come with me . . ."

"You have work to oversee, Papa, but I have work to do. We've guests for supper tonight."

"True," said her father, chucking her chin.

"Wait for me on the terrace," Maria Christina said to Francesco. "You'll find the newspaper there; it came just a few minutes ago."

Angelo nodded assent, turned on his heels, and walked away. He saw that the two young people were in love and he did not oppose their feelings. Although they had never discussed it, he realized that their marriage was in the offing. But he was reluctant to lose his daughter. If Maria Christina married Francesco, she would follow him wherever he went, far from Norbio, and without her, he, Angelo, would feel utterly alone.

Francesco sat down on the terrace, between the peonies and the dahlia beds, and picked up the newspaper. Every now and then, Maria Christina came to sit beside him, but she was occupied by her household responsibilities. The prospect of Francesco's overseas assignment weighed upon her mind. As long as he was "on the continent"—in Italy—she could hope to see him from time to time; but if he went off to Africa, it could mean a prolonged separation. All of a sudden she envied Carmela. For looks or charm, Alfonso Pizzuto couldn't be compared to Francesco, but Carmela loved her little man, he was there close to her, and they were officially engaged. Maria Christina's love for Francesco, on the other hand, had no official status. Moreover, one day Margherita, without meaning to be discouraging, had remarked to Angelo that army officers were permitted to marry only girls who brought them a certain substantial dowry. Maria

Christina recalled that her father and stepmother had commented upon the unfairness of this ruling and had pondered how they could get around it. It would be simple enough to find an appraiser who would set a value of forty thousand liras on a vineyard of sizable acreage. Hearing them then, and now again as she thought back to the episode, Maria Christina's eyes filled with tears. She missed her mother whom she knew only from the faded daguerreotype in her father's study, the image of a girl who, when not much older than herself, had given birth to her. The emptiness she had felt from her earliest years had been filled, at last, by her love for Francesco. The tears in her eyes as she looked up at Francesco's tanned, virile face were tears of tenderness and joy—he was there, within reach, beside her. A postcard from him from the mainland, or a quick hug when, as now, they were alone together, were enough to reassure her of his love. No one, she felt quite certain, had ever cared or could ever care for her in the same way.

They sat with their arms around each other until Maria Rosaria called out to her from the kitchen. Under the eyes of her old nurse, she planted a kiss on his lips and ran away.

Maria Christina had appointed the best linen, china, and silver to be laid, and the table when set looked festive enough for a wedding supper. Carmela and Alfonso sat side by side, as if they were already married, while Maria Christina and Francesco exchanged glances from a distance, glances which seemed to say, once more, that they would marry, dowry or no dowry.

"If your father doesn't give you a dowry, I'll give it to you myself," Francesco had told her, and she smiled happily over the echo of this promise.

For many years, Sante Follesa had been a day laborer in the big citrus grove at Lugheria and had eaten the bean-and-hambone soup served in Don Tommaso's kitchen to all the farm workers. As a boy, he had been timidly but deeply attached to the whole Fulgheri family, with a special mute and hopeless love for Carmela. He left Norbio for the mainland while he was still very young, under the pretext of finding work, but with the secret hope of making his fortune and then returning to declare himself to Carmela. As a laborer he found that life in the big cities was harsh. In Milan he had just escaped death in the riots of 1898. Afterward, he had worked in Genoa as a longshoreman, had joined the Workers' Leagues, and had taken part in the major strikes. When he left for Marseilles, he was a revolutionary socialist, ready to fight at the least provocation. The French police kept him under surveillance and, finally, shipped him back to Italy. He returned to Norbio, then left again to look for work in the mining basin of Iglesiente, where some fifteen thousand shepherds and farm workers had flocked to the lure of easy money. This time he set out without illusions, carrying a knapsack that contained all his worldly goods: a razor, a shaving brush, and a cake of soap—an emigrant's baggage. His youthful love for Carmela Fulgheri had given way to a passionate commitment to social struggle. Among the many mines in the area only the smallest had any openings. The pay was low, as everywhere else; the miners had to buy their kerosene for the lamps that lit the galleries and their groceries from a company store, where prices were higher than those of the mainland. Housing, too, was a company monopoly, and the miners paid high rents for miserable shacks. The Buggerru Mine, which belonged to a French company called Malfidano, was close to the village of the same name, whose eight thousand inhabitants had no other occupation besides transporting the coal from the mine on crudely constructed barges to the nearby island of San Pietro, where the harbor was deep enough to permit the loading of the colliers that transported the coal to France. The bargemen, too, were underpaid, and they were the first to organize the unions called Workers' Leagues. The founder was actually a Piedmontese physician, one Doctor Cavallera, who was as poor as his patients and a convinced Socialist. There was no one else to whom workers could turn for medical care.

The local administration ignored the people's needs—schools, streets, lighting, and sanitation—but took good care to collect taxes. Discontent was rife, and grew deeper every day. The miners' only hope lay in the Leagues, which, during the last years, had increased in number, patterning themselves on the one founded by Dr. Cavallera. But the mine owners countered the miners' protests by firing all those who belonged to the Leagues and by dispossessing them of the shacks they built on company-owned property.

Sante Follesa left Norbio on September 3, 1904, shortly after taking leave of Francesco Fulgheri and Angelo Uras. His brief encounter with them had left him feeling bitter. Among the "gentry" they were the two persons he respected, and yet even they were indifferent to the condition of the miners: indeed, it was clear that they disapproved of the miners' strike in spite of the obvious and solid reasons behind it.

Sante walked for a good part of the day, then got a ride on a wagon, and fell asleep on its cargo of mastic twigs. When the wagon went through San Silvano, he jumped out and took a shortcut through the mountains to Buggerru, where he arrived at twilight. A full moon floated in the September sky, lighting up the countryside and the ugly, smoky mining village. Houses two or three stories high, carelessly plastered, characteristic of neither city nor country, were huddled together around the square. Their fronts were marred by black drainage tubes, the balconies were transformed into places for food storage, wash hung drying outside the windows, and broken garbage cans lined the sidewalk below. Only the office building of the mining company had a certain quiet dignity, which contrasted with the rest. In the solid wall of house fronts there was an occasional break, created by a narrow alley that wound its dark way into the rest of the village.

Sante made straight for the League headquarters. There he found the miners who had summoned him to their aid. Negotiations were deadlocked. All day long the committee had argued with the "Turk" without success. Among those present was Felice Littera, a miner from Norbio and a friend of Sante.

Felice had been fired that very afternoon and dispossessed from the house, which, after years of self-sacrifice and saving, he and his wife had managed to build on the land of the Malfidano Company. Littera was desperate because his wife was pregnant and had no place to go. The League leaders had tried to obtain a postponement, but Georgiades was obdurate. Sante's first impulse was to take up his friend's cause immediately, but he knew that he would get nowhere, and he had to keep cool for the battle of the next day.

"For the time being we must drop our other demands and concentrate on the maintenance of the old working hours," said Sante. "We have to win one point at a time, and the rest can come later."

He walked out of the League headquarters with Felice, and they found his wife Antonietta and three children sitting on a stone doorstep at the far end of the square. Antonietta was crying. Sante tried to cheer her up; he knew a place where they could sleep that night. And to Felice he said:

"You'll find work at Norbio, more secure and for better pay. Norbio's changing these days."

And he told him about the watering troughs and the washhouse. Felice had only to go to the mayor, and he would get a job. He himself intended to leave the mine eventually and go back to the village.

"But for the time being I want to stay here to organize a protest against this business of firing."

The Litteras stayed that night at the house of Sante's friend.

Sante, thankful that he had taken care not to acquire a wife and children and was accustomed to camping practically anywhere, wrapped himself in his shepherd's cape and slept soundly under an army tent, dreaming of the world of the future—a world without mine- or land-owners, where miners ran the mines and workers the factories, where the police took orders from the trade unions. Cradled by such dreams, he was happy: even if his feet stuck out from under the tent, so tall was he, he was safe from any notice of firing or dispossession.

The next day Felice escorted Antonietta and their children on their way toward Norbio. The sun had barely risen above the dark Linas mountains, and was shedding a dusty light over the rooftops of the crowded houses. As they walked along the road, they could see stretches of pale green prickly-pears and, beyond, the dark green mountains. In the distance were sand dunes, covered with thick brush and, still farther away, an intensely blue sea turning into an expanse of transparent green. The mountains had to be crossed or circled in order to reach Norbio and the wide Capidano plain. The little family was near the crest of a hill when a wagon's harness bells sounded behind them. Felice recognized the driver's voice. Then the wagon, drawn by four horses, with a heavy load of brown cork, appeared from beyond the roadside hedge. The wagoner, a tall, bearded man, was walking beside one of the shafts, cracking his whip in the clear air.

"Hello there, Compare Giuseppe!" Felice called out. "Will you give my wife a lift to Norbio?" And, in a low voice, he said to Antonietta: "What luck! It's my friend, Giuseppe Lisca."

Felice explained their plight, and Giuseppe replied he would welcome company on the journey. The children, squealing with joy, were hoisted onto the wagon. Antonietta climbed up after them, disdainful of the men's assistance.

"I'm not happy about going," she whipered into her husband's ear.

"Don't worry. I'll be with you soon, perhaps even tomorrow."

The wagoner checked his harness, jumped onto the wagon, and urged the horses on. Felice waved, then walked briskly back downhill. He found the square filled with people staring up at the company building. There were miners, bargemen, and women and children as well. The committee must have already gone in, for he saw Sante hurrying to catch up.

When Sante entered the room, he was shown to an empty chair opposite the "Turk," Georgiades. Already seated was the Sub-Prefect of the Province, Signor Valle, who had come from Iglesias, as well as a police official and other government people. The seven members of the workers' committee exchanged looks with Sante, in mute confirmation of the agreement they had reached the evening before. Now that he was there, they felt more confidant. If they had failed to win any points at the previous meetings, perhaps it was because of his absence.

"Very well, then," the "Turk" began, "you're here on behalf of the workers in the Malfidano Mine . . ."

"Yes," said Sante, arranging some sheets of paper scattered on the table before him. "We"—and he made a sweeping gesture that drew in his companions—"represent the three thousand miners who work for the company."

"How do you know what these three thousand men are thinking?" asked the Sub-Prefect. "Have you held meetings?"

"We live together," said Sante, "and see one another every day."

"Do you hold meetings?"

"Yes."

"And where do these seditious gatherings take place?"

"There's nothing seditious about them, sir. All over Italy there are authorized workers' leagues and trade unions."

"Tolerated, you mean."

"No, sir, authorized by the government, in Genoa and Milan . . ."

"Here we're at neither Milan nor Genoa!" said the Sub-Prefect abruptly.

"True enough. This is Buggerru. But, even if it doesn't seem like it, it's part of Italy." And he continued coolly: "If you want to talk directly with our fellow-miners, there are two thousand of them out on the square."

"For the present, I'm talking to you. Do you represent the Workers' Leagues?"

"We represent the totality of the workers of Buggerru, and also the Leagues, of course."

"The Leagues, eh?" muttered the "Turk." "*Je m'en fiche.*"

"No, I don't think you will," said Sante, digging his hands into his broad, red wool sash, and feeling his stomach rumble under the pressure of the fingers. He had had only a cup of coffee early in the morning and the hands of the big clock on the wall stood at ten. The clock mechanism hummed and rasped, and the chimes played the first notes of the *Marseillaise*. The revolutionary anthem contrasted so strongly with the attitude of Monsieur Georgiades that Sante wondered if there was something here that had escaped him.

"Well, then," the manager continued in his heavily accented Italian. "You've presented a memorandum in which you make a number of claims. For instance . . ." He paused to pull some papers out of a leather briefcase . . . "Increased wages, lower rents, improvement of housing and sanitation facilities . . . But the Malfidano Company isn't a charitable organization!"

"We know that," said Sante firmly. "Our demands aren't for charity, they're for our rights, for what's owed us."

"I can't permit such language," shouted Georgiades, pounding the table and turning to the Sub-Prefect for support.

"It's not permissible," the Sub-Prefect echoed.

"I didn't ask your permission," answered Sante deliberately.

"And then," Georgiades went on, "you insist that the stores shouldn't be run by the company, as they are in every mining area."

"The lack of competition enables you to squeeze the last penny out of the miners and their families. The necessities of life cost more here than in either Rome or Milan, and I can prove it. In any case, we're here this morning to demand the restoration of the old working hours. We'll come back to our other claims later."

Once more the "Turk" pounded the table with his clenched, chubby fist.

"What's the fellow talking about?" asked the Sub-Prefect.

"The reason for the strike that's gone on for the last five days," said the manager, before Sante could give an answer.

"I can tell you the whole story," Sante interrupted. "For over thirty years the custom of this mine has been to suspend work from noon to three o'clock . . ."

"Which seems to show the company's concern for the miners' health and well-being," put in the Sub-Prefect.

"That's not the reason," Sante retorted. "After the three-hour break in which to wash up and eat their lunch, the miners were twice as productive. Now, all of a sudden, 'Monsieur' Georgiades has decided, although it is contrary to company interests, that the men should go back down into the mine at two o'clock, an hour at which you gentlemen are drinking your after-lunch cup of coffee and getting ready to take a nap."

"How do you dare . . . ?" shouted the assistant manager, Mancuso, who was sitting almost directly opposite him. He was in his thirties, with pomaded hair, parted in the middle, and a narrow mustache that formed two rings, one on either side of his somewhat effeminate mouth. He wore a white ribbed cotton vest, spotted by the ashes that fell from his Virginia cigarette.

Sante was tempted to stretch out a hand and choke him. For a moment he lost his self-control, his chest swelled under his rough shirt and, with his fingers, he slowly lifted up his side of the heavy oak table, causing papers and pencils to slide in disorderly fashion onto the laps of his opponents. Mancuso pushed back his chair and leaped to one side, and the others followed his example. A moment of confusion followed. At a gesture of the Sub-Prefect the two *carabinieri* standing, stiff as ramrods, on either side of the door moved into position at Sante's back. Suddenly aware of their presence, he cautiously lowered the table into its former position, and everyone returned to his place.

Georgiades was deathly pale. Upon his orders, three building employees brought in trays loaded with bottles and glasses. The odor of a tavern pervaded the room and *filuferru* restored color and self-assurance to the negotiators' faces. The miners nervously refused to drink. Nothing had been decided, and the clock marked half past noon. From outside, there could be heard the shouts of the crowd. Sante said impatiently:

"Our comrades have been waiting for nearly five hours."

"Too bad, but it's not my fault," said Georgiades. "I've sent a wire to Paris almost every day, but there's been no reply. In fact, I wired early this morning, calling attention to the gravity of the situation. No answer. It may be that the board of directors will meet your demands. But that's something I can't decide on my own. I have to wait for orders."

"Quite understandably," said the Sub-Prefect, thrusting his thumbs into his vest pockets.

Georgiades got up, bowed, and excused himself for once more leaving the room. At least five times in the course of the morning he had repeated the same manoeuver. Under the pretext of sending a telegram to Paris, he had actually telegraphed to the Prefect at Cagliari, who had promised to send two companies of soldiers. Meanwhile he was trying to gain time until their arrival.

Soon there was agitation on the square. The soldiers had arrived and were forcing a passageway through the crowd. Eventually they closed ranks and drew up in front of the company building. The shouted orders of the officers drowned out the confused clamor of the miners. One officer went inside. Entering the meeting room, he came to attention.

"Sir," he said, from under his dust-covered mustache, addressing himself to the Sub-Prefect, "I am Captain Bernardoni from the garrison of Cagliari. By order of His Excellency, I am yours to command."

His mouth clamped shut and he stood motionless, his fingers still raised to his cap. Georgiades appeared, in his turn, at the door.

"I didn't want to bother you," he said to the Sub-Prefect, "but I telegraphed to His Excellency the Prefect, just on my own, *en amitié*, if you'll allow me to say so."

"En amitié, my eye!" shouted Sante, who as an emigrant had acquired a smattering of French, jumping up from his chair and pushing Georgiades back through the doorway. He had a sudden intuition of what might happen, and rushed downstairs, followed by his companions.

The Sub-Prefect decided to barrack the soldiers in the sheds occupied by the municipal carpentry. The soldiers were covered with dust from the long march, and their uniforms were spotted by perspiration. What they most wanted was a drink of water, and they waited only for the order "Break ranks!" before they fanned out to look for it. The miners, after their initial dismay, felt sorry for them, and the women let them drink from their pitchers the brackish water of Buggerru. They gulped it down greedily, paying no heed to the officers' remonstrances. The heat was as intense as that of summer.

The workers who had instructions to ready the soldiers' lodgings slung their tools over their shoulders and went off, dragging their feet, in the direction of the carpentry sheds. In his usual devious way, Georgiades had imported some unemployed and hungry men from the neighboring town of Nebida, who were ready to do anything for money. Now, if ever, was the time to use them. They had been recruited at random and were totally unskilled; for this very reason, they were willing to follow management's orders.

When the miners who were still in the square heard the saws

and hammers, they advanced, shoulder to shoulder, and yelled at the strike-breakers, "Scabs! Scabs!" From the carpentry sheds there came an equally pungent reply that only fomented their irritation. Sante tried to explain that the strike-breakers weren't miners, that they had been brought in as a group from the outside. He appealed for calm, but no one paid him any attention. It would be the scabs' fault, the miners insisted, if the strike were to fail.

A rock hurled from the far end of the square flew over the crowd and struck a window of one of the sheds. Another followed, and another, until rocks were falling thick and fast. In a momentary panic, a never-to-be-identified individual gave a curt order which the soldiers automatically obeyed. Like a single man they leaned the butts of their rifles against the ground, retracted the bayonets, operated the loading mechanism and inserted a cartridge. Not all of them fired their rifles, but many did, and seemed glad to have done so, as if the shots had saved their lives. Later on, during the investigation, it was said that the rifles went off of their own accord and that the Prefect didn't even know that the soldiers had cartridge pouches on their belts.

Felice Littera clearly saw the movements of the soldier he was facing. He swung his long-handled hammer and hit his enemy over the head at the exact moment when he felt the heat of the exploding lead in his face and fell, unconscious, to the ground.

Sante, his face smeared with blood and his jacket in tatters, reached the confrontation point and looked around him. Almost all the miners' faces were familiar. One of them lay prone, with his face in the dust; Sante knelt down, gently turned him over onto his back, and broke into sobs. He got up, clasping his hands in front of him, staggered toward the company building, and went upstairs to the meeting room before anyone could stop him. The Sub-Prefect, Georgiades, and the others were all there. Sante displaced a chair, leaned over the table, and spat deliberately in Georgiades' face. The Sub-Prefect signaled to the two *carabinieri,* who promptly seized Sante by both arms while Georgiades walked away, clumsily wiping his face with the sleeve of his jacket.

"No!" Sante muttered to himself, resisting the handcuffs, and he swung at the *carabinieri* so hard that they both lost their balance and fell back against the conference table. With a single leap, he mounted the sill of the open window, where, for a moment, he stood on one foot. After a quick glance at the dismayed face of the Sub-Prefect, he calculated the ten-foot drop to the ground, then sat on the sill and slid down, landing gracefully on his feet. Immediately he ran diagonally across the square in the direction of the road winding up the hillside beyond. Only at the top did he pause to look behind him and make sure that he wasn't followed. He stood stock still, catching his breath. At the moment of his jump he had thought he heard the Sub-Prefect say: "Don't shoot!" to the *carabinieri*. Now he was quite sure that this order had been given, in a low voice, to be sure, but decisively. The Sub-Prefect had repeated the single word: "No! No! No!" Probably even he had enough of killing for the day.

At this point, Sante heard a wagon's harness bells and the cracking of a whip on the Arbus road. Cautiously he followed a narrow passageway through the hedge of prickly pears and then lengthened his steps until he found a hiding place in a clump of mastic trees. The fellow cracking his whip was Francesco Zedda Lumbau, known as Carrabusu. Physically Carrabusu was strikingly like Sante Follesa, tall, agile, and unusually strong. But where Sante was quiet and even-tempered, Carrabusu was boastful and overbearing, always ready to pick a quarrel. More than once they had come to blows. On the Piazza Frontera, a few years before, over a petty matter of precedence, they had had one of the roughest fistfights Norbio had ever seen, and Carrabusu had come out of it considerably battered. Ever since he had brooded because there had been no chance for revenge. Now Sante glimpsed him almost overhead, as if he were on the rim of the world, standing on his wagon behind four husky horses. Had Carrabusu seen Sante, he wouldn't have hesitated to report him to the first squad of *carabinieri*.

He freed himself from the handcuffs, weighed them for a moment in the palm of his hand, and then threw them far away. He saw them rise up in the air, their metal shining for a second in the sun, and then fall into some blackberry bushes. He remained hidden until the wagon was safely past, then cautiously made his way back to the road. The countryside was empty and silent except for the rustle of the wind. Only the day before, he had been in Norbio: nothing had yet happened, the two companies of soldiers had not yet marched to Buggerru, the violence might still have been avoided, and those were alive, twenty-four hours ago, who were now dead. He detached his long knife from his sash and cut a stout stick of arbutus. A deep feeling of frustration and failure beset him. If he had not insulted Georgiades and had run away, perhaps he might have taken advantage of the negotiators' confusion and obtained some concession from them. As it was, he had had the satisfaction of spitting in the "Turk's" face, and that was the end of it or, rather, there had been no end, because he was now a fugitive and if he were to avoid imprisonment, he would have to leave the country, to travel surreptitiously to Corsica, and thence to Marseilles. But meanwhile, he must go back to Norbio, speak to Angelo Uras, and make arrangements for Littera's widow and children. Felice was beyond his help: the comrades who had braved death beside him would see to his burial.

After a moment's pause, he turned his back on Buggerru, left the road, and went down from the crest of the hill in the opposite direction, cutting through thick woods. Even if the Sub-Prefect had ordered the soldiers on guard in the meeting room to hold their fire, Sante knew he was not going to be let off scot free. The only way to be safe was to stick to the paths traveled by goats and fugitives from justice. Not very far away he could hear the clatter of Carrabusu's wagon and the driver's shouts as he whipped on his horses, regardless of the fact that they were lathered with sweat and the load was precariously balanced. The lesser track, which Sante finally reached and followed, ran parallel to the road so that the sound of the wagon, although fainter, never left him. Whenever he stopped, the wagon got ahead of him, but when he started walking again, he overtook and went beyond it until his next pause. Coming to a brook, he stopped to bathe his feet, which were hot and dry in his heavy miner's shoes. A minute later, he arrived at a hut where a goatherd was standing astride a nanny-goat and squirting her foaming milk into a cork bucket.

"Look at this!" he said proudly, glancing up at the visitor. "To think I already milked her this morning! She's no ordinary goat, I can tell you!"

"What makes for so much milk?" Sante asked him.

"It depends on a lot of things, the breed of the animal, the quality of the pasturage, and also on the moon."

Sante gulped down some milk and felt immediately refreshed. He looked up at the diaphanous, fuzzy moon that seemed to be melting into the still daylit air above the summit of Mount San Michele.

"It depends on God, when you get down to it," the goatherd concluded.

"On God? What's God got to do with it?" Sante never thought about God. God didn't enter into even his childhood memories.

"He's got to do with it, yes, he does," the goatherd insisted.

They chatted for a while, and then Sante thanked him and went on. The wagon had gone far ahead of him and he no longer heard the noise that might have guided him on his way through the darkening woods.

Toward evening, lamps were lit and there were signs of life in the houses of Buggerru. Smoke rose from the chimneys, over the rooftops, blackening the sky except over the sea, which still shimmered in the last rays of the dying sun. All the familiar household noises could be heard throughout the evening hours, until they faded away into the silence of the night.

News of the massacre traveled like an electrical shock through the working class over all Italy. In Milan, it was announced at a protest meeting, and there was a general strike from one end of the Peninsula to the other. But in Sardinia, it roused no echo. The silence of that sorrowful afternoon of September 4, 1904 at Buggerru was symbolic of the mute role that Sardinia played in the overall life of the nation.

Sante came to Norbio the next night. In the black sky, he recognized the mass of Mount Carmelo and the tall twin rocks of Giarrana. When he crossed the Castangias end of the town, with its narrow, cobbled streets, he had, at last, a feeling of reassurance. At home his mother was waiting, with a pot of hot bean soup in one corner of the fireplace. She said that Angelo Uras had inquired about him. It was known that he wasn't dead, that he had escaped from the *carabinieri*, and for this reason she had stayed up and kept the soup ready. Then she asked him about Felice Littera.

"If you ask, it means you already know. . . ."

"Yes . . . but how did it happen?"

Sante shrugged his shoulders. The old woman pulled off his shoes and put his feet into a basin of hot water. With a feeling of great relief, he lay down on the straw bed, covered with skins, where he had been born some thirty years before. He fell asleep at once, like a baby, with no cares, watched over by his mother. In the morning he awakened, rested, to find his mother sleeping with her head on the table. Rickety old pieces of furniture and everyday household objects stood out clearly and without shadows in the transparent light of the early October morning. He went outside, bare to the waist, to wash in the good well water. It had an earthy smell. A paper-thin layer of ice had formed over the water during the night and was now melting under the first rays of the sun. With his eyes shut, a man could guess at the weather by plunging his hand into the well. After he had dried himself, Sante put on a clean white shirt, drank a cup of hot coffee, and left the house. His mother made no more than a half-hearted effort to hold him back. From what he had told her she knew he risked arrest, but she let him go, with a silent prayer.

On the streets there were only women, an occasional old man, and schoolchildren carrying their books in torn bags and cases. There was also a wagon, loaded with twigs to be used as kindling wood, driven by one of Angelo Uras' farmhands, Saverio. Sante gave him a knowing wink and leaped up on the wagon. From Saverio he learned that news of the strike and the massacre had arrived at Norbio in an exaggerated and distorted form. Rumor had it that all the miners of the Iglesiente region had revolted and that all the soldiers sent from Cagliari had been killed, together with a large number of miners. It was known, of course, that the *carabinieri* were after Sante Follesa. Concealed under the twigs, Sante was driven in the wagon straight into the courtyard of the Uras house. Angelo was happy to see him and immediately offered him a cup of coffee.

"They lost their heads," he said, with a long sigh.

"That's no excuse," Sante shot back, looking at him obliquely.

"No excuse, no," the mayor admitted. "In certain posts, there's no excuse for losing your head, and that's what they did . . . you fellows, too, for that matter."

In a fury Sante put down his cup.

"Us? There were two thousand of us, and we'd been waiting for five hours. One man alone can be patient, think things out, exercise some self-control. But in a crowd of two thousand, someone's sure to crack."

They looked each other in the eye, and then Sante added:

"The man who called the soldiers and the man who sent them are responsible for what happened. The soldiers, poor devils, can't really be blamed."

They walked up and down for some time under the overhanging portico. Angelo did not hide his sympathy for the massacred miners, but he sought for a justification, or at least an explanation, of the authorities' behavior. His whole life, after all, had been a passage from the peasantry to the bourgeoisie, or, as they said in Norbio, to the "gentry." Toying with the gold chain of his pocketwatch, he tried to get a clear idea of the events. Coming to a sudden halt, he asked: "Didn't you fellows suspect that the soldiers might shoot?"

"I was in the meeting room, with the miners' committee, the manager, and the Sub-Prefect. I became aware of the soldiers' arrival when I heard the officers shouting orders. But it didn't occur to me they'd shoot. At that moment, we were discussing the question of the lunch break . . . you know the living and working conditions at Buggerru."

"Yes, I know."

"Well, we'd been arguing this point for hours, and down on the square our men were waiting to hear the results. Then rocks began to fly . . . ."

"Rocks?" Angelo queried, dropping the watch chain.

"The miners were throwing rocks at the scabs who had consented to turn the carpentry sheds into soldiers' barracks. But we can't be blamed. They shouldn't have brought in the scabs and set them against us. And there was no need to send for the soldiers. A discussion was in progress and we were thrashing things out. That damned 'Turk'! If he'd only agreed to go back to the old lunch schedule, everything would have quieted down. Of course, the Prefect, too, is to blame."

Sante had stopped walking and was looking intently at his interlocutor.

"It seems to me," said Angelo, "that both sides should have been more moderate. Some of the rocks hurled at the scabs hit soldiers, and it was natural that they should react. Any men in their place would do the same thing."

"That's just it. The soldiers shouldn't have been there. They were brought to Buggerru to shoot, and shoot they did. Not exactly the way to settle a dispute, is it?"

Angelo nodded gravely. In his heart, he was on the side of Sante and of all the miners.

"The Prefect was in cahoots with the 'Turk.' They were set on what they call 'giving us a lesson.' Too many lessons of this kind are being given in Italy these days, I tell you."

The two men were standing shoulder to shoulder, until Sante took a step forward and stretched himself, with something like a groan.

"Very well," said Angelo, "but someone should have used his head. Violence won't help the working class."

"I know," said Sante, gazing up at the sky. "I know you hate violence and that you understand what I've been saying. You treat your workers well; you give them fair pay and see that they have enough to eat. But your horror of violence doesn't prevent you from condoning war, from supporting an army that not only kills miners but conquers colonies as well."

"All the European powers . . ." Angelo started to protest.

"I know that line of reasoning, too, but I'm on the side of the Negus of Abyssinia and of all the black and yellow peoples. They're 'colonized' in Africa and Asia, and we workers are 'colonized' right here at home. You're an honest man, the best sort of man we can hope for in this filthy country, but you're tied to your class and also to your property."

They resumed their pacing up and down. Saverio was unloading the pile of twigs near the wood shed, and Maria Giuseppa was stacking them. Angelo's attitude toward Sante was one of genuine friendliness. No argument could cast a shadow over this feeling, one which took him back to his childhood. When he got the first news of the massacre, his impulse was to mount his horse and ride to the aid of "his own people." Only prudence had held him back. He could help them more, he realized, if he didn't seem too precipitate in protecting their interests vis-à-vis the law. And so he simply asked, as mayor, that the body of Felice Littera be sent back to Norbio, and at the same time, took emergency measures for immediate financial aid to the widow. Angelo had a deep concern for justice, a concern he had learned from his parents and that was part of his peasant heritage. He wanted justice for Sante Follesa, this man walking beside him and occasionally bumping his shoulder, this man who had survived by a miracle, this man whose life pattern might have been his own and which was, perhaps, one he secretly envied.

"You hate violence, all of you," Sante repeated, "but you accept the calling in of the soldiers. Humbler men stick it out, or they emigrate; they don't vote because they're illiterate and pay no property tax, and if they gather in the square to obtain a hearing, they're mowed down. You're a good man, Angelo Uras, you run this village as if it belonged to you, like the father of a family. But that won't change the world. And the world has got to be changed. Certain rights are the same for all. And I'm ready to get them by violence."

"Do you want to start a revolution?" Angelo asked half-seriously.

"If it's necessary, yes," was Sante's firm reply. "I don't like it any more than you do, but I see no other solution. And when the real shooting begins, I won't be lined up on your side."

"You're making a speech where there's no need of it," said Angelo, trying to maintain a light tone. "Anyhow, you can't start a revolution all by yourself and, this minute, neither here nor in Buggerru will you find many followers. And if you're caught, they're going to throw you in jail. I can always get you a lawyer, and you wouldn't stay shut up for long, because they'll want Buggerru to be forgotten. But what I'd rather do is give you a good job. I need men like you."

Sante stood stiffly, digging his fists into the pockets of his patched trousers. His face, too, was like a clenched fist, and there was a hostile look in his eyes.

"Thank you, Angelo Uras, but I can't accept. I came to say good-by and to entrust Felice's wife and children to your care. I'm going to make for Corsica and then for Marseilles."

"Are you sure that's what you want to do? Have you thought it over?"

"I don't need to give it a second thought," said Sante.

"Well, sometimes a man's will coincides with his fate. I wish you the best of luck. There's a shipload of cork going straight to Marseilles next week. If you like, you can go with it."

"That offer I can accept, and I'm grateful."

They clasped hands, and then Sante went away, walking with measured, deliberate steps through the village as if in the direction of his imagined future.

Before Francesco left for Massawa, Don Tommaso had asked Angelo, on his behalf, for Maria Christina's hand, and the engagement had been officially announced to family and friends. This announcement, which both young people would have liked to keep simple and intimate, turned out to be a public event. The town councillors all came to offer their good wishes and congratulations, and even Serrasogu kissed Maria Christina on both cheeks. Angelo's consent was not as willing as it seemed: he was worried about the dowry, without which Francesco could not marry. It troubled him to part with some of the property that by hard work and good luck he had managed to put together and that seemed like an integral part of himself. Now that he had lost the vigor of youth, the thought of giving up land weighed heavily upon him. He didn't need to count up the years to realize that he was growing old; he felt it every time he put his foot in the saddle or rode for too long or even when, as often, he indulged in memories of the past. The course of his early life was clear in his mind: his mother, Don Francesco, Valentina, and all the feelings he had had about them. And he was aware of having changed since those faraway days.

However, he made an agreement with Don Tommaso and handed over the vineyard of Pranu Mesu to his daughter. Knowing and loving her father as she did, Maria Christina understood his reluctance and worked to make up to him for his "great sacrifice." To her, money and property had little importance; she cared only for the love of Francesco and was saddened, as she had been before, by the prospect of his going away. Francesco, on the other hand, seemed almost happy. It was some time since the idea of wearing a uniform had bothered him. He now felt very much at ease, and during the three years at the Military Academy, he had become completely adjusted to army life. In spite of loving Maria Christina, he was glad to be off and, without showing it, he was waiting impatiently for the moment when he could pull down the lid of his campaign chest and go. This last stay at Norbio had dragged; village life seemed tedious and monotonous now that he had come to enjoy the city, the company of his comrades, and even the discipline to which he was committed. His political ideas were elementary; perhaps he had no ideas at all, but only feelings. He was thrilled by the sight of the flag, the strains of the Royal March, the cadenced tread of the regiment when it was on review, even if he was intelligent enough to understand the rhetorical nature of superficial patriotism. At the moment, Africa fired his imagination. He was called to an almost bureaucratic assignment, in an old fort baked by the tropical sun. But, unaware of this unromantic reality, he dreamed of the Africa of Pierre Loti and the explorer, Captain Bottego, of exotic women and hunting expeditions.

When Francesco left, Angelo went with him to Cagliari, saying, quite vaguely, that he had "business" to transact there. A man called Silvestri had written to him as representative, he said, of the heirs to the wealth of the Sanguinetti family, which owned the forests of Fontana Nera, Mazzani, and Mudegu. Already the year before, Silvestri had tried, unsuccessfully, to make a sale. Now Angelo, without speaking of it to anybody, couldn't help dreaming, in his turn, of "liberating" these great woods. He asked Maria Christina to help him pack his valise, a portmanteau he had bought years before. Then he took a hot bath, and dressed with special care. Margherita pursed her lips as she watched the preparations for departure. She did not understand her husband's mood, his mysterious urgency to go to Cagliari. In all the years of her marriage, she had lacked the intuition to sense what her husband might have on his mind, and even when he spoke of it, she did not always grasp the meaning. She had never been capable of the kind of love that develops grace, sensibility, and intelligence.

Angelo and Francesco traveled by carriage to Acquapiana and there took the train to Cagliari. Francesco was in uniform, and Angelo in a linen duster. Under the train shed of the Cagliari station, they were surrounded by a swarm of *piccioccus de crobi*, ragged, barefoot boys who, for a very small sum, were ready to carry parcels and small pieces of luggage in their big, yellow reed baskets. When Angelo returned home with purchases made at the market, he usually made use of their services. But on this occasion, he was tired and pushed them aside. He and Francesco boarded a horse-drawn tram, loaded with sweating, impatient people; everyone felt their nerves were on edge because of the sirocco wind that wafted the hot breath of the North African desert over the sea. It might have been a summer day. The tram ran down the Via Roma, bordered on one side by massive buildings with a shaded arcade in front of them and on the other by tall fig trees whose thick foliage was encrusted with dust. Through the leaves, the harbor, where railway locomotives were backed up alongside the red-and-black steamers, was visible. The rounded sterns of sailboats were so close to the docks that they nearly touched them, and porters and longshoremen were running to and fro. The whistle of a steamer or a locomotive sounded at intervals above the metallic din of the traffic and the confused hum of human voices. The Via Roma was crowded with people who seemed not to know where they were going or what they were doing at this stiflingly hot, late afternoon hour. The sun was hidden behind a pile of clouds, suffused, in turn, with yellow, orange, red, green, and blue. The façades of the buildings, the highest towers of the Castle, and the houses crowded together on the intervening hillside, among tufts of palm and agave and the buttresses of the medieval fortifications, were tinged with the same fantastic hues, which soon would fade away, leaving the city under an amethyst evening sky.

Angelo and Francesco, wearied by their journey and annoyed by the tumult around them, refused to surrender themselves to the familiar city. Every time they came, it revealed itself for what it was—crowded and hectic, with spectacular sunsets and a feverish gaiety that prevailed over the heat, the dust, the sirocco, and the stench of rotted seaweed from both the seashore and the inland backwaters. The people in the streets chattered in singsong voices, very different from the dry, hard speech of the country folk. Cagliari had nothing in common with the rest of the Island. From ancient times it had served as the conquerors' stronghold, and its heterogeneous population of mixed blood looked down on everyone from the back country. When Angelo came to the city he felt like a peasant, and, like any good peasant, he had an acute feeling of inferiority; he became timid and vulnerable.

Francesco was sitting beside him, and Angelo saw sweat pour down his tanned cheeks into the stiff collar of his jacket and soak his impeccable white ribbed cotton tie. "Who knows what the fellow is thinking?" he said to himself, wishing that he could read his future son-in-law's mind. He knew nothing about him, really, although he had seen him grow up under his own eyes. At the end of the broad Via Roma, the tram turned to the left, without slowing up, and climbed the less crowded Viale Regina Margherita, bordered by smaller trees and lower houses. He recognized the reddish building of the tobacco factory. The gas street lamps had been turned on, and the street seemed to stretch endlessly in the direction of the higher part of the city. After the Piazza Indipendenza, the tram climbed, with greater effort, up to the Piazza Martiri, which was the end of the line. Angelo and Francesco got off, embraced each other, and said good-by. Then Angelo walked briskly toward the "Iron Stair."

Silvestri was waiting for him in the hall. He was a tall, thin man with gray eyes and sparse, faded hair. They sat down by the window and began, immediately, to discuss the business that had brought them together.

"Signor Uras, you know better than I the forests of Fontana Nera, Mazzanni, and Mudegu, and you certainly aren't unacquainted with the name of Sanguinetti. My clients are anxious to sell, and I wanted to propose the purchase to you before anyone else."

Angelo was nervous, but he kept his feelings under control. So the woods were actually up for sale. He lit a cigarette and said: "May I offer you a glass of beer?"

"I'd rather have Malvasia wine," said Silvestri, taking a pipe and a tobacco pouch out of his pocket. The waiter brought a bottle and two glasses, poured the wine and backed away, bowing.

"Not a bad drink," said Silvestri, after a sip. "So . . . what do you think of my offer?"

"I'm glad you are offering it to me, but you'll have to be more definite. How much are your clients asking? I must have a few days to think about it. But," he added after draining his glass, "I'm interested."

"My clients won't wait very long."

"I don't ask for very long," said Angelo. "But the idea requires some thought. And there's the matter of raising the money, of arranging for a bank loan. That is, if it's really worthwhile."

"It won't take much money," Silvestri assured him.

Angelo put out his cigarette and lit another, accompanying the gesture with a subdued, ironical laugh.

"Don't hurry me," he said, with his face wrinkling like a winter apple around the slanted eyes and drooping mustache that gave it a Mongol cast. "I've never liked being rushed. You simply must give me time to think."

"All the time you want, Signor Uras. I'll be waiting for your decision."

The prospect of becoming a large-scale landowner danced in Angelo's mind the length of the return journey. The sale was legitimate and he could raise the money by mortgaging Aletzi. "Everyone looks out for his own interests, what the devil!" he said to himself. But there was something unclear and unsatisfying. Somehow the "deal" didn't make him happy, and yet he couldn't discover the reason. There was no risk involved; in only a few years the forests would be paid for.

All alone, except for Basilio, the watchman, he spent a whole afternoon in the town hall studying the files and reconstructing the story of the woodland tracts, which had been sold, long ago, by inept administrators to buyers who had handled them no less ineptly. The real losers had been the shepherds to whom pastures had been rented for exorbitant sums. As he leafed through the old land registers, the words of Sante Follesa, who was now sailing away under a false name, echoed in his ears: "You're a good man, Angelo Uras . . . but that's not enough. . . ."

That night he slept badly. The next morning he went to the town hall and told Cavaliere Frongia to summon the Council. While drawing up the agenda, he was momentarily uncertain but resolved his doubts with a vague phrase: "No. 1—Supplementary communal land acquisitions," whose exact meaning even he himself did not quite know. And while the town clerk looked at him in a puzzled way, he added: "No. 2—Request for loan from the Savings and Loan Bank." Cavaliere Frongia stared at him, gaping. He had never drawn up a request of this kind and had no idea of how to go about it. The matter called for further study.

Angelo went slowly down the granite steps that led from the front of the town hall to the Piazza Frontera. Men lifted their caps respectfully in greeting, and women nodded, with a light in their eyes, in his direction. They were all people who trusted him. He went into the café, ordered a glass of brandy, gulped it down in the peasant manner, and asked for more.

"How was the hunting, Mr. Mayor?"

"Good. Very good. They caught two boars."

"What do you mean by 'they'? Weren't you the leader?"

"I went with them, but I didn't shoot. I'm too old for that kind of thing."

"Nonsense! You're just as healthy and strong as you were twenty years ago. Have another drink!"

He let the barman fill his glass and downed the contents as rapidly as he had before. The fellow was right; he was healthy and strong, even if, in the last day or two, his ideas had been somewhat muddled. How bracing was the air of Norbio this autumn! All of a sudden the town crier's horn sounded, and he called out:

"By order of the Mayor, the following announcement: the Council is summoned to meet at four o'clock tomorrow afternoon. Members are urged to be present!"

"Tomorrow" he would speak at the meeting and inform the councillors of the woodlands offer. The township should buy the forests, not he! This conviction had slowly grown within him and now his happiness was complete, with no shadow of doubt across it. And he felt genuinely young, as in the days of his love for Valentina.

The councilmen would surely be against his proposal and he prepared to fight hard and aggressively to convince them of its worth. He could easily understand the crude thinking of Serrasogu who, as a cattle owner, could see no advantage in the township's purchase of woodland areas. But owners of sheep and goats should take a different view; they would pay less rent for pasturage, and eventually it would be free, as in the days when land belonged to everybody, like air and clouds and sun.

Angelo knew that owning a little herd of animals was a very different thing from possessing land or money. Although he himself was a land-owner, a passionate grower of trees and, like a tree, rooted in the land, he understood the mentality of the herdsman. A flock of sheep or goats is alive, it has eyes and horns and legs, every animal is different from the next, with its own way of grazing and even of giving milk. The Enclosure Law had forcibly created private property. It had destroyed the balance of communal life and made for an irreconcilable conflict of interests between peasants, who suddenly became landowners, and herdsmen, who were compelled to live a nomadic existence, always in search of a pasture for the sheep or goats from which they made a living. Out of sympathy for the herdsmen, Angelo looked back to the time before the law as to a mythical golden age. But it was not so remote that it could not be brought back to life for the good of the people of Norbio.

At the Council meeting, he fought vigorously. He clothed his dream in hard facts and statistics and, although at moments he feared he would be voted down, in the end he won, and there was a unanimous vote for the purchase. At table, in his own house, he admitted that he had foregone a great business opportunity, one that might have made him a very, very rich man. Filippo, his eldest son, who at thirteen looked more and more like his mother, did not hesitate to voice his disapproval. "You mean we could have had more money than anyone else in Parte d'Ispi?" he asked regretfully. "A lot of money doesn't mean much," said Angelo, in melancholy fashion. Maria Christina appeared pleased with what her father had done. As for Margherita, she continued to eat her dinner without betraying any emotion whatsoever.

Too much, you try to do too much," Senator Loru said when he heard about the project of reforesting the foothills of Mount Linas. But Angelo would not let himself be discouraged. He had a very keen awareness of time, he knew that he would not live long enough to see the mountainside covered with trees. This awareness enabled him to conceive of time in a dimension infinitely greater than of an individual's life span, of that brief cycle during which dust takes on the shape of man before returning to dust. Trees last longer, he reflected; unconsciously, he associated them with the enduring link that binds one generation to another. He was thinking specifically of the giant, hundred-year-old olive trees of Balanotti and the magnolia that shaded the washhouse.

"Do you want to go on being mayor?" the senator asked him.

"Yes, just for the sake of planting pines," Angelo answered calmly. "You politicians have allowed the destruction of the forests, and I want to re-create them."

"But why pines? Why not oaks? Pine trees have no fruit; they have little timber value."

"They're beautiful to look at. They cleanse the air, they check the flow of water, and their wood can't be burned in the foundries."

"Madness, pure madness!" said the ninety-year-old Loru.

"So far it's only a plan. I hope to carry it out."

"Why should you push yourself so hard?"

"For my own pleasure. A hundred years from now this country . . ."

"A hundred years from now, the people of this country will be just as flinty-hearted as they are today."

"Hearts . . . and souls . . . they're not my concern," said Angelo, drinking down a glass of *filuferru*. "That's why I didn't want to be a priest."

And so, for the whole of his twenty-year mandate, Angelo worked at changing the face of Norbio. The people were always behind him: only the councillors, although they elected and reelected him, always opposed his projects at the start, and in the end, they always gave in.

No one would have thought of erecting lampposts, one every two hundred paces, as Maria Christina wrote to Francesco, but once they were there, everyone was pleased. It had been the same thing for the washhouse, the slaughterhouse and, finally, for the pines. Indeed, after the first saplings had been planted near the Carmel chapel, the village schoolchildren undertook to water them every day. In the afternoon when school let out, they were to be seen walking, single file, with earthenware pitchers, up to the church where each one took care of the tree for whose growth he had promised to be responsible. This was more than even Angelo could have hoped for. He never held mass meetings, but he had a gift for finding the right word and the right tone with which to present a project. On this occasion, he had the idea that every child should have a pitcher for a toy.

The school superintendent hailed this a real discovery, "one that you would expect from a professional educator."

Nor did it happen, as the town Council had predicted, that the pine saplings were devoured by goats. Goatherds gave the area a wide berth, and if one of their animals was attracted by the green patch which, from the Piazza Frontera, looked like moss growing on rocks, they drove him back into the flock. The saplings grew, unharmed, and others were planted beside them, until every child had two, three, and four to look after, and they grew in height as they grew in number. After a few years, there were fifteen hundred pines, a young and vigorous pine forest. And today, a century later, in spite of inefficient government and the repeated menace of "developers" and sub-divisions, the pines are a hundred and fifty thousand. When the wind blows, their tossing branches roar like the sea. Walking up toward the chapel, a visitor sees enormous specimens, with gnarled, gray branches, that might have been buffeted by a cosmic wind but, like the wind, are everlasting and indestructible.

Part Five

With the passage of the years, Angelo felt increasingly alone, cut off, as it were, from the life that went its way around him. Many things had happened. Don Tommaso was dead, Carmela and Alfonso had married and had a daughter, Giovanna, as pretty and lively as her mother; Angelo's and Margherita's three sons, Filippo, Oreste and Amedeo, were grown men; Maria Christina's little boy, Marco, was Angelo's favorite grandchild who, with the others, filled the house with noise and chatter. The life of Norbio was the life of its young people, and he was an old man who had no friends left with whom to joke and in that indirect way to express personal and private concerns. His mother had been a great one for jokes and laughter, but now everyone around him was deadly serious, including Maria Christina. Francesco was in the trenches and, although she was not tearful, she was devoured by anxiety.

People hailed Angelo with respect, lifting their caps and saying: "Greetings, Angelo Uras! God bless you!" but he never knew exactly what they were thinking.

Often, looking at the Manno house, he remembered it as it was when the sisters were young and charming and Valentina, the loveliest of them all, had worked over her embroidery on the great covered veranda; he remembered when, for the only time in his life, he had been genuinely in love. Now Valentina had been buried for years in the cemetery on the other side of the river, where worn stone crosses clustered about a tall cypress tree. Her grave was marked by a marble cross, indeed by a shaft with two sculpted hands, one a man's, the other a woman's, clasped in a gesture of friendship rather than love. And yet there had been love between them, real love, which lived on in Angelo's heart, even while he was an old man. He felt as if his life were a long succession of years or, rather, one long year, complete with all its seasons, droughts, sudden storms, and some serene and perfect days, few and far between, and most of them long gone by.

The reason for Marco's desperate weeping every time his father went away was not, as Uncle Oreste would have it, an infantile "psychosis"; it was simple and honest despair, because every separation, under war conditions, could be permanent. Francesco was in the front lines and the little boy knew what this meant. Every day his grandfather read the casualty list aloud, and every Sunday more women came to church with black shawls on their heads. Marco realized that his father was running the same risk as the others and that his house, too, could go into mourning. Although he knew nothing of death except its outward appearances, he knew that the dead don't come back, that they disappear forever. If his father were to die, he would never see him again and he could never again be happy. Every time Francesco left, Marco was keenly aware that it might be for good. Everyone in the household tried to persuade the others to the contrary, but those who cared the most had a hard time holding back their tears. Concealing their worry, they watched Francesco smilingly button up his long gray-green coat; they looked at his black mustache and gay, carefree blue eyes. "Is it possible that he isn't thinking the same thing?" they wondered. Perhaps he would never set foot again in the old house which he was leaving so lightheartedly. Healthy and strong as he was, he could die the next day, the minute he set foot in the trenches, like so many young men who hadn't had time even

to write a postcard announcing their arrival at the front. Uncle
Oreste, when he said good-by, he so thin and sickly, embraced
Francesco as if to ask forgiveness for the fact that he too wasn't
in the fight (although he would have been hard put to it to say
what it was all about, really) and overcame his emotion by saying, in his musical voice, that by spring it would all be over.
The others, too, aunts, uncles, cousins, and the friends who had
come to see him off, all tried to cheer up Maria Christina by
saying the same thing, as if this were the last winter of the war
because it would surely end by spring. They lied because they
were sorry for Francesco's wife and child and because they were
so fond of him. These difficult moments united them, and they
became affectionate in a way that contrasted with their usual
reserve. Even in Uncle Oreste's skeptical laughter there were
echoes of an emotion which gripped him like a sudden pain.
Marco understood this, too, just as he understood that, no matter how much they all loved his father, and perhaps for this
very reason, when the day of departure drew near they were
anxious to get it over. And when the day actually came and the
carriage drew up at the door, their sorrow was such that eventually all of them—except for Marco and his mother—were impatient to see him drive away.

When the moment of parting came Maria Christina fainted;
she fell to the floor and had to be carried to her room. At this
point Marco, who was no longer so very little, was entrusted
to Annamaria, his former wet nurse, and was led away so that
when his mother revived she would not find him crying. Everyone spoke up for "getting him away from his mother," but
actually the sound of his hopeless, childish weeping frightened
them like an open wound and, because they couldn't stop it,
they wanted to banish it from their hearing. Annamaria picked
Marco up and took him to her house, in the Castangias section,
the oldest part of the town, with its small stone dwellings and
narrow courtyards heaped high with piles of dried twigs,
bundles of reeds, and long poles. The houses, looking like blackened shells, got their light from small windows and from a door
opening onto the courtyard. Annamaria sat in front of the door,
threw her shawl over Marco, and sang lullabies to him, just as

Maria Christina sang to the new baby, little Emanuele, until finally he calmed down. But for days after he had gone back home, there were sobs stored up inside him, and a stray thought or mental picture caused him to burst into tears. Then, little by little, he grew accustomed to his father's absence. Despair turned into melancholy, and prolonged melancholy melted away in the long, monotonous winter nights. And yet there was always the fear, a reflection of that so obvious in his mother, that bad news might be on the way.

The other men of the house, partly through the influence of Francesco, had managed easily enough to keep out of the war. Uncle Oreste because he was so delicate, Uncle Filippo because he was a dealer in army supplies, and Uncle Amedeo because, in view of his father's old age, he was needed to look after the land. All this was quite proper, but Marco envied his cousins, the children of Uncle Amedeo; beside them, he felt cheated. Uncle Amedeo didn't merely look after the land, he went hunting as well. Coming back from a whole day's absence, he scooped up his three little ones, who had interrupted their games to run and greet him. When Marco heard their laughter and happy voices, his eyes filled with tears and he ran to seek consolation from his mother. At no other time of his life did he suffer as much as during those long, winter afternoons when he was a child.

No, it wasn't a "psychosis," as Uncle Oreste told Maria Christina; it was a sorrow too deep for a mere child to cope with. If anyone laughed, he wished him dead. His child's hatred was as compelling as his precocious sorrow.

Every Sunday, the Uras family—that is, the women and children—went to Mass and, in the evening, to vespers. Their contact with the Church was regular and continuous, but not so, it seemed to Marco, their relationship to God. God was far away and high above, on an invisible throne. Whereas the saints to whom his mother and grandmother and aunts addressed themselves with veneration, but also with a certain ease and familiarity, were people like themselves. The churches of Norbio were crowded with images, one for every chapel, and, on festive days, more than one, just as the drawing room of Grandmother Margherita was crowded with portraits. The paintings and statues occupied shadowy places in the church; they were mysterious in their holiness, but dressed like the villagers, with eyes, hands, beards, and feet like those of the people who knelt down or made the sign of the cross as they went by. Everyone chose a saint of his own to whom to pray, as an intercessor with God, the God who dwelt beyond the curtain of clouds around Mount Homo and also beyond the most secret thoughts of his creatures.

Everybody in Norbio suffered from the war, but there were degrees of suffering and, to Marco's mind, injustice in their difference and distribution. In the evening, when the family and friends gathered around the table burst into laughter, Marco resented them. As for the gentle and defenseless Maria Christina, she felt the separation from her husband so deeply that she withdrew from the people around her. At the very moment when they raised their glasses to toast some future happiness, in which Maria Christina and Marco felt they had no part, hundreds and thousands of men were dying. Even if Francesco was not killed at this particular moment, a bullet might pass within inches of his heart. Marco saw his mother's eyes fill with tears as she rose to her feet. There was silence for a moment as she left the room. Then the drinking went on. Later, Marco remembered none of his mingled feelings, except for the sheer hatred, so very terrible in a child.

Angelo's wife, children, servants, and even the smallest of his grandchildren were ready and eager to follow him every time he went down into the courtyard. They wouldn't let him out of their sight, and this was burdensome to him. He wanted to be his own master, to go where he pleased without accounting for his movements. He was satisfied with a juniper stick to lean on, the money with which to buy a glass of sweet wine, and some lumps of sugar in his waistcoat pocket.

But this morning as he started to leave the house, nobody gave signs of life; he could not hear even the children. He stopped and turned around to look up at the windows of the apartment of Edvige and Amedeo. At this hour his daughter-in-law Edvige must be bathing her last-born, Carlina, who was only a year old. Mentally he measured the span of time that included the baby's tender age and his own decline. Not very far removed from either end there was darkness, pre-natal darkness and the unknown darkness of death. He walked unhurriedly toward the gate. Suddenly he was disappointed, almost hurt that no one had followed or stopped him, that nobody was worrying about his safety. "Perhaps," he thought to himself, not for the first time, "I'm already dead." And he imagined his own body lying inertly in the big leather armchair, the head thrown back, the throat exposed. The part of him that now walked, thinking and seeing, across the courtyard, was pure spirit, transparent, silent, light as air, invisible, and happy to go away. This thought made him feel happy and free.

He searched his waistcoat pocket for a lump of sugar, and put it on his tongue. What a gorgeous winter day, the sky swept clear by a warm wind, fragrant with the smell of freshly cut grass! Soon, in the valley and in village courtyards, orange trees would blossom; he felt as if he were already sniffing the delicate perfume that contrasted with the rough granite of the houses and the red and brown roof tiles held down by rocks or tree trunks. Going through the gate, he turned to the right and took the street leading up to the square, where a crowd had gathered. He could hear, above the murmur, one man's powerful voice, at moments shrill and threatening, at others bland and wheedling. One of the usual political orators from the city, he thought. Still he paused to listen, but could not catch the words. Better so, he reflected, because if he had understood them clearly he would have been tempted to show them up for the lies they were. He couldn't bear to have his people misled.

It had been a long time since he felt so well, and he knew from experience that such well-being couldn't last. Usually it marked the passage from one period of fatigue or prostration to another. "So it can't last . . . well, what of it?" he said to himself. "While I'm in good form, there's no reason for complaint." In life we grow old and feel young several times over, but we die once and for good. So much the worse! The voice shouting in the square was certainly that of an outsider, and Angelo resented politicians who came to sell their candidacies at Norbio. Their presence offended him, and he would have liked to force them off the platform and warn their listeners: "Don't believe a word they say!" He restrained himself for fear that it might seem he had something to gain from discrediting them. He himself had never deceived the voters; he had kept all his promises. He had promised to save the trees and he had saved them; he had lowered taxes and Norbio had become a prosperous town. He had promised public works and brought them into being. He had even foretold, somewhat rashly, that water would run again from the springs at the foot of the mountains, and after the mountains had been reforested the springs did, indeed, abound in water. The peasants had come to consider him a saint or a magician, who by raising his hand could command the elements. They didn't realize that his achievements were due to patience and perseverance.

Now, all of a sudden, he detected the smell of brandy flavored with licorice and he remembered that it was Carnival time. If the peasants and herdsmen were shouting down the orator, it was not because of any political conviction but simply because they had been drinking since dawn—the poor people's disorderly celebration of Carnival, which as mayor he had vainly tried to restrict, had begun. In fact, this was the last day, Shrove Tuesday, when the celebration grew wildest and always ended in violence and murder. Years ago, Angelo had forbidden the wearing of masks and the sale of strong liquor, and he had been accused of being a spoilsport and a traitor, an ally of the priests and the *carabinieri*. His struggle had been all in vain; somebody was always killed on Shrove Tuesday.

That morning Marco woke up of his own accord and slipped noiselessly, on bare feet, into his grandmother's room. Margherita Fulgheri Uras, in a long, lavender dressing gown, was making her morning toilet, with the aid of the redheaded servant girl Aurelia. Marco enjoyed being present at this ceremony; he liked the minty smell of the toothpaste, the odor of roses of the face cream and, above all, that of the "Acqua di Felsina" toilet water, which stood out over the rest. On tiptoe he glided behind his grandmother's back, bending down so that she should not see him in the mirror and making a conspiratorial face at Aurelia before he wended his way into his Uncle Oreste's room. Oreste had gone out, but his room was still redolent of the camphorated oil he used to combat his headaches. Marco was intent upon the pleasure of being alone in this room, the most mysterious in the whole house. Amid the smell of camphor, he picked out the more pungent odor of the grease with which his uncle oiled his pistols and the carbine he kept in a wall closet. Then his attention was caught by another marvelous object within his reach: a pair of field glasses that belonged to his father. He picked them up, slipped the leather strap over his head, and opened the window giving onto the balcony. Adjusting the lenses as he had been taught to do, he sighted a woman in a faraway house on the edge of the pine wood hanging up her wash in the courtyard. He could see even the clothespins that she held in her hand before attaching them to the wet clothes and linen on the line, and he made out an undershirt, shorts, and socks. Then he shifted the focus of the glasses to the crowded square. The men were dressed, as always on holidays, in black, and sported on the lapels of their jackets strange cockades of colored paper, decorated with shooting stars. Some of them wore long-nosed cardboard or papier-mâché masks, others brightly colored, patched pantaloons, motley vests, women's dresses or else sheets, with holes for their eyes and arms and a belt around their waists. From a balcony a man from the city was speaking in a loud voice, while his hearers shouted and whistled at him. At certain moments, the entire crowd burst out laughing, with one voice. The warm wind from the mountain brought with it the rank smell of the crowd and the sweetish odor of orange blossoms. "Orange blossoms?" Marco wondered. No, it was brandy flavored with licorice, because this was Shrove Tuesday. The womenfolk had made honeycakes, which they would offer, together with a glass of wine, to any costumed or masked reveler who came into their courtyard; the gates were thrown open for the day. No one would tell a child to stand still or be quiet; on the last day of Carnival, there was complete freedom and, as a result, confusion both indoors and out.

Suddenly a "hunter" darted out of the crowd, as if expelled by it. The "hunter's" costume is typical of Norbio. It is like that of a regular hunter except for its bright colors, ranging from yellow to blue, and for the fact that it is made up of patches. The "hunter" carries over his shoulder a pouch filled with bran and a gun with a hollow rod inserted in the breech, which scatters bran into people's faces. Anyone who is hit has to pay for a round of drinks. Now Marco recognized the "hunter" as Luciano Cambilargiu, the village lamplighter, who was in love with the Uras maidservant, Aurelia. He wore a pair of riding breeches, with one leg yellow and one red, tucked into coarse wool gaiters, and carried a long gun with a polished wooden butt encrusted with mother-of-pearl. Luciano was an extraordinarily light and agile fellow; he proceeded by long leaps, and no sooner did one foot come down on the ground then he bounced back up into the air, as if he were a puppet on a string. Marco saw him stuff a handful of bran into the barrel of his gun, swing down the street, and pick out his victim. The victim was a man wearing a long cape, whose pointed hood hung back over his shoulders, and a cap with an oilcloth visor. This turned out to be the swineherd, Sisinnio Buscas, who once a year, at about this season, came to butcher and cut up the family hog, thereby creating another festive occasion for the Uras children. Just now Sisinnio was listening to the orator; his mouth hung half open and with one hand he stroked his long blond mustache. The "hunter" arrived with a leap at a crouching position nearby, slowly straightened up, took deliberate aim, and at just the right moment blew bran into the swineherd's gaping mouth. Sisinnio was half choked and could not stop coughing. Although his friends shook him and slapped him on the back, he was unable to catch his breath. Meanwhile the "hunter" shouted triumphantly and did a sort of grotesque victory dance. Sisinnio, a practiced bandit and rustler, was no easy prey, even on the last day of Carnival. Now he would have to pay for a round of drinks and take down one of the hams from the smoky beam where he kept them hanging. Even at a distance Marco saw the "hunter" reload his gun with bran and prepare to make another hit. He leaped up in the air and landed in a crouch, swinging the blue tassel of the fez he had worn as a *bersagliere*, then took aim and blew another barrelful of bran into the swineherd's mouth. Sisinnio caught his breath, raised himself to his full height, took a long knife out of its sheath, and started after the "hunter," who fled down the hill.

A ngelo was walking slowly down the middle of the street, leaning on his light, strong juniper stick. All of a sudden, like a landslide provoked by an exploding mine, a large segment of the crowd poured into the street and filled it. Angelo braced himself and stood his ground, swaying slightly from one side to the other. He heard the beat of hobnailed boots, like the clatter of a flock of sheep, and saw outstretched hands, angry red faces, and mouths opened for shouting. "What the devil is up?" he wondered. Were they chasing somebody? Who could it be? The speaker? He gripped his stick as if it were a club. The "hunter" was running out in front of all the rest, with his red fez on his head.

"Stop! All of you stop!" ordered Angelo, hardly raising his voice.

The "hunter" stopped short, as if he had run into an obstacle, and bounded backward, with outspread arms, until he actually did run into the sweeping tide of people and seemed to float, like a wooden puppet, against the compact human wall behind him. The crowd, too, had come to a halt; the men in the front lines rapidly lowered their masks over their faces. Angelo took two steps backward, assured his balance, then twirled his cane and, with unexpected vigor, tossed it beyond the rooftops. The light, white stick rose straight up in the air, still turning, and passed so close to Marco that he stretched out his hands from the balcony in an attempt to catch it. At the end of its trajectory, it revolved like a kite propeller and fell in a leftward direction over the edge of a roof. The crowd breathed a long

"Ohhhh!" of surprise and admiration. As for Angelo, he held out a threatening forefinger:

"Wearing masks is forbidden!" he said.

The crowd dropped back, grumbling.

"It's forbidden by law!" Angelo repeated. "I'm going to call the *carabinieri* and have you arrested, all of you!"

"*All* of us?" said a mocking, provocatory voice, and other men laughed. There were far too many of them to be arrested by the four *carabinieri* of Norbio.

"Look out!" Angelo shouted, turning purple in the face. "I know you, and I say you may get into serious trouble."

The "hunter" was the only one not wearing a mask, but his face was daubed with paint, and this too was forbidden.

"I know you, too, Luciano Cambilargiu," Angelo added, "and I'm going to see to it that you lose your job."

Suddenly he saw blood spurt from the "hunter's" mouth; the fellow staggered and fell to the ground. At this moment Angelo, too, felt unsteady on his legs and realized that it had been a mistake to throw his stick away. He would almost certainly have fallen, had not hands been stretched out to hold him up, hands which he pushed away as he attempted to tear the hated masks from his would-be rescuers' faces. All he succeeded in doing was to pull an insignificant cloth from the flushed face of Giovanni Concas. "He's going to have a stroke," Angelo said to himself, as the deep flush traveled upward to Concas's forehead. "A stroke . . ." he repeated under his breath, aware that this was happening to himself. "A breath of evil air is going to move in and strike me down . . ." He raised his face and voice toward the balcony and shouted:

"Marco, come give your grandfather a hand!" before falling back into the arms of the men around him.

Someone went for a chair, and they eased him into it; then, in step, they slowly carried him to the house. As soon as they had got him through the gate, his sons took over the chair. For a second Angelo thought he was going to fall out of it, and his right hand clung to Amedeo's jacket, while the left hung helplessly at his side. Maria Christina, her face flooded with tears, asked: "What is it, papa?"

303

"I'm all right," he answered, with an ironical smile. "It's nothing . . . I'm dying, that's all."

They carried him up the stairs from the porch and into the drawing room, where they laid him on the sofa. He was relieved to feel a soft pillow under his head. Marco came quickly to his side.

"Did you see, Grandfather, what they did to Luciano?" He struggled to tell about the terrible thing he had witnessed without really understanding it. When Luciano had stopped short in front of his grandfather, the man with the blond mustache had stuck his long knife into his back, and now the "hunter" lay in a pool of blood on the street.

"What *did* they do?" Angelo stammered, suddenly aware that he was unable to speak clearly. This fact frightened him more than the limpness of his left arm and leg.

"Did you understand what I said, Grandfather?" asked Marco, staring at him out of his round eyes.

Suddenly Angelo saw, above the child's head, the head of Dr. Alfonso Pizzuto. Marco was lifted up and deposited in the arms of Annamaria, while Alfonso ordered the others clustered around to draw back. He told Maria Christina to take off her father's jacket, and he himself cut off most of the shirtsleeve from the right arm. Then he took out a lancet, which he kept in a slender box, as if it were a fountain pen, and plunged it into a conspicuous blue vein, releasing a spurt of black blood. By turning the arm he directed this spurt into a basin held by Annamaria. Amid the general silence, there was a tinkling sound like that of a faraway bell. At a nod from the doctor everyone left the room. Marco went to the kitchen in search of Aurelia, took her by the hand and led her first into the courtyard and then up the street.

On the street, nothing was left but a pool of blood. But a group of men stood in front of the barber shop. Inside, the "hunter" had been placed sideways on a chair, because of the knife that was still stuck into his back. Aurelia saw his reflection in the barber's big mirror, but the barber, Antonio Zaccheddu, would not allow her to come any closer. Soon the crowd outside made way for the ruddy-faced, self-assured little doctor. He wiped the wounded man's face with a wet towel and shifted his body so as to look at the back.

"God almighty!" he exclaimed. "We'll have to operate. Get him to the clinic right away."

The sergeant of the *carabinieri* and two of his men arrived on the scene.

"Who did it?" asked the sergeant. "Did any of you see?"

Marco was about to say that the knife belonged to Sisinnio the swineherd, and that he had seen him with his own eyes stick it into Luciano's back, but Aurelia clapped her cold, hard little hand over his mouth and whispered: "Be quiet!" in his ear. Marco couldn't understand why he shouldn't tell the truth. And why should Aurelia, who was in love with Luciano, be the one to stop him? His grandfather had said that he would have the lot of them arrested, just for wearing masks, and surely there was far more reason for arresting the swineherd.

"Do you think he'll live?" the sergeant asked the doctor, nodding in the direction of Luciano, as some of the men started to carry him away. The barber was hastily throwing sawdust on the floor.

"He's lost a lot of blood," said the doctor, "but these fellows are a tough lot. He'll make it."

He grasped Marco's arm so abruptly as almost to lift him off the ground.

"Always underfoot, are you?" he said, but not unkindly, giving him an affectionate spank and pushing him out the door. Marco once more took hold of Aurelia's hand and after watching the men take Luciano away, they went home together.

In the house everyone was walking on tiptoe. The dining room table was set as usual, except that neither his mother nor his grandfather was there. The old man had been carried to his bedroom on the second floor and Annamaria was guarding the stairs to prevent anyone from going up. Marco ran to look for his mother. His Uncle Amedeo caught him on the wing, but he broke loose and managed to elude Annamaria as well and to dart up the stairs.

Maria Christina was sitting on the edge of a chair, as she often did when she talked to her father. Her knees were leaning against the bedstead; she held an open prayer-book in her hands, and her lips moved almost imperceptibly. Without taking her eyes off the book, she held out one hand, and Marco glided silently toward her. His grandfather's eyes were shut and his face in repose, except that the left side was slightly contracted, as if in a grimace. His mother held a finger to her lips to impose silence.

Street noises reached the old man's ears in a muffled form, but he vaguely heard them. He lay in a torpor from the bleeding and the drugs with which Alfonso had treated him. The torpor was agreeable, like a half sleeping condition, in which sounds evoked moving, colored images.

Maria Christina had a cot placed beside her father's bed, and kept Marco with her. The little boy could not forget the wide-open glassy eyes of the "hunter" and the way his head had rolled to one side when they put him on the stretcher. "Perhaps he was already dead on the barber's chair, and nobody knew it," he thought to himself. "He could have died, without saying a word, amid all the commotion. . . ." Perhaps his grandfather might die the same way, without anyone's notice.

"Mama," he whispered, "why don't you turn on the light and have a look at Grandfather?"

"Papa, how are you?" asked Maria Christina gently.

In the darkness, the old man's white hand reached out toward the cot. Marco stretched out his own and brushed it caressingly with his fingers. The hand was warm, warm and alive.